Lovers Lane
10 Christmas Romances

Sandra Edwards
Regina Duke
Colleen Ladd

PUBLISHED BY:
Lovers Lane Romance

Lovers Lane: 10 Christmas Romances
Copyright © 2017 Lovers Lane Romance. All works in this collection remain the sole and separate property of their respective authors.

Print ISBN: 978-1-981610-61-7
Digital ISBN: 978-1-944746-26-1
Kindle ASIN: B074HQT6CL

ALL RIGHTS RESERVED. With the exception of quotes used in reviews, this book may not be reproduced or used in whole or in part by any means existing without written permission from the authors.

All works contained within this collection are a work of fiction. Any resemblance to persons, living or dead, is purely coincidental. Any references to places, events or locales are used in a fictitious manner.

Formatting by StevieDeInk.
Edited by Marian Kelly and Linda White.

Lovers Lane: 10 Christmas Romances cover design © 2017 StevieDeInk. Cover photos from Fotolia.com.

Christmas Past by Sandra Edwards
Copyright © 2017 Sandra Edwards

Christmas Present by Sandra Edwards
Copyright © 2017 Sandra Edwards

Christmas Future by Sandra Edwards
Copyright © 2017 Sandra Edwards

The Christmas App by Regina Duke
Copyright © 2017 Linda White

The Christmas Beau by Regina Duke
Copyright © 2017 Linda White

The Christmas Sweets by Regina Duke
Copyright © 2017 Linda White

The Christmas Light by Regina Duke
Copyright © 2017 Linda White

The Christmas Carnival by Colleen Ladd
Copyright © 2017 Marian Kelly

The Christmas Champion by Colleen Ladd
Copyright © 2017 Marian Kelly

Christmas Magic by Sandra Edwards
Copyright © 2014 Sandra Edwards

Please Note: It's not necessary to read the first book in the series to enjoy and understand the story that encompasses Christmas Past, Christmas Present, and Christmas Future. Although, for maximum reading pleasure, check my website at SandraWrites.com to learn how to pick up a #FREE read of Holiday Romance (Book 1 in the series).

Christmas Past

Joseph's Point Romance: Book 2

Sandra Edwards

One week before Thanksgiving

LIZ Stephens stared at the faded and worn envelope the postal lady had placed in her hands. "Thank you," she said mindlessly, paying no attention to the woman as she walked away.

The addressee's name glared up at her. *Elizabeth Turner*.

She didn't need to read the address under her name or the sender's info to know *who* the letter had come from. Even though she'd been a teenager when the letter was written, she still recognized the handwriting.

But *he* never wrote her any letter. That's what she had believed all these years. That's the only thing that had kept her sane...thinking that Jackson had betrayed her. Sure it sounded crazy, but the idea that he did ask her to wait for him — that their future had been robbed from them by, of all things, a lost letter — well, that was just too much for her heart to bear.

Liz sucked in a breath, tucked the letter inside her sweater and headed back toward the elevators. If she was going to read this thing, and she was, then she wanted to be alone because if this was *the letter*, she knew she'd never keep her composure.

Liz couldn't let Lucky see that. What would she think? What would she do with the knowledge that her mother had loved another man before her father?

She stepped inside the elevator, went upstairs to her penthouse and locked the door behind her. Very few people could get up here, but those who could knew Lucky. Liz's daughter had a way of talking secrets out of people. This was one that Liz intended to keep hidden.

She opened the sliding door, stepped onto the balcony and settled into her favorite chaise lounge chair. A brisk bite from the November chill and the scent of pine settled around her. She pulled the afghan off the back of the chair and wrapped it around her shoulders.

The day Jackson left for boot camp forty-five years ago still clung to Liz's thoughts as if it'd happened yesterday. At sixteen, she hadn't handled it well, and they'd fought just before he left. For six months, they'd bickered back and forth in letters that were few, far, and in-between. Then nothing.

Her hands shook (but not from the cold) as she broke the seal on the letter that was written so long ago. Gingerly, she unfolded the paper and was bombarded by the words that now pierced her heart. In short, Jackson had sent her a declaration of undying love and the promise to return and marry her after his tour overseas, if she'd only write back and say yes.

Every emotion that she'd kept locked inside her all these years—hurt, anger, betrayal, loss, feelings of inadequacy—they all steamrolled over Elizabeth Turner Stephens and left her feeling...empty.

She could still see him standing on her parent's porch in the rain, just days before she graduated from high school. The distraught look on his face—the one she'd thought was worthy of an Academy Award—had etched itself onto her brain. Him trying to explain about the letter he'd written her nearly two years earlier.

But Liz hadn't gotten any letter. She'd thought he was lying. Trying to make himself feel better about running off and marrying somebody else. Jackson had claimed that he'd waited a year before he considered moving on. Then he met *her*. And now it was too little too late. *She* was his wife now, and she was very pregnant. In that moment, standing on her parent's porch in the rain, Liz had realized that it didn't really matter about any damned letter. Their fate had been sealed.

In the here and now, Liz sucked in a deep breath and peered out over the Sound. All these years, thinking Jackson had lied to her about the letter. That alone had allowed her to hate him, and it had allowed her to find love again. It had allowed her to move on.

But Jackson hadn't lied. He was telling the truth when he said he'd written her. The problem was that it'd taken the damned thing forty-five years to show up.

All the hopes and dreams of the missed opportunities that fate had cruelly snatched away, pooled around her eyes and spilled over onto her cheeks.

Something inside Liz Turner Stephens quietly died that day. At the same time, the love she'd once felt for a man she'd ended up hating for the better part of her life began to awaken.

Everett, WA
Day After Thanksgiving...

Liz Turner.

Jackson Ruiz hadn't heard that name in years. Oh, it'd crossed his mind often enough, but that had never felt so intimidating as seeing it in a text message on his cell phone right now.

Of course, he knew her name wasn't Turner anymore. It hadn't been that in a very long time.

Jackson slid on his glasses to read the text once more, just to make sure he hadn't misread.

Hi Jackson, I'm looking for an old friend. Does the name Liz Turner from Joseph's Point mean anything to you? If you're not the Jackson I'm looking for, please accept my apologies. ~ Liz.

All sorts of notions and ideas began rolling around inside his head, but the most prominent one was, *isn't that just like her, being so magnanimous and all*. But why was she contacting him now? After all this time? Hell, Jackson had grandchildren and he suspected she did too. The odds were in favor of it.

He didn't want to know how perfect her life had turned out. And surely, she didn't want to know about his family with Angela. As he recalled, Liz hadn't been too happy about Angela to begin with. Of course, he'd lost his wife over a decade ago, but they'd had two beautiful children (sons) who had in turn given them five grandchildren—all boys.

Jackson couldn't complain.

Even so, that hadn't stopped the ghost of Liz Turner from creeping back into his thoughts, front and center, at least weekly. He hadn't intended to dwell on it. It just happened that way. She'd been seared into his heart long ago, and as of yet he'd found no real way to erase it.

The way Jackson saw it, he couldn't help who he loved, but he was damn sure capable of controlling what he did about it. And what he'd done, over the years, was nothing. He'd accepted long ago that he and Liz just weren't meant to be. Fate had intended him to be with Angela, and that's where he'd stayed.

But Angela was gone now, and apparently Liz was back. Question was, if the guy she'd married was still in the picture.

Joseph's Point, WA

Liz Stephens' nerves twisted into a ball in her gut. As soon as she'd sent the text, she regretted it. She hadn't talked to Jackson Ruiz in years, and the last time they met face-to-face wasn't pretty.

Standing at the sliding glass door in her suite at Serenity Pines, Liz gazed out at the Sound. Snow drifted along on a gentle breeze outside. Today was not unlike *that* day—the last time she'd seen Jackson—only it was rain then, not snow, that had been falling. She'd been out in it too, not tucked away inside (like today) where it was warm and dry. But that was so very long ago...back when she was a teenager. And she still remembered it all. Word for word. Everything that was said and everything that was left unsaid.

Jackson Ruiz walked away from her that day and never looked back. Not even when she yelled, "Go to hell!" after him.

Over the years, Liz had come to realize the childish part she'd played in their breakup. The arrival of the long-overdue letter had simply drove it home for her. That was probably why she'd reached out to him. She just wanted to tell him she was sorry, and that she didn't hate him anymore. Not even by a long shot.

If she was being completely honest, Liz had wanted to tell him that for years, yet it hadn't seemed appropriate when Larry was alive. She loved her husband and the life they'd built together, but Larry was gone now and Liz was still here. Still alive. Still lonely.

What if *she* saw the text? Oh god. This could cause him all kinds of problems. Liz should never have reached out to Jackson.

Should she send another text? One stating that her intent was not to disrupt his life? Hell, she didn't want to disrupt her own life. This was just something that was eating at her, and had been for years. The letter had brought it to the surface. That's all it was.

Liz sucked in a breath, hoping for a little courage too. She straightened her blouse, smoothed down her hair and headed out. She and Lucky had a hotel to run, after all, and she suspected that Lucky was going to need her mother more than ever this year because Lily (Lucky's daughter) had decided to spend winter break in Seattle. Working.

Plus, there was that thing with Lucky. She'd gone and gotten herself pregnant and was due in early January. Not that Liz was upset about it. It's just that it was shocking. Ever since having Lily, Lucky had never expressed a desire to have more children. Liz had decided long ago that Lily would be her one and only grandchild. Then Lucky married her high school sweetheart Tim Holliday and along came Ella—his stepdaughter who'd tragically lost her own mother. Lucky adopted Ella, and she, Liz, and Lily fell in love with the little girl.

Maybe this time Liz would finally get that boy she'd always longed for.

The elevator doors opened to the first floor. The lobby was overrun with boxes of various sizes—most were opened and holiday decorations had been laid out on the floor, while the staff busied themselves with the business of decorating.

She found Lucky in Creekside Cafe, having breakfast alone. She looked miserable. Liz knew it was more than just the pregnancy, though. She was upset because Lily was staying in Seattle straight up until the day of the Christmas party, and she was going back to Seattle the day after Christmas. Two days. That's all she was giving her family for Christmas this year.

"You know," Liz said, sitting down at Lucky's otherwise empty table. "I hate to bring this up but..." She didn't exactly hate it, but she did hate seeing Lucky hurting. Still, the best thing she could do for her daughter was make her see the truth of the matter. "Do I really need to remind you about the first time *you* didn't want to come home for Christmas? You'd just met Daryl...remember?"

Lucky's head snapped toward Liz. "You think she has a boyfriend?"

Liz chuckled. "I don't know if she has a boyfriend." She shrugged and shook her head. "But she's a grown woman and she has a life outside her mother and grandmother's view. Let her live it."

"Well, that's easy for you to say," Lucky said. "I'm right here."

"Plus, it's not like she's goofing off with her friends." Liz eyed Lucky. If she took that as a personal jab, then Liz had done her job. "She's actually working so she can keep her apartment on campus." They both knew this. Lily and her roommates had opted to stay in Seattle during the winter break so they could get jobs to hold onto their apartment through the spring semester. Otherwise it would've been snatched up by other students.

That was a better reason than Lucky had had when she ditched her mother to spend Christmas with a guy she'd just met. Granted, she married him...but still. Liz had been bitter about it back then. Perhaps there was a still a bit of that resentment lingering around.

"It's not like I wouldn't pay the rent for her," Lucky said, bringing Liz back to the present.

"And what life lesson exactly are you teaching her by doing that?"

Lucky rolled her eyes. "It's not like she's not gonna inherit this whole place from us one day."

"Well," Liz said, "she's not going to inherit the whole thing now." She let her gaze fall to Lucky's bulging belly. Plus, there was also Ella to consider now, as well.

Frustration rolled across Lucky's eyes. "You know what I mean, Mom."

Liz instantly felt bad. Upsetting Lucky had not been in her plans. There was the baby to consider. "Dear, I'm just trying to remind you how it feels to be young and full of hope." She gave her daughter a mother's smile. You know the type. The one that says, *I love you no matter what,* then added, "We lose that as we mature into adulthood. Especially after we have children." Liz shrugged, wanting to comfort Lucky, yet knowing that her words would not. Even so, she said, "Let Lily have her fun...so she doesn't live to regret it."

Lucky's piercing gaze cut into Liz. "Is there something you're regretting these days, Mom?"

Liz closed her eyes, hoping it'd hide any sorrow that she might be feeling over Jackson. When she reopened them, she had effectively pushed back her regret for the moment. She knew she'd succeeded because her heart wasn't about to let that secret escape. "No dear," she said with so much confidence that Lucky wouldn't dare object. "I just don't want her ending up with any."

Lucky eyed Liz for what seemed like forever, before finally saying, "You always want Lily home for Christmas...what gives?"

Liz's cell phone jingled with an incoming text message. She left her phone in her pocket, but grinned at Lucky as she stood, saying, "Saved by the bell."

Liz strolled away from Lucky, and when she was far enough, she pulled her phone out of her pocket and glanced at the display. Silently she read the text and her heart leapt into her throat.

Lizzie, is that you?

Seattle, WA
Monday following Thanksgiving

Lily Peterson hugged herself to keep warm as she made her way down the sidewalk. She should've worn a thicker jacket, but the weather report had said not to. Go figure.

She pulled open the door of Uncommon Gifts & Fine Liquors. She was there to interview for a job to take phone orders through the holidays. It was either this or the local coffee shop. Frankly though, she'd take either. Emma and Celina, her roommates, had already landed their jobs. Lily had to do her part.

The receptionist's desk was dressed up in holiday decor. Red and green streamers hung along the edge, and a pack of Snowbaby figurines sat perched on a blanket of fake snow, alongside a little Christmas tree.

At the receptionist's desk, she said, "Hi, I'm Lily Peterson. I have an appointment with Mitchell Grant." She glanced at the girl's name plate. *MaryAnne McDonald.*

The receptionist was a pretty brunette with a nice smile. Her voice was pleasant when she said, "I'll let him know you're here." She gestured toward the row of chairs near the door. "Go ahead and have a seat. I'm sure it'll only be a minute."

"Thanks." She turned, then glanced at the figurines once more. "Love the Snowbabies."

"Thanks. We sell them here." Jeanette's enthusiasm escaped in her bright eyes. "If you take the job, you get a discount."

"Tempting." She nodded, then claimed the nearest chair. She didn't know why she was so nervous. She'd interviewed for jobs before. It's just that none had been so important as this one. She had to do her part to secure the apartment with her friends. And the last thing she was going to do was ask her mom or grandmother to give her the money. It was bad enough that they were paying for it during semesters. Some day she was going to pay them back. Lily Elizabeth Peterson had come from a long line of strong, independent women. She wasn't about to break that mold now.

Moments later, a guy in his late twenties came out. He looked at her, asking, "Lily?" She nodded. He smiled, then said with a friendly nod, "Come on back."

She followed him through the doorway and down a corridor. He wasn't a bad looking guy. He just wasn't Lily's type. Good. She didn't need the distraction right now.

She followed him through a doorway on the left. He closed the door and she claimed the nearest chair at the table in the room. Mitchell Grant took a seat across from her.

"Thanks for coming in, Lily." He glanced up at her every once in a while, but mainly his eyes stayed locked on her one-page resume. "What we're looking for is someone to process online orders for delivery mostly along the west coast, including the greater Seattle area. It's important to note that while this job is full-time—in fact, it's helpful if you can do overtime—but it is temporary. It's just for the holidays. And it will end in early to mid-January." His tone made Lily suspect that this had been a problem in previous years. Most people aren't looking for temporary work, they want permanent. And they hate to lose a good job.

"Would I be required to deliver anything?" she asked.

"Not unless you want to."

"Where do I sign up?" At fifteen bucks an hour, this job would go a long way to paying her share of the rent.

He laid her application on the table, folded his hands over it and looked up at her. "So you're wrapping up your fourth semester at Seattle U?"

She nodded. "Yes."

"Double major in Business Management and Marketing. Very ambitious."

Lily hesitated, then said, "I'm expected to help with the family business after college."

"I take it your family's business isn't in Seattle."

"No it's not." Lily decided it was time to put her cards on the table. She leaned toward Mitchell. "Look...I need this job so I can keep my apartment through the semester break." She shrugged. "I can be here twenty-four-seven, save Christmas day."

"So I'm not going to have any problems with you in mid-January when the job ends?"

"Not a bit." They both knew she would be far too busy to work, even part time, once school started back up. "We'll smile and part ways amicably."

"When can you start?"

"Now."

"What about your classes?"

"I'm prepped and ready for finals next week. I'll work around those days. I'll make sure I get at least eight hours in on my test dates."

"You want to do a dayshift otherwise?" he asked. "But you can stay longer if you want."

"Perfect."

"You have classes today?"

Lily shook her head, saying, "No."

"Great. Let's get you started."

Liz hurried to her office on the second floor of Serenity Pines. That and her penthouse were the only two places she trusted herself to look at Jackson's messages. She had to learn to control her facial expressions.

She cued up the text and reread it. *Lizzie, is that you?*

"Yes," she whispered, "it's me." Her hands shook as she began one-finger typing. She wouldn't dare use the speech-to-text feature for fear that someone might hear her.

Hello Jackson. How are you?

I can't complain. You?

I'm still here. Right where you left me.

How did you find me?

With the advent of the internet, it wasn't that hard. lol.

:) same old Lizzie, huh?

Yeah...and the keyword being OLD!

How are you Lizzie? Really? How's your family? Do you have children?

I have a daughter. Her name is Lucky.

Lucky? That's an unusual name...

She's my lucky charm.

I'm curious...how so?
Her birthday is July 7th.
You're kidding? came his answer, and they both knew why.
Yes, Jackson...she was born on your birthday.
Well then, she's my lucky charm too.
How about you Jackson...how many children do you have?
Can I call you? Or you can call me, if that helps.

It hadn't escaped her that he didn't answer her question. She began typing: *Yes, whichever way works best for you.* As she hit the send button, she knew in her heart that this was a mistake.

Her phone dinged again. Jackson asking, *What is the best time to call?*

She suggested tomorrow, a late-morning call around eleven. He agreed.

Ten long moments had passed since receiving his last text. Liz's hands were still shaking.

This was such a bad idea. What if his wife found out? Liz couldn't imagine that she'd take it well. After leaving the Marine Corps, Jackson had brought her home to Joseph's Point, but once she found out about his and Liz's history, she insisted they move away. Jackson had complied.

That evening, Liz chose to eat alone in her apartment upstairs. She just didn't think she could dine with the family tonight. She was on edge, and her very perceptive daughter would see that. This was best, she told herself. At least until she could get a handle on her emotions.

As she finished her meal of roasted chicken, carrots, and mashed potatoes, her phone jingled. She checked the display. A text from Jackson.

Lizzie, I need to ask you something.

She typed the word *okay,* and hit send. A cloud of anxiety settle around her as she waited for his question.

Where is Lucky's father?

Liz sucked in a deep breath. How was she supposed to tell him about Larry? Somehow it seemed almost sacrilegious to talk to Jackson about her marriage. She knew firsthand how hard it was to find out that your first love had moved on. And why would he want to know about it anyway? It's not like she wanted to hear all about his life with *her*.

Liz began typing again: *He passed away a few years ago.*

I'm sorry. Do you think I could call you now?

Sure, so long as it's not a problem for you.

Uncertainty swelled inside Liz. He was going to call. Right now. And when the call was over, he'd retire for the evening with his wife. Liz had been here before. Over forty years ago. Why was she putting herself through this again?

The phone rang.

Anxiety pumped through her entire body. As she reached to connect the call, she knew it was a bad idea. She was setting herself up for another fall. "Hello." She barely breathed out the word.

"Lizzie?" His voice was deeper than she remembered, but still recognizable. "Are you okay?"

She'd found her strength now, if only for her voice, and said, "Hi, Jackson...it's good to hear your voice."

"I'm sorry about your husband," he said. "I can relate."

"Oh...?" Liz found herself saying. The thought that Jackson may have lost his wife, just like she'd lost Larry, finally found its way inside her head.

"Angela's been gone more than a decade. Cancer."

"Oh, Jackson...I'm so sorry." And she was. Sure, it hurt to think that he'd chosen another over her, but she never wanted Jackson to hurt the way she had when Larry passed.

"Thank you. But enough about me...I want to hear all about Lucky."

Liz's heart swooned. "Do you remember the Holliday family? They lived about half an hour, forty-five minutes north of here?"

"Sure, sure...they had that Christmas tree farm up there, right?"

"Yes. She's married to Pete and Caroline's son, Tim. They're expecting their first child together. They each have a daughter from a previous marriage, so it's not their first rodeo." But what Liz really wanted was more information about Jackson. Like her friend Martha Triplett had always said, *if you want to know something...just ask.* Liz decided to give it a try. "How about you, Jackson? How many children do you have? Any grandchildren?"

"Two boys." There was pride in his tone now and it reached through the phone and swathed her in a measure of peace. Liz was glad that Jackson was proud of his family. That meant he had no regrets. He added, "And five grandchildren."

"Five...oh my goodness." Liz couldn't imagine having five children around at once.

Jackson's laughter poured through the phone. "Yep. All boys."

Liz shook her head. "I can't imagine. Are they spread out in age, at least?"

"Only one, my oldest grandson Jake is the only adult of the bunch. The others are teenagers."

Liz's thoughts soared back momentarily to when Lucky was a teenager. She couldn't imagine a whole slew of them in the house at once. "You have my sympathies," she said with a hint of laughter.

"Thank you." Silence settled between them for what felt like forever before he added, "So how are you Lizzie? Are you happy?"

The thought crowded inside her head. Was she happy? She said into the phone, "I'm not unhappy."

"I'm sorry."

"What are you sorry for?"

"I just want to apologize for any part that I may have played in robbing you of any happiness that you had coming."

Okay, he deserved that. As far as Liz was concerned, he did have it coming. He had after all brought his wife to her parents' house, expecting her to jump for joy over his good fortune. He had no idea how that had damaged her outlook on life. "Okay...since we're apologizing," she said, "I need to apologize for being a childish brat." Liz kicked at the table leg while composing her next thought. Finally, she said with a shaky voice, "I got your letter."

Seconds passed, feeling like hours, before he said anything. Her heart was about to pound out of her chest when he asked in a confused tone, "My letter?"

"The one I've spent the last forty-five years thinking didn't exist." Liz's voice was no more confident than before. "I'm really sorry, Jackson."

"You have nothing to apologize for."

Liz chuckled before saying, "That's very kind of you, but yes I do."

"Do you think it'd be okay if we stayed in touch?"

"I'd like that, Jackson." But even as she said it, she knew it was a really bad idea. How was Lucky going to react to the news that she'd gotten her name because she was born on the birthday of her mother's old flame?

A few days into December, the staff had decked out Serenity Pines to the nines with Christmas decorations—to eight-year-old Ella's delight. That morning, Liz had dined in the Creekside Cafe with Lucky, Tim, and Ella, who loved the French toast. Tim and Lucky had left for a doctor's appointment, and now Liz and Ella walked through the lobby hand-in-hand as the child gazed around in delight.

Ella's eyes fell on the towering Christmas tree perched in the center of the lobby. It had about a bazillion presents stashed underneath it. She gazed up at Liz. "Who are all those presents for?"

"Those are gifts that'll be distributed to children in our community who might not otherwise receive a present for Christmas."

She squeezed Liz's hand. "Is there one for me?"

"My dear, I don't think you'll have a thing to worry about." She gave the child a wink. "I happen to know that Santa is bringing you about a gazillion presents!"

Her eyes widened. "A gazillion...? How many is that?"

Liz reached for the elevator button. "More than you can carry."

"Wow." Ella's voice trailed off as they stepped into the lift. After the doors closed, she looked back up at Liz. "If you need to put some of my presents under the tree for the children, I'd be okay with that."

"That's very kind and generous of you, Ella," Liz said. "But I don't think that's going to be necessary. Santa picked your presents out especially for you."

They went to Liz's office on the second floor. A few weeks ago, she'd had a little desk brought in for Ella, since she'd been spending so much time with Liz during the later part of Lucky's pregnancy. Ella would sit there and draw, color, or practice her penmanship, while pretending to be Liz or Lucky. At first, Lucky was her go-to choice, but lately, Liz had overheard Ella pretending to be her. It made Liz's heart swell.

Lily had grown up in Arizona, so Liz had missed out on times like this with her granddaughter. She was grateful for the do-over with Ella. And now the new baby was coming. Liz was hoping for a boy. She had her little girl now.

As Ella settled in at her desk, Liz did the same and her phone jingled with a text. Glancing at the display, she tried to contain the smile she knew was tipping the corners of her mouth. Eagerly, she read Jackson's message.

Morning Lizzie! How's the world treating you?

Liz glanced around, making sure Lucky wasn't lurking somewhere in the shadows, just waiting to unearth her secret. When she was confident that Lucky hadn't somehow managed to sneak into the office when she wasn't looking, Liz let the smile tip the corners of her mouth and she started typing.

Fine thanks. And you?
Not bad. Didn't sleep much last night.
Me neither. lol.

A couple of minutes passed, then an image came through. It was a picture of two men about Lucky's age. One looked like Jackson, the other did too, but to a lesser degree. *My sons.*

Looking at the picture made Liz's heart hurt. She started typing, *I don't have many pics on my phone,* she lied. *I'll look around for one of Lucky.* She didn't want to see anymore pictures right now. She was still longing for her own child with Jackson. If she avoided sending one of Lucky, maybe he wouldn't send anymore for now. She had to get used to the idea that she and Jackson were never going to have a child and she had to get to the point where she was okay with that. Right now, she wasn't.

No worries, came back from Jackson. *Does she look like you?*
Liz laughed out loud. *No. But my granddaughter Lily does.*
Then she's lovely.

Liz fell into the grip of his charm. Once again. Shaking her head, she began typing, *I forgot to ask yesterday...where are you living?*
Everett.
Washington?
The one and only.
How long have you lived there?
Ever since I got out of the Marine Corps.

Holy shit! All this time, Jackson had been living on the other side of the sound. So close, yet so far away. Before Liz could respond, another text came in from Jackson.

I'll get straight to the point, Lizzie. I'd like to see you.

She glanced around, her eyes landing on Ella. She smiled at the little girl, then started typing. *When? Where?*

Today? Lunch?

Sorry, I'm a little tied up right now.

I can come to you.

No, no, no. That couldn't happen. Liz hadn't yet figured out how to explain all this to Lucky and Lily. She texted back, *How about dinner this evening?* Even though she knew it was a bad idea. Lucky would never be okay with this.

I'd be honored. Name the time and place.

"No, no, no," she said softly, then begin typing. *7:00 pm. And Everett is your town. You choose the place.*

Liz closed the messaging app, looked at Ella and said, "I have to make a phone call." She stood. "Do you think you could man the office for me?" After Ella nodded, Liz stepped toward the doorway of her private lounge. "I'll be right in the next room and I'll only be a minute."

Stepping into the room, she pushed the door shut, but not all the way. She sat down in the chair by the door and cued up Martha's number. Silently, she urged her friend since childhood to answer her phone.

"Liz, what's up?" Martha asked, then added, "Everything okay with Lucky?"

"Yes," Liz answered in a gentle tone. "You're not gonna believe who I talked to last night."

"Who?"

"Are you sitting down?"

"Do I need to be?"

"I'd suggest it."

Seconds passed, then Martha said, "Okay, I'm sitting down."

"Who's the last person in the world you'd think I'd be talking to?"

"Larry." Martha wasn't trying to be cheeky, that's just who she was. She could find humor in most any situation.

Liz ignored her. Instead, she said, "Jackson Ruiz."

"You're shitting me!" Martha's shock reached through the phone and wrapped around Liz, feeling much like a straightjacket. "How did this happen?"

Liz blew out a sigh. Thank goodness *she* was sitting down. This was harder than she'd anticipated. "Remember when Jackson returned home from overseas with a wife?" She guided Martha down memory lane, back to when Jackson had come home from his military service. "And how he said he'd written me that letter two years earlier, asking me to wait for him...but I never answered?"

"Do I ever!" Martha's voice barked through the phone. "Rat bastard."

It hurt to say it out loud, but she carried on. "The letter came last week."

A full fifteen seconds fell between them before Martha spoke and there was no room in her tone for a sliver of belief when she said, "It did not."

"Oh but it did," Liz said, raining on both their parades.

"And it was like he said?"

"Yes." Liz knew there was helplessness and hopelessness in her tone, but she couldn't help it. For as much as she loved Larry, Lucky, Lily, and now Ella and pretty soon a new baby, she couldn't help feeling that she'd somehow been robbed of what could have been.

That feeling ate at Liz Turner Stephens. She wasn't supposed to have any lingering thoughts over what could have been—not when she'd spent a lifetime with a man who had loved her beyond measure, and she had loved him in return. They'd had a beautiful daughter, who in time had given them a beautiful granddaughter.

Liz Stephens had wanted for nothing.

Yet every now and then she found herself thinking about Jackson and the fun times they'd had when they were kids. But that had all changed straight out of high school. And for decades, she had chalked it up to *she and Jackson just weren't meant to be.* Now she was faced with the knowledge that maybe it could've been—if only she had received the damned letter in a timely manner.

"Well shit..." Martha's complaining voice pulled Liz out of the pity pool she was sinking into. "I guess I gotta take back that rat bastard bit." Turned out, Jackson wasn't quite the bad guy they'd both labeled him as over the years. "You okay?" Martha asked.

"I'm fine." But Liz had to admit that she might feel differently if his wife hadn't already passed.

As if she could sense Liz's thoughts, Martha asked, "Is he still married to her?"

"He said she died something like a decade ago."

"Oh my God." Her tone was soft, but there was strength in her words. "Lizzie, I'm so sorry." Martha *never* called her "Lizzie", but she got why she did it now. Martha knew. She knew what it was like for Liz when Jackson went into the Marine Corps. She knew what it was like for her when he stopped writing. And she knew what it was like for her when he came home with a wife and some lame story about having written a letter that had gone unanswered. "So what now?"

"He wants me to have dinner with him tonight," Liz threw out there, half hoping Martha would talk her out of it.

"Is he back?"

"No. He lives in Everett."

"You're going...right?"

"Girl, don't you know that's such a bad idea?"

"Yeah, probably." She laughed, then added, "But you're going. Right?"

And then the two old friends proceeded to cook up a scheme—just in case Lucky found out. Liz would be with Martha that evening.

That afternoon, Jackson had texted Liz the address of a steakhouse in Everett. Ella appeared at Liz's door while she dressed for her evening out. As every little girl does, she looked on in wonder as Liz applied her makeup.

To Ella's delight, Liz smudged some peach-colored eye shadow on the child's eyelids. "So..." Liz said, "you haven't told me yet what you want. A little brother or a sister?"

"Mommy and Daddy want me to have a baby brother," she said.

"How do you feel about that?"

Ella shrugged. "It's okay, I guess."

"Might be fun to have someone to play with."

She shrugged again. "By the time the baby's old enough to *play*, I'll be too old."

Fair enough. "But you know what you will be?" Liz waited until she was sure she had Ella's attention, then added, "A big sister."

Ella's eyes widened as if she hadn't thought of that. "Is being a big sister important?"

"Very." Liz gave a dramatic nod. "Who else is going to teach the little tyke how to dunk cookies in milk?"

"That's my job?"

"Absolutely!" Liz glanced down at the child. "It's a rule."

"It is?" Ella was on the hook now.

Liz nodded. "The job goes to the best cookie dunker in the family." She did a one-shoulder shrug. "That, my dear, is you."

"Me?" Ella said with a measure of wonder.

Liz picked out a tube of hot pink lipstick. "That's right?" She said, then painted her lips.

"Can I have some lipstick too?"

She looked at Ella, considering how Lucky and Tim would react. "Tell you what..." She rummaged through her colors and came out with a light pink color called cotton candy. "How about this one?" She asked, opening the tub up and showing her the color.

Ella nodded and Liz painted her lips for her. "Miss Liz...?" she said, looking up at her.

"Yes?" She put the tube of lipstick back in its slot and shot Ella a smile.

"Is the new baby gonna call you grandma...like how Lily does?"

Liz wasn't sure what point Ella was trying to make, so she treaded lightly. She began with a nod, saying, "I suppose so, since I'm Lucky's mom." Liz wanted Ella to call her grandma—if that's what she wanted. But it had to be a decision that Ella came to all on her own. The child fidgeted in her chair, telling Liz that she needed to open the door. "You know, Ella...I'm your grandma too."

"You are?" She asked hopefully.

"Most definitely. Lucky's your mom now, and I'm her mom. So that makes me your grandma." Liz tapped her finger playfully on the end of Ella's nose. She giggled.

"Miss Liz...?" She looked up at Liz with hopeful eyes. When Liz's gaze met hers, Ella continued. "Do you think I could call you grandma?"

Liz bent down and laid her hands lovingly on Ella's cheeks. "Oh, sweetie..." She paused to contain her emotions so she didn't break out in tears and ruin her makeup. "Nothing would please me more."

Ella wrapped her arms around Liz's neck, hugging her. "I've always wanted another grandma."

Liz's car rolled up in front of the Steakhouse at 6:58 pm. She'd used a car service, just not Serenity Pines, to drive her there. She had a feeling she was going to need a drink once she got to the restaurant. The odds were favorable. Pretty much a fact. And she didn't want any of the resort's drivers spilling the beans to Lucky. There was always a chance that she wouldn't ever see Jackson again after tonight, anyway, so why buy trouble?

The driver opened Liz's door and offered her a helping hand out of the car. Heading toward the entrance, she smoothed down her dress. Liz had turned sixty this year, so her vanity had faded long ago, right along with her youth. Even so, she at least wanted to look presentable. After all, she was only eighteen the last time she saw Jackson. Liz could barely remember that girl.

A blast of warm air blew past her as she entered the restaurant. Butterflies stirred in the pit of her gut. God, why was she so nervous? She felt like a schoolgirl again.

Lizzie, get ahold of yourself, breezed through her thoughts as she smiled at the girl behind the hostess podium. She sucked in a breath, hoping she didn't sound as nervous as she felt. "Hi, I'm meeting a friend for dinner...Jackson Ruiz."

The girl grinned, obviously remembering him. Liz wasn't surprised. Jackson had been a charmer since day one. "Right this way." She beckoned Liz with a wag of her finger.

She followed the hostess through the restaurant, trying to pick out a much older Jackson from the room full of diners, but she couldn't see him in any of their faces. Liz followed the girl around a corner and as she scanned the new area of the dining room, her eyes landed on a man in the back corner as he stood.

Jackson. Liz's heart jumped into her throat. He'd been cute when he was a boy, but now, even at the age of sixty-two, he was every ounce a man.

A man who could still turn her knees to mush—just like when she was a teenager.

Jackson had decided he shouldn't ask about pictures of Lucky again, or Liz's granddaughters until she was ready to show them to him. Obviously, she was uncomfortable with the idea. He thought it better to wait until she brought up the photo swapping again.

He got that. Jackson had hurt Liz deeply. He'd have to be willing to wait until he could rebuild his trust with her again.

She strolled toward him, the purple dress she was wearing swayed with her curves. Her red hair was a little darker than he remembered, and it hung just past her shoulders. When their eyes locked, she grinned and raked her hair behind her ear—just like she did when they were kids.

Jackson embraced her. "It's good to see you, Lizzie," he said, welcoming that old feeling that was washing over him. It was familiar and exciting.

She laid her head on his shoulder. "It's good to see you too." She wrapped her arms around him and hugged him tight. After a moment, she lifted her head up to look at him. She smiled sadly, then pulled away. "It's been a long time."

Jackson pulled out Liz's chair. She took her seat, then he reclaimed his own across the table from her.

The hostess said, "Jim will be your waiter this evening. Can I get you some drinks to get started?"

"Wonderful," Jackson said. "I'll have a scotch, neat with a splash of branch." He wasn't from the south, but he had seen the TV show Dallas enough to know that this was now a universal signal for the bartender to use plain water instead of soda water. Jackson glanced at Liz, hoping she'd be okay with him having a drink.

She was looking at the hostess. She said, "I'll have a Rosé martini."

Jackson relaxed, taking her drink order as confirmation that she wouldn't judge him for one of the few joys in life that he still held onto—a dram of good scotch. Angela had never liked him drinking. Even though he'd never had more than one or two drams two or three nights a week. She'd always thought it would turn him into a drunk.

"Great. I'll get those right out," the hostess said, then walked away.

Jackson waited until she was out of earshot, then looked at Liz and said, "You haven't changed a bit." He knew he was staring but he couldn't help it. "You're just as beautiful as ever."

Liz laughed. "And you've obviously gone blind in your old age."

She looked into his mahogany eyes, catching them with her intense gaze. She was looking for answers or maybe explanations. Jackson said, "I'm sorry, Lizzie." He shrugged, then shook his head. "If I had known it would take this long for you to get my letter...." He looked away as his words trailed off.

Her tone held a measure of helplessness when she said, "How could you have known that would happen?" Silence fell between them long enough to induce Jackson to look back at her. She continued, "Fate wasn't on our side, Jackson." Her eyes seemed to smile at him now. "But it didn't make my feelings for you any less real."

"I never wanted to hurt you," he said. Then the words he hadn't even expected to say, fell from his mouth, "I wanted to marry you." Inside, he was just as horrified as she looked on the outside. He shook his head. "I know it doesn't help to say that now, but I need for you to know it, all the same."

"Believe it or not, in some weird way, it does help knowing that." She paused, her attention drawn behind him as the hostess returned with their drinks.

After delivering them, she said, "Jim will be right with you. Enjoy your dinner." And she was off again.

Jackson said to Liz, "And believe it or not, it does help knowing that I was wrong, too."

"What were you wrong about?" Her brow furrowed, outlining her confusion.

"I thought you didn't care enough to even decline my offer."

Oh my God. Liz hadn't thought of that. But why couldn't it be so? She'd spent decades thinking he'd lied about writing the letter in the first place. It should be just as easy for him to think that she'd gotten the letter—he did write one after all—and hadn't cared enough to even say *no*.

"I hate it that you've spent all these years thinking I'd blown you off." She searched out his eyes, their gazes met and locked. She felt like crying. Instead, she shook her head, hoping to gain control of her emotions. It didn't work, so she flashed him a weak smile.

"Well, I don't think it anymore. So all's well that ends well." His face said he meant it. That left Liz feeling hopeful.

She said, "I wish I'd gotten your letter." She shrugged. "But I didn't." And she wasn't about to back herself into a corner where she spent the rest of her days regretting something that didn't happen a long time ago. She wasn't going to do that to herself. And she wasn't going to do it to Lucky either. Even so, Jackson Ruiz was in her heart. Still.

He didn't say anything. He simply gave her that smile of his, the one she hadn't seen from him in years, and it melted her heart.

"Jackson..." Nearing tears, she went silent long enough to regain her composure. Once she was confident in her success, she said, "We have full disclosure now. *We* didn't tear us apart...circumstance did." She looked him in the eye. "Can we ever be friends again?"

Jackson shook his head. "We can never be friends, Lizzie." He reached across the table, touching her hand. "We're so much more than that. We're connected." His brow furrowed, and Liz was overcome with an uneasy feeling. "Don't you feel it?"

"Yeah." She nodded. "But we've got to heal...to become friends again." She glanced away, overrun with the memories of their demise. Getting over Jackson had been incredibly hard. It'd taken Larry to help her move on. Larry wasn't here anymore so what was she supposed to do if things went south again?

"I messed up, Lizzie," he said. "Let me make it up to you." In between sips of scotch, Jackson said, "You want us to be friends again?" He set the glass down on the table. "Done." He shot her a wink. "Just like old times."

Liz shook her head, all the while hating it. "It's not like old times, Jackson. It's not just you and me anymore. I have a daughter and grandchildren. You have children and grandchildren." Liz glanced away, guilt overcoming her. "I don't want any of them feeling like we're somehow invalidating their entire existence."

He said confidently, "They'll all get over it."

Yes, but would Lucky?

Oh God. Liz had to tell Lucky. It didn't look like Jackson Ruiz was going away. Nor did Liz want him to. She'd tried that before, yet he'd never left her heart. It appeared that Jackson was on a mission now—to reclaim what he'd lost all those years ago. Her love.

And Liz was okay with that. Sure, she was a little worried about Lucky, but wasn't it time to follow her heart?

Sitting across the table from him, she realized she'd been away from Jackson Ruiz for too long. She didn't know if she could live without him in her life anymore, or if there was even anything left to salvage.

But she was damned sure willing to find out.

Christmas Present

Joseph's Point Romance: Book 3

Sandra Edwards

December 10th....

LIZ Stephens reread the text she'd just received from Jackson Ruiz. *I want to see you, Lizzie.*

And she wanted to see him. She just didn't want to appear too eager. *I can possibly get away to meet you in Everett again.*

How about I come to you?

That couldn't happen. Not yet. Not until she was sure about Lucky. Liz started typing. *Soon. After I talk to Lucky and Lily.*

Lily is Lucky's daughter, the older one...right?

Yes.

So talk to them. They're grown women. They can handle it.

It's complicated. Liz blew out a deep sigh and started typing again. *Lucky's been having a tough pregnancy. I'm a little worried about her.*

Understood.

Seconds fell around Liz and settled into silence as the messages from his ceased. *I'll tell her,* Liz typed, *just as soon as I know she and the baby are okay.*

It's fine, Lizzie. You'll tell her when the time is right.

Thanks Jackson. I appreciate that.

And she did. Liz didn't need to be pressured by him on top of everything else that was going on. She would tell Lucky when she thought Lucky was ready.

What night are we getting together again?

I'm free tomorrow night.

Can't do it tomorrow night. Have a standing dinner date with my oldest grandson. How about Friday night?

Friday night it is.

Liz had no room to complain. She was after all the one who insisted they wait to tell Lucky. But this went so much deeper than simply telling her daughter about her old beau. No, with this one, she'd have to explain to her daughter why she named her Lucky.

Lucky waddled her way across the lobby at Serenity Pines, heading for Creekside Cafe, figuring that's where her mother was. She needed her to keep an eye on Ella while she and Tim went for yet another doctor's visit.

Lucky hadn't wanted to go today. She'd wanted to put it off a day or two, but Tim wasn't hearing it. Doctor Claiborne wanted her in today and so did Tim. They'd even argued about it earlier that morning. Lucky had Christmas shopping to do still. And really, she was almost thirty-seven weeks along...so what could go wrong?

Strolling toward the entrance, Lucky caught sight of her mother at the counter of Creekside Cafe with her nose buried in her phone. Lucky glanced at her watch, then laughed to herself. *Martha must be up early today.*

She was at her mother's side now and Liz still had no idea she was there. "Wow, that must be some conversation," Lucky said over her shoulder.

Liz shielded her phone against her chest. "Lucky! I didn't see you there."

"Apparently not." She chuckled as she slid onto the empty stool at her mother's side. "What are you and Martha up to?"

"Martha?" That's what Liz did when she was being evasive. She had a habit of repeating what the other person just said. This may have been a tried and true method back in the day, but Lucky was on to her. Liz said, "Oh, just the usual stuff, you know...."

Uh huh. As Lucky prepared to counter argue, her own cell phone pinged with a message. *Probably Tim.* She glanced at her phone. *Yep, Tim.* He had the car around front waiting for her. "Can you keep an eye on Ella when she gets home from school? It's an early day. She'll get here about eleven-thirty."

"Sure." Liz eyed Lucky. "What's up?"

"Just another doctor's appointment," Lucky said. The last thing she wanted was to worry her mother. "It's no big deal."

Liz cut her mother's gaze toward Lucky. That was never a good sign. "There's an old saying...now how does it go?" She paused, as if pondering it. After a moment, she said, "Oh yes...me thinks she doth protest too much." The words bit at Lucky as her mother's steady gaze settled on her.

Lucky's phone dinged again. She held it up, showing Liz the new text from Tim. "I've gotta go, Mom," she said, rising from the stool. "I'll fill you in on everything the doctor says when I get back."

Lucky made her getaway, hurrying off to meet up with her husband. For as bad as Tim could be right now, Elizabeth Turner Stephens could be far worse.

It was far better to wait until she saw the doctor. No use worrying her mother if everything turned out fine.

Ella arrived home from school at 11:45 am, so she and Liz went into the Creekside Cafe to have lunch. Liz ordered a salad with seared-chicken, green beans, almonds, and dried cherries. Ella went for the tried-and-true grilled cheese and chocolate milk.

Ella took a bite of her sandwich, then a gulp of milk. Setting the glass down, she looked up at Liz. "Grandma...."

The title made Liz smile. She was enjoying every second of this. It was something she'd missed out on with Lily, so now she was making up for lost time. "What's up, little bit?" she asked, giving the child her full attention. But Ella didn't say anything. The pain peering out in the little girl's eyes reached out and wrapped around Liz, squeezing her heart. "What's the matter, dear?"

Tears pooled around her eyes. She said, "Is my mom gonna die?"

"Oh, honey...no." Liz pulled Ella into her arms and hugged her tight. "What's got you thinking that?" She had to ask because she had no idea how the child had come to this conclusion. Was it because of the frequent doctor visits? After all, that's what had led to her biological mother's passing—at least in the child's eyes. Liz reached for Ella's hands and held onto them as she asked, "Is it because of all the doctor visits?"

Ella nodded, still whimpering softly. She threw her arms around Liz and clung to her.

"Look, honey...your mommy's not sick." She made it a point to look into Ella's eyes. "She's pregnant. She's having you a baby brother," she added with a smile.

Liz's thoughts drifted off to the gender reveal party they'd thrown when Lucky was in her fifth month. They were all thrilled when Lily and Ella pulled apart the cupcake, revealing the blue cream filling inside.

Ella whimpered again. "But she is sick. I heard mommy and daddy talking this morning about her doctor appointment today."

"Honey." Liz brushed the eight-year-old's bangs away from her eyes. "I know it seems scary because your mommy's always going to see the doctor. But that happens with all pregnant ladies." She summed it up as if it were no big deal. It definitely wasn't the big deal that Ella seemed to think.

The child shook her head. "But daddy said he was afraid of what might happen to mommy or the baby."

For the first time, alarm reared its fearful head inside Liz. "What did mommy and daddy say…exactly?"

It took Ella a moment to gather her thoughts, then she said with certainty, "Mommy said that daddy shouldn't worry so much. Then daddy said something about the doctor warning them."

Liz wasn't liking the direction this conversation was taking. She asked in a soft, smoothing voice, "Do you remember about what?"

Ella's face skewed with confusion. "It was a weird word. Pre-clampsure or something like that."

"Preeclampsia?" Liz asked in a fragile tone.

"Yeah," Ella said with a nod. Her gaze veered off for a second. When she glanced back at Liz she asked, "Is that going to kill mommy?"

"Sweetie…" Liz raked Ella's hair behind her ear, gave her a soft tap on the nose, then smiled. "Your mommy would never willingly leave you. So don't you worry about that."

Tears welled up in Ella's eyes again. "My first mommy didn't want to leave me…but she had to go anyway."

Liz pulled Ella back into her arms again. "I don't want you to worry about that. If something was wrong with your mommy, I'd know it. And you know why?" Liz hugged her, whispering, "Because I'm her mommy. If she was sick, I'd know it."

A light flickered in Ella's eyes, like she understood. "Is Repeat gonna be okay?" she asked of her unborn brother.

"Repeat?" Liz asked.

"That's what daddy's been calling my baby brother."

Then it hit Liz. Her new grandson's name was going to be Peter Lawrence Holliday. Named after both of his grandfathers. Liz chuckled, then said, "Oh yes, he's going to be just fine."

"Will he be here for Christmas?"

Liz shrugged. "Probably not. More like a New Year's gift." She sucked in a breath, then added, "Most likely."

In the kitchen of his home in Everett, Washington, Jackson Ruiz, sliced up some red and yellow bell peppers for the steak and potatoes foil wraps he was preparing for this week's dinner with his grandson. Jake had brought the beer. Sierra Nevada Celebration Ale. It was his favorite.

Jackson didn't mind it. He could appreciate a good beer every now and again, but if he had his druthers, he'd rather have a dram of good scotch for an after dinner drink. He understood where Jake was coming from, though. Back in the days of his youth, he been quite fond of a cold bottle of Brown Derby often enough. Truth be told, he didn't mind the beer tonight, it reminded him of days gone by...and the girl he'd left behind.

Jake was busy quartering red potatoes for their foil wraps. "I gotta tell you what happened at work the other day..." he said, barely able to control the laughter that was already bubbling up in his gut. As a first year resident, Jackson's grandson had some pretty crazy stories to tell. "This lady comes into the ER, complaining of pain in the lower abdomen and pelvic areas." He tossed a handful of quartered potatoes into the small colander for rinsing off later. "As it turns out, she has cervicitis, but she has no idea what that is. So I tell her, it's inflammation of the cervix. You'd think that'd be the end of it, right?" he asked with a nod. "But no." Jake locked eyes with Jackson. "She wants her husband tested for it too. She wants to know if he gave it to her."

It was Jackson's turn to laugh now. "I'm guessing she's not well-versed in human anatomy."

"No," Jake said. He began rinsing off the potatoes in the colander. "I told her there's no way her husband has cervicitis.

That it's impossible. You know what she said?" Jake's eyes were full of wonder now. "She tells me...how do you know? You haven't examined him yet."

Jackson shook his head. "You're making this up."

"Truth is stranger than fiction. You can't make up shit like that," Jake chuckled.

"Well, if this doctor thing doesn't pan out for you," Jackson said, "you can always fall back on a career as a story teller."

Jake shrugged innocently, then said, "Oh, by the way…" He divided the potatoes in half and tossed them into the foil pouches. "I dropped into the Dixon's the other day." Jake was far too amused over his visit to a local diner. That could only mean one thing. Jake confirmed his suspicions when he said, "Mrs. Parker asked about you."

Jackson asked jovially, "Oh, how is Edna?"

Jake picked up his beer, saluted Jackson, took a swig, then said, "Wanting nothing more than to be my new grandma."

"Well, you gotta give her an E for effort." Jackson chuckled. "She is persistent, if nothing else." Both men broke into full-blown laughter.

Edna's husband had passed about five years before Jackson's wife. Hell, even at Angela's funeral, there was Edna, front and center, cozying up to Jackson. It annoyed his children and amused his grandchildren.

His children, James and Robert, had been worried that Jackson might be afraid to be alone or something, and immediately assumed that he'd want to find himself a new wife right away. And there Edna was, ready, willing, and waiting. And waiting, and waiting…and waiting.

Trouble was, Jackson wasn't looking for a wife. He'd already had one of those. And now? Now he was just looking to reclaim his long lost love. He'd mess that up once, he wasn't going to let that happen again.

Jackson could feel Jake's steady gaze as he said, "You seem preoccupied. You okay?"

Jackson nodded. "I'm fine." He paused, as thoughts of Liz flittered around in his mind. Memories of what it felt like when he held her and kissed her played with his emotions. Even so, he couldn't help but smile right before glancing at Jake. "Just thinking about the days of my youth." He hoped his smile wasn't as hollow as he was beginning to feel. The good news was, every text message that he received from Liz helped to fill that hole.

Jackson closed up the foil on both wraps and took them out to the hot grill on the patio. He was glad Jake was standing behind him as he placed the wraps on the hot rack. He really didn't want to be face-to-face with him right now. Not when Jackson was wondering what his kids and grandsons would say when Liz finally agreed to start dating him out in the open. Again.

Jackson went back inside the kitchen. Jake followed.

"You know, Grandpa." Jake's tone had mellowed, just like his grandmother's used to when she wanted her way. It always worked for her, and it was beginning to work for Jake now. "It wouldn't be the worst thing in the world if you'd find someone for, you know…companionship."

Inside Jackson laughed. But he kept it to himself. On the outside, he peered at Jake, saying, "I think you and I both know how to take care of that."

Jake grabbed another beer from the refrigerator. "All I'm saying is, I remember you being happy with grandma. And now…" He shrugged. "You just seemed…lonely."

"You think dating will fix that?" His question sounded evasive, but what he was really after was approval.

Jake rolled his eyes around the room, like he was thinking about it. "Sure." One of his shoulders dipped into a one-sided shrug. "Why not? What's the worst that could happen?"

Jackson said, "She steals your inheritance?"

Two full seconds passed, then both men broke into hearty laughter.

Jackson had never talked it over with James and Robert, so he had no idea what they'd think of his *moving on*, but it was encouraging that Jake was open to the idea.

But there was a big difference between Jackson starting to date again after all these years, and him starting to date his first love again.

While they may be okay with the former, he doubted they'd ever be okay with the latter.

Later that evening, after Liz was sure that both Lucky and Ella were safely tucked away across the hall in their own penthouse, she pulled out her tablet to check her email. Just one real message, from her cousin. Everything else was junk.

She headed over to Facebook. Martha, her friend since childhood, had mentioned that her daughter Olivia had posted new pictures of Martha's grandchildren. Olivia's husband was in the Navy and stationed in Florida. So these days, Martha lived on the social media site.

Liz fought the urge to search for *Jackson Ruiz*. She'd bite her fingers if she had to.

She didn't figure Jackson for the social media type, but stranger things had happened. Still, she wasn't sure she was ready to see any more pictures of his children and grandchildren. Not yet. It'd been hard enough looking at the pictures he'd shown her at dinner the other night. *His* children. With another woman.

And why did it get under her skin so much? It wasn't like she resented his children. It's just that seeing their pictures for the first time left her mourning the children that she and Jackson could've had, had things gone differently.

Liz busied herself with the new photos on Olivia's wall. Most of them were of the kids and all of them were at the beach. In swimsuits. Liz glanced at the flames in the nearby fireplace and shivered. Now she understood why Martha was going to Florida in a couple of weeks.

An ad on the website's sidebar caught her eye. It wasn't the ad so much as the color of the image, a bright golden color, advertising Uncommon Gifts & Fine Liquors. The ad claimed they had whatever it was you were looking for. And she did have a few more items left on her shopping list.

Liz clicked on the ad.

She wasn't sure what she was looking for, so she started browsing. Liz had never been the decisive type when it came to gift giving. In that respect, she could have given the queen of procrastination a run for her money. Committing to a choice had always been a chore for her when it came to buying presents for those she loved.

Except for Jackson. When they were kids, she'd always known exactly what to get him.

She checked out their perfumes (for Lucky) and the Snowbabies (for Martha). Perfume always made Lucky smile. And Snowbabies were like crack for Martha. She could open her own store.

Course, if she were shopping for Jackson—the last time she'd bought him a Christmas present they were just kids. These days he'd probably enjoy a bottle of fine scotch more than a model car kit—his favorite gift to receive as a boy.

Ooh! What about the MAC lipsticks Lily had been asking for? Luckily, the site had colors and kits. Liz couldn't decide on one, so she picked out three or four that she thought would complement Lily's skin and hair color and tossed them into her virtual shopping cart.

And pretty soon she was perusing the booze. Liz found several brands of fine Scotch whiskey on the site—that's what Jackson had been drinking the other night—and any one of them should work just fine, but she had no idea which one he would prefer.

She grabbed her phone and begin typing out a text. *Do you think it'd be okay if I sent you a Christmas present?* As she hit the send button, she wondered what Jackson would say.

It didn't take long for his response to ping back. She looked at the display. *Sure, but it's not necessary. Can I just see you instead?*

Delight spilled through her body. *Nobody said you had to choose between the two,* she typed, adding a "smiling devil" emoji at the end.

Well, in that case....

Good. Now send me your mailing address for delivery.

Jackson texted his address over, but soon another message followed. *And where can I deliver yours to?*

Liz texted him the address to Serenity Pines, wondering if he'd ever heard of the resort. Being the owner of a five-star hotel wasn't something you led off with when you were becoming reacquainted with a former flame. Not Liz anyway.

Isn't that a ritzy hotel?

Yes.

Are you working there, Liz? Back in the day, it wasn't often that he called her *Liz*, but when he did, he was usually serious.

Aw, he was worried about her. She chuckled as she typed. *I guess you could call it that.* But then, she didn't want to paint herself in a worse off light than she was actually in, so she added, *but I don't do much working these days.*

Liz turned her attention back to the website where she settled on a bottle of twenty-five-year-old Glenmorangie. At five-hundred a bottle, it wasn't so expensive that one might hesitate to drink it, yet it still suggested that the recipient was important to the giver.

Lily Peterson sat down at her desk, ending her lunch break. While signing back into her computer, she hoped she didn't regret the cheesecake she'd had for dessert. Sweets tended to make her drowsy, and there were still a lot of hours between now and when she got off. Seven o'clock.

She processed a few orders. They were mostly routine. Buyer's info, recipient's info, payment info, and the occasional note that some senders opted to include. Uncommon Gifts & Fine Liquors was based in Seattle, and had a healthy reach along the west coast and western United States, and had begun to stretch its way across the country.

The next order up was local. Everett. Her eyes darted to the optional note box because there was text in it, which wasn't always the case. Something about the passage made Lily choke up as she read it.

Merry Christmas, Jackson! Here's to ancient memories and long forgotten music. Love always, Lizzie.

For a second, Lily was taken aback by the woman's name because it was so close to her own grandmother's. Come to think of it, didn't she always get mad when Lucky called her that?

Curiosity pushed Lily's eyes to the sender's name. Confusion tightened in her chest as she read it. Elizabeth Turner Stephens. She'd even included her maiden name, further confirmation that there was no doubt as to the identity of the sender. Her grandmother was sending an expensive bottle of whiskey to a man that Lily had never heard of, and yet a man she obviously had a special fondness for. Who sends strangers or casual acquaintances five-hundred-dollar bottles of booze?

Lily glanced at the sender's address…just in case there was a blue moon out tonight. There wasn't. Damn it. She knew the address well. Serenity Pines. Lily looked at the recipient's name. Jackson Ruiz.

Who is he? breezed through her thoughts. Was he someone from her grandmother's childhood? Lily scoured her memories, trying to recall if her mother had ever mentioned a Ruiz family.

After a moment or two, Lily had to admit to herself that there was nothing about the name Ruiz that struck a familiar chord.

Her thoughts drifted back to the note, and her eyes soon followed. *Merry Christmas, Jackson! Here's to ancient memories and long forgotten music. Love always, Lizzie.* The words etched themselves onto Lily's psyche where they slowly faded into secondhand feelings of bittersweet memories.

Lily was hit with an overwhelming desire to know more about this man — specifically who and what he was to her grandmother.

Then the lightbulb flicked on. She had his address, thanks to her grandmother sending him a very expensive bottle of scotch.

Lily glanced at the delivery date. Thursday. Two days away.

She glanced toward Mitchell Grant's office, wondering if he would let her deliver it herself.

Lily entered the apartment, arms filled with items she'd bought off her holiday shopping list during her lunch break, and the dinner she just picked up at the burger joint around the corner. Her roommates, Emma and Celina were out for the evening. Not unusual for a Thursday. It was, after all, ladies night somewhere.

She took the Christmas loot to her bedroom and stashed the bags in her closet until she could wrap the presents. After all, some of the things she'd bought were for her roommates. She closed the closet door and went back into the living room, where she grabbed her burger and fries and headed for the couch. Five minutes later, she was chowing down and watching a Jeff Dunham show on TV.

The comedy on the television should have steered her thoughts away from the day's events. But considering it involved her grandmother, the particulars were still there, lingering on her mind.

She grabbed her phone and queued up the app she'd noted the mysterious recipient's name and address in. The delivery date was set for the following Thursday, but Lily was thinking of delivering it herself on Wednesday evening (the night before). She'd already checked with her boss Mitchell, and he said he didn't care.

She reread the message her grandmother had sent to this man (she'd copied that down too).

Merry Christmas, Jackson! Here's to ancient memories and long forgotten music. Love always, Lizzie.

The words wrapped their loneliness around Lily again. *Ancient memories* and *long forgotten music*. Neither of those were things you said to just anybody. They suggested intimacy.

Lily sucked in a breath. Who was this? She picked up her phone to queue up Crystal Sanderson's phone number. Who better to ask than her mom's best friend—not to mention, she was also the town's mayor, which in Lily's eyes meant it was her job to know something about the town's history.

The phone rang twice. "Lily," Crystal's chipper voice poured out, "to what do I owe the pleasure?"

"Crystal, I'm sorry to be calling so late."

"It's fine." There was something in her voice, a pleasantness that set Lily at ease. "And it's not that late. So what's up?"

"This is probably going to sound weird, but have you ever heard of a man named Jackson Ruiz?" Lily tried — ineffectively — to calm the anxiety in her voice.

"Ruiz...?" Crystal remained silent for a few seconds, then added, "There was, a long time ago, a Ruiz family here in Joseph's Point. I don't remember any of their names though. Your mom and I were just kids when the last of the family moved away. Why?"

Why? Lily hadn't anticipated that. But she was known for thinking on her feet. "Just doing a little research on my mother's hometown. No biggie."

"Come to think of it," Crystal said, "part of Serenity Pines property used to be the Ruiz family's land." Of course they both knew that part of Serenity Pines property had also belonged to the Turner family. Liz had inherited it when her parents passed away.

"My grandpa and grandma bought it from them?" Lily had trouble reining in the alarm that now flooded her voice.

"Oh no," Crystal dismissed the idea. "It's traded hands a couple of times before landing in your grandma and grandpa's."

Lily didn't know why, but that made her feel better. The more distance she could put between her grandmother and the Ruiz family…but hell, Lily laughed at herself, that was nothing more than wishful thinking.

Crystal said, "Are we going to see you at the Christmas party?"

Lily smiled. "I wouldn't miss it."

"Good." She sighed dramatically. "Your mother will be insufferable if you're not there."

Oh, she'd be there all right. And maybe by that time, she know exactly who and what Jackson Ruiz was to her grandmother.

The following Wednesday evening, Lily shifted her car into park, killed the engine and glanced toward the two-story, wood-frame house as she reached for the box of scotch on the passenger seat.

Well, you've come this far, she told herself. She open the car door and stepped out, bringing the scotch with her.

As she headed up the walkway a cool, brisk December chill danced around her. Even so, she climbed the steps up to the porch and paused briefly before ringing the bell.

This is probably a bad idea, breezed into her thoughts just as she hit the button.

Lily heard laughter—an engaging male voice—coming from inside. She sucked in a breath as the door opened.

Her eyes rolled up a torso that made her smile, and straight to the face of an incredibly handsome man. When their eyes met—his were a deep obsidian color—he grinned in such a way that Lily's heart did a little flip-flop.

His dark eyes sparkled when he said, "Well hello there. What can I do for you?"

Lily hesitated, having momentarily forgotten why she was there. Then, as if a lightbulb had gone off in her head, she remembered the booze she carried. She said, "I have a delivery for Jackson Ruiz." She didn't know much, but she knew this incredibly handsome (not to mention young) guy was not the man that her grandmother was sending notes to that mentioned *ancient memories* and *long-forgotten music.*

He nodded. "Hang on a second." He turned away from the door and called out, "It's for you." He stepped back, opening up the door as he turned back to face her. "Come on in. It's chilly out there."

Lily stepped across the threshold and said, "Thanks." He was right, after all. She was cold.

An older gentleman strolled toward her, somehow reminding her of the younger one who'd just answered the door. If she had to guess, she'd say they were grandfather and grandson.

The senior of the two said, "I'm Jackson Ruiz."

Lily offered a smile, hoping it kept her from ogling. "Mr. Ruiz, I have a delivery for you," she said, holding the boxed gift out to him. "Merry Christmas."

Jackson's smile was pleasant enough as he took the box and handed it off to—God, she wished she knew his name—he'd been standing behind the older man this whole time. Jackson said to Lily, "Merry Christmas to you too." He pointed to the oblong box that he'd passed off, adding, "If I'm lucky, that's a bottle of scotch." Then he laughed, and his younger look-alike joined him.

Lily chuckled and handed him her phone and a stylus. "If I could just get you to confirm receipt?" she asked, and waited for him to comply.

As Jackson signed, he said, "Jake, give the young lady a tip. And a big one." Handing the phone and stylus back to her, he added, "It's Christmas, after all."

Lily felt her cheeks sting, and hoped it was from the chill that had followed her inside—and not the embarrassment that was now burning her face.

Jake Ruiz had a hard time dragging his eyes away from the red-haired beauty standing just inside the front door of his grandfather's home. As an idea popped into his head, he said to her, "Hang on a sec. Let me grab my wallet."

Jake went to the kitchen, fished a twenty out of his wallet and grabbed a Sharpie out of the junk drawer. He wrote his name and cell number across Andrew Jackson's face, and left the marker on the counter when he headed back toward the delivery girl with a grin.

She pointed to the label on the package. "Your receipt is in the address envelope."

"Thank you, my dear." Jackson nodded as Jake handed her the twenty.

He thought she blushed a little when his hand skimmed over hers. He felt it, the electricity from her touch, run up his arm. It sent a good feeling rolling through his body.

"Thank you." She graced him with a smile that made him want to kiss her.

Jake glanced down at the twenty in her hand, as if willing her to see his phone number. He closed the door as she turned and headed down the porch steps.

He hoped she picked his phone number up off the money. He'd like to hear from her again.

When he looked up at his grandfather, the man had lost that cheerful demeanor he'd displayed just seconds before. Jake asked, "What's up?"

Jackson pointed to the package that Jake had set on the counter. "Open that up. We're gonna need a drink."

Jake asked, "What makes you think it's booze?"

"Because I know where it came from," he said, bringing out two of his favorite scotch glasses.

Liz had told Jackson about the gift yesterday. She never could keep a secret when they were kids. He'd bought her a Swarovski figurine, and what he really wanted to do was deliver it himself. He decided to wait until they met for dinner on Friday. He'd give it to her then, rather than have it mailed to her. He'd given her a necklace for Christmas, when she was fifteen, of glass forget-me-nots. It was all he could afford then. The figurine he was going to give her on Friday also had forget-me-nots, and Jackson wanted to see her face when she opened it up.

A jolt of shock ran through Jackson when he saw the girl standing just inside his front door. She was the spitting image of Liz Turner—straight down to the ginger-red hair and tawny-brown eyes. Jackson needed to know if that was Lizzie's granddaughter.

In one of their many text conversations, Lizzie talked about her granddaughter Lily and how much she looked like her. And boy did this girl ever. But what were the odds that Liz's granddaughter would be up here in Everett, delivering booze to strangers? Now he wished he'd asked for a picture, but it'd been hard enough looking at the picture of her daughter Lucky—who didn't look a thing like Liz. And he couldn't very well ask for one now though without raising suspicions.

Liz had said that Lucky was upset about Lily's decision to stay in Seattle to work over the holidays—delivering booze, it was starting to look like.

Jackson poured himself and Jake healthy portions of some very expensive scotch—thanks to Liz—and prepared to open an old can of worms.

An hour and four drams later, Jake said, "So you're telling me that you think the girl who delivered this scotch—" He pointed to the bottle on the kitchen counter. "—Is your high school sweetheart's granddaughter…?" His tone showed concern more so than anger. "And you think this all because she looks like your old flame…when she was young."

No amount of talking was going to sway his grandson's opinion, so Jackson did the only thing left to do. He slid off the barstool and headed for his bedroom. "I'll be right back," he said to Jake.

Jackson went to the back of his closet and dug out the shoe box that he'd hidden in the far corner. He'd had the box all these years, but he'd only begun keeping it at the house after Angela died. Before that, it'd been stored in a safety deposit box. And all because Jackson couldn't bear to throw its contents away.

He headed back to the kitchen with the box and reclaimed his barstool at the counter. He sorted through the contents, and came out with *the* photograph. The one of him and Liz at his prom. She'd worn a floor-length dress in emerald green. The color had been the perfect complement to her ginger-red hair and her golden-brown eyes.

He placed the picture on the counter in front of Jake, leaned back in his chair and crossed his arms over his chest, and waited for the look on his grandson's face.

It took about two seconds. Then Jake's mouth dropped open. All he could do was look at Jackson with his mouth gaping as he pointed to the photograph. Finally, he managed to string a few words together. "On second thought…you might be on to something."

"I need to know for sure," Jackson said.

"Why?"

"Liz hasn't told her family that we're back in touch."

"That you're aware of anyway."

Jackson shook his head. It was pointless to even entertain the notion. Liz had been adamant. "We don't know for a fact that the girl actually is Lily."

"You know her name?" A look of surprise flickered in Jake's eyes.

"Have you been paying attention?" Jackson narrowed his gaze.

"Yes, Grandpa." Jake sighed heavily. "You're back in touch with your old flame." He raised an eyebrow and leaned toward Jackson. "Even looks like you might have the hots for her...still." Jake grinned, enjoying the predicament his grandfather had gotten himself into. His expression turned solemn, then he added softly, "I just wasn't expecting you to remember her granddaughter's name." His apologetic expression set Jackson's mind at ease. Jake wasn't trying to fight. He was just being honest.

Jackson said, "Look, I know this is hard for you to understand..." He went silent to choose his words carefully. How was he supposed to explain that he still had feelings for a woman he'd known before his deceased wife—the mother of his children, grandmother to his grandchildren. He shook his head. "It's complicated."

"Look, I'm not knocking you, Grandpa," Jake said. "Grandma's been gone for over a decade. And if you've become friends again with your old high school flame...hell, I don't care. If she makes you happy, who am I to complain?"

"I appreciate that, Jake." After a second, Jackson chuckled. "But I get the feeling you're going to be the exception rather than the rule when it comes to the families."

Jake stayed silent for a bit, like he was pondering the notion. Finally, he said, "Well I guess you'd better find out if that's actually your friend's granddaughter." He gave Jackson a knowing look. "If it is...it's better that your friend hear it from you."

True. And Jackson knew exactly how to find that out too. With a grin, he fished the packing slip out of the box the scotch had come in and reached for his cell phone.

Curiosity peeked out in Jake's tone as he asked, "What are you doing?"

"Watch and learn," Jackson said, then dialed the number on the packing slip and hit the speaker button. While he waited for them to answer the phone, he look at Jake and smiled. After two rings, a young woman answered the call with the standard business greeting. When she finished her spiel, Jackson said, "Good evening. My name is Jackson Ruiz and I received a delivery this evening from your esteemed business."

"I do hope everything was satisfactory, Mr. Ruiz."

"Oh, yes," he said. "Very." He chuckled to lighten the mood. "I'm afraid that I forgot to tip the delivery girl before she left. Lily was her name, wasn't it?" he asked off-handedly.

"Do you have the order number?" she asked. "I can look that up for you."

Jackson located the number on the packing slip and read it off to her. She put him on hold, giving him time to wonder how he could end this call without raising red flags. Who calls a service to ask a delivery person's name?

After several seconds, the girl at the other end of the line said, "Yes. The delivery agent's name is Lily."

The implications of what that meant washed over Jackson and pushed everything else—except the phone call—to the back of his mind. Even though the bottom was about to fall out of Liz's world, his voice remained calm when he said, "Thank you." But he couldn't just leave it at that. Calling to find out the name of the girl he'd supposedly stiffed for a tip, would raise red flags, if he offered no solution. "I'm going to be in Seattle next week," he said, making it up as he went along. "I'll drop by your office and leave her a tip."

Hell, by the time this girl had a chance to talk to Lily, he would have—hopefully—already talked to Liz.

Liz. Jesus, he needed to get off the phone and call her, text her, or something. No, maybe not. This was a job that was better handled in person.

Jackson was happy when the girl on the phone said, "Is there anything else I can help you with, Mr. Ruiz?" That meant she was ready to end the call.

So was Jackson. "You've been more than helpful, dear," he said, mainly because he couldn't remember her name, and because of that, he added, "Goodbye," before hanging up. He laid the phone on the counter and glanced up at Jake. "The delivery girl's name is Lily," he said. "That was Liz's granddaughter."

Jake asked, "What are you gonna do?"

Hell, there was only one thing left to do. He had to go warn Lizzie. He didn't want her blindsided by Lucky or Lily. He'd worry about his sons, James and Robert, and the other grandchildren later.

Lucky was lying in bed watching television when her phone vibrated. She was fortunate that Tim hadn't confiscated that too. He'd taken her tablet and e-reader. The only thing he'd allowed her was the TV, and that's because more often than not, she usually fell asleep watching it. The doctor had said bed rest, and Tim intended to see that she followed through. She'd turned the sound off on her phone when she realized he would take that too, once he remembered she had it.

She looked at the door. No sign of Tim. He was in the kitchen with Ella, eating. Lucky chanced it and took her phone out from under the covers and checked the display.

A text from Crystal. *What's up? How're you feeling?* While Lucky was reading, another message came through. *The warden have your phone?*

Lucky laughed to herself and typed back, *Nope. Not yet.*

Are you okay?

Yes, I'm fine. They're still worried about the pre-eclampsia though.

Do you for sure have it?

Maybe. They're not sure. But how bad could it be? Lucky was due in a couple of weeks, and the doctors had all said the baby was fine. She wasn't worried.

Well, as long as you know you're okay.

You know me…I wouldn't jeopardize my baby.

I know that's true.

Except for Lily. I'm gonna kill her if she doesn't come home for the Christmas party.

Oh, she's coming. I talked to her a couple of days ago.

Seriously? How odd. It wasn't unheard of, but Lily and Crystal weren't in the habit of talking unless it involved Lucky somehow. *What about?*

She was asking about Joseph's Point's history.

Why on Earth would Lily be asking about that? *Specifics?*

She wanted to know about a Ruiz family.

Ruiz? The name rang no bells for Lucky. *Must have been before our time.*

Had to think long and hard to remember them. We were kids when the last of the family moved away.

And Crystal knew that much because she'd probably looked it up for Lily. *Why is she asking about a family that you and I can barely remember?* It didn't make sense to Lucky.

IDK. I told her the only thing I really knew about them is that part of Serenity Pines sits on property that the family once owned.

That wasn't entirely strange, since Serenity Pines property encompassed more than one hundred acres. Still, Lucky couldn't imagine why or how Lily had come to need this information. But that wasn't her main concern right now. Lucky messaged back, *she said for sure that's she's coming home for the party?*

Yes. She promised she'll be at the Christmas party.

That settled it. Lucky would ask her about it at the party—just as soon as Lily started badgering her about how much rest she wasn't getting.

Lily arrived home from Everett a little after ten o'clock that evening. She'd stopped at the corner market to pick up a few personal items. Closing the door behind her, she listened briefly to see if Emma and Celina were home. Dead silence.

She went to the couch, setting her grocery bag on the coffee table as she sat. Her purse strap fell off her shoulder and her bag dropped to the couch. She dug out the twenty dollar tip she'd gotten from Jake Ruiz. He'd written his name and phone number on it. She stared at the inscription. She couldn't call him. Could she?

Are you nuts? swirled through her thoughts. Lily certainly didn't want to be the one to tell him she thought there was something going on between her grandmother and his grandfather.

Oh well, he would've been fun. Lily stuffed the twenty back into her purse.

The front door opened. She glanced over her shoulder. Emma and Celina. Lily said, "You guys are home early."

"Got work tomorrow." Emma gave a one-sided shrug.

Celina dropped onto the couch next to Lily. "Plus it was boring down at Patty's."

"No hot guys?" Lily asked.

"Not a one." Celina shook her head.

"I met a hot guy tonight," Lily said slyly.

"Where? You were at work, weren't you?"

Lily nodded. "I made a delivery tonight. Up in Everett. You should've seen this guy." The excitement coursing through her veins found its way out in her exuberant voice. "He was so incredibly handsome."

Emma had taken the chair at the end of the couch where Lily was sitting. She asked, "You get his number?"

Lily nodded and tried not to grin. She had nothing to grin about. She couldn't call him—not without giving their grandparents away.

"When are we calling him?" Celina asked.

Lily shook her head. "We're not."

"Oh come on," Emma said, "you know we're joking."

"Still can't call him."

"Why not?" Celina wanted to know.

"Isn't anybody curious as to why I'd drive all the way to Everett to make a delivery?" Lily asked.

Emma looked at Lily. "Yeah, why'd you do that?"

Lily laughed at the irony of it all. "I wanted to know who my grandma was sending a five-hundred-dollar bottle of scotch to."

Emma and Celina looked at each other, to Lily, then back to each other again. They said in unison, "Huh?"

Lily hadn't intended to share this bombshell just yet, but now that her friends were home, she couldn't help herself. "There is this man...he lived in my mom's hometown a long time ago. Way before she was ever born. Like back when my grandma was a kid." She paused only long enough to take a breath. "Anyway, my grandma sent him a Christmas present...from Uncommon Gifts," she said, using the pet name she'd concocted for her employer.

Celina said, "How do you know it was a Christmas present? Maybe it wasn't a *gift* at all."

"Merry Christmas, Jackson..." Hell, Lily had memorized it all by now. "Here's to ancient memories and long forgotten music. Love always, Lizzie."

"Okay," Celina said. "So it was a Christmas present." She gave Lily a questioning look. "Maybe your grandma's just having some fun. It's allowed. Your grandpa's been gone a while now."

True. Going on three years now. "But don't you find the note she sent along..." She paused, searching for the right word. All she could come up with were the words her grandmother had used, "*Ancient memories* and *long forgotten music?*" Lily shrugged, feeling the weight of the words on her shoulders. "It's just sad."

Emma's eyes opened wide. "What if they're long lost lovers?"

Lily scoffed at the notion. Her grandmother was only twenty-one when she had her mom. She also knew her grandfather wasn't from Joseph's Point. It was starting to look like her grandmother and this man might have been high school sweethearts.

"I wonder how long they've been in contact," Emma said to no one in particular.

"Long enough for my grandma to feel comfortable enough to send him a pricy present," Lily said.

Celina asked, "Do you think he recognized you?"

Lily looked at her. "Why would he?"

"Well, my guess is..." Celina said, "if she's sending him expensive bottles of scotch, then he probably knows all about you."

"Still don't get why or how he's supposed to recognize me," Lily said.

"Wait...I got this." Emma raised her hand at Celina, then went into her purse and came out with a compact mirror. She opened it and held it up so Lily could see her face. "Need we remind you?"

No. They didn't have to, but even so, she had forgotten that one clear and crucial fact.

Lily had inherited her grandmother's good looks. Straight down to the red hair, tawny eyes, and classic features. How could she have forgotten that?

Staring at herself in the mirror, Lily realized there was a storm coming to Joseph's Point, and it was headed straight for her grandmother.

The worst part of all was...Lily was partly at fault here for sticking her nose in before her grandmother was ready to come clean about it herself.

Christmas Future

Joseph's Point Romance: Book 4

Sandra Edwards

December 20th

"So...what did Jackson think of your gift?" Martha looked across the table she and Liz were brunching at in the Creekside Cafe. The sounds of Brenda Lee 'Rocking Around the Christmas Tree' had Martha dancing in her chair.

It made Liz tap her feet. "I don't know," she said. "I haven't heard from him yet." The online tracking said the package had been delivered last night. Liz had told Martha as much when they were chatting on the phone last evening.

"Maybe he got drunk and passed out…?" Martha shrugged, then laughed it off. "Which would totally be your fault."

Liz drilled her glare into Martha. "When are you leaving for Florida again?"

"Oh, you know you're gonna miss me when I'm gone," Martha teased.

"You keep telling yourself that."

"Have you told Lucky about Jackson yet?"

Liz shook her head adamantly. "No. Lucky has enough on her plate as it is." They both knew Liz was talking about her pregnancy and the complications that seem to be accompanying this one.

"Look, we both know there are far more implications here than simply you dating your old high school sweetheart."

Yes, and now Liz and Martha weren't the only ones who knew what that was, but they were the only ones who knew why Liz had named her daughter Lucky—because Liz had felt incredibly fortunate that her child had been born on Jackson's birthday, even though she'd missed out on the one thing she'd always wanted. Jackson's child. She hadn't gotten that, but it felt like fate had given her a little piece of him to hold onto after all.

Liz glanced up at Martha. "We're not dating."

"Semantics," Martha said. "You're dating."

"Do you have anything useful to add?" Liz asked.

Martha skewed her mouth as she thought about it. Her head began shaking, and she laughed right before saying, "No."

Liz's cell phone rang. She checked the display. Serenity Pines staff. She answered the call, "This is Liz."

She kept her eyes on Martha as she listened to Katie, who worked the registration desk. "There's a gentleman here to see you. His name is Jackson Ruiz."

"Where is he?" Liz asked in a weaker voice than she'd anticipated.

"We're at the front desk."

"I'll be right there," she said and ended the call. She looked at Martha. "He's here," she said, pushing herself up from the table.

Martha did the same and walked out of the restaurant with Liz. She said, "I thought you told him not to come here?"

"I did." Liz kept her gaze straight ahead, looking for Jackson. She saw him leaning against the check-in counter. He smiled when he saw her.

"That's Jackson?" Martha's voice showed her approval.

Liz followed her gaze, then said, "In the flesh."

"Holy smokes!" Martha stated. "No wonder you're dating him again." Then she let out a devilish flow of laughter. "He looks even better now than he did in high school."

Through tightened lips, Liz said in a firm tone, "I'm not dating him."

"Then you won't mind me taking a stab at him?"

Liz laughed. "What's Ted gonna say about that?" she asked of Martha's husband of thirty-five years.

"You spoil all of my fun," she said when they were mere steps from Jackson.

"Jackson..." Liz's voice held a measure of alarm. "What are you doing here."

"Lizzie, I'm sorry," he said, "but I had to come. Is there somewhere private that we can talk?" Jackson glanced at Martha. His brow furrowed, then he asked, "Martha?"

"In the flesh," she said, and elbowed Liz.

He laughed, then said, looking directly at Liz, "You girls haven't changed a bit."

"Neither have you," Martha said. "You still lie as good as ever."

She meant it as a jab, but Jackson didn't take it that way. He gave her a genuine smile when he said, "It's good to see you, Martha." Then he looked back at Liz. "We need to talk."

"Come on," Martha said, grabbing his arm. "We're having lunch. Join us."

"I don't want to impose," he said to Liz.

"It's all right," Liz said, even though she didn't like parading Jackson around Serenity Pines, but what else could she do? He was here now, and she couldn't turn him away. "If a pregnant brunette comes up," she said to Jackson, "let's be discreet, please."

"It's not like Lucky knows who he is," Martha whispered to Liz as the three of them headed back to their table on the Creekside Cafe's terrace.

While Liz and Martha finished their brunch, Jackson ordered a cup of coffee and relayed the previous night's events in detail, including how he'd called the store to confirm that the delivery girl's name was Lily.

Maybe not sharing pictures of the grandchildren had been a bad idea. Liz grabbed her phone and pulled up a photo of Lily. Turning the display toward him, she asked, "Is this the delivery girl?"

"Yep" Jackson's demeanor suggested he wasn't surprised to see his suspicions confirmed.

"Hey, I gotta great idea," Martha said with a hint of enthusiasm. "You should come to the Christmas party, Jackson." She nodded. Liz cut her eyes to Martha, drilling her with her stare. Martha gave her a one-sided shrug, adding, "Let's be real...Lucky's gonna know all about Jackson Ruiz before dinner time tonight."

True. But all Liz could think about was having to explain to Lucky about the true origins of her name.

Jackson asked, "Why are you so afraid to tell Lucky? Didn't she marry her high school sweetheart recently?"

A wave of sorrow washed over Liz. The remnants of the teenager she once was peered out, saying, "Oh Jackson, I'd love for you to come to the Christmas party. It's three days away, though." She shrugged. "That's not much notice."

"I'd be honored." His black-coffee colored eyes drew her in, just like they used to. His grin roped her in even further. Just like back in the old days, one smile from him and she was gone. Hook. Line. And sinker. "Say, listen...is your granddaughter spoken for?" he asked.

Mildly curious, Liz said, "Not that I'm aware of." Then she had to ask, "Why?"

"My grandson," he said. "I think he's slightly enamored with her." Jackson winked at Liz.

She felt her heart slipping away as this feeling washed over her, but she couldn't quite name it. All she knew was that it had originated from somewhere deep in the neighborhood of *bittersweet* and *lonely* streets.

"Oh, love is in the air," Martha said, standing, then announced, "I've got to go." She glanced toward the man at the table. "Jackson, it was nice seeing you again. I'm sure we'll be seeing a lot more of you now."

"You can count on it," he said.

Before she walked away, Martha bent down to whisper in Liz's ear. "There's no law that says you have to tell Lucky where her name came from."

Liz looked up at Martha. "It's not hard to put two and two together."

"Oh, what if she does?" Martha said in a dismissive tone. "Doesn't mean you have to admit it."

"You want me to lie to her?"

Martha shook her head and rolled her eyes. She glanced at Jackson and smiled, "As you can see, *Lizzie* is still a drama queen."

Jackson chuckled. "It's great seeing you again, Martha."

Martha said to Liz, "I'll see you at the Christmas party." She turned to Jackson. "You too."

Liz and Jackson watched Martha stroll away, then he said, "Lizzie, I'm sorry about all this. I had no idea that your granddaughter would come waltzing up to my front door."

They both understood the implications for why she'd showed up at his door—because her grandmother had given him a very expensive bottle of scotch for Christmas.

"It's not that I don't want to tell Lucky and Lily about you," she said. "I'm worried about Lucky. She's been having a difficult pregnancy and I don't want to do anything to add more stress on her plate."

"Is she all right? The baby?" Concern colored Jackson's tone.

"She's at thirty-eight weeks, so I think she'll be fine. They can't decide if she has pre-eclampsia or not."

Jackson stood. "I'll leave right now...if that helps."

Liz reached for his hand, lacing her fingers around his and urging him to sit back down. He did. "You leaving now isn't going to accomplish a thing." She let out a heavy sigh. Shit was going to hit the fan, no matter what she did now. Lucky was bound to be upset, yet Liz couldn't stand the thought of never seeing Jackson again. Never touching him again. "I don't want to give my daughter any added stress right now, but what's done is done."

"It's better coming from you than someone else, don't you think?"

"Yes, I know..." Liz looked up at Jackson and couldn't help but smile. "My time is running out."

"Maybe this will cheer you up." A grin spread across his face as he pulled a festively wrapped box out of his coat pocket and offered it to her. "I figured since I was coming, I might as well bring your Christmas gift."

Liz felt her cheeks burn as she took the box, which covered the palm of her hand and most of her fingers. She said, looking at it, "Jackson, you didn't have to do that."

"That makes it all the more fun." He winked.

"Should I open it now?" she asked, playing with the red ribbon around the snowflake wrapping paper.

"Of course." He smiled, encouraging her.

"All right." She peeled the ribbon away carefully and tore the tape off the ends. The Swarovski emblem on the blue box sent a little shiver of anticipation up her spine.

Jackson had given her the Flower Dreams figurine with the sparkling blue forget-me-nots perched in their own crystal vase.

"It's beautiful, Jackson," Liz said, hoping she didn't sound like the teenage girl she'd turned into on the inside at the sight of the flowers. When she was ten and he was twelve their classes shared the same classroom (a product of small-town life), both classes had sung happy birthday to her that morning. At lunchtime, Jackson had gone into the flower beds lining the front sides of the gymnasium and picked out a bunch of forget-me-nots and presented them to her in the cafeteria. From that moment on, little Lizzie Turner became known as Jackson Ruiz's girlfriend.

Then when she was fifteen and he was seventeen, he'd given her a sterling silver necklace with a row of forget-me-nots cut out of blue glass for Christmas. Did he even remember the necklace? She could always wear it to the Christmas party. Maybe she'd even break with tradition—Liz Stephens had always worn either a red or a green dress to the Christmas party. Maybe she'd wear something blue. She wondered if it was still Jackson's favorite color.

Jackson's deep, grown-up voice broke into her private thoughts. "When I saw it...I immediately thought of you." He was smiling now, and she got the feeling he wasn't aware of it.

"Well..." She let her eyes drift away shyly. "I've always been partial to them you know." Liz glanced back up at Jackson. "Since I was little."

Jackson's wistful smile and faraway gaze lingered for the longest time, long enough to make her feel vulnerable. "Lizzie, I'm really sorry about all this." His apology was so genuine that it wrapped its melancholy around her. "The last thing I ever wanted was to cause you anymore heartache."

"I know..." She let her words trail off to gain some composure. Then added, "And it's okay." She shrugged, accepting what she couldn't change. "It was bound to happen sooner or later anyway."

"I know you were just being generous by extending Martha's invitation to your Christmas party...but I can decline the offer—respectfully of course—if you want me to."

"No Jackson," she said, "I want you to come." And she did.

"Are you sure?"

"Absolutely," Liz said. "I'll talk to Lucky today—" She cut

her eyes toward Jackson. "—I'll tell her about you, and I'll let her know that she can expect to meet you the night of the Christmas party."

He reached for her hand, wrapping his around it. "Do you think I can bring my grandson?" he asked, then laughed before adding, "He's sweet on your granddaughter."

"Right," she said softly. If Jackson's grandson was even half as handsome as Jackson had been back in the day, then Lily was most likely already smitten. And boy was she ever going to be embarrassed. Liz chuckled. "Sure, sure...bring him along," she said as an even better idea came to her. "How about you bring your entire family. We encourage children at our parties, so bring any little ones. We have a kids party for them as well." Liz studied Jackson, trying to gauge where his head was at. Unable to pick up anything, she said, "I know it's really short notice, so let me send helicopters to fly your family to and from the party."

"Elizabeth!" He didn't need the sharp tone. The fact alone that he had called her *Elizabeth* was more than enough to rattle her cage. Now that he had her attention, he continued. "You don't need to impress me or my family."

"I'm not trying to impress you...or your family," she said. "I'm just trying to make it easy for everybody." And then, like a fair-weathered friend, her mouth betrayed her by saying, "I want to make it easy for them to *want* to come."

"Hell..." Jackson laughed out loud. "You're going to make it so enticing that they'll never want to leave."

Liz caught up with Lucky that afternoon. She found her up in her penthouse resting. "Where's Tim?" Liz asked, sitting on the edge of the bed.

"He and Ella went up to Holliday Farms." She sighed, as if happy to be free of her warden, if only for a few hours.

"And you're still in bed?" Liz found that ironic, since Lucky had been fighting bed rest for months now.

"Yeah, I'm feeling a bit tired today. Go figure." She chuckled. Liz could see that she was tired of being pregnant. Those memories for Liz were fleeting, but even so she conjured up some genuine sympathy for her daughter.

"Maybe you should skip the party," Liz said. It was in three days after all.

"I have a plan. I'll be fine."

"Is that right?" Liz asked in a light-hearted tone.

"Yes. I'm going to rest today and tomorrow and possibly the day after," she said. "I figure I'll be plenty rested for the party by then."

It could work. There was a slight chance of it. "I'll keep my fingers crossed for you," she said and glanced away, looking for any excuse to put off the inevitable. But Martha was right, Liz didn't have to tell Lucky where her name had come from. She didn't have to tell her that it was because she felt *lucky* that her child had been born on her old flame's birthday.

But she did have to tell her something.

"Thanks, Mom." Lucky chuckled. "I really want to go to the party, though. I've missed so many of them."

"And I want you to be there," Liz said, even though she knew it was for very different reasons. "I've invited someone. Someone I want you to meet."

"I knew it!" She ground the words out as if she'd just discovered some state secret.

"You know...?" Liz asked weakly.

"Well, I know you've been texting someone. That's pretty obvious." Lucky rolled her eyes. "You're not fooling anybody, Mom." She stared at Liz for a moment, then added, "Plus Ella told me she heard you talking to your *boyfriend*. Her words, not mine."

Liz sighed. "I was afraid you would react like this."

"Like what?" Lucky asked. "If you have a boyfriend, don't we deserve to meet him?"

"It's not like that. And he's not my boyfriend." Liz found the term ridiculous. Hell, she and Jackson were in their sixties now. Boyfriend seemed appropriate enough when they were kids, but not now. Now she wasn't sure what they were. "We're just old friends who've reconnected."

"Old friends...?" That got Lucky's attention.

"I did have a boyfriend in high school," Liz said. "I told you that years ago."

"Yes." Lucky nodded and a smile tipped the corners of her mouth. "Mom, if an old friend of yours has come back into your life...who am I to complain?" And they both knew she was talking about her and Tim. They were once high school sweethearts too. "If he brings happiness to your life, Mom, I'm all for it."

"Well, good...because there's more," Liz said. She was going to take Martha's advice and not tell Lucky where her name came from, but she had to tell her about Lily.

"More...?" She went silent for a beat, letting the implications of what more there could be fill her head. "He's not my father, is he?"

"Jesus no." Liz was mortified that she'd even think that. Sure, Liz had always secretly wanted Jackson's child, but she didn't want that child to be Lucky. No, Lucky was all Liz and Larry. And the fact that Jackson had come back into Liz's life after all this time, it didn't take anything away from the life she'd lived with Larry. No, he wasn't Jackson Ruiz. But Larry Stephens hadn't ever left Liz *wanting* for anything—at least not until he died. When Larry passed, he'd left a hole in her heart, and now she was lonelier than ever. It was a hole that only Jackson's presence seemed to fill. "I loved your father with all my heart."

"I know, Mom," she said. "Just like I loved Daryl with all my heart," she said of Lily's father. "So if this man is not my father, what else is there?"

"I sent him a Christmas present. Do you want to take a guess where I ended up ordering it from?"

Lucky's stare was empty. She raised her hands. "I give. Where?"

"Uncommon Gifts & Fine Liquors," Liz said. "I had no idea that's where Lily is working when I placed the order." If she'd known that, she could've avoided this whole mess—until a later date anyway.

"So I'm taking it that Lily knows?" Lucky continued looking at Liz like she was still waiting for the *more* part.

"She delivered the gift."

Alarm shaded Lucky's golden-brown eyes darker. "Why in the hell would she do that?"

Liz shrugged. "Curiosity maybe."

"What exactly did you send him?"

"Bottle of scotch."

"Oh shit!" Lucky's eyes opened wide. "Wait...is your old friend a member of the Ruiz family?"

Liz felt anxiety creeping back in. "How did you know that? Did Lily already call you?"

Lucky shook her head. "No. She called Crystal, asking about the Ruiz family, with some lame story about how she was studying up on Joseph's Point's history."

"Maybe I should call her...before this gets out of hand."

"I don't know, Mom." Lucky shook her head. "I'm not sure how she'll take it that you had a boyfriend before dad."

Lucky had a point. Lily hadn't yet experienced life enough to know that there's room in the human heart for many loves. She probably wasn't going to take it as well as Lucky had.

Of course, Lucky was assuming that Jackson was simply an old friend, but Lily had seen the note that accompanied the scotch—a note that was meant for Jackson's eyes only.

Liz was going to have to do some damage control.

December 23

Lily passed through the entrance of Serenity Pines. The conversation she'd just had with her mother was still fresh on her mind. Okay, so Grandma had invited her *special friend* to the Christmas party tonight. Special friend. That was rich.

Lily didn't know why she was so upset. Her grandfather had been gone three years now. She didn't begrudge her grandmother companionship, but Lily couldn't get the specifics of the note that had accompanied the scotch out of her head. *Ancient memories* and *long-forgotten music.* Those words spoke volumes and suggested that this man was much more to her than just an old flame.

And because he came before her grandfather, Lily felt like him coming back into her grandmother's life now would somehow invalidate her entire existence.

She rode the elevator up to Liz's office on the second floor. Her grandmother's secretary, Gloria, nodded as if expecting Lily. It was her cue to go on in.

Inside the spacious office, her grandmother was standing at the windows behind her desk, peering out over the Sound. Lily eased the door shut, not wanting to disturb her. She said, "Hi Grandma."

Liz turned to face Lily and smiled, but kept her arms crossed at her waist. "Lily dear. Thanks for dropping by. I really wanted to talk to you before the party tonight."

Lily went to the couch against the far wall and sat. "I need to talk to you too, Grandma," she said as Liz took the chair to her left.

"I understand that you made a delivery to a friend of mine's house," she said, getting straight to the point. Lily liked that about her grandmother.

"Who is he, Grandma?" She too could get straight to the point.

"Jackson and I grew up together."

"Like you and Martha?" Lily knew she was trying to downplay the relationship, and she wasn't going to let her sugar coat it.

"Yeah." Liz shrugged. "Well, not exactly like that. No."

"Did you love him?" The thought of what the answer could be, burned Lily around the edges. Still, she looked to her grandmother for an answer.

Liz nodded solemnly. "Yes...I did." A distant sort of smile succeeded in brightening her face. "He was my first love."

"And grandpa...?"

"Your grandfather was my husband. The man I chose to marry. The man I had a child with." Liz studied Lily's face, then added, "I don't regret any of that. I loved your grandfather."

"And you obviously still have feelings for Mr. Ruiz, too."

"Lily." Liz reached for her hand. "You still have your whole life in front of you, so I don't expect you to understand this...but the human heart is capable of a lot," she said. "It has room for many loves across a lifetime."

"I'm sorry, Grandma. I'm trying to be okay with this." How could she tell her the truth? That she was scared.

Liz flashed a knowing look her way. "Why do you feel so threatened by Jackson?"

Another thing Liz Stephens was good at. Reading people. Lily shook her head and looked away, saying, "I'm scared."

Liz moved to Lily's side on the couch and draped her hands over hers. "Scared?" Curiosity pushed out the word. "What are you afraid of?"

"That you'll end up wishing you'd had his family...instead of me and Mommy...and my baby brother." Lily's vision blurred, obscured by the tears she wanted desperately to cry.

Liz pulled Lily into her embrace. "Look, a part of me has always loved Jackson. And I can't change that," she said. "But I wouldn't change a thing about the last forty years. You. Your mother. The new baby. Ella." Liz shook her head. "I wouldn't change a thing." She raked Lily's hair back out of her face and swiped at her tears, then added, "But I won't apologize for revisiting what Jackson and I once had. He's the only one who can fill the hole left in my heart by your grandfather's departure." She reached for Lily's hands again. "I'm lonely Lily. I need to feel happy and whole again. He does that for me."

"And you don't think Grandpa would feel betrayed that you still harbor feelings for this man?"

"It didn't bother him when he was alive," Liz said. "Your grandfather knew all about Jackson. And he told me often enough that the fact that I could still carry love in my heart for someone who had broken it was something he'd always found endearing about me." She was smiling, albeit sadly, now, talking about Lily's grandfather. "My history with Jackson made me who I was…the woman your grandfather loved."

Lily felt bad about the tears that had welled in her grandmother's eyes. For the first time, she was seeing Liz Stephens not just as her grandmother—but as a woman. She threw her arms around Liz. "I'm sorry, Grandma. I hope I haven't messed this up for you."

"It's all right dear," she said with a chuckle. "No harm, no foul."

Lily leaned back. "Oh, yes there is." She laughed at herself. "I've made a complete ass of myself."

"Well, it's in your blood, honey." Liz patted her on the back. "Jackson understands you were just curious."

Jackson wasn't what—or more precisely *who*—she was worried about. "Oh, Grandma…if only it were that simple."

Liz peered at her now. "Okay, what aren't you telling me?"

Lily fished the tip out of her pocket that she'd gotten from Jake. She handed the twenty to Liz, who unfolded it and looked at it.

She looked back up at Lily, confusion lighting her eyes. "What's this?"

"He told his grandson to give me a tip," she said. "He wrote his name and number on the money."

"Oh...." Liz's tone took on a lighter quality. "You like him."

Lily sighed. "Yeah but now that he knows I'm not just some random delivery girl...that I'm actually the basket case granddaughter of the woman who sent his grandfather a Christmas present..." Lily shook her head. "Jake must think I'm crazy."

"Well, he must not think you're too crazy."

"Why's that?"

"He's coming to the Christmas party tonight."

"You invited him too?" Lily's tone gave away her anxiety over the matter.

"The entire family."

"All of them?" Lily's tone had grown weak. "Even Jake's parents?"

Liz nodded. "Yep."

Oh God. It was bad enough that she had to climb out of her pit of embarrassment where Jackson and Jake were concerned. But did her grandmother have to throw the whole family at her at once?

Everett, WA

"You guys are going, right?" Jake Ruiz sat across the kitchen counter from his parents, James and Barbara Ruiz, waiting for an answer. He and his grandfather had agreed not to give Lily's part in this away, so he had said nothing about her.

Jake's mother looked at his father and said, "I'm not sure it's such a great idea." She paused, shaking her head. "Your dad's old flame?"

"They were high school sweethearts. Big deal." Jake's dad shrugged. "Honestly, I'm kind of encouraged that someone from his past is still around...and somebody who still cares about him."

"What if she's after..." Mom said.

"After what...?" Dad dismissed her fears. "Anybody who sends a fleet of helicopters to take your family to *their* Christmas party, isn't after anything Dad may have saved up over the years."

"He's got a point, Mom," Jake threw his support behind his dad's position, because he also knew about the incredibly expensive bottle of scotch his grandfather's old friend had sent him.

"Why do you always take your father's side?" Mom asked.

"I don't always take his side," Jake said. "But in this case he happens to be right."

"And you know this how?"

Jake shook his head. "This is not my story to tell, but since you're acting like we're on an episode of *Dateline*, I'll tell you what I know."

Dad raised his eyebrows and his mouth fell open. "Yeah, I think you'd better start talking."

"She sent Grandpa a very expensive bottle of scotch. I was there when it was delivered."

"How expensive?" Now Mom was interested.

"A bottle of twenty-year-old Glenmorangie."

Of course, Mom didn't really know what that was, but Dad did. He asked, "Did you get a taste of it?"

"Oh yeah..." Jake grinned. "Never seen anything like it."

"It's not all gone, is it?"

Jake shrugged. "I don't think so." He shook his head. "We didn't drink it all."

Mom cut in. "Would you two listen to yourselves?"

They both looked at her with innocent shrugs. Dad said, "Do you know how long it will be before I'll ever see another five-to-six hundred dollar bottle of *anything*?"

The Ruiz family wasn't poor, not by any means, but to categorize them as anything more than upper-middle class would be a total fabrication. "Grandpa obviously didn't tell you," Jake said.

"Tell us what?" Mom asked.

Jake said, "You know that swanky resort over on the peninsula?"

Jake's parents nodded. His father said, "The one in Dad's hometown?"

Jake nodded. "Grandpa's old flame owns it."

Liz latched the hook on the choker of forget-me-knots around her neck. The string of blue glass set in sterling silver's only value was of the sentimental sort. She'd received it as a Christmas present when she was fifteen.

She could still feel Jackson's hands resting on her shoulders after he'd fastened it around her neck for the first time. That was such a long time ago, but the way it had made her feel still lingered on today.

She opened her jewelry box and pulled out an emerald ring (her birthstone) and slid it on her ring finger, left hand to cover the mark where her wedding band used to sit. Liz had taken it off when she decided to look for Jackson.

On her way out the door, Liz grabbed her Michael Kors clutch in electric-blue saffiano leather and stepped out into the hallway, where she knocked on Lucky's door. Lily came out first, then Lucky.

"Where's Tim and Ella?" Liz asked.

"They went to pick up his parents." Lucky raised her hands in a surrendering fashion as she stepped into the elevator. "I know, I know...we have cars and helicopters for that sort of thing." The helicopters were new. Lucky had added them last year, and begun offering suite and room packages that included a helicopter shuttle to and from the airport. Serenity Pines had purchased six helicopters, and all were in service daily. "But you know..." she said as the elevator doors slid shut. "Tim hates the receiving line. He'll do anything to avoid it."

The lift began moving down. Liz said, "I know." She wasn't

exactly fond of it herself. "But it was your father's tradition." And that, in a nutshell, was why she kept it going.

"That's a beautiful dress, Grandma," Lily said, with an admiring smile. "You look gorgeous in blue."

"Thanks, sweetie." Liz ran her hands down her sides, as if she could smooth out the dress. Thirty years ago, she wouldn't have flinched at showing off her figure, but hell, now she was somebody's grandmother. It seemed like the time for that sort of thing had come and gone. Even so, she hoped Jackson liked the dress on her. Blue was his favorite color. And the purple Lily was wearing was gorgeous on her. If Jake wasn't a fan before, Liz was sure he would be after just one look at Lily wearing it. She said, "Love the sparkling lavender on you." It made her red hair pop. Liz looked at Lucky, "The green is beautiful on you this year."

"Thanks. I'm trying to downplay the fact that I look like a beached whale." Lucky paused, then added, "You're not wearing your typical Christmas party dress color, Mom." No she wasn't. Usually, Liz wore red or green. Tonight she wore a floor-length sheath gown with a beaded overlay in electric-blue.

"New year, new tradition," Lily said as the elevator doors opened up on the eight floor in the passage way that led into the Serenity Pines ballroom.

Liz glanced at Lily, who smiled back at her. She draped her arm around Lily's. "You know..." she said, "I couldn't have asked for a better granddaughter." Liz tangled her free arm around Lucky's and the three women—three generations—stepped out of the elevator.

The staff began opening the ballroom doors. Two sets of double doors on each side of a row of restrooms. Women's in front, men's on the back. Inside the ballroom, mother, daughter, and granddaughter were perched against the wall behind the restrooms in a receiving line. An armed and padded stool had been brought in for Lucky. Because Lucky was pregnant, Liz cut the receiving line, which was fed from both sets of doors, down to just twenty minutes, and noted such on the invitation. After that, Lucky would be ushered to the family's table where an incredibly comfortable chair awaited her.

Liz turned to Lucky. "Are you sure you're okay?" She asked as Lucky struggled to lift herself onto the stool.

"I'm fine, Mom," she said. "I could use some punch though."

"Uh huh," Liz said. "Nice try." Knowing full well that Lucky was asking for punch of the alcoholic variety. Liz also knew that Lucky was only joking. Well, mostly.

But she looked tired. Something about her demeanor wasn't quite right. Liz didn't think she was going to last till her due date—January 1st.

Lily leaned in against Liz's ear, saying, "Grandma...?" Liz cut her eye toward Lily, who said, "What time do you think Mr. Ruiz and his family will be here?"

Liz glanced at her watch. 7:08 pm. The helicopters were scheduled to arrive on the helipads at 7:10. "Any moment now," she said. "Have you thought about what you're going to say to Jake?"

"I'm probably gonna be too terrified to speak." Lily's tone suggested she was joking, but Liz knew the exact opposite could well be the case.

The first of the helicopters carrying the Ruiz family touched down on one of Serenity Pine's helipads. James and Jake climbed out first. Then James offered his wife Barbara a helping hand while Jackson shuffled out on the other side.

While they waited for the other helicopters to unload, Jackson checked that his tie was tucked neatly inside the jacket of his tux. He liked the vivid blue color of the tie. Normally, he'd choose a darker blue, but Liz had sent the tie over, saying it would match her dress beautifully. That and only that had induced him to wear it.

"Oh my goodness," Barbara said to James, gazing around at her surroundings. "How can your father ever compete with all this?"

"He doesn't have to," Jake said. "I'm pretty sure she needs something from him that she can't get at this resort."

"Barbara, all you need to know is that Lizzie and I go way back," Jackson said. "She doesn't have a selfish or a lofty bone in her body."

She asked, "How will we ever fit in here?"

The thought had never occurred to Jackson. He said, "Like a hand in glove." There was no other option. He'd lost Liz once. He wasn't willing to do that again. Jackson looked at James. "You're awfully quiet, son."

James chuckled. With his eyes fixed on the other helicopters, he said, "I'm waiting to see Robert's reaction to...all this."

"You didn't tell him?" Jackson asked.

"Nope." James let out a bit of devilish laughter.

Jackson had assumed that James would run straight to Robert with the information he'd unearthed. That was Jackson's mistake. He said, "I'd like you two to be on your best behavior, please." And it was no question.

Jackson's son Robert climbed out of another helicopter and offered his hand to his wife, Marlene. They're children—three of them, all teenage boys— and Jake's brother poured out of the third helicopter.

Standing on the sidelines, Jackson watched the rest of his family make their way toward him and the others. What would Liz think of them? How would they react to her? Jackson prayed this went well.

He slid his hands inside his pockets and waited for Robert to look his way. When he did, Jackson gave him a gesturing nod, encouraging him to get a move on. He didn't want to waste time getting inside. He knew Liz, her daughter Lucky, and her granddaughter Lily were keeping the receiving line open until Jackson and his family came through. Considering Lucky's condition, he figured the sooner they got her settled in at her table, the better.

Robert coaxed his family along. "Come on kids..." he said, gazing around at the resort before them. Then his eyes fell back on Jackson again. Robert said with a laugh, "Let's go meet your new grandmother."

Liz saw Jackson pass through the right hand entry, and said to Lily, "I'll be right back." Walking away, she glanced over her shoulder and mouthed, "Tell your mother."

As she drew closer, she recognized something in Jackson's smile. He was no longer the boy she knew. Now he was very much a man. But here, in this older Jackson's smile, she saw the boy he'd once been peeking out at her. "Lizzie..." He reached for her hands, then leaned in to kiss her cheek. "You look beautiful," he whispered against her ear.

"And you look as dashing as ever." She paused, waiting until their eyes met before continuing. "I hope we don't live to regret this." She gave him a weak smile, hoping to hide her nervous chuckle.

He wrapped her arm around his. "Well my crew has promised to be on their best behavior." He winked at Liz and before she knew it she was smiling. "Come on." He tugged on her hand. "Meet my boys."

Jackson introduced James and his wife Barbara, and Robert and his wife Marlene. Then he introduced the grandsons, ending with Jake—his namesake.

Liz took him over to Lucky and Lily. Jackson's family followed. After introductions, Liz showed them to their table, which adjoined her own (where Jackson and Jake would be sitting for dinner tonight). She made it a point to be nothing but polite, cordial, and gracious to the entire Ruiz family. This had to go well. She didn't know if she could watch Jackson walk away from her again.

After half an hour and a couple of drinks (for the adults), Jackson's sons and their wives were chatting and laughing and looking like they were genuinely enjoying themselves. Jake's brother and his eldest cousin had met Belinda Gentry's teenage daughters and had become *otherwise engaged*. His two youngest cousins, twelve and thirteen-year-old boys, had discovered the arcade in the center of the ballroom.

The band began playing 'Always On My Mind', and old Willie Nelson tune. Jackson laced his fingers with Liz's and tugged her out of her chair and to the dance floor. He wrapped her in his embrace and Liz felt like she'd finally come home.

She looked into his coffee-colored eyes and was instantly bombarded with all those old feelings she thought she'd left in the past a long time ago. "It sure is good to see you again, Jackson." It also made her say stupid things.

"Well," he said, "since the sky didn't fall in...you want to have dinner with me New Year's Eve?"

"I'd love to." Liz felt herself starting to gush and she consciously tried to stop it before it got too far, where she ended up looking ridiculous.

"Should I come here?" he asked. "If you can get us a table in your best restaurant—" He winked. "—I'll pick up the tab."

"Jackson..." She laughed and glanced away, feeling like a teenage girl all over again. Now she was beginning to remember what she hated about those formidable years. Everything in this moment felt like nothing short of life and death. "I see you haven't lost an ounce of your charm," she managed to say, but she kept her eyes away from his captivating gaze.

"You bring it out in me, Lizzie." His playful tone set her at ease. "You fix us up with a table, and I'll take care of the rest."

Liz had stopped throwing caution to the wind when Jackson

returned home with a wife years ago. But here she was ready to do just that when she said, "Okay, Jackson, I'll get us a quiet table...where it's just you and me."

"You leave everything else to me," he said. They danced a few seconds in silence, then he asked, "Where's Martha? I was expecting to see her front and center."

"She and her husband left on a earlier flight today. They're spending Christmas with their daughter and grandchildren in Florida," Liz said. "They were going to fly out tomorrow, but decided to take a flight today since we're supposed to get that snow storm in tonight."

Tonight's snow storm was also the reason that Jackson's family would be staying in the two guest penthouses on Liz and Lucky's floor. They kept them open for family and friends when they came into town. Each penthouse was a spacious three-bedroom, so those two apartments could house a lot of friends and relatives.

"Ah yes, the snow storm." Jackson looked around then said, "Who do I see about sleeping arrangements? I'd like a room to myself so I can sneak out later."

Liz's giddy laughter poured out. "I told the staff to put James and his family in one apartment and Robert and his family in the other. You and Jake will take the guest bedrooms in my apartment." She paused, glancing up at Jackson. "I hope that's okay."

"It's perfect." He smiled, then winked. "Better lock your bedroom door."

"Can't have any fun like that," Liz said as the song ended. She led him back to their table near the southern wall of windows. He pulled out her chair, but before she sat, she pointed to the parking lot and said, "See the second lot back? That's where the field was that we used to play in that was between our houses."

Jackson laughed and laid his hand against the small of her back. "That's not where it was." He shook his head as she looked up at him.

"Yes it is," she dismissed his objection.

"Don't you think I know where my own childhood home used to be?" He chuckled.

"I can prove to you that you don't," she said, wanting desperately to kiss him. She hadn't felt like this in ages. Alive. She felt alive. It felt good.

"You think so, huh?" He was laughing now.

"I hope you brought a coat with you," she said, leading him out into the main hallway.

"Why?" He teased her. "Am I gonna need one?"

Liz shrugged. "Depends on your tolerance for the cold."

"Well I guess if I get cold I'll just snuggle up to you," he said, nestling her in closer.

She laughed, grabbing his hands. "You haven't changed a bit."

"That too is your fault," he said, holding her coat up so she could slip her arms into the sleeves. He draped his own coat over his arm and escorted her outside, where it had begun to snow.

Jackson sleeved into his coat and shoved his hands inside the pockets. Liz pulled gloves out of her pocket, slipped them on and wrapped her arm around the crook of his as they prepared to go for a walk down memory lane.

Jake walked up to Lily's side. She was still standing in the receiving line area. "You didn't call me," he said.

She looked at him and smiled shyly. "No, I didn't." She sucked in a breath, hoping for some courage. "I ah…all things considered, I just didn't think it was a good idea."

All hope faded from Jake's face. "I'm sorry," he said. "Obviously I misread your signals."

Lily shook her head, feeling her cheeks burn. "No, you didn't misread anything." If Lily had learned anything from their respective grandparents' situation, it was not to let misunderstandings dictate their future. "I was just too embarrassed to call you." She shrugged. "I would've had to admit who I was."

"My grandfather and your grandmother were high school sweethearts. It's not that big of a deal really."

"I keep telling myself that," Lily said. "And really, my heart hurts for my grandmother...but I can't wish that she'd gotten your grandfather's letter on time." She shrugged. "If she had...none of us would be here."

"But we are here." His soothing voice consoled her. "Nothing can change that either."

"Which is why I'm choosing not to stand in their way," she said. "The only reason they aren't married today is because my grandma received your grandfather's letter forty-something years late." Loneliness invaded her heart as she added, "Fate played a cruel, cruel joke on them—I'm not complaining about that, mind you—but if they're still feeling it, they deserve a shot at happiness just like everybody else."

"I completely agree." Jake grinned. "How else would I have met you?"

Every cloud *did* have a silver lining. It may have rained on their grandparents' parade all those years ago, but maybe something could be salvaged from all the heartache. "Can I show you something?"

"Sure," he said with a measure of curiosity.

"It's outside," she said, "Let's grab coats."

"Now I'm definitely intrigued," he said, following her out into the lobby where they collected their coats.

Lily had hoped for the chance to take a walk with Jake, so she'd brought her coat down into the coat room earlier. There she saw that her grandmother had done the same thing. Now Liz's coat was gone. As Jake helped Lily with her coat, she said, "Did you know that part of Serenity Pines property is where the Ruiz family used to live here in Joseph's Point?"

"My grandfather said something about that," Jake said. "Is the house still standing?"

"No." She shook her head. "It's been gone for decades," she said as they left the ballroom entryway and waited for an elevator to arrive. "But I'd like to show you what my grandmother built on the spot where the Ruiz family home once stood." Lily had figured that out after Crystal Sanderson had told her that part of Serenity Pines property had once belonged to the Ruiz family. Lily had gone to look at the town's old records. That's when she learned where Jackson's family home used to sit.

"Again, I am intrigued," Jake said as they stepped into the elevator and rode it down to the lobby.

When the elevator doors parted, Lily and Jake stepped out onto the first floor. Katie, one of the hotel staff, rushed up to Lily. "Thank God I've found you," she said breathlessly.

"What's up?" Lily asked, wondering why Serenity Pines staff was looking for her. They never had before.

"Martha Triplett, came by this morning." Katie shoved a five-by-seven sized manila envelope at Lily. "She told me to give it to you."

Lily took it and shrugged. "Okay. Well, thank you." She looked at the envelope while Katie took off. Lily looked at Jake. "Martha is my grandmother's best friend. She knew your grandfather too." But Lily couldn't get the question out of her head, "I wonder why she left this for me, though?"

"What is it?" he asked.

Lily opened the envelope and found a folded sheet of paper and another note-sized letter in a sealed envelope. Her mother's name was scribbled on the exterior of the new letter. Lily took the sheet of paper out to read it.

Lily, I had hoped to do this myself...but since I had to leave early, this is up to you. Tonight at the party, if things start to go south after you and your mother meet the Ruiz family, give this letter to your mother. It's from her father. Merry Christmas! Martha.

Lily looked at Jake. "What do you think this letter says?"

"I don't know." He hesitated, then said, "Maybe we should go back upstairs and give it to her?"

Lily wanted to show Jake the tribute that her grandmother had built, but it could wait until later. Of course, he wouldn't see the Ruiz family name on it anywhere, but it hadn't been hard to figure out why Liz Stephens had built it on that spot—now that Lily knew the whole story.

Liz looked up at Jackson as they stood in the gazebo in the middle of Serenity Pines Botanical Garden. "So what do you think?" she asked, gazing around at the gardens surrounding the gazebo. Because the entire building was essentially a greenhouse, varieties from dozens of exotic flowers appealed to both the senses of sight and smell. Beautiful butterflies in a multitude of colors flittered about.

"This is where the house stood?" Jackson asked.

She nodded.

"Well this is a hell of an improvement." He chuckled.

"You like it?" she asked. "I was afraid you wouldn't."

Jackson let his gaze settle on hers. "After everything I did to you," he said, caressing the length of her cheek. "All these years...you still made room for me in your heart."

"You've always been there, Jackson," she said, unable to pull her gaze away. "Always."

"Same here, Lizzie. Same here."

"So..." Liz let the word drag out. "What do you think about a table right here? Nobody but you and me." She glanced up. "I can arrange for a little music to be filtered in. Maybe you'll even ask me to dance. How about it?" she asked. "New Year's Eve? You and me?"

Jackson cupped her face in his palms. "I wouldn't miss this for the world."

"Now, let's go eat. I'm hungry."

"All right." Jackson grinned. "All this talk about food's making me hungry anyway."

Liz got the feeling that he was using food as a metaphor. She laughed devilishly and turned for the exit. "One of these days...you know I'm gonna call your bluff, don't you?"

"I'm counting on it," he said as they stepped out into the cool, brisk December night's air.

Liz and Jackson returned to the resort tower, where they took the elevator back up to the ballroom on the eight floor.

Liz stopped in front of the restrooms. "I'm gonna drop in here for a second," she said. "I'll meet you inside?"

"Perfect," Jackson said, then kissed her cheek before heading out.

Entering the ballroom, Jackson saw Lucky coming toward him. "Lucky, hello..." was all he could think of to say.

"Mr. Ruiz." She offered a gracious smile, but for some reason Jackson thought she looked tired. She laid her hand on her stomach. "I seem to have lost my mother and my daughter Lily. Have you seen either of them?"

"Your mother is in the restroom. I'm afraid I haven't seen Lily since we first arrived." But hell, he hadn't seen any of them since then. He and Liz had been down at the gardens. "Have you seen my grandson Jake? He may know where Lily is," he added with a hint of a chuckle.

"Ah, that explains it," Lucky said as if relieved. "I do hope your family is having a good time, Mr. Ruiz. We'd really like to see more of all of you."

"Thank you, Lucky." Jackson decided it was a good time to build a bridge with Liz's only child. Something *they* could share. "You know, I understand that you and I share the same birthday."

"Holy shit!" Lucky's mouth dropped open as she looked down. With a much shakier tone, she asked, "Can you get my mother, please?"

Jackson studied Lucky's face. "Are you all right?"

"Mr. Ruiz..." she was holding her very large belly now. "This isn't the way I wanted our first meeting to go, but could you find my mother? Tell her my water broke."

"Should I call for an ambulance?" he asked, reaching for his phone.

She stopped him. "No. The snowstorm is setting in. We need to find out if there's a doctor here at the hotel." Inclement weather was not unusual in a place like Washington state. They knew the storm was coming, and since most of the guests were Joseph's Point residents, they knew they could get home before things got too bad. In the event that a storm came in quicker than anticipated—like tonight's—well, Serenity Pines was a resort after all. Invited guests to the annual Christmas party never had to worry about where they were going to sleep if they couldn't make it home.

Jackson ushered her to a nearby chair, then called for the attention of one of the waiters. "Bring one of the waitresses over to sit with Mrs. Holliday. Then go find my grandson Jake Ruiz. He's a doctor." The waiter took off. Jackson turned back to Lucky. "I'm going to go get your mother. I'll be right back."

"All right." Lucky nodded, uncertainty shading her eyes. "Thank you Mr. Ruiz."

Liz followed Jackson into the elevator. He'd just told her that Lucky had been taken to a two-room suite on the fourth floor. Olympia and Gig Harbor were the closest hospitals, and they were too far away to drive to in the winter storm. Liz asked, "Did you find Lily?"

"Yes. She's with Lucky," he said, pushing the number four button. "And so is my grandson."

Oh sure, they'd said Jake was a doctor. A first-year resident over in Seattle. But Liz's question was, "How many babies has he delivered?"

"I wouldn't know," Jackson said as the elevator stopped at the fourth floor. "Relax, dear. He's a surgeon. He can deliver a baby if need be."

Liz blew out a sigh as the elevator doors opened. "I'm sorry, Jackson." She shook her head, chastising herself silently for insinuating his grandson wasn't capable. "That came out wrong."

He laid his hand against the small of her back as they made their way to Lucky's room. His touch felt good, comforting. He opened the second door on the right and led Liz into the living room of the suite where Lily, Ella, and Tim's parents were waiting. Lily jumped up and ran to Liz.

Liz asked, "What's going on?" She held onto Lily's hands, hoping to pass on some serenity to her.

"She's having the baby now," Lily said in a wrecked tone. "They're in there." She pointed to the suite's interior room. "Mom, Tim, and Jake." She looked at Liz wide-eyed. "Jake is delivering my mother's baby." Distaste shook her voice now.

"Come sit down." Liz draped her arm around Lily's shoulders and began guiding her back to the couch. "Everything's going to be fine."

"I didn't get a chance to give her the letter," Lily said.

"What letter?"

"Martha dropped it off earlier today," she said. "Katie gave it to me a little while ago." Lily fished the note Martha had written out of her pocket and handed it to Liz.

Lily, I had hoped to do this myself...but since I had to leave early, this is up to you. Tonight at the party, if things start to go south after you and your mother meet the Ruiz family, give this letter to your mother. It's from her father. Merry Christmas! Martha.

Oh Lord, flew through Liz's thoughts. Her gaze slid back to Lily. "Your grandfather wrote Lucky a letter?" Liz had no idea. Lily nodded. Liz asked, "Why do I not know about this?"

"I think it has something to do with Mr. Ruiz," Lily said.

That's what Liz thought too. And she didn't like where this could be headed either. She'd better just tell Lucky about her shared birthday with Jackson and let the chips fall where they may. Liz held her hand out. "Maybe you'd better let me give the letter to your mother."

At 2:28 a.m., Jake peeked out of the door of the suite's interior room. "Grandpa," he said in a low voice.

Jackson sprang up and in two strides landed at the door. "Everything okay?" he said as Liz appeared at his side.

Jake nodded. "Mother and baby are fine. Lucky can rest here until we can get an ambulance out here to get them. I'll monitor them both until we can get them to the hospital." He looked at Liz and offered her a smile. "It's time to meet you knew grandson."

After a few moments of oohs and aahs over the baby from both sides of the family, Lucky said to Lily, "You want to hold your baby brother?"

Over the next few minutes, the baby was passed from family member to family member, becoming acquainted with each. When the Hollidays excused themselves, Liz said, "Could Lucky and I have a few minutes?"

Tim gave the baby to Lucky, then followed the others into the suite's outer room.

Liz retrieved the letter from her handbag. "Your father wrote this to you after he found out he was sick," she said, offering the envelope to her. "I didn't know about it. He gave it to Martha for safe-keeping, with instructions for when to deliver it."

Lucky looked at the envelope, at Liz, back at the envelope, then back to Liz where her gaze stayed. "Daddy wrote me a letter?"

"Apparently, dear."

Lucky acknowledged the baby in her arms. "Read it to me?" she asked in such a way that it made Liz think about when Lucky was a little girl.

Carefully, she broke the seal on the envelope and pulled out a single piece of paper that had a handwritten letter inscribed on the front and back.

My dearest Lucky, there are some things I want to say to you. I'm entrusting the timing of the delivery to your mother's best friend Martha.

By now, you know that I was not your mother's first love. The thing I want you to know is that I knew all about Jackson Ruiz from the beginning. Your mother and I were always completely honest with one another. I want you to know, your mother never made me feel anything less than one-hundred percent loved.

After all, she gave me you! The day you were born was the best day of my life, and the luckiest. That's why I begged your mother to name you Lucky...because we were incredibly LUCKY to have you come into our lives. The reason I bring this up now is because I also know that you were born on your mother's old flame's birthday. I've always known this. I say these things to you now because I want you to know I don't feel in any way betrayed by your mother's past relationship with Jackson Ruiz. And if he happens to come back into her life after I'm gone, please know that I am all for it if it brings her the slightest measure of happiness. I will always be with you Lucky, and Lily. Forever your loving father....

Liz watched Lucky as she folded the letter up and stuffed it back inside the envelope. Then she turned her sights on Liz. Lucky's lips moved slightly every so often, as if she were going to say something but just couldn't figure out what. Finally, she managed to get out, "So Jackson is your Tim." It was more of a realization for Lucky than a question.

Liz hadn't been sure what to expect from Lucky, but that wasn't it. She said, "Yeah." It felt good to admit that. "I guess he is."

"If he makes you happy," Lucky said. "That's all I care about."

Liz felt herself smile as she said, "I'll confess, it feels really good to have Jackson back in my life."

"Good." Lucky grinned. "Now bring him back in here. I have questions for him." She laughed, and Liz joined her.

Liz headed for the door, but stopped long enough to point a finger at her, saying, "Behave yourself."

Once the family gathered around Lucky and the baby, Liz and Jackson stepped back, taking in the sight.

Tim scooped up the baby, gave him a kiss and then handed him to his grandmother (Tim's mother). Tim's father was holding Ella, who was cooing over her new baby brother and touching his forehead and cheek ever-so-gently. After a couple of minutes, Tim's mother handed the baby to Lily.

A moment or two later, Jackson rested his hands against the small of Liz's back. "Would you look at that?" he said softly, pointing toward Lily and Jake. "You and I just might end up with a child in common after all."

It was a beautiful sight, Lily holding her little brother with Jackson's grandson Jake standing behind them. Jackson's grandson. The man who'd delivered Lily's brother, Liz's grandson.

For the first time in her life, Liz was starting to feel like things just might come full circle for her after all. Liz looked on as Jake doted over Lily while she chatted with her baby brother about nothing and everything.

Full circle. Liz and Jackson, together again. Maybe one day they'd be welcoming their mutual great-grandchild—from the looks of things with Jake and Lily—but preferably in a hospital next time.

Liz didn't bother trying to tear her gaze away from Jake and Lily. They were so full of hope and optimism, she decided, as her thoughts wandered off to the New Year's Eve dinner date she had coming up with Jackson.

It was officially Christmas Eve now, and she couldn't ask for a better present than to be with Jackson tonight, welcoming her grandson into the world.

"Merry Christmas, Jackson," she whispered against his ear.

He kissed her cheek. "Merry Christmas, my love."

Elizabeth Turner Stephens smiled. Life in Joseph's Point was good again.

The Christmas App

Regina Duke

Camryn Talbott held her head high as she sashayed past the cubicle workers to her private office. She knew she looked good. Her short blond hair was exquisitely styled, her shoes were way beyond her budget, and thanks to her generous sister, she was able to wear the very latest in…the previous year's fashions.

But that was okay. After all, it made smart business sense to keep clothes that looked great. And her sister had superb taste, matched by a superb salary. Her sister, Aiden, was the Vice-President of a major corporation and she wasn't even forty yet. The role model she represented had haunted Camryn since she was old enough to understand the word "competition."

She reached her office and closed the door softly. Only then, in her private space, did she slump and let her purse slide to the floor. She lowered her computer bag by its strap and dragged it toward her desk. Her spotlessly clean desk.

Aiden's desk never seemed to have any paper on it. And someone must wax it every night. But Camryn was not a clean-desker. She was an out-of-sight-out-of-minder. That meant she needed her projects in view at all times so she wouldn't forget one. But if Aiden had made it to the top with a clean desk, then darn it,

Cam would empty that sucker every night. She'd ordered three dozen magazine holders, and at the end of the day, she tidied each pile on her desk and deposited it in one of the holders, which she then placed on a bookshelf by the window. Then, every morning, she moved her work back to her desk and wasted precious minutes setting her projects out where they had been the day before.

And Christmas was coming. That meant she would get to hear all about Aiden's most recent towering achievements. Oh, goody.

She toyed with the idea of using nail polish to delineate their space on the desk top, but the boss would probably object.

She plopped into her chair and wondered if middle management was as high as she would ever get. She liked her job well enough. Okay. Kind of. Sort of. But she went home late every night and often had to take work with her. Every time a new position opened in the company, she would consume every word of the job description, hoping against hope that one line might read, "Personal happiness guaranteed."

So far, no luck.

What she really, really wanted was to go home every night to a slobbery dog and two perfect children and a husband who looked at her the way other men looked at a thick-crust pizza. Someone hungry for her. Someone who would say, "Don't worry, babe. We got this. We're a team."

That was her big secret. No way she would admit those desires at a family gathering. Can you imagine the ridicule Aiden would heap upon her?

When Camryn was born, Aiden was a sophomore in high school. Fifteen years between them. Camryn knew she shouldn't compare herself to her sister. After all, Aiden had a huge head start. Their professional parents had prepped her for college, coached her in business techniques, and did all they could to ensure her success in the working world.

By the time Camryn came along, they were tired. She was

grateful if they made it to her school awards ceremonies. But where her parents had lagged, Aiden seemed driven to pick up the slack. "Make your mark in the world, Cam. Get out there and build your own security. Once that's done, you can think about a home life."

Camryn stared glumly at her desktop computer. Her laptop was okay for home, but the company wanted her hooked into the system. Every time she set her fingers on its keyboard, she could feel invisible shackles clamping around her wrists. She sighed heavily and turned it on.

It took two or three minutes for all the shared programs to prepare themselves for action, so she unbuttoned the jacket of her tailored suit and slipped into the lunch room for a cup of coffee. Seven others were doing the same, and they all greeted each other silently, with nods and half-smiles.

"Aren't we a happy lot?" thought Camryn. The three men in the room let their eyes linger a bit on the lines of her suit. One of them blushed when she caught him looking, and that made her smile. She took her coffee mug—"World's Greatest Manager"—and returned to her office.

When Cam was just one of the girls in the office, she had dated now and then. Aiden had scolded her. "Never date inside the company! Recipe for disaster."

Well, that eliminated a lot of people because Cam didn't have the time or the inclination to bar hop. She was too busy taking night classes. When she finally made manager, she despaired when she discovered she would be working evenings, because there was so much to do. Still no date time, and on top of that, she had to drop her night classes.

Cam sipped her coffee and leaned back in her chair. She stared glumly into the dark brew. "I think I'm miserable," she confessed.

Her computer beeped. Odd. It usually played the company

logo and theme music, seven annoying chimes that ran up the scale like a reminder that she should be climbing the competitive ladder.

But this morning, it beeped. She frowned at it. A small box in the middle of the screen blinked at her. She leaned toward it and read, "Click here for a special greeting from IT."

Information Technology? She'd been down there a few times, mostly when she was in a cubicle. Her finger hovered over her mouse. What if it was some kind of dangerous worm?

She got up and looked out the door. Thirty conscientious heads were bent over their work, and three others were probably cruising porn sites. They'd be sorry when IT—Information Technology, the computer techs—initiated their recently announced crackdown on those naughty little behaviors. But no one appeared to be having a computer crisis. If the little box on her screen was malware, surely it would have affected the eight-a.m. crowd first.

Management arrived at nine.

She closed the door and returned to her desk. She took another sip of coffee to fortify herself, then clicked on the blinking box.

Her computer screen turned into a glorious snowy Christmas scene, with reindeer peeking out of a barn and shadows of chubby people passing behind curtained windows. An oboe played "Silent Night." And as she watched, a winged angel appeared at the top of the screen and tapped a wand—did angels have wands?—three times. On the third tap, a decorated Christmas tree began to form, beginning with the top of its crowning star on down to the base, where squirrels ran back and forth with tiny gifts.

"Awwww." Cam surprised herself. Had that come out of her? She thought she'd lost whatever Christmas magic she'd been born with. Aiden had schooled it out of her. Marketing, that's all it was. Marketing.

And yet...no ad popped up to destroy the lovely scene. Instead, a bar of text ran slowly across the bottom.

"This greeting comes with a full heart. It will disappear in ten seconds…unless you hit the space bar. Ten…. Nine…. Eight…."

Cam hit the space bar. The text disappeared, but the graphic remained. So lovely.

"Great," she sighed. "How am I going to get any work done?"

As if it had heard her question, the image shrank to an icon on her desktop, leaving all her other business-related programs accessible.

"Son of a gun." She cocked her head to one side and clicked on the icon. It took over the screen again. She clicked again and it minimized. She smiled. "Okay," she said to herself. "Maybe everyone in Management got one."

She dove into her work and every time she needed a break, she clicked on the icon. Lovely.

At noon, she went to the lunchroom, carrying her meager little granola bar. She bought a diet soda out of the machine and sat down in a chair by the wall. She refused to eat at her desk, regardless of Aiden's advice. Instead, she picked up a Good Housekeeping magazine and began reading about homemade Christmas ornaments. Well, she'd never have time to make them, but they were very cute. Little leftover ball ornaments decorated to look like Santa and his elves. The half hour sped by. She left the magazine open on the chair and returned to work.

The afternoon moved by as easily as the morning had, thanks to her little icon friend. And when she left for her apartment, she decided that tonight she would watch the Hallmark channel and leave her work at the office.

The next day Camryn went to work feeling a little more comfortable about her job and not as depressed about Christmas. Truth be told, a tiny part of her was hoping she might get another Christmas card, or at least be able to revisit the digital card from the day before, on and off during her day.

She said, "Good morning!" as she filled her coffee cup, leaving three of her workmates opened-mouthed with disbelief. She also looked around a little more carefully than usual to see if anyone looked curious. Was anyone watching her for a reaction? If so, she thought that might give them away. No, she didn't see anyone with that special gleam in his eye.

Slightly disappointed, she went into her office, closed the door, plopped down at her desk, and sipped her coffee. No point in waiting any longer. She turned on her computer and stared at the screen as it went through its usual dance in preparation for loading programs. Then it played "Jingle Bells." Her coffee frozen halfway to her mouth, she listened to the quick xylophone rendition of "Jingle Bells." After a few seconds, the music faded and a new digital Christmas card bloomed from the center of the screen. It started out with the Christmas scene from the previous day. However, when the Christmas tree appeared, it was covered with decorations that looked incredibly familiar to her. Suddenly, she realized the ornaments on the tree were the same as the ones that she'd been reading about in the lunch room the day before. Cute little balls of elves and a fat jolly Santa.

How that could be? How could they be the same? Was it some kind of weird coincidence? Had they been there the day before and she just didn't notice? She waited for the Christmas card to reach the point where she was instructed to press the spacebar in order to keep the card or let it fade away. She pressed the spacebar. The card minimized. She set her coffee cup down and struggled to keep from running out of her office. She paused at the door, opened it carefully, and stepped calmly past the numerous cubicles to the corridor. Once she was out of sight of her coworkers, she couldn't help herself. She broke into a trot. She went straight to the lunch room, where she spotted yesterday's magazine right where she had left it. She went over and quickly found the page that described how to make the ornaments that she would never have time to make, and in her haste, she ripped the page from the magazine. She could not pull her eyes away from the illustration. She walked right into the door, then realized that she needed to be more careful. So she tucked the page inside her blouse and then walked with purpose back to her office.

Once she was sitting in front of her computer again, she tried to calm herself by sipping at her coffee. She took a deep breath, then unfolded the illustration from the magazine and laid it on the desk. She clicked on the icon for the e-card and the Christmas tree in all its glory showed up on her screen. Sure enough, her instinct had been correct. The ornament that she loved so much in the magazine was now part of the digital Christmas card. How could that possibly be? She wracked her brain, trying to remember who had seen her in the lunch room yesterday, but frankly, she hadn't paid any attention to the other occupants, as usual. Now she had a mystery on her hands.

She let the card run from beginning to end. It was so adorable, and she knew how much work had gone into it. She'd been studying computer graphics at night school, before she took a shot at her middle management position and actually got hired. She frowned at the screen. Was the message at the end of the card slightly different? This time it said, "Sent to you with a full heart from a secret admirer. Wishing you holiday joy."

She leaned back in her office chair and wondered how she was supposed to think about business when she had this glorious gift from an unseen admirer on her screen. With a deep, longing sigh, she minimized the card and got to work.

But she could hardly wait for lunch time. By 11:30 she had convinced herself that she should test her theory. She would pick a different magazine and find a different Christmas ornament to admire. When no one thought she was looking, she would take a mental inventory of everyone in the room. She was so excited now, she could hardly wait for lunch time. She never had a secret admirer before.

I wonder what he looks like?, she thought. The anticipation she was feeling made everything move in slow motion. At five to twelve, she could stand it no longer. She took her purse, walked normally past the cubicles outside her door and moved at a dignified pace toward the lunch room. Once again, she couldn't stop herself from trotting the last few feet. She grabbed the handle of the door and opened it.

No one. The lunch room was empty. She felt depression descend upon her. Oh well, it was a lovely fantasy. How could she have thought that anything would really come of it? But she was a person who carried her plans through to completion, so (with much less enthusiasm) she moved to the table where magazines were spread helter-skelter. She selected a copy of *Home Beautiful* and sat down to eat her granola bar. She flipped past one page at a time. Someone came in the door. Her heart pounded as she glanced up. It was just Olive from down the hall.

She kept paging through the magazine until the door opened again. She barely even looked up this time. Sigh. Wasted effort. It was Reuben, that sky-high former basketball player, who went and got an MBA so he could find a job in the real world, blah, blah, blah. She hoped he didn't sit down next to her to tell her all about his struggles in graduate school. She sighed again.

At last, the magazine took an interesting turn. Suddenly, there was a beautiful Christmas tree on the page. She turned the page. "For the crafty among us," it read. "Do try to make this lovely little angel for your tree."

It had a stockinette head and beautiful lace doily wings, and its tiny crocheted body hung gracefully below its praying hands. *Okay*, she thought, *this is really cute*. She munched her granola bar, running her finger over the little angel as she chewed. She glanced up. Where did these four other people come from? She hadn't even noticed the door open. She tried to identify them, feeling a spark of excitement reignite within her. She would eliminate the two women, she decided, laughing softly at herself. That would never work out.

That left two guys. One was five foot seven, chunky through the middle with polyester trousers. She thought she recognized him from human resources. She hoped and prayed he had not sent her the card. The other fellow was about six feet tall, broad shouldered, slender but not skinny. He was taking the lid off a plastic container. That was a good sign, a male human being who actually consumed salad for lunch. She waited for him to turn around, but he stared into his salad bowl. Even when he sat down to eat, he was careful not to make eye contact. She couldn't read his name tag from where she was.

I know. I'll get up and get a soda out of the vending machine. Then I'll be able to read his name tag.

Nonchalantly, she stroked the page lovingly, stood up, and tried to draw attention to herself by stretching and yawning. Then she said aloud, "I guess I have to go back to work now." No reaction from anyone. She moved to the soda dispenser, selected a diet soda, pulled it out, and turned around quickly to see if anyone was looking at her. But no one was, and she still couldn't see the name tag of the salad eater. He was hunched over that bowl like he was disarming a landmine.

Well, back to work. It had been a fun and exciting morning, and that's all she could ask for. When she got back to her desk, she found a phone message from her sister the VP. That certainly cast a cloud over the rest of her day. She hoped everything was okay. She loved her sister, and she didn't want anything bad to happen to her. But she suspected that the phone call was not an emergency but rather an opportunity to share some great accomplishment or career move…maybe a huge raise. She wasn't sure. Glumly, she pressed the button to play back the call. Her sister's voice was efficient and brisk, as always.

"Hi, sis, just wanted to give you a heads up. I believe I'm going to be CEO before Christmas. Just wanted you to know ahead of time because I didn't think it was fair to spring it on you in front of the family. You know how they compare you to me. Just thought I'd let you know privately. Okay then, can't wait to see you at Mom's."

And she now she was really depressed. CEO? The rest of the day was like walking through a dark cloud of anguish. The thought of listening to her parents exalt her older sister for all that she had accomplished filled her with dread.

By one the next morning, Camryn realized she was not going to sleep at all. She'd tossed and turned, wondering who her secret admirer could be. At last she turned on the lamp by her bed and made a list of all the men in her department. One by one, she checked them off. She knew it couldn't be Tim, who occupied the front desk. She was pretty sure it wasn't Roger either. Roger slicked his hair down to his head and wore plaid trousers to work. The other three men in her department— Cyril, David, and Jerome— had very little to offer her, and she hoped beyond hope that none of them were involved in her e-cards. Cyril was bald and had glasses thick as Coke bottles. David was a nice enough guy but he was younger than her by four years and was the boss's nephew. Jerome was sixty-two if he was a day. His hair was white, his tummy hung over his trousers, and he coughed and made rude noises a lot. She lay back on her pillow and closed her eyes. Who else could possibly be involved?

Maybe she needed to look outside the department. After all, the fellows that she had on her list didn't seem at all capable when it came to computers. They could barely run the software required by their office work. The card was signed "from IT," so she needed to think about the possibilities there. The problem was, she had no idea who they were. Then she had a brilliant thought. She pulled out her cell phone and looked them up online. It took her a while, but she wasn't going to sleep. That was obvious. So why not?

She finally found a listing for the personnel in the IT department. This was more like it. She scrolled down and realized there were a lot of people working in IT. She saw at least twenty-three names there. She immediately eliminated the women and jotted the names of the men on her notepad. Somehow writing them down made them more substantial. Okay, let's see, Norman… Richard…. Casey…. She paused for a moment. She liked the name Casey. Maybe Casey was her secret admirer. And maybe she just wanted it to be Casey because she liked the name.

She clicked her tongue at herself and continued. Riley… Harry… She was in no way a "Harry" person, so she crossed him off the list and hoped to God that he had not sent the e-card. She ignored the names of men whose photos showed mustaches or beards. She wanted her secret admirer to be clean shaven. Once she compiled her list, she promised herself that, the next day, she would go to IT and check these guys out. Knowing that she had a plan allowed her to fall asleep at last.

The next morning, for the first time in weeks, Camryn actually showed up at the office thirty minutes early. No one had even made coffee yet. But she had stopped at Starbucks on her way and got herself a latte. After all, it was the Christmas season. She should treat herself. She went into her office and closed the door.

It was very quiet. The cubicle workers outside her door, who had theoretically been at their desks since eight, were not thumping away on their computers and answering phones. In fact, she didn't even hear a phone ring. For a while, she sipped her latte and stared at her computer screen. What if there were no more e-cards? What if it was the same one as yesterday?

As if testing to see if a burner was hot, she flicked on the computer.

And there it was. A beautiful e-card blooming in the center of her screen. When the tree appeared, she almost dropped her latte. All the ornaments were now angels with lace doily wings and sweet painted faces.

Her heart pounded with excitement. The tag line at the bottom had changed again. "Wishing you angels and love this Christmas. Your secret admirer."

She pulled her list out and flattened it on the surface of her desk. Then she took a red pen. She numbered the guys one by one. And then she tried to come up with a really good reason for going down to IT.

After all, when one had a computer problem, one called IT to one's office, she thought. One didn't run down to IT. It was unheard of. Especially for middle management. It took a while, but at last she thought she'd come up with a reason to go. Just in time, because she could hear people starting to pound keyboards and answer phones outside her office. She put her plan into action. She unscrewed the cable from the printer and unplugged it from her computer. Cable in hand and feeling quite self-sufficient, she opened her office door and walked sedately past the cubicles and into the hallway, down to the elevator, where she punched the call button for the next floor. Once the doors opened on IT's floor, she began to get cold feet, but then she reminded herself that it was just another department in the company. No one would think anything about it.

She walked down the hall until she saw the big sign next to the door: Information Technology. She wasn't surprised to find it gave her a warm fuzzy feeling. After all, IT had been the field she'd aimed for when she started night classes. Then she got interested in computer graphics, and she had so much fun in those classes. But with the constant competition going on between her and her sister, when that position came up in middle management, she felt like she had to apply. If she hadn't, the family would have said she wasn't even trying. Besides, it was her sister who noticed the ad in the first place, circled it, and left it for her at the family's Fourth of July picnic.

She took a deep breath, straightened her spine, and opened the door to IT. More cubicles inside. That was no surprise but there was a registration desk near the front of the room with three women working behind it. Darn. She pulled out her list of names and, with the list in one hand and her cable in the other, she went up to the friendliest-looking woman and said, "Hi. I'm Camryn from downstairs, and I was wondering—"

The other woman stopped her. "I'm Kelly. Nice to meet you. You look so familiar. Didn't you ask for tech setup for that presentation last week?"

Camryn blushed. "Yes, I did. Thanks to you guys, the computer equipment all worked perfectly."

"What can I do for you?"

Camryn held up her printer cable and said, "I was wondering if you might have another one of these? Or if I could talk to a technician about it?"

Kelly said, "No problem. I'll see if we have one in stock." Before Camryn could say anything, she was gone.

Well, rats.

Okay, she thought. Let's see, Norman… Richard….

A tall man with dark wavy hair and black horn-rimmed glasses came around the corner. He stopped when he saw her and almost did an about-face. Then he seemed to realize that such an action would probably seem rude, so he approached the counter instead.

"Welcome. Have you been helped?"

Camryn smiled and said, "Yes. Someone's checking on something for me, but actually…." She peered at his name tag. "Riley?"

He said, "Yes, that's me. That's my name. Nice to meet you."

Camryn squinted at him. "I think we've met before."

Riley looked around as if there were someone else behind him whom she might be talking to.

Camryn studied him carefully. He had broad shoulders and a narrow waist, like the salad eater she'd spotted the day before. "Were you in the lunch room yesterday?"

Riley rubbed his face and said, "Gosh, yes, I probably was. I often go there. Usually to eat lunch."

Camryn felt like an idiot. Of course he went there to eat lunch. She tried again. "I just can't quite place you. You look so familiar somehow."

Riley shuffled his feet and gazed down at the carpet. He finally tilted his head sideways, almost looked her in the eye, and said, "I may have met you in school."

Camryn snapped her fingers. "We shared the same computer graphics class!"

Riley nodded. "That's right. What can I help you with?"

She held up the printer cable. "Look, Riley, I'm here on false pretenses."

Riley's brows rose, a question mark over his stunning sky-blue eyes. "So…what kind of false pretenses?"

Camryn thought to herself, *Okay, so he's not a great conversationalist. Who cares? Look at those dreamy eyes!*

Besides, she'd learned in her computer classes that guys who loved tech would often prefer to communicate through their keyboards instead of engaging in witty chit-chat. Then she realized that she'd put her finger on how and why her secret admirer could very well be Riley!

"I came here with this hijacked printer cable so I could say something was wrong with my computer. But I'm actually trying to solve a mystery. Can you help me?"

"A computer mystery?" Riley sounded doubtful. "I've never found them all that mysterious."

Camryn wasn't sure but she had the distinct impression that he was playing with her. Maybe it was the glint of a tease in his eye or his quirky almost-a-smile.

Two could play at that game. "I remember you now. You were the lanky know-it-all in graphics class, weren't you? The one with all the answers?" She smiled and moved her head as if to flip her hair, but it wasn't long enough. Even so, it had the desired effect.

Riley's color rose. His perfect nose and sensitive mouth almost twitched. After a few awkward seconds, he came back with, "Lanky?"

Camryn laughed. Then she said, "Will you be my Sherlock and help me solve my mystery?"

Riley's eyes flicked up and down, as if assessing her total package. Without taking his eyes off her, he raised his voice. "Donna? I'm making an office call. Be back later."

Riley couldn't believe his luck. The woman of his dreams had just walked in and told him she needed him. He had spent numerous hours in graphics class slouched sideways in his chair so that he could keep an eye on that striking blonde huddled over her keyboard. When they demonstrated the projects that they were working on, it was obvious that she had a knack for computer graphics. He would even say she was gifted. He had almost worked up the courage to talk to her when, all of a sudden, she stopped coming to class.

The instructor told him that she'd gotten a job at Hyper Tech Inc. At first Riley was little disappointed and a tiny bit jealous, because Hyper Tech was the company he'd set his own sights on. He'd submitted three different applications there for various positions in their IT department. At that point, he was only a few credits away from his degree in Computer Graphics and IT.

He had a hundred questions for Camryn, but her very presence tied his tongue in knots. In the elevator, she made an attempt at some conversation.

"How long have you been working here, Riley?"

"Just a couple of months. I had to finish my summer courses."

That was all they had time for before the doors opened.

"My office is this way," said Camryn.

Riley blurted, "Why did you leave? You were a genius in class."

Two spots of color rose on Camryn's cheeks. "I was sort of pushed into applying for a middle management job. My family wanted me to have the security of a job with a future." She snorted derisively, then fell silent when two coworkers approached, deep in conversation.

Riley waited for them to leave. "That was my logic as well. Get a day job, and work on the apps at night."

Camryn's face lit up. "You're actually using your classes?"

Riley shrugged and nodded. "I'm entry level at IT, but I've always dreamed of starting my own business and selling my apps all over the world."

Camryn stopped, her hand on her office door. "That was my dream, too! When I started with computers, I was so excited." She opened the door, let Riley in, then left it ajar about six inches.

Riley went straight to her computer. He held out a hand for the cable, reinstated it, and sat down in her chair. "Your excitement was contagious in class." He pushed his glasses up his nose and pretended he didn't see the Christmas card icon at the bottom of the screen. "Before you left, I was sort of hoping…." He let it trail off.

"Hoping? For what?" Camryn sounded interested, and she moved to stand beside him.

Suddenly nervous again, Riley cleared his throat and reverted to his junior high days. "A lot of our course work felt like hoops to jump through in order to get the degree. I've been working with computers and graphics and such since seventh grade."

"I see. So you were hoping…the instructor would discover one of your apps and help you promote it?"

Riley shriveled inside. He wasn't making much personal progress. "Um, not exactly. More like, hoping you might have coffee with me after class."

He could have sworn Camryn's body heat increased by at least five degrees. He peeked at her out of the corner of his eye and added, "No pressure."

Camryn's response was the sweetest he'd ever heard. "I wish you had asked me. Say, if you can solve my computer mystery, I'll raise your coffee to a lunch date."

Riley's heart was in his throat. "Okay." *Gee, that was suave*, he thought. "Where's the mystery?"

Camryn leaned close to cup her hand over the mouse. She clicked on the icon and the e-card bloomed on the screen.

Riley blinked at it.

"Does this look familiar?" asked Camryn. "I mean, did everyone in the office get this?"

Of course it looked familiar. He'd created the darn thing. He scrambled for words. "Is it annoying you?" he asked. He peeked upward in time to see Camryn roll her eyes.

"No, of course not. How can I be annoyed when something this beautiful is signed 'your secret admirer'?"

Riley relaxed a bit. "Only one person received it. You."

Camryn pushed his chair gently around. "Is there something you want to tell me?"

Riley suddenly ran out of air. Instead of speaking, he put his hands on the keyboard and typed with lightning speed, *I think you're beautiful.*

Camryn nudged him sideways and typed, *I think you're the cutest geek I ever met.*

Now Riley's hands were shaking so hard he couldn't type. He looked up at her hopefully and almost squeaked, "Does this mean we can have lunch together?"

Camryn giggled and nodded.

Riley grinned from ear to ear. Then he asked awkwardly, "Any other questions for your IT guy?"

"Yes," said Camryn. "Can we leave right now?"

They left the building like two kids skipping school. When they emerged on the sidewalk, they were both laughing. After half a block, Camryn took a chance and let her hand brush against Riley's. A moment later, he was holding her hand, and they walked on in silence.

At the corner was a coffee shop promising quick service, and they went in.

"We should eat," said Riley, "if this is a lunch date."

Camryn giggled. "Good thinking." Even if it was only nine-thirty. They settled at a table for two against the back wall. No sense in flaunting their truancy by sitting next to the window.

A waitress approached and poured coffee without asking if they wanted any. When she left, they shared a moment of disbelief. Camryn whispered, "Do you think she even saw us?"

"She looked but didn't see. Very Holmesian, don't you think?"

Camryn was delighted. "You're a Sherlock Holmes fan?"

Riley's brows rose. "You, too?"

"Totally!"

Riley looked pleased. "That's a very good sign."

Camryn nodded. "We'll always have something to talk about."

"Excellent!"

Camryn realized Riley was looking deep into her eyes, and she was transfixed. She could have sat there all day, just staring into his eyes. The waitress had other plans.

"What'll you have?"

"Hmm? Oh. Right," said Camryn. "I'll have a cinnamon roll."

"Me, too," said Riley.

The waitress left, and they scrunched their shoulders and tee-heed at each other. "What now?" asked Camryn.

"We eat our rolls while you explain to me why you gave up on graphics and app building."

Camryn made a face. "I loved those classes. I wanted to finish, but when they gave me this job, they said, 'Surprise, you get to take hours of work home with you' because no one had been filling my position for almost a year."

"That's terrible."

"Oh, that's not the worst part," she said glumly. She lowered her voice. "I don't even like the job." Before she knew it, the cinnamon rolls were gone and an hour had passed while she unburdened her soul to Riley.

"You must think I'm really pitiful," she said at last. "Letting myself be bullied out of what I loved to do, just for a paycheck."

Riley shook his head. "Not at all. We have to pay the rent." He glanced around. "Let's get out of here, okay? Let's go do something worthy of playing hooky."

Camryn felt a thrill. "Like what?"

"Let's go look at Christmas windows! And we definitely need to buy candy canes."

"Big ones!"

Riley grinned, and Camryn's heart soared. The rest of the day was filled with fun. After finding the biggest candy canes in the city, they decided to buy slightly smaller ones because the biggest were too large to carry. Later, after critiquing all the Christmas windows they could find, they sat down on a bench next to an outdoor ice rink.

"Do you skate?" asked Camryn.

Riley looked aghast. "On ice?! No way. A person could break an ankle…or even worse, a wrist." He mimicked typing at a keyboard.

Camryn laughed.

Then Riley took her hand and pulled her across the street to a bus stop, just as a large green-and-white bus slowed to a stop.

"Where are we going?"

Riley paid both fares and tugged her down the aisle to the back of the bus. "Skating."

Camryn's forehead scrunched in confusion. "On a bus?"

"You'll see."

Five minutes later, he buzzed for a stop and pulled her to the door. They stepped onto the sidewalk in front of Roller World.

Camryn's mouth fell open.

With a wave of his hand, Riley announced, "Roller skating, the sport of kings. And geeks."

It was the best fun Camryn had had in years. They skated nonstop for two hours, then feasted on foot-long hot dogs. By the time they left the rink, it was three in the afternoon. The pale winter sun cast a cold light on the city streets. Camryn shivered inside her coat. "That was great," she said happily.

Riley had a glazed look of happiness. "I think I may be getting serious. You roller-skated with me. That is a rare trait in a female of the species."

Camryn smiled and let him encircle her in his arms.

"Shall we walk?" he asked.

"Where? Back to the office?" Her smile faded.

Riley shrugged, a delaying tactic he seemed to use when he was nervous about asking a question. "Would you like to see the apps I'm working on? We can pick up my laptop and go somewhere neutral," he added quickly. Then he blushed, "Besides, my apartment is a mess. I'd rather tidy up before inviting you in."

Camryn was floating on air. "I'd love to see your apps."

"Do you think we'll still have jobs in the morning?" he asked.

"Who cares?"

Riley laughed out loud. Then he pulled her hands up so he could kiss her fingers. A moment later, his arms were wrapped tight around her as he kissed her warmly on the lips. They stood there, gazing into each other's eyes, until the jingle of a horse-drawn carriage caught their attention.

"Perfect!" shouted Riley, waving the cabby down.

Camryn sighed dreamily. Perfect, indeed.

Two weeks later, Camryn gathered up all her office knick-knacks in a backpack and waved farewell to her officemates. "Enjoy your Christmas party!"

"Do you have to go so soon?" asked Roger.

Just then, Riley stumbled through the door, carrying a rucksack stuffed with papers and equipment. "Is there cake?" he asked.

Camryn set her backpack on the floor. "I guess we have time for cake." She held up her hands and the room fell quiet. "Thank you all for being so good to me these last six months. Most of you already know Riley, but if you don't, here he is, my future business partner."

One of the cubicle girls said dreamily, "I'm so happy for you. Leaving the cube farm to start your own business. You're a brave woman." She offered Camryn a small piece of Christmas cake.

Camryn took the plate and passed it to Riley. "Gee, thanks, I think." But she gave the girl a brief hug. "The courageous part is yet to come."

Riley looked confused for a moment. Then the light came on. "Oh! You mean, Christmas at your parents' house."

Everyone laughed.

Riley cleaned his plate in three bites. "Okay, we'd better get going."

Camryn was ready. Five minutes later, they were strolling along the sidewalk, headed for Grand Central. They'd already stowed overnight bags in a locker, and once they retrieved them—filling the locker with their office things, except for their laptops—they caught the train for White Plains.

Riley drummed his fingers nervously on his laptop. "I hope your family likes me."

"At this point in my life," said Camryn, "I'm more concerned about you liking them. Just be yourself. That's the guy I fell in love with."

That deserved a kiss, so Riley gave her one. Then they both giggled like teenagers. In White Plains, they took a taxi to the Talbott home.

Camryn stood in the driveway as Riley paid the cabby.

"What's wrong?" he asked.

Camryn pointed to a Lincoln Continental parked at the curb. "My sister's already here. I was hoping to show you off to my parents before she arrived."

But there was no time to change her plans, because her mother was coming out the front door to greet them.

"Camryn, dear! So good to see you." Her hair was obviously died a rich brown, her wrinkles making it clear that her roots were gray. "Is this your young man?"

Camryn gave her mother a quick hug. "I don't own him, Mom."

Riley chuckled. "Not yet anyway." He extended a hand. "Riley Atwood, ma'am."

"Oh, aren't you polite! Come on in, your father doesn't want to be out in the cold. And Aiden is already here! She brought a carload of gifts, too."

Camryn suppressed a sigh of irritation. "Oh, goody."

Once all the introductions were made, they stood in the dining room, looking awkwardly at each other. Aiden, an older, taller, thinner version of her sister, pressed her hands together and announced, "Mom? Dad? Camryn already knows, but I have a surprise for you." She cleared her throat. "I was just made CEO of the company!"

Camryn's parents looked genuinely pleased. Her father clapped and nodded. Her mother made a fuss and insisted they all drink a cup of Christmas punch.

Riley smacked his lips. "This is great. I suspect someone spiked your punch, Mrs. Atwood."

That struck everyone as hilariously funny, and Camryn knew right away they'd all started toasting before she and Riley arrived.

Mrs. Talbott waved her hands in the air. "Let's all sit down. Aiden, dear, help me serve. No, no, your father has begun dropping things. We don't want him carrying the turkey platter."

Camryn and Riley sat down beside each other at the table. Camryn leaned toward him and whispered, "I hope this isn't too uncomfortable for you."

Riley squeezed her hand reassuringly.

Mr. Talbott began the inquisition. "So…Riley, is it? What do you do for a living?"

"I design computer apps, sir."

Silence.

Camryn translated. "He works with computers, Dad."

"Oh. Well, now, that's supposed to be a darned good way to make a living. What company are you with?"

Camryn froze.

But Riley took another drink of his punch and leaned back in his chair. "Brand new business called RiCam Apps. A startup, but there are excellent people there. Sure to be a winner."

"Glad to hear it!" Mr. Atwood was hard of hearing.

Aiden and her mother came in carrying platters of food. "Here we are," said Mrs. Talbott. "So delightful to have you girls home for the holiday." She faltered when she looked at Riley. "And you, too, of course," she added.

Camryn pressed her lips together to keep from saying something she'd regret later. But Riley was unfazed. "Mrs.

Talbott, after dinner, I hope you'll give me a tour of your lovely home. What I've seen so far is really special."

Mrs. Talbott beamed. "Why, thank you. I would love to."

Aiden cleared her throat. "Cam, weren't you able to bring your gifts with you on the train? I've already put mine under the tree."

Before Camryn could say anything, Riley bumped her knee with his and spoke up. "Oh, don't worry. We have a few surprises."

Mr. and Mrs. Talbott were obviously tickled. Aiden, however, only pretended to laugh politely. Once she finished buttering her Parkerhouse roll, she addressed Riley in a confidential tone. "I hope you don't fall too hard for Cam. She's a rising star in the management world, you know. It's hard to reach the top when you're hitched to…other obligations."

Camryn snapped, "Aiden! That's an awful thing to say."

Aiden drew back, as if Camryn were the one being rude. "Really? Well, I'm just looking out for your interests, little sister. After all, if I had given in to…temptation…and married my college sweetheart, I never would have had the time and energy to make CEO."

Riley nodded as if he understood completely. "I can understand what you're saying. That's why Camryn and I quit our humdrum jobs so we can concentrate on our business startup."

"What? What'd he say?" Mr. Talbott had a hand behind one ear, straining to hear.

Mrs. Talbott looked surprised.

Aiden laughed out loud. "Oh, you must be joking! You gave up a middle management position to play with your computer games?"

Camryn said icily, "Apps are not games, Aiden."

Riley held up a finger. "Although we will probably develop some in the future. They can be very lucrative." He finished off his punch. "For now, we'll have to make do with the million-dollar loan the bank just offered us."

Aiden nearly choked on a piece of roll. "How much?"

Riley shrugged. "Starting a business takes capital. Otherwise, we'd just use our own money."

"Ha! Camryn has money? Don't you know she's wearing my hand-me-down wardrobe? She can't even buy her own shoes."

Camryn blushed hotly.

Riley pulled her hand into his. "That was before," he said.

"Before what, dear?" asked Mrs. Talbott.

"Before we started selling our app online. It's only been up ten days, but we've already sold fifty thousand."

Aiden's eyes nearly popped out of their sockets. "Fifty thousand dollars?!"

Riley shook his head. "Fifty thousand apps."

Camryn began to relax. "At eight dollars each." She couldn't help herself. She used the retail price.

Mrs. Talbott clapped her hands for joy. "That's wonderful, dear! So you will both be working on your new company?"

"That's right, Mom." Camryn let her eyes settle on Riley's handsome face. "Working together, we should have our next app on the market in six months or less."

"The bank is excited," said Riley. "We want to get as much done in the first year as we can."

Aiden sat stunned.

Mrs. Talbott asked, "Why is that, dear?"

Riley pulled a small velvet box out of his pocket and set it in front of Camryn. She knew what was in it, so she smiled like the Mona Lisa. "Because," she said, revealing the huge diamond ring, "we want to slow down a bit when we have our first child." She let Riley put the ring on her finger. "But first, we'll be getting married right after New Year's." She wiggled her fingers so the ring would catch the light.

Mrs. Talbott was ecstatic. She leaned toward her husband. "You hear that, old man? We're going to have grandchildren!"

Aiden seemed to shrink in her chair. "I'm very happy for you," she said calmly. "I guess the family will have to settle for one CEO."

"Yes," said Camryn, "and one old fashioned girl with a husband and kids and a dog."

Riley added, "Who is Chairman of the Board at RiCam."

Aiden scooted her chair back. "Excuse me." She left the room.

Camryn looked from her mother to her father. "Uh-oh. I'd better go talk to her."

She found Aiden standing in front of the Christmas tree, her arms folded, staring into space.

Camryn said, "I'm sorry, Aiden. Sometimes Riley is perfect and sometimes he's all geek. But I love him. We didn't mean to hurt your feelings."

Aiden turned, tears in her eyes. "It's okay. I'm so happy for you." She hugged Camryn tight. "I'm going to tell you something I never told anyone." She made sure they were alone. "I dedicated myself to my career because…my college sweetheart decided to marry someone else."

"No!"

Aiden wiped her eyes. "Yes, it's true. I just never found anyone else. But listen up, little sister. You'd better plan on more than one baby. I've waited all my life to be someone's rich auntie."

The rest of their visit was like a dream. Camryn didn't even mind when Aiden put herself in charge of getting them married and throwing a small reception afterward.

"But Aiden, you have less than a month," cautioned Camryn.

Aiden tossed her head and said teasingly, "What good is it to be CEO if you can't get important things done?"

A year later, Camryn cooed at the baby in her arms. She juggled the baby and the bottle, as Riley gave her a pen. Together, they signed a card for Aiden.

"We are delighted to announce the birth of our first daughter, Aiden Atwood. Love, RiCam."

The Christmas Beau

Regina Duke

"WE'RE here!"

"Mother, it's about time we shared a shopping spree!" Holly Howell picked up her purse, and prepared to get out of the car.

"Wait until I get parked, please." Margaret Howell was driving, and that meant they never went over forty miles an hour. At last, she turned off the engine and engaged the emergency brake.

"No one uses those anymore," said Holly.

"Better safe than sorry. Remember when Teddy Bear accidentally knocked the car into drive?"

"I know, I know." Holly found her lip gloss and rolled it on with the blind expertise that some young women are born with.

"He was a great old boy, wasn't he?" Margaret said tenderly.

Holly said, "He was sweet." She stuffed her phone and the gloss in her purse. "But then, pugs were bred to be sweethearts." She slipped out of the car, full of excitement because she had not even begun her Christmas shopping yet. Her mother had assured her that the Christmas Circuit was the best place to shop for both her family and her friends. Holly turned and headed toward the front of the massive building. Then she stopped, confused. She didn't see any signs indicating a Christmas extravaganza.

She said, "Mom, I thought we were going to a craft fair. Christmas Circuit, right?"

Her mother nodded eagerly. "Yes dear, there are all kinds of vendors here, and they'll have beautiful gifts for you to choose from."

Holly planted her hands on her hips and turned to read the sign over the parking lot entrance. "Christmas Circuit. Three days, three dog shows. You promised me you were not going to bring me to any more dog shows," said Holly.

Her mother locked the car and approached her daughter, patting the air to calm her down. Now, now, sweetheart. I couldn't just not show up. I'm showing three dogs for three different people. They pay me to do this. You know this is how I always used to make my extra money."

Holly sighed deeply. "Oh, Mother, I should've known we'd end up at a dog show. Why can't we just do a cat show once? You know. Surprise me." She made googly eyes at Margaret.

Margaret pretended to laugh. "Very funny dear. Cat shows do not hire handlers to show cats. Now, you come along with me. And try to be nice to the dog owners. After all, they're paying me a handsome fee to show their dogs in the ring and if their dogs win, I get a bonus."

Holly decided, since it was almost Christmas, that maybe she should surrender. Or at least not fight with her mother. After all, not a single Christmas carol said, 'Tis the season to argue with family.' "All right, Mom, but there had better be a lot of vendors here."

Her mother was instantly happy. "Come on, sweetheart, I'll show you where I'm going to be and where the vendors are." She led Holly up the steps of the huge arena, through the front doors, and onto the vendor floor. Holly tried not to show that she was somewhat impressed by the hundred or more vendors that had set up their displays.

"And where will you be, Mom?"

Her mother pointed down to the arena that was usually used for horse shows, but today it was divided into smaller rings for the dog show. "I'll be down there," she said. "Mostly by ring number four because that's where they're showing Shelties. And I'm handling two today."

Holly eyed her mother suspiciously. "You said you were handling three dogs."

Her mother humphed. "Well, I am, two today and one tomorrow."

Holly folded her arms across her chest. "Mom? How many days are you working? What are you not telling me?"

"Oh, come on, dear, let's go in and see what the vendors have. I have to be down at the ring in about an hour, so we have time to get a cup of coffee and see what the sellers are offering."

Holly trudged after her mother, still complaining. "Is this another one of your great plans to introduce me to somebody special?" She tried to keep the sarcasm out of her voice.

Her mother looked offended and hurt. "Why, don't be silly, dear. You don't even like dogs. Why would I try to introduce you to somebody at a dog show?"

"Who knows how that incredible mind of yours works? I figure you must have some ulterior motive." Then, as her mother's comment registered, she objected, "Who says I don't like dogs? I like dogs just fine. It's dog poop I hate."

Her mother laughed and waved a hand in the air as if such things were so silly, she shouldn't even consider them. "Let's go over there and get ourselves a latte. Oh look! They have croissants."

Holly decided she might as well have a latte because it was obvious that she was stuck here for most of the day. She knew she should've brought her own car. But her mother had insisted on driving.

"Okay, Mom, a latte and a croissant, and then I'll shop. When do you finish showing dogs today?"

Her mother looked away evasively and said, "Oh, I'm here until about three."

"Three o'clock?" Holly was horrified. "It's only seven-thirty in the morning!"

Her mother shrugged. "That's the way it goes, dear. If my dog qualifies in the first class, then I have to hang around and show it in the next class and so on. If we make it all the way up through the breeds to best-in-show, you should be proud of me."

Holly glared at her mother. "When is best-in-show?"

Her mother changed the subject. "Look over there. They have chocolate eclairs. Let's splurge. Let's have a chocolate eclair." And off she went.

Holly decided she was too mature to stamp her feet, but not too mature to roll her eyes, so she did so. Her mother obviously had something in mind besides showing dogs or she never would've brought Holly along. And Holly was certain it wasn't for the shopping. Still, she might pick up some dog-oriented gifts for Christmas. She had to admit there was a tremendous selection of crafts and gifts and artwork of all kinds. She would have no problem at all completing her Christmas list. After all, the rest of her family and many of her friends were dog people. But she had never gotten the bug. Maybe it was because she was around it so much as a child.

She'd spent so many weekends, as a little girl, following her mother around the dog show circuit, helping load and unload the car, even helping with the grooming of some of the dogs. All of that had left a sour taste in her mouth. She just wasn't sure that she wanted to get involved in it herself. Wasn't it enough to watch her mother do it?

The chocolate eclairs were delicious.

"How is your coffee?" her mother asked.

"Frankly, it's a little watery. But the eclair is heavenly." She smiled. She had to admit that a nice pastry first thing in the morning tended to sweeten the entire day.

"Now before I go shopping," she said to her mother, "why don't you just tell me who it is you're trying to set me up with so I can talk to him for five minutes, find out how much I hate him, and get it over with?"

Her mother lifted her nose in the air and sniffed. "You seem to think I have such bad taste, perhaps I won't even point him out to you."

"Oh Mom, don't be like that. I know you're going to be busy all day, and I know I need to leave you alone to concentrate on the dogs. I'm a big girl. I can find things to do to entertain myself. You don't have to go setting up dates for me."

Her mother reached out and squeezed her arm. "Holly dear, if I don't help you look for someone new, you'll just be an old maid the rest of your life. You have no interest in anything since Doug left. I'm telling you, you need to get out there and find someone to spend your life with. Not all men are thoughtless doofuses."

Holly suddenly found her lap to be of great interest and began pulling threads off her slacks. "I know," she said sadly. "But I thought Doug was the one. He he was perfect for me."

Her mother's voice was filled with sympathy. "Sweetheart, he left you on the steps of the church. He obviously was not the perfect man for you. The perfect man would never do that to you."

Holly tried to pull herself together. Thinking about what Doug had done to her just made her trembly inside, and she didn't want to be trembly while she was Christmas shopping. It took all the fun out of. In fact, she hadn't really gotten into the Christmas spirit at all because, well, she didn't have anybody to go to Christmas parties with. She didn't have a special guy to buy a present for. She was facing the entire holiday season all by herself. Suddenly she realized that she was deep into a pity party. After all, she wasn't really alone. She had her mother, and she had her siblings, and her dad was…. Well, she had her mother.

"Don't worry, Mom, you go do your dog thing. I know the money is helpful and seeing your dog friends is important for you, so I'll just stick to the vendors, okay?"

With that, Holly picked up the last bite of her chocolate eclair, popped it in her mouth, and rose from the table.

Margaret reached out as if to stop her, then pulled her hand back. "All right, dear," she said sadly. "But you know where I'll be if you change your mind."

"Thanks, Mom, I know you love me." Holly moved closer to give her mother a kiss on the cheek. Then she hefted her purse and strolled toward the first of the many vendors lining the mezzanine.

Behind her, Margaret called, "Keep your cell phone on!"

Holly nodded, but her mind was elsewhere. It was hard being jilted. Of course, that had been six months ago. They had planned a June wedding. Three hundred people were there. So no big deal, right?

She muttered to herself, "Really, Holly, sarcasm is not your strong suit."

Doug had broken her heart and, more than that, he had humiliated her in front of everyone she knew. She was still having trouble dealing with the whole thing. If she ever did find someone new, how could she risk even having a wedding? No one would think it was really going to happen. All three hundred people on that first guest list would just laugh if she sent them another invitation. That image erased all the joy she'd gotten from the eclair, and she practically pouted as she examined the crafts in the first vendor booth. Swarovski Crystal dogs and Swarovski crystals on dog collars. Very cute. Dutifully, she looked at everything in the booth and found herself open-mouthed when she encountered a collar so huge that it could have served as a belt for her. Somebody's mastiff would be very happy. On to the next booth.

After visiting a vendor offering hand-sewn dog clothes, kitchen towels, and pillowcases, all with doggie themes, she couldn't help but cheer up a bit. She knew her mother would adore a set of pillowcases with pugs on them. And in fact, her sister would love that set of kitchen towels with corgis on them. She tucked all her purchases into the same plastic bag and decided that maybe this was a good place to shop for Christmas after all. Everyone in the family had dogs except her. Did that mean that they were all nuts? Or did it mean that she was the oddball? Oh well, it didn't really matter at the moment. Here she was, and here she'd stay until three o'clock at least. The show would last three days. Tomorrow she would come up with an excuse to stay home and let her mother come by herself. It's not like she was showing her own dogs. She didn't need help with crates and set-up and all of that. All she had to do was come and handle someone else's dog. Yes, that's exactly what Holly would do. She would get all her shopping done today, and then tomorrow she would stay home with a good book. What a lovely thought.

Having sufficiently cheered herself up, Holly continue to stroll from vendor to vendor, trying to decide what to get for her sisters and her brother. Occasionally she would pick up some little thing and add it to her bag for her mother. She was at vendor booth number ten when she heard a lovely baritone voice saying, "Can you hold this for me, ma'am? I need to be in the ring in five minutes."

The sales lady behind the table said, "Of course. I'll set it right here and save it for you. Good luck."

Holly turned to see if she could locate the source of that beautiful baritone voice. And in doing so, she practically knocked the fellow over.

He, however, was very gracious. "Oh, I'm so sorry," he said. "I didn't even see you there." He stopped for a moment to pick up the plastic bags she'd dropped, glancing up at her as he spoke. Then he did a double take and let his eyes linger for a few moments. Obviously, he was in a hurry to get to his assigned ring, but at the same time, he seemed drawn to Holly. "I have to go," he said apologetically. He started to leave, then turned back. "May I ask your name?"

Holly took her bags out of his hand and figured, why not? She'd never see the guy again. "I'm Holly," she said.

"It's nice to meet you, Holly. My name's Tanner." He shook her hand, then just kept holding it. "I'm going to show a dog, and then I'm coming back for my stuff at this booth." He finally loosened his hold on her fingers. "I would love to have coffee with you later, if you're going to be shopping for a while?"

Holly decided it wouldn't hurt to sip coffee while looking at this good-looking guy over the rim of her cup. "I'll be around somewhere," she said. "I'll probably make it to booth twelve or thirteen by the time you're finished with your dog."

"Okay," he said, "I'll be back." And he left. Holly had to laugh when she saw him break into a run as soon as he had enough clear space to do so. These dog lovers took their competitions so seriously, she thought. But he was nice-looking. In fact, she had to admit to herself that he was probably the best-looking man she'd seen in a very long time. Much better looking than Doug.

Maybe her mother was right. Maybe she had settled for Doug. He was a little on the short side and he'd already developed a tiny potbelly before he was even thirty. Maybe she should be glad he left her standing on the church steps.

This fellow Tanner seemed interested in her. Maybe he even thought she was attractive. It was hard for her to accept. After all, when a girl is jilted at her wedding, her self-confidence takes a huge hit.

"You'll never get over it, will you?" she said to herself. "Well, I'll just keep shopping. If he comes back, we'll see."

As soon as Tanner left the building, he skipped down the stairs three at a time and broke into a full run across the parking lot to the other long, low building with Exhibition painted on the side. He was due in the Rally Excellent B ring, and he had spent far too much time looking at dog collars. He skidded to a halt on the cement floor in front of the check-in table. He hadn't missed his turn, but he had cut it very close. His little Cavalier, Charlene, did her best, but halfway through the course, Tanner started thinking about Holly. That distraction made him miss a sign, and they didn't qualify.

Charlene seemed miffed.

"Not talking to me, eh? Well, let's go outside. And I'll take you next door and introduce you to a very pretty lady. If she's still there."

His cell phone pinged. He groaned and checked it. It was a veterinarian he sometimes worked for. He had told everyone he was going to a dog show. He silenced the phone to ignore the message and hoped that Holly was still shopping. He tucked a disgruntled Charlene under one arm and ran up the cement steps to the arena.

There she was, in booth twelve. His heart thrilled at the sight of her, and that caught him off guard. What was so special about her? How come he was so attracted to her? Yes, she was cute, but he'd seen lots of cute girls in his life. He began to wonder if all that talk about "chemistry" between people might be true. He approached quietly and tapped her lightly on the shoulder.

"I'm back."

Holly jumped, but turned around with a big smile. "Hello again." Her gaze dropped to Charlene. "Oh my goodness, what an adorable face! Is this the dog you were showing? I haven't seen any other Cavaliers on the arena floor."

"Points for recognizing her breed." Tanner was pleased. "She's my little diva. We're competing in Rally in the other building."

"How did she do?"

"Great. But I missed a sign, so we didn't qualify."

Holly made a sympathetic noise and petted Charlene. "Poor little girl. Papa messed up, did he?"

Charlene's tail wagged furiously.

"She likes you!" Tanner beamed. "Where are you set up? Are you doing conformation?"

"No, that's my mother's thing." Holly was still petting Charlene. "I'm the black sheep in the family. I don't have any dogs."

Tanner was stunned. "How do you get through the day?"

Holly laughed, a sweet tinkle of a sound that vibrated in Tanner's heart. "Well, I'm around a lot of them because everyone else in my family is into dogs." She was totally focused on Charlene, now petting her with both hands. "It doesn't seem fair to leave a dog alone all day while I'm at work."

Tanner loved the fact that Holly just kept talking. The more she talked, the more he liked it. "Come with me to pick up my collars, and then we can find a place to sit down and chat. I promised Charlene a hot dog."

He led the way to booth ten, letting Charlene work her magic on Holly. He couldn't believe she didn't have a dog. She seemed like a natural with his Charlene. "You're going to spoil her," he warned.

"Me? Look at you, carrying her around like a little princess. She has four legs, you know," teased Holly.

Tanner pretended to be offended. "I'll have you know that she may be one of the few dogs at this show who is actually doing what she was bred to do. She's being my little companion."

"You have a very good point there," Holly conceded with a smile.

After they picked up Tanner's purchases, he ambled toward

the snack bar. "May I take you to lunch? This place has top-notch hot dogs. Just ask Charlene."

"Sounds like a culinary delight," joked Holly. "Lead on."

Tanner ordered three hot dogs. "Make one naked," he said. "It's for my dog. And we need two sodas." He glanced at Holly. "Is that okay?"

"Sure. The sun is shining, there's no snow on the ground, and the sky is a lovely December blue, so definitely a cold drink."

Tanner paid for their lunch. "I like a woman with wit," he said. "It keeps things interesting."

Holly looked suddenly wary.

"Is something wrong? What did I say?"

She shook her head. "Very long depressing story. But I have to ask. Are you married?"

"Nope. I am dismally single."

They sat down, and he unwrapped a hotdog for Charlene, who sat perkily on his lap, drooling on the edge of the table.

"Dismally?" Holly tilted her head to one side. "Explain, please." She spread her napkins out on the table.

"Oh, you know. I'm surrounded by beautiful females all the time, and most girls get jealous."

"Are you a photographer?"

Tanner chuckled. "No, I'm a veterinarian. And a dog fancier. You'd be surprised how many women find that combination incredibly boring."

"No way! I just took my CPA exam!"

"Wow." Tanner pretended to listen for something, one hand cupped around his ear.

"What are you doing?"

"Can't you hear it? Every time a jingle bell rings, a CPA passes her exam. That's a lot of work."

Holly laughed. She used a plastic fork to push onions off her hot dog. "Us single people have lots of time on our hands." She made a face. "I needed something to occupy my mind after my fiancée left me at the altar."

"What kind of idiot would abandon you on your wedding day?" He touched her hand instinctively. "I'm so sorry. I hope you don't hate all men."

Holly's brows rose in silent comment. "Well…."

"Even the ones with adorable Cavaliers?"

Holly grinned and stabbed at her hotdog. "I guess if Charlene thinks you're okay, I could probably give you a chance." She gave him a flirty sidelong glance.

Tanner's pulse raced. "You have the most gorgeous auburn hair," he blurted.

Holly gave him a come-hither wiggle of fingers. "Tell me more." Her eyes sparkled with mischief.

"It's a perfect match with Charlene's sable."

Holly laughed with delight. "Oh my gosh, you really are a dog lover." She reached out to pet Charlene again. "She is a lovely color. Well, colors. Maybe I should have a patch of hair bleached white so we're a total match."

Tanner cleared his throat to hide his embarrassment. "I didn't mean…"

Holly let him off the hook. "Don't worry. I'm from a dog family. I know you meant it as a compliment." She squeezed his hand, then pulled back suddenly, as if she'd gone too far.

Tanner opened his palm, inviting her hand to return.

Holly obliged, a blush coloring her cheeks. "Your hair is more Afghan hound, I think," she said playfully.

Tanner pulled a few strands of dark blond hair forward and made a comical effort to look up at them. "Does this mean I have to change breeds?"

"Oh, I hope not! Charlene is adorable." In fact, Holly was surprised at how her heart reacted to Charlene's pudgy little face.

Not as smooshed as a pug, but so expressive. Then she realized she was even more attracted to Tanner.

The hours flew by as Holly grew fonder and fonder of Tanner. It was the most fun she'd ever had at a dog show. When she grew weary of the noise in the conformation arena—dogs barking everywhere—he suggested they stroll through the obedience building.

"Oh my, it's so quiet!"

Tanner was amused. "You spent your life following your mother around the country to dog shows and you never saw anything but the beauty pageants?"

Holly laughed. "Mother would cringe if she heard you say that." She pushed her nose in the air with one finger and said haughtily, "The word is 'Fancy,' you peasant. 'The Fancy' is how we refer to ourselves."

"We're making progress," teased Tanner. "You said 'ourselves.' You included yourself!"

They were strolling, arms linked, past the obedience rings and toward the rally rings. Tanner said, "My setup is over there." He set Charlene on the cement floor and let her prance ahead of them on her leash. She knew exactly where she was going.

"Uh-oh," said Tanner. "My puppysitter looks pissed."

Holly followed his gaze and saw a middle-aged woman with short hair and a military manner about her marching to and fro in front of an exercise pen against the back wall. She tapped her wrist as they approached, even though she wore no watch. A banner hung over the front of the pen, announcing: Cavalier King Charles Spaniels Rescue.

Tanner went up to the woman and kissed her on the cheek. Holly admired his courage because that woman did not look kissable. "Aunt Ruthie, I'm sorry. This is Holly, and I've practically converted her to Cavaliers. Holly, this is my aunt, Ruth. She used to breed Cavaliers."

Holly extended a hand. "Used to?"

Ruth's expression softened as she shook Holly's hand. "Years ago. I decided I could do more good by rescuing than breeding."

Tanner lifted Charlene over the wire fence. "Are you mad?"

"No," barked Ruth. "Just tired. You ready to pack up and go home?"

"Just about. I wanted to introduce Holly to my harem." He stepped over the side of the wire pen and eight wagging Cavaliers all jumped on him at once, begging for attention.

Holly helped him pet them. "My mother's last dog passed away last month. It's been really hard on her. Now she handles for other people."

"Good for her. It'll give her a chance to find another dog."

Holly nodded. "Ruth, are you showing at all?" She'd been hoping to have Tanner to herself for a while longer.

Ruth solved her problem. "I'm taking these flirty bitches home." She glanced in Holly's direction, then asked Tanner, "Will you try Charlene in the rally ring again?"

"I'll be out there, humiliating her again," he joked. "Holly, you'll be coming back tomorrow, I hope?"

"Definitely. I haven't finished my Christmas shopping yet."

Ruth busied herself with putting leads on the dogs. Tanner picked up Charlene, saying to Holly, "This one, I sleep with." Then he blushed. "I mean—"

Holly laughed. "I understand." Her phone beeped. "Oh darn. It looks like my mother is ready to go. We're sharing a car."

Tanner looked disappointed. "Okay, I can take it," he said. "So what if I was building my entire future around you and the possibility of dinner?" His tone was lighthearted.

Holly looked hopeful. "Maybe tomorrow?"

Tanner grinned. "Perfect. Charlene and I compete at 8:45, if you want to come over and cheer us on."

"I will," said Holly. "Sorry. I have to go. My mother says she can't see me anywhere." She stabbed furiously at her phone, sending a text. "So nice to meet you Ruth."

"Same here. See you tomorrow."

Holly didn't want to leave, but her mother was heading for the car already. She stopped at the big glass doors to try to catch another look at Tanner, but he was focused on his aunt's Cavaliers.

Out in the parking lot, Margaret look tired.

"How did it go, Mom?"

"Not so good. I don't think the Shelties like me."

"What about the third dog?"

"I handle him tomorrow." She got into the car and Holly followed suit. Margaret said wearily, "I supposed you want to skip the rest of the show?"

"Not at all," said Holly. She smiled a secret smile. "I've discovered a new breed. I can't wait to come back tomorrow."

Tanner tried to control his impatience as he helped his aunt load all the dogs in the car. She had installed a pet barrier between the front and back seats, and she folded all the back seats flat so the Cavaliers could move about a bit, rest on their blankets, or stand up at the windows and watch the world go by. Charlene traveled on Tanner's lap. Once they reached his aunt's house, he was in a hurry to get in his own car and head home. There was something he needed to check.

Just like Holly, Tanner had been carted around from dog show to dog show since childhood, but his reaction had been the opposite of hers. He loved it! When his aunt was younger, he would accompany her to local shows on the weekends and out-of-state shows in the summer, when he was out of school. His parents were dog lovers as well, but his father preferred the working breeds. After being pounced on and dragged by one of the family boxers at a tender age, Tanner had decided he preferred small dogs, and Aunt Ruthie was right there, presenting him with his first Cavalier.

He lived on the outskirts of town, just over the county line, on property his aunt was going to leave him in her will. She'd insisted he go ahead and use the house and the kennels after she'd broken an ankle a few years back and had to move closer to medical help. He set Charlene gently on the floor, and she ran to her water bowl, slurping and splashing as her long ears dipped in the bowl.

Tanner went straight to his bedroom closet. It took him about ten minutes to find what he was looking for, a sturdy box filled with memorabilia. He hauled it off the high shelf and lugged it into the living room. Charlene curled up next to him on the sofa.

"It's got to be here somewhere, Char," he said, ruffling her coat. "Let's see….sixth grade? No, junior high, I think. Seventh grade. Yes! That was the summer, because I came home and had to face all the tall guys in eighth-grade gym. Here it is!"

He opened the pages of the album carefully. The passing of years had dried out the glue holding the photos to the pages. Leaf by leaf, he examined the summer of his twelfth year.

"There it is!" He point to a page with three photos on it. Charlene panted at his elbow. "There's Aunt Ruth, and there's your great-great-grandmother winning best-in-show. And there's the judge…Margaret Howell. And down here…" He moved to the other two photos. "Ruth took these pictures of us kids at that show. Gosh, look how cute she was. Still is, as far as that goes." He sighed heavily. "If only I'd had the courage to ask her name back then! Holly," he said to his twelve-year-old self. "Her name is Holly. And it took me another twelve years, but I've found her again." He shook his head in wonder, a sentimental smile lingering. "I don't think she has a clue about who I am or that we met before."

On a whim, he took the photos out of the album and laid them on the coffee table. "I'll take these along tomorrow," he said.

"Assuming she actually shows up. Then I can jog her memory with these pictures."

Charlene whimpered, her tone ending in a question mark.

As usual, Tanner pretended they were having a conversation. "If she doesn't recall, I'll just tell her all about that day. Don't be such a doubting Thomasina. Come on, I'll get you a biscuit."

The next morning Holly was eager to return to the fairgrounds.

Margaret was puzzled, but pleased. "I thought you didn't like dog shows."

Holly smiled like the Mona Lisa. "Part of me had forgotten that there are nice people there. And I'm still shopping for Christmas."

Margaret gave her a sidelong look. "And you don't mind riding with me?"

"Not at all. Oh! I forgot to ask what time you go into the ring today, and what breed are you handling?"

"Ring six, about eleven, if they don't run late. I'm handling a working breed."

Holly waited, but no specific information was forthcoming. Before she could ask, Margaret changed the subject.

"There are certainly a lot of vendors at this show."

Holly agreed. "One of the booths has leashes and nothing but leashes—handmade leather leashes of all kinds, braided leashes, leashes with snaps on the end, leashes for conformation. leashes for tall dogs, leashes for small dogs, and tiny six-inch leashes."

"Tabs," said Margaret.

"Right. I never understood why you used them when your dogs were so tiny."

"Tabs aren't for holding onto. They're for letting the dog think a leash is still attached to its collar."

Holly thought if she got her mother a couple of those, they might please her. And then again, they might just break her heart. Teddy Bear had passed away only the month before.

Holly decided not to get leashes for her mother. The hurt was too recent, and she didn't want to pour salt in her mother's wounds. Her little pug had been adorable, although frankly, he had been a very noisy breather during the last year of his life. Then Holly felt bad for thinking such a thing. He'd been a wonderful little pet. Teddy Bear, her mother's little heartthrob, registered name, Howell's Picnic in the Park, and call name "Teddy Bear."

No wonder Margaret wanted to get back into the dog show scene. So many of her friends were here, and she needed their comfort and support after losing Teddy.

As they pulled into the parking lot, Holly said, "I hope you don't mind, Mom. I want to go into the Obedience building and watch a friend in the Rally ring."

"Male or female?"

"Both. I mean," she stammered, "the friend is male, the dog is female."

"Excellent." Margaret seemed pleased. "Making new friends is a good idea."

Holly wasn't sure where her mother was going with her comment, but on the other hand she wasn't bringing up anyone else that she wanted Holly to meet. That might be a good sign.

"Do you need me for anything before I go?" asked Holly.

"No, dear, you go along and have fun. I've been trying to reach someone but they must've changed their phone number. But that's okay. I've run into six other old friends that I haven't seen in months. I hope you don't mind, but I told them I would join them for lunch today." She hesitated, then asked, "Would you like to join us?"

Holly was desperately hoping to spend the whole day, including the lunch hour, with Tanner, but she didn't want to say that to her mother. Instead, she said, "No, that's all right, mom. You need to have some reunion time with your friends. Besides I know all you'll talk about is dogs, dogs, dogs." She made a comical face as if that was the last thing in the world she ever wanted to hear. She didn't want to admit to her mother that she was falling in love with a certain little Cavalier King Charles Spaniel, not to mention her overwhelming attraction to the dog's master.

Margaret smiled knowingly. "Yes you're probably right, dear. All we talked about yesterday was dogs, dogs, dogs. Today will probably be the same. It's at least day three before we start gossiping about other dog owners." Then she laughed at her own joke and left for the arena.

Holly felt a thrill of excitement as she approached the exhibition building. It was already eight o'clock, and she remembered enough to know that the excellent classes were usually the first in the ring. Was Charlene in excellent or in advanced? Or was she doing both? How could she forget so much about dog shows? Exasperated at herself for having shoved all that dog show knowledge to the back of her brain, she decided it didn't matter. All she knew what was that she was extremely comfortable with Tanner. He talked to her as if he had known her all her life. Had she ever met him before? She was virtually certain that she would have remembered a man as handsome and graceful as Tanner. She wondered if he liked to dance. Would that be too much to ask?

It took her a moment, once she entered the exhibition hall, to locate the corner where Tanner and his aunt had set up their exercise pen for the Cavaliers. When Tanner saw her coming, he waved and grinned from ear to ear. Holly was delighted. She navigated the other setups, moving through the narrow aisles, and at last reached the corner with the Cavaliers and Tanner.

"Where's your Aunt Ruth?" she asked.

Tanner said, "She said something about watching the Cavaliers next door. There are twenty-five entered in this show."

Holly raised her eyebrows. "Are you afraid she's going to

acquire another dog? My father used to beg Mom not to bring anymore home."

Tanner laughed out loud. "No no, she's totally into rescue now." He stopped as if he wanted to say something but wasn't sure how to put the question. He stared at his feet.

Holly noticed and dipped her head to look him in the eye. "Is something wrong?"

"Not wrong, but I'm not sure how to share this with you. Hypothetically, if you had a mad crush on someone when you were in junior high, but you never had the nerve to speak up about it, do you think the person you had a crush on would want you to admit it and let them know years later?"

Holly pulled back as realization crept up her spine. "Are you trying to tell me something about yourself, Tanner, or are you asking for a friend?" She put air quotes around the last part.

Tanner pulled three photographs out of this equipment bag. "I brought these to show you, because I am ninety-nine percent sure that you are the girl in these photographs. Especially since your mother is next door handling in the show ring. Do they look familiar to you at all?" He handed them over.

Holly glanced at the first photo and smiled. "That's my mother when she used to judge." Then she looked at the other photos and her eyes widened in disbelief. "Gosh! This is me," she said. "And... and... this good-looking blond kid here... is that you?"

Tanner nodded eagerly. "Remember when our parents put us in a corner with a deck of cards and told us to play Fish, and we ended up learning poker?"

Holly laughed out loud at the memory. "Yes, indeed. That skill served me well at college. You wouldn't believe how many times I won at Saturday night poker in the dorm." She paused and took a closer look at the photographs. "This mad crush you mentioned," she said. "Are you trying to tell me that way back then you had a crush on me? Fair warning. If you say the crush was on this other girl—" She pointed at a dark-haired girl with chubby cheeks. "—then I may never speak to you again." She gave him a flirty look.

Tanner blushed. "Not Gloria!" He looked horrified. "She's my cousin."

Holly caressed the photos. "My favorite is this one. We're all trying to look so innocent for the photo, but as I recall, we had huge rolls of cotton candy behind our backs. And you," she said softly, "are staring right through me."

Tanner nodded. "I was trying to communicate with telepathy."

Holly pressed the photos to her heart. "That is so beautiful."

"Thanks." Their eyes met and, for a long while, they just stood there enjoying their silent communication.

Their moment ended when a ring steward called out, "Rally Advanced B, number 32! Last call!"

"That's me," said Tanner, stooping to pick up Charlene. He paused for a second. "Will you go to a Christmas party with me tonight?"

"Yes!" Holly put a hand to her mouth to keep from laughing at the look on his face. He was so darn cute!

Two minutes later, he and Charlene emerged victorious from the competition. He picked her up and kissed her muzzle, then trotted back to Holly. "You are definitely good luck! It's the first time she actually stayed with me off leash!"

"Congratulations!" Before she knew what was happening, Tanner pulled her close and kissed her on the mouth. The sparks from their connection made Charlene bark. Or at least that's how it felt to Holly. When the kiss ended, she was breathless. "Wow."

Tanner's eyes were full of feeling. "Wow, indeed. I was definitely not mature enough to handle that at twelve."

Holly giggled.

The rest of the day whizzed by. Lunch was hamburgers and

fries, shared with Charlene. The little dog plunked herself down on the storage compartment between the front seats of Tanner's Subaru to make herself more available for petting and snacks. Holly could not remember the last time she'd laughed so much in one hour.

She notified her mother that she was going to a party after she helped Tanner take Ruth and the rescues home.

"Ruth? What's her last name?"

Holly stared at her phone. "I don't know," she said at last. "I can ask her and let you know."

"Good. Have fun at the party. Got to go."

"Well, gee," muttered Holly. "Glad you're happy for me." But her mother was probably due in a ring, so she shrugged it off.

At Ruth's, Tanner broke the news that the party was an Ugly Sweater party. He had one ready to go for himself, but he offered to change their plans if it wasn't Holly's cup of tea.

"It would be fun to go to a Christmas party," she said. "What a shame I have nothing to wear." She said it half-jokingly, but Ruth held up an index finger and headed for the stairs.

"Wait right here," she said.

Holly and Tanner shared a quiet laugh at Ruth's intensity. Tanner whispered, "The Great Ugly Sweater Quest."

A few moments later, Ruth reappeared. "It's actually a sweatshirt. Will it do?" She held up a baggy red sweatshirt bearing the image of a full-sized pug wrapped in Christmas lights, which lit up when Ruth pressed a tab in the sleeve.

Holly felt tears welling up. The little pug looked exactly like her mother's late Teddy Bear. "Oh, it's precious."

Tanner touched her shoulder. "Are you okay?"

Holly tried to fan her tears away. "I'm sorry. My mother just lost her dog a few weeks ago, and this sweatshirt…well, I guess I was more attached to that smooshed little face than I realized."

Ruth stepped in and gave Holly a hug.

Before leaving for the party, Holly paused and asked, "Ruth, may I ask your last name? My mother asked me, and I didn't know."

Tanner pulled the photos from his pocket and showed her the one of the Judge. "We've been to dog shows with them both."

"Oh my goodness," said Ruth. "That's Margaret Howell! You're Margaret's daughter?"

Holly wasn't sure how she should react. "Yes, unless you hate her. Then no."

Ruth laughed loud and long. "One of my old friends from my breeding days told me last night that an old friend of hers was trying to locate me but couldn't seem to get a response on the phone number she has. I'll bet it was Margaret. Is she going to be at the show tomorrow?"

"I think so, although I don't know if the dog she was handling today actually won its class. Here. I'll give you her phone number. I'm sure she'd love to reconnect." She took the pen and paper that "Ruth offered and jotted down her mother's number. "I think she's still grieving for Teddy Bear. You know how it is. No one is as sympathetic about the loss of a pet than other dog owners."

"You two go on and enjoy the party. I'll give your mother a call. Poor thing. No one should be without a dog."

Holly cleared her throat, but decided she'd better not confess that she didn't have one either.

Ruth asked, "Can you wear this sweatshirt without being sad? I've had it for years. But the batteries are new."

"It's perfect," murmured Holly. She pulled it on over her head. It went well with her blue jeans. "Ta-da!" She spread her arms.

Tanner grinned. "We are definitely going to win a prize."

Holly would never have gone to a party with a stranger, but she felt she'd known Tanner forever, and she was so attracted to him, she couldn't bear for the evening to end. He danced like a dream. His brown-and-white patchwork sweater with Rudolph on the front complemented her sweatshirt perfectly, because Rudolph's nose blinked in time to the music!

And Holly was thrilled when Tanner turned to the hostess—a chubby woman with dark hair—and said, "Gloria? You remember Holly, don't you? The girl I fell in love with twelve years ago?"

Gloria jumped up and down. "Omigosh, you were the daughter of the judge!"

Holly smiled. "I still am, actually."

Gloria laughed long and loud, and Holly was instantly transported back in time. She half expected someone to bring out a deck of cards.

Gloria squeezed Holly's hand. "Where did he find you? Did you go to vet school, too?"

Holly shook her head. "I could never stand the sight of blood. I think it's great that Tanner is a vet."

Tanner said humbly, "I just graduated last spring. I don't have my own practice yet. I'm sort of a rotating vet for local animal hospitals."

Gloria said proudly, "He graduated top of his class. He's just trying to decide which of his offers he wants to make permanent."

Holly was impressed. "Why didn't you mention that earlier?"

Tanner leaned close. "Because every time I look at you, I am thinking of other things."

Holly felt a thrill race through her middle. "Well, I don't have a regular position yet either. So we're even."

Tanner looked puzzled. "But you're a CPA. That's a huge skill. Why haven't you been snapped up?"

Holly looked away and fiddled with the blinking lights on her sweatshirt. "I was pretty broken up after my disaster at the church. Interviews don't go well when you burst into tears at unexpected moments."

Tanner took her hand as the stereo began playing "Jingle Bell Rock." He led her to the middled of the room — Gloria's family room was packed with guests — and pulled her close.

"Umm, Tanner? This song is rock-n-roll."

"And this," he replied softly, "is slow dancing. Much more satisfying." He pulled her even closer.

"And this," she murmured in his ear, "is the best Christmas party ever."

The week after that party was the best week of Holly's life. Tanner was kind and funny, and they had that ridiculously wonderful link from the past, spending weekends at dog shows and having mutual crushes. Now they were making up for lost time.

The fact that neither of them had full-time jobs at the moment made courting a joy. Tanner picked her up on Monday morning so she could help him take Charlene for a walk in the park. The weather was being kind, and they only needed fleece jackets as they followed little Charlene on her leash, while she investigated one light pole after another. Everything was worth sniffing, and while she wagged for joy, Holly and Tanner indulged in the simple pleasure of holding hands and sharing personal information with each other. Holly wanted to know every detail of the Tanner's life during the twelve years since they'd last seen each other, and the same appeared to be true for Tanner.

He asked, "So after your mother's accident, she withdrew from showing dogs?"

"Yes. Breaking a femur is horrible. She was chasing a loose dog in the hotel parking lot. Someone had lost hold of their leash, and it was headed into traffic. Mom caught the dog just in time to keep it from being hit by a car. She had just returned it to its panicked owner, when the pickup hit her and destroyed the bone. Recovery was long and slow, and by the time she was feeling well enough to be active again, some of her friends had moved away, including her best friend, the one she used to travel to shows with. I was heading off to college and wasn't able to ignore my studies every weekend, so she fell out of the loop."

"Ruth was telling me stories last night about what a great group they used to have. She knew Margaret but it was one of those things where you would love to get to know someone, but if they were judging at a show, Ruth was afraid people would think she was currying favor."

"I understand," said Holly. She headed for a secluded bench. "Do you think Charlene would mind if we take a short break?" She wagged her eyebrows invitingly.

Tanner was already an expert at reading certain signals. Holly found she could only go an hour or so without kissing Tanner. The chemistry between them was thrilling. But she'd been badly hurt when her former fiancé abandoned her on her wedding day. She didn't want to move too quickly.

For a while, they communicated silently on the bench. When they were forced to stop for air, Holly asked huskily, "Does this count as learning to read lips?"

Tanner smiled. Charlene barked and tugged at her leash.

Holly pretended to be irritated. "Oh fine. I should have known there was another woman in your life."

They kept walking. Tanner said, "It's so sad that your mother lost her last dog. I'm glad she's doing shows again. She needs to reconnect with her friends."

Holly tilted her head in a question. "Are you speaking from personal experience?"

"Yes, only it was my knee and it happened in college in competition skiing."

"Ouch!"

Tanner lifted his wrist to his forehead and moaned, "My career as a professional athlete ended that day." Then he added under his breath, "Thank goodness. I was a terrible skier."

Holly squeezed his arm. "Somehow I doubt that. You had to be pretty good to make the ski team."

"By the time I was up and about, it was summer, and my grades were spectacular. Who knew that sports were taking up huge chunks of my time?" He laughed. "My grades improved so much, they got me into vet school."

"I've heard that's not easy."

"Neither is the CPA exam," he said, returning her subtle compliment. He planted an arm around her shoulders as a cloud floated in front of the sun. The breeze felt much chillier without the sunshine.

Holly leaned her head against his shoulder as they strolled. "I always loved math, but physics? Not so much. Otherwise I would have gone into engineering. And my mother thought I could make a much better living as a CPA than as a math teacher."

"Brilliant advice."

Their eyes met, and they stopped on the path for another kiss. There were very few other dog walkers around, and even the stalwart joggers and bicyclists were being discouraged by the drop in temperature. Charlene wound her leash around their legs and barked insistently.

Holly said, "She wants attention."

Tanner said, "She wants the dog biscuits in the car. Come on. Let's go get lunch."

The rest of the week seemed like a dream. They attended another Christmas party—this one hosted by one of the veterinarians for whom Tanner had worked—and before leaving, Holly had passed out half a dozen business cards. They attended a bell-ringer concert, and they spent wonderful hours revisiting their childhoods while eating popcorn in front of Tanner's big-screen TV. They binged on Rudolph, *The Santa Clause,* and two different versions of *A Christmas Carol.*

Lovers Lane

On December 20, they went Christmas shopping together. They discovered they were both last-minute shoppers. Holly swore she would have finished her list at the dog show if she hadn't met Tanner, so she blamed it on him.

"Ha. Ha. No way. You had plenty of time to peruse those vendor stalls. Let's see." His gaze shot skyward as he counted on his fingers. "Yep. Between arriving and meeting me, you had a good…two hours at least."

Later that day, they shared an early dinner. "I hope you don't mind if we put off dancing until tomorrow night," he said, running his fingers through her auburn hair.

"Actually, that works out great, because I'm too tired from wandering the mall to spend the evening on the dance floor." She turned her face so she could kiss his palm. "I hope everything is all right."

"Aunt Ruth texted me, asking for some help with a new rescue. Poor little guy. He needs to be bathed and maybe even shaved. And he is terrified of everything."

"Oh no! Of course you should help." She gave him a teasing smile. "Besides, that will allow me to find a gift for you without you seeing it."

"Perfect." He planted a kiss on her cheek. They were still in the restaurant, and neither of them felt like entertaining the other diners with a floor show.

Holly still had hold of his hand. She wiggled it back and forth, not sure how to ask her question. "Tanner…."

"Right here." He pulled her hand close for a kiss.

Holly was pleased, but she still had to ask. "Most couples these days…well, I heard on a talk show that most couples are…intimate…on the third date. That just doesn't work for me. But I don't want to disappoint you. Are you?"

"Am I what? Disappointed?"

"Mmm-hmmm."

"No. Some things are worth waiting for. Besides, it's not like I have a harem lined up and waiting for me."

Holly laughed. "Actually, you do. All those beautiful little Cavaliers."

"Don't worry," said Tanner. "I'm having a wonderful time. Getting to know you, after all these years, has been a joy. And if we're both waiting for something wonderful, I guess I'd better do some extra shopping of my own." He leaned forward and kissed her softly on the lips.

The couples at the surrounding table applauded. Holly blushed, and Tanner laughed, then stood up and took a bow. He caught the waiter's attention. "Check, please."

They stood on Holly's front porch, necking like teenagers, until the porch light came on.

Tanner grumbled, "I forgot you live with your mother."

Holly gave him one last kiss. "I came home from college with a fiancé and no job, remember? I figured I'd be in my own place by now. But Mom really needed some cheering up. And after being jilted, so did I."

"Completely understandable. You're a good daughter." His phone beeped. He took it out of his pocket, then groaned, "I'm coming, Aunt Ruth."

"You go. Help your aunt. Will I see you tomorrow?"

"I have to cover for another vet tomorrow. Would dinner be okay?"

"Ah, the truth at last." Holly pulled away, doing her best imitation of a petulant movie star. "The almighty dollar is more important than spending time with me. Alas!"

Tanner appreciated the humor and came back with a tease of his own. "Well, I could skip work and feed you fast food...or go to work and feed you shrimp and sirloin."

Holly gave him a warm hug and said with a giggle, "In that case, don't forget to set your alarm. Shrimp and sirloin? Yummy!"

Tanner thought about Holly all the way to his aunt's house. He'd never been left at the altar, but he'd had a couple of young ladies laugh in his face before, and that was bad enough. His thoughts circled around the gift he was hoping to find for Holly. He wanted it to be extra special. Maybe Ruth would have some ideas.

But once he arrived, there was no time for chit-chat.

"Thanks for coming," said Ruth. "Help me fish him out from under the bed."

"What's he doing under the bed?"

"He's hiding. Spooky little guy. No one ever took the time to show him that people can be nice. He's a mess."

That part was certainly true. The poor little guy was supposed to be white and tan, but his fur was past repair and his ears were a forest of mats.

After an hour of bathing and grooming, Tanner said, "What a sweet little dog. As terrified as he is, he hasn't complained a bit."

"Amazing, isn't it? Who could neglect such a sweet little soul? He's going to need a lot of attention to bring him out of his shell. Someone with experience." Ruth's voice trailed off as she pondered the situation.

"What's his name? Do you know?"

"The previous owners called him Beau. I figure we should stick with that. So much other stuff is changing in his world. When we find him a home, his new owner can change it, or not, as they please."

"Come here, little Beau." Tanner wrapped a warm towel around the dog and carried him in his arms. He cleared his throat. "Say, Ruth, I've been meaning to talk to you."

"Hmm? Oh." She grinned from ear to ear. "You're in love with Holly, aren't you?"

Tanner gaped at her. "How can you tell?"

Ruth laughed. "I've been around the block a few times. I know love when I see it."

Tanner set Beau down on the new dog bed Ruth had placed in a wire crate. "I need to figure out what to get Holly for Christmas. Any ideas?"

"Oh, I might have one or two. Say, I called her mother a couple of days ago, and we had a lovely conversation. I invited them to come over for Christmas dinner, and Margaret said yes. It was a feeble yes, so I expect you to back me up and have Holly urge her mother to come."

"I'd be glad to. Holly said she was so sad for so long, and her mother, too, that they did very little decorating. I didn't see a tree inside. Just a little crèche on a table. And there aren't any lights outside, either. I think they could use some Christmas cheer. Now, about that advice…."

Holly was thrilled at the thought of spending Christmas day with Tanner, and she was totally on board with urging her mother to go as well.

But Margaret wasn't sure. "Oh, honey, you and Tanner are a couple now, and he might want some privacy with you on the holiday."

"Well, we'll be with Ruth, and trust me, she's not what you would call a private person."

Margaret laughed. "I remembered so much about her when we spoke on the phone. Life is strange, isn't it? We shared the same group of friends, but the two of us never really had a chance to get to know each other. It was sort of a wave-as-you-go-by kind of acquaintance." She hunched her shoulders, a sure sign to Holly that she was going to share a secret. "Shall I make a little confession?"

"Okay. I guess. You didn't do anything wild and woolly when you were young, did you?"

Margaret laughed and slapped her knee. "Silly girl. As if I would tell you that kind of thing."

"Mom! Is that a yes?"

Margaret waved it away. "My confession has to do with Ruth. I went to the Christmas Circuit show to find her, because I remembered her son, Tanner, from back in the day, when you kids were parked in a corner while all the adults went out to show their dogs." She took Holly's hand. "Isn't that a miracle? I couldn't remember his name, and I'd forgotten her last name, and none of my phone numbers worked. I wanted you there so I could introduce you to a new young man. And you went ahead and found him yourself!"

Holly beamed. "Mom, that is so sweet! Now you *have* to come on Christmas day, because I can't wait to see their reaction when you tell them that story."

Holly's heart was so full at Christmas, she didn't even know if she was making sense. Were her words comprehensible? Her face hurt from smiling so much. She had encouraged her mother to bake a stollen like she used to do when Holly was young, and the two of them had spent Christmas Eve elbow deep in nuts, fruit, flour and sugar, singing along to Christmas carols on TV.

Tanner had excused himself from their baking madness because his parents lived on the East Coast and he had promised to Skype with them on Christmas Eve.

So Christmas morning—although Holly thought she should say Christmas noon, because that's when they arrived at Ruth's—was a joyous gathering. She hadn't seen Tanner in twenty-four hours and it felt like a month. They had plenty of opportunities for stolen kisses while Ruth gave Margaret a tour of her house and kennels.

"I used to live on the big property, but I turned that over to Tanner. He was always my favorite, you know."

Tanner teased, "My siblings had better never hear you say that."

Holly was delighted with the kennel setup, and she couldn't stop talking about how cute the Cavaliers were.

"I just do rescue now," said Ruth. "I was breeding dogs, and then one day, I found one of my pups—maybe two years old by then—at the animal shelter! I was so mad, I couldn't see straight. I got him out of their and started scouring all the local shelters."

"It's a noble cause," said Margaret. Then she shared her story about trying to connect Holly with Tanner, and they all had a good laugh. "Oh wait," said Margaret. "Who is this?" She approached the crate where little Beau shivered in one corner. "Poor little baby." Moving on instinct, she opened the crate and pulled Beau into her arms. He seemed confused at first, but as she soothed him and cooed at him, he began to calm down.

Ruth explained how he'd come into her possession. By the time she finished, it was obvious that no one was going to take Beau out of Margaret's arms.

Ruth looked infinitely pleased as she tossed a wink at Tanner. "How about a Christmas toast? And maybe gifts?"

Margaret rocked Beau in her arms. "I've got mine."

Tanner retrieved a bottle of sparkling cider from the fridge. He wrapped it in a white towel and played the perfect sommelier, filling the stemmed glasses halfway, then using militaristic precision to park the bottle in a bucket of ice.

Holly giggled and raised her glass in the air. "A toast to old friends reconnecting."

"I'll drink to that," said Tanner, draining his cider.

"Good thing this is non-alcoholic," quipped Ruth.

Tanner topped off everyone's glass again.

Ruth said, "A toast to new love."

Tanner slipped one arm around Holly's shoulders and gave her a gentle squeeze. Then it was Holly's turn. "A toast to forever homes." Her eyes filled with tears when Margaret leaned over

Beau and planted a kiss on his little head. He wagged his tail for the first time since his rescue, and everyone cheered, very softly so as not to frighten him.

"Well," said Margaret, "I guess it's my turn but I don't know what to say. And I'm sorry, Ruth, but I didn't bring a gift."

Holly made a face worthy of a doubting twelve year old. "Yes, you did. You made stollen!" She stepped to the table and opened the Christmas box they'd brought it in.

"You made that?" asked Tanner.

"It's lovely," said Ruth.

"And delicious," said Holly.

"Well, I'm sure Holly has a gift for Tanner," said Margaret.

Holly covered her mouth, trying to tamp down her excitement. "I put it under the tree." She went to get it, and they all followed. "I hope you like it," she said tentatively to Tanner. "It's going to be very useful."

Tanner had to set his glass on the mantel to open the package. "It must be a book, it's so heavy." He looked to Holly for confirmation, but she just giggled and hid behind her hands. Once Tanner had the wrapping off, his expression turned to one of serious admiration. "Holly! This is fantastic." He held up the polished bronze plaque. It read: "Tanner O'Neill, DVM".

"Holly, this is great. Thank you so much." He pulled her close for a hug and a kiss. Holly felt shy all of a sudden.

"I figured soon you'll have your own practice, and this can go on your office door."

"It's perfect," said Tanner softly.

Before Holly could steal another kiss, Ruth blustered, "Well, come on, Tanner, give her your gift."

Tanner smiled apologetically at Holly as he reached for a small box the size of a CD case. "Now I hope *you* aren't disappointed."

Deep inside, Holly was a wee bit disappointed. She had been secretly hoping her gift would be an engagement ring. She forced herself to maintain the cheer of the moment. She shook the little package and held it to her ear. "No rattles." She sniffed it. "No chocolate."

Tanner was now hiding a smile behind his hand.

At last, Holly tore the paper off and gently pried the lid off the little box. She tilted her head and frowned a question at Tanner as she lifted out a greeting card.

Tanner mimed for her to read it.

She opened the card cautiously, wondering what might spring out of it. Then she began to read. Within seconds, tears coursed down her cheeks. She was unable to speak. All she could do was nod, yes, yes, yes. She handed the card to her mother and fell into Tanner's arms.

Tanner had written inside, "Dearest Holly, Thank you for making my childhood fantasy come true. Now I hope you'll make my grownup wish come true as well, and say you will marry me. P.S. If you say yes, we'll go pick out rings together."

Margaret handed the card to Ruth. She pulled the Cavalier close and, with tears in her eyes, said, "Oh Holly, we both got 'beaus' for Christmas!"

The Christmas Sweets

Regina Duke

TATUM Price loved the holidays, and this year was no exception. She had already watched "It's a Wonderful Life" three times, and it was only December 15th. Her apartment was decorated from floor to ceiling, and she had a Christmas music channel playing on the radio. Her third-grade class had made a paper chain for her tree, and every child had signed their links. Fall had been a thrum of activity, and her life felt rich and full.

Until her school broke for Christmas vacation.

This morning, she slipped her red horn rims onto her nose, as usual, and she was half-dressed before she realized school was out until after New Year's. Seventeen days, all alone, left to her own devices. She kept the layers of pink she was wearing on top, but slipped out of her skirt and into a pair of jeans and running shoes. The weather had blessed southern New York with a stretch of dry cold. She wouldn't need her snow boots.

The apartment was quiet and still. She'd left the tree lights on the night before, and they blinked weakly in the morning light, as if to say, "Look at all these kids you won't get to spend the holidays with."

She sighed. Just as she was about to slip into a pool of the blues, her phone rang.

"Hello?"

"Hey, TaterTot, you coming to our house for Christmas this year?"

"Dad! What a nice surprise."

"Your school is out for Christmas, right?"

"Yes, it is."

"Good! We'll see you soon then?"

"Oh dear." She scrambled for a reason not to go. If she told the truth—she couldn't afford to fly clear across the country on her beginning teacher's salary—her parents would insist on buying her a ticket. She did not want them to do that. They were already helping out her brother, and one of her sisters was saving up to spend a year abroad in Italy. "I'm so sorry, Dad. I'm volunteering to help low income children over the holidays." She could swear her nose grow half an inch, but when she touched the end of it, it felt normal. Maybe it was just her imagination. Or her guilt.

She managed to make it through the phone call, but darn it, now her mood was ruined because she'd lied to her parents. If she could beam home, she would have gone. But the price of a ticket was outrageous for a woman who barely had grocery money left after paying for rent and other necessities. She'd already run her credit card up buying and mailing Christmas gifts. The idea of putting an airline ticket on that card scared her half to death.

She stood there for a few minutes, holding her cell, and staring at her tree. Time to turn off the lights. She did so, and the room looked even lonelier. She combed her thick dark hair and brushed her teeth, then stared glumly at herself in the mirror.

"No pity parties." She wagged a finger at herself. "There are tons of things for a single woman to do during the holidays. Alone. By herself. Crap." She left the bathroom and shook the contents of her purse out on the little table in the kitchen alcove. Her mother would be so proud to see how tidy her apartment was. Of course, when you owned one plate and a box of plastic picnic ware, it was easy to keep your sink clean. She found her wallet and opened it to count out her cash. She was determined to get to her next payday without using that credit card again. It would take her most of the year, as it was, to pay off the balance she'd created while Christmas shopping.

Her personal wealth was limited to one hundred and twelve dollars and sixty-nine cents. She might be able to afford a movie if she snuck in her own treats. But what fun was that? She was in good shape, so she could walk most places, and working at a small private school an hour from New York City meant she had trains and buses and subways to get around on. But she wouldn't be able to go into the city every day. And once there, she wouldn't have much spending money.

The credit card whispered in her ear, "Use me. Use me. It's only once a year."

Naturally, that was her imagination again. If her credit card could really talk, she'd sign with an agent and take it on the road.

She laughed at the thought.

Then she sobered again. Her best friend Tina had left the night before to catch a flight home to Florida. And her baptism by fire as a new teacher had eliminated the possibility of a social life, so she didn't even have a boyfriend to hang out with and possibly depend on for an evening on the town.

She put everything back in her purse, and sat heavily on the kitchen chair. Seventeen days. She drummed her fingers on the table.

"Oh! What's the matter with me? What would I tell my students?" She took a notebook out of her purse and wrote down, "Library books."

"I can spend my vacation reading! I can walk to the village

library from here. And I can bake myself some cookies, too." That made her feel better. She added cookies to her list.

She could start her day by window-shopping at that local second-hand shop she passed every day on her way to school. What was it called? Oh yes. One-Two-Three. Strange name. It wasn't open at seven in the morning, and by the time she headed home, it was usually closed. She had always wondered what was inside.

She bounced with excitement as she realized she could also buy herself a Christmas splurge at the Village Candy Store. They made chocolates by hand, and the place was packed, floor to ceiling, with every kind of candy she could imagine, including all of her favorites from childhood. Five dollars would buy her a pound of loose candies. The handmade chocolates were much more expensive. But at least it was a fun item to add to her list. She wrote "Thrift Shop" and "Candy store" on her list.

Certainly, that was enough for one day. She would think about tomorrow, tomorrow. She shoved her arms into her red down coat, slung her purse over her shoulder, and headed out the door.

Braydon Farmer cringed every time his son, Jake, missed a note. He could hear him practicing upstairs, even over the hum of the machinery in his candy kitchen. He was working with caramel, and his white apron was spattered with the sticky stuff, and of course, he'd managed to get it on his hands.

Plink, plink, plonk. Sometimes he wondered if the boy didn't mess up on purpose, just to get on his father's nerves.

But no, that wasn't fair. They'd both agreed that Jake would try piano lessons for a year. They'd promised his mother, Shelly, that he would study music. But Braydon was certain of one thing. He'd never let his son fly all over the country to concerts. Those small planes routinely rented by her band had been the death of her.

Then he wondered if it was his fear of losing Jake to some struggling chamber orchestra or rock band that was causing the boy to hate his lessons. Was he subconsciously sabotaging his son's musical progress? He felt a headache coming on as Jake began another half-hearted scale. The jingle of the bell over the candy store door out front announced the arrival of a customer.

"Oh no. Brenda? Are you out there?" He lifted his hands in the air, stopping just short of pushing his stubborn forelock out of his eyes. His hair and eyes were the same color as the caramel, but Jake had his late mother's dark hair and brown eyes. He backed into the swinging door, hoping his teenage clerk was doing her job.

No such luck. She was sitting at a table with her boyfriend, making googly eyes over an ice cream cone. Ice cream? In December?

"Hello?" A sweet female voice called from the door.

Braydon swung his attention to the customer who'd just come in. "May I help—?" He sucked in a breath. "Hey! Come in, come in." He'd only met her twice during the fall semester, but he'd burned her face and name in his memory. He hadn't been stirred by a woman since Shelly's death five years ago. "Tatum Price, right?"

Tatum looked confused. "Do I know you?"

Braydon was crushed, but he put on a brave smile. "You're my son's teacher. Third grade? Jake Farmer?"

Her face lit up with recognition. "Oh, of course! I should have seen the resemblance. How are you?" She came close to the counter and reached over it to shake hands.

Braydon's hands were sticky with caramel. "Ummm...."

"Oh, sorry," said Tatum. "Is Jake enjoying his first day of Christmas vacation?"

Upstairs, plink, plink, plonk, plink. Braydon's gaze moved upward. "Oh, not yet, but he will."

Tatum laughed. "I didn't know he was studying piano."

Braydon thought "studying" was a generous term, but he nodded. "Yes. He started in September." He glanced at his hands. "If I go clean my hands, will you promise to wait right here? I'd love to talk to you."

"Sure." Her tone was light. She moved to one of the little tables where customers were encouraged to sample the product.

"I'll be right back," said Braydon. "Don't move."

Tatum laughed sweetly.

Braydon ducked back into the kitchen and scrubbed caramel off his hands. He had been going to fire his young counter help, but he was in such a good mood after seeing Tatum, he decided to cut her some slack. He forced himself to breathe calmly as he dried his hands. Her hair was gorgeous—thick, straight, and dark. She was adorable in those red glasses. They set off her steel-gray eyes. So unusual. Those eyes had grabbed him by the heart and shook him hard the first time he met her at Jake's school. He'd meant to make time to get to know her, maybe ask her out, but running his own business ate up his days and nights. Two parent-teacher meetings, and neither of them felt like the right time to ask her out, not while they were surrounded by dozens of other parents and kids.

He took a deep, cleansing breath and headed out front.

"Jake! Why aren't you practicing?"

Jake was chatting eagerly with his teacher, piling handfuls of gummy worms and bubble gum on the table in front of her. He swung around, looking guilty, when his father called his name.

"Daddy! Look who came to see me." He was wide-eyed and obviously delighted.

Braydon's heart melted. "You must be extra special," he said. He settled his hand on Jake's head and smiled at Tatum. "Thanks for waiting."

The look on her face when her gaze settled on Jake was more than Braydon could have hoped for. This woman loved kids.

She said, "He was telling me he wanted to play drums, but you already had a piano."

Braydon ruffled Jake's hair. "It was his mother's."

Jake offered, "Her plane crashed when I was a little kid."

Braydon felt a twinge of sorrow at the mention of the plane crash, but at the same time, he was relieved that for Jake the memory was just a story to tell. He doubted that his son—only three years old at the time—had a clear memory of the tragedy.

Tatum said, "I'm so sorry." She started to stand.

"No, please," said Braydon. "Please stay. A little while." He sat down to encourage her. "Jake, you only practiced for fifteen minutes. I thought we agreed on half an hour a day."

Jake's pout was worthy of an Academy Award. "My fingers hurt."

Braydon wasn't buying that one. "You can finish later, okay?"

Tatum pushed her red glasses up her nose. "Jake, do you remember the fancy word we learned for drums?"

He nodded eagerly. "Precaution."

Braydon laughed.

Tatum smiled. "Very close. Percussion."

"Percussion," repeated Jake. "Percussion."

"Good," said Tatum. She glanced at Braydon. "Do you know what kind of instrument the piano is?"

Jake sagged. "Boring?"

This time, Tatum laughed with Braydon. "I think he's going to be a comedian," she said. Then, "No, Jake, it's a member of the percussion family."

Jake looked at her as if to say, *You grownups will do anything to make me practice.* "No way."

"Way," said Tatum. "Haven't you ever looked inside?"

The bell over the front door rang, and two women entered, bundled against the cold.

Braydon lifted a finger in the air. "Please stay. I need to take care of these customers."

Tatum smiled. "Sure."

By the time Braydon returned to Jake and Tatum, it was obvious that she had almost convinced Jake about his percussion piano. Before he could sit down, three more customers came in.

"Merry Christmas! We need homemade peppermints."

"I'll be right with you," said Braydon, giving up hope on the love-sick teen in the corner. He backed toward the candy counter. "We're closed tomorrow. Jake and I would love to see you without interruptions. Be right back."

Tatum laughed softly. At least she didn't seem to be in any hurry to leave.

Jake squealed, "I'll get those peanut butter candies for you!"

Ten minutes later, Braydon was still greeting customers. He couldn't complain about the rush of sales, but he wasn't happy about the timing. The next customer stepped up to the counter. "What can I do for you?"

It was Tatum. She tossed her head and her gorgeous hair swung from side to side. "I have collected what I hope is a pound of candy from your barrels, with Jake's help," she said, setting a white bag on the counter.

Braydon knew at a glance that it was closer to three pounds, but he didn't weigh it. "That will be five dollars," he said.

Tatum eyed him suspiciously. "Are you sure it's only five?"

Braydon pretended to calculate in his head, then snapped his fingers. "Oh, I forgot the Christmas surcharge. Five dollars, and a promise that I can see you tomorrow?"

Jake jumped up and down. "Yes, yes, yes!"

Tatum looked pleased. "Ah, the surcharge. Well, I promised myself Christmas candy, so I guess I have to pay it." She handed him a five. "What time tomorrow?"

Braydon's heart swelled in his chest. "Ten a.m.?"

Tatum looked surprised.

"I was hoping we could spend the day together," he said.

"Gee," said Tatum, "that actually works for me. On one condition. Jake, will you play your piano for me?"

Jake wilted.

"How about if I show you what's inside it?"

"You can take it apart?" Jake's eyes widened at the thought.

"We can open it," said Tatum, glancing at Braydon for permission.

Braydon nodded. "That sounds wonderful. Shall I pick you up?"

"I can walk," said Tatum. "I have to if I'm going to eat any of my Christmas candy."

Braydon scribbled his phone number on a sales slip. "Here you go. Just in case. We live upstairs, so just push the bell outside that's labeled 'Farmer.' And we'll be on the lookout."

Tatum grinned from ear to ear. "Okay. See you then." She had to wend her way through half a dozen customers to reach the door.

Braydon watched Tatum exit until he couldn't see her anymore. He handed Jake a peppermint stick, then turned to his customers. "Merry Christmas! Everyone gets an extra half-pound of barrel candy with their purchase today." He couldn't believe his good fortune, and he wanted everyone to be as happy as he was.

Tatum practically floated all the way home. Once there, she dropped off her library books and her candy, then headed out again. The sun was shining, and she hadn't made it to the second-hand store yet. Besides, she felt so good, she just had to move.

She hummed "Jingle Bells" as she browsed through the shop. When she found a clerk, a young woman dressed in what appeared to be a selection of clothes from the shop itself, she paused. "Excuse me, but could you tell me what the name of the shop means? Why One-Two-Three?"

The woman smiled brightly, holding up her fingers as she spoke. "One, brand new. Two, second-hand. Three, new-to-you."

"It's much bigger than I expected from the narrow shopfront."

"Are you looking for anything specific?" asked the clerk. "We have mostly clothes up front, but there's furniture and household items in the back, and musical instruments, and books and knick-knacks. Take your time. Holler if you need me."

"Thanks, I will." Musical instruments? Tatum was intrigued. Her piano—well, her family's piano—was on the west coast with her parents. She'd been playing since she was six and had given piano lessons to help defray the costs of college. But when she got a job in New York State, she couldn't just up and pack the piano to take along.

Meanwhile, she'd been so busy adjusting to her teaching duties, she hadn't had time to think about it, but upon learning that Jake Farmer was trying to learn, all her musical yearnings returned in force. It wouldn't hurt to look around a bit. She didn't expect to find much—people usually traded up for better pianos because their resale value was so high—but she couldn't stop thinking about Jake (and his handsome father), so she ambled through the store, running her fingers over every chair and couch and desk, until she found the music section way in the back.

"Oh my." The Yamaha electric keyboard took her breath away. It looked brand new. That couldn't be right. She approached cautiously, afraid it was an illusion that would evaporate if she got too close. But here it was on a folding stand. She peeked behind it and saw it was plugged in, so she turned it on. The power light worked. But surely there was something wrong with it.

She had to know. She pulled up a chair with an orange sticker on the seat that read "$5.00" and sat down, her fingers poised over the keyboard. She pressed down with a C chord, which came out perfectly, and gave a little squeak of delight when she realized the keyboard was weighted to feel like an acoustic piano. She let her hands take over and played "Mary, Don't You Know" with her eyes closed.

When she finished, five listeners applauded. "Wonderful!" "You play beautifully."

The store clerk was one of them. "You need that keyboard," she said. "Can you play 'Oh Come All Ye Faithful'?"

Tatum obliged, letting her fingers caress the keys and feeling the music soothe her soul. An hour passed as she played one Christmas favorite after another. When her back began to ache from sitting on the hard wooden chair, she stood up to stretch. There were now ten customers applauding.

"Thank you for letting me play," she said to the clerk. "I miss my piano so much."

The clerk said, "You should have this. You're the first person who has actually sat down and made music on it. Really, it was meant for you."

Tatum flipped the dangling price tag over and shriveled inside. Three hundred dollars. She shook her head. "I can't afford it."

The other customers began to wander away, and the clerk pulled a marker out of her pocket. She drew a line through the price. "What can you afford?"

Tatum's eyes filled with tears. "I have one hundred seven dollars to last until payday."

"Where do you work?"

"I'm a teacher at the Barnhart School. First year."

The clerk smiled. "Do you believe in Christmas miracles?"

Tatum's mouth opened but she didn't have words. At last, she choked out, "Yes, I guess I do." After all, she'd just met Braydon and her Sunday was going to be filled with fun and good company. "I definitely do."

The clerk wrote $120 on the price tag. "Payable at ten dollars a month over the next year, or whenever you can pay it off."

"Oh my gosh! You're kidding!!"

"No kidding. It was brought in years ago by a professional musician who had acquired a newer model and wanted it to go to someone who would love it and play it."

Tatum's hands trembled as she pulled out a ten dollar bill. "Do I need to fill out paperwork?"

"No. You live and work here in the Village. I've seen you peeking in my windows while I'm stocking merchandise." She gave an impish smile. "I trust you."

Tatum laid her hands on the keyboard again. "How will I get you home?" she murmured.

"I'll be here tomorrow," said the clerk. "Between noon and three. Marking prices down for Christmas. Perhaps you have a friend who can help you? I'll loan you a dolly and I'll put the keyboard in its case."

Tatum couldn't help herself. She embraced the woman. "This is a Christmas miracle! Thank you, thank you! Oh. What's your name?"

"Joy," said the clerk. "Can I expect you tomorrow?"

"Definitely! And I'd like to look through your stash of music books," she added.

"Take your time." Joy pocketed the ten-dollar bill. "I'll be up front."

Tatum could barely contain her excitement. She was going to have a piano again! Well, an electric keyboard, but with weighted keys, it was every bit as good, and it would actually fit in her apartment. She fought back tears of gratitude as she looked through the rack of used music. The prices on the piano books were ridiculously low. And one of them, she just had to buy for Jake. Maybe it would get him a little more excited about his lessons. Besides, by helping Jake, she could feel a lot better about telling her father she was working with disadvantaged kids over the break.

She stopped at the cash register with ten music books in her arms.

Joy rang up her purchases. "Great choices. That will be ten dollars."

Tatum handed over another precious ten. "You have just made my entire Christmas," she said.

"Wonderful," said Joy. "So you'll come shop here again?"

Tatum laughed with delight. "You can count on it."

She spent the rest of the day rearranging her meager furniture to give the keyboard a place of honor when it arrived. She hoped Braydon wouldn't mind helping her move it.

She dug through her closet, looking for the last scrap of wrapping paper. She'd sent most of it to her family, carefully taped around their gifts. But she had one piece left, a bright red print with reindeer and Santas on it. She used it to wrap the book she'd found for Jake.

She cooked rice for dinner and settled in front of the TV to watch "A Christmas Carol." Her library books sat unread on the tiny kitchen table.

Sunday morning, Braydon left Jake at the breakfast table with a box of cereal and instructions to practice for thirty minutes before Tatum arrived. Then he ran downstairs to check on his kitchen and make sure all was well in the shop. He got caught up in re-stocking candy barrels, some of which had been seriously depleted by his offer of barrel candy with any purchase of homemade chocolates. When he glanced at the clock, he realized he hadn't heard any piano playing while he was downstairs, and it had been nearly forty-five minutes.

He found Jake sitting cross-legged in front of his PlayStation, stuffing dry cereal into his mouth whenever he lost a life in his game.

"Jake, you promised you'd practice. And why aren't you dressed yet? We're going out with Tatum today."

"I'm so close to the next level, Daddy. Just a few more minutes."

Braydon shook his head. But he couldn't be angry. Instead he removed the cereal bowl from Jake's lap, then picked his son up in a fireman's carry and headed for the boy's bedroom.

Jake laughed and screamed as they went, and it all ended in a tickle fight on his bed. The game was cut short by the front door buzzer.

"She's here," said Braydon. He selected a couple of items from Jake's dresser. "Put these on. I'll go let her in."

A few moments later, he was at the side door of the shop, which led up the stairs to the apartments above. He didn't have a jacket on, so he jogged to the corner and caught Tatum's attention.

"We use this door for our living quarters," he said, waving her over. She looked fantastic. Her red scarf framed her dark hair and complemented her red glasses. Her down coat covered her jeans all the way to her calves. "Gosh, you're beautiful," he sighed.

Tatum's cheeks reddened. "I think I like you," she said teasingly. "You can tell me I'm beautiful any time you want."

"You must hear that a lot," he said, holding the wooden side door open for her. The staircase was brightly lit, and he led the way upstairs.

"Actually," said Tatum, "I'm the plain one in the family." She shrugged. "Boys don't make passes at girls who wear glasses. Remember that from junior high?"

Braydon laughed and ushered her into his apartment. Only then did he realize what a mess the place was. Jake's toys were everywhere, his bowl of cereal sat in front of the TV, and most alarmingly, a carton of milk sat precariously on the piano. Braydon grabbed the milk carton, sighing with relief that Jake hadn't knocked it over. "Sorry about the mess," he said.

Tatum shook her head. "No apology necessary. I understand. I have a whole roomful of kids Jake's age, remember? I spend at least thirty minutes straightening up before I leave for the day."

"Don't you have janitors?"

"Sure, but they do the floors and empty the trash. I pick up books and pencils and crayons and tubs of paste…the usual."

Braydon grinned. "Jake is getting dressed. May I take your coat? I promise to hang it up out of reach."

Tatum grinned and unzipped her coat, revealing a skinny package wrapped in Christmas paper. "I brought Jake a present."

Jake's voice called from the other room, "I heard that! I'm coming!"

His clothes were on, but he was still barefoot.

Braydon stopped him. "Socks and shoes first. Go on."

Tatum studied Braydon with a practiced eye. "Can I borrow you for my class? I have a few kids who assume all my instructions are for everyone else."

Braydon hung her coat in the entryway closet, the tidiest part of the apartment. "Don't worry. You'll get the hang of it. You have to sound tough, but be sweet enough that they want to please you."

"Is that what you do?"

He closed the closet door and considered her question. "Well, I'm pretty good at sounding tough. Trouble is," he said, lowering his voice, "Jake knows I love him so much, he can almost get away with anything."

"That's a great quality in a father. Mine is like that, too." She looked away and fell silent, folding her arms across her chest.

Braydon was puzzled. "Did I say something wrong?"

"Oh, no, of course not." Tatum unfolded her arms and moved to the piano. "I just told my dad a little bitty fib to keep him from scraping up airfare for me for Christmas. I guess I feel a little guilty about it."

"Don't worry," said Braydon. "Those little white lies we tell to protect the people we love? That's what angel wings are made of."

Tatum smiled. "I never thought of it that way." She marveled at what a sweet man Braydon was. She sat down at the piano and let her fingers drift over the keys. They seemed to want to play "I'll Be Home for Christmas" and she let them take over.

Jake's voice startled her. "You close your eyes when you play."

Tatum turned to him. "You will, too, someday. Your fingers will make friends with the keys and you won't even have to look at the music."

Braydon leaned an elbow on top of the piano. "Right now, he and the keys have more of a karate chop relationship."

Tatum laughed. "That's a good one."

Jake persisted. "You said yesterday that my piano is a precaution...I mean, a percussion instrument. I tried to look inside but nothing moved."

Tatum said, "That's because it's sort of a puzzle box. You have to know the secrets before you can open it."

Jake's face lit up. "No kidding?"

Braydon echoed, "No kidding?"

Tatum stood up and flipped the top of the piano open.

"I got that far," said Braydon.

"I'm too short," said Jake.

Tatum gave them an all-knowing look. "If your dad will let you stand on the piano bench so you can see, I'll show you the secrets."

"Yay!" Jake was already on his knees on the bench. Braydon caught his arm to steady him as he stood up.

"This should be interesting," he mused.

"Didn't you ever watch your piano tuner?" asked Tatum.

"Um, no, not really."

She found the catch inside the front panel and popped it loose. "This one is heavy and takes two hands." She lifted it carefully and set it on the sofa.

"Wow!" Jake stared intently at the strings and other wooden parts. "What are those?"

"Those are hammers."

"Really? They're made of wood," said Jake in disbelief.

"Metal hammers wouldn't sound as good, and besides, they might break the strings. Go ahead and play a note."

Jake did so.

"See? When you press a key, you're really hitting the strings with a drumstick. Kind of."

"Oh, I get it. Cool. Look at all those strings. Like a big guitar."

"Like more than thirty guitars, actually."

"Neat-o!"

Tatum smiled. "And there's another secret underneath. Braydon, would you help me put the upper panel back, please?"

"Sure."

Once it was secure, Tatum said spookily, "Are you ready to see the rest of it? Or is your mind already blown?"

Jake giggled. "Show me, show me."

Tatum glanced up at Braydon and was caught off guard by the affection she saw in his eyes. She cleared her throat. "Here goes. You can get down now. I need to move the bench." She proceeded to unfasten the lower panel.

"What are those long things?" asked Jake.

"Those are called the trapwork. When you press one of the pedals, they move the levers to make the sound louder or softer." She gave Braydon a little shrug. "That's a simplification, but you get the idea."

Jake was squatting to get a better look at the workings of the piano. "Awesome," he said softly. "It's like I'm playing a Transformer, only it's not a car."

"I like that," said Braydon. "And lucky for you, Jake, because you're too young to drive."

Tatum refastened the lower panel. "Now do you feel better about your piano?"

Jake nodded eagerly. "And you brought me a present?"

Braydon rolled his eyes, but Tatum matched Jake's enthusiasm.

"Yes, I did! Look what you can play…someday…with a little practice."

Jake ripped the paper off the music book and squinted at the cover. "Oh my gosh! Star Wars! Does it really sound like the movie?"

"You tell me," said Tatum. She opened the book and began to play.

Jake was ecstatic. "When can I start? Why doesn't my piano teacher give me good stuff like this?"

Tatum beamed. "I'm glad you like it. We can start today, but I need to ask your father a favor."

Braydon nodded. "Anything."

"I found a keyboard for myself at the One-Two-Three, and I need help getting it to my apartment. Joy said she'll be there between noon and three."

"No problem." He tilted his head. "You mean you play like this and you don't have an instrument?"

"It was my parents' piano. And it wouldn't fit in my suitcase."

Jake thought she was hilarious.

Braydon glanced at the time. "Why don't we start with breakfast? Or brunch? After that, we can go move your keyboard."

The rest of the day flew by. Tatum found Braydon so easy to talk to. And he seemed to feel the same way. For every story she told, he told two. By the end of the day, she felt like she'd known him all her life.

They bought Jake a Christmas tree and spent three hours decorating it. Then they went ice skating on the Village pond.

"Don't worry," said Braydon. "It's artificial. No one falls through the ice here."

Tatum found ice skating a challenge, but Jake thought she was the funniest skater ever, and Braydon had lots of opportunities to pull her into his arms, as she flailed about on the ice. She'd grown up in California. They didn't ice skate much.

After hot dogs for dinner, and Tatum's confession that she was down to eighty-seven dollars until payday, they headed home. Jake was ready to be carried, and Braydon hefted him up on one arm.

They stood in front of her apartment building. It was getting dark, and Jake was asleep on his father's shoulder.

Braydon said softly, "I had the best time ever."

"Me, too," said Tatum, letting him squeeze her hand. "I think Jake had fun, too."

"I'll probably pay for letting him have that extra hot dog. I expect a tummy ache at three a.m."

"Oh, what a dear. He's got the greatest personality." She dropped her eyes shyly. "Just like his dad."

Braydon bent at the knees and leaned in to plant a soft kiss on her lips.

The spark that rushed through her made Tatum's eyes glow with feeling. "Wow." She put a hand behind his head and kissed him softly back.

"Double wow," whispered Braydon. "Will I see you tomorrow?"

"I'm free until school starts. But you have a candy store to run."

Braydon nodded, then brightened. "How would you feel about a part-time job during the break. I need counter help in the worst way. You'd get some extra cash, and I'd be able to find out…"

"Find out what?"

"Find out whether you can stand to be around me all day at work."

Tatum felt like another miracle had fallen into her lap. "What time shall I arrive?"

The next five days made Tatum feel she'd made the right decision about not letting her dad fly her home. In the morning, she was up at six, playing her keyboard. At nine, she was selling candy. Some of the customers were parents of the kids in her class, and that made for great conversations.

Braydon's teenage helper took over at one every day, and Tatum had Jake waiting impatiently at his piano, desperate to learn some Star Wars music. His regular music teacher had taken December off, so she didn't feel like she was stepping on anyone's toes. Besides, Jake needed some help to make him fall in love with his Transformer. She taught him some riffs and a boogie-woogie beat. Her talent for teaching extended to music, and after giving lessons for four years during college, she had a lot of tricks up her sleeve to use on the young ones.

When the weather allowed, while Braydon made candy, she took Jake for long walks, window shopping, and ice skating. She would watch from the parents' bleachers, where electric heaters provided some comfort.

And every day, she felt closer and closer to Braydon. By Friday, they were dancing around the subject of a possible future together.

Jake was hunched in front of his PlayStation with a bowl of popcorn at his elbow while Braydon made dinner for Tatum, proving that candy wasn't the only thing he could cook.

"This is delicious," she said. "How did you know lasagna is my favorite?"

"You told me on Wednesday."

Tatum laughed. "Well, at least you listen. It would be great to have someone around who actually enjoys cooking." Then she blushed and looked away, afraid she'd gone too far.

Braydon took her hand across the table. "I've been thinking about that," he said. "I'm so fond of you."

"Uh-oh," said Tatum. "Why do I hear a 'but' coming?"

Braydon pulled his hand back and picked up his glass of wine. "It's not doubt," he mused, his forehead creasing in thought. "And you are perfect for Jake."

Tatum felt a sliver of heartache. She hugged herself tight. "You're tired of me already?" She tried to keep her tone light, but her voice wavered.

"No, no! Not at all!" Braydon got up and moved to her side. He pulled her out of the chair and into an embrace.

Tatum argued with herself about whether she should enjoy the closeness or break it off…for about one second, then wholeheartedly hugged him back. "Thank goodness!"

Braydon smoothed her hair. "I just have this memory of Jake's mother, haunting me. Is it okay for me to bring someone else into my life?"

Tatum leaned back to look in his eyes. "Do you need some time to think? Shall I stay away for a while?"

Braydon looked tortured. "I don't want to lose you," he whispered, "but I keep waiting for permission to move on. Does that make sense?"

Tatum hated to say it out loud, but she couldn't lie to Braydon. "Yes, it makes sense. You're still tied to her through Jake. Her spirit is still in your heart and your house."

"Maybe…maybe just one day," said Braydon. "Let's see if I can stand to be apart from you for one whole day. If I can't, that's my answer."

Tatum's heart teetered on the edge of a cliff, but she pulled herself together. "All right." She held out her hand, and they shook on it. "But you know what this means, right?"

Braydon shook his head, bewildered.

Tatum moved to the coat closet for her things. "It means you get to do the dishes all by yourself." She forced a playfulness into her voice that she wasn't feeling, and managed to hold it together until she was safely down the stairs and on the sidewalk.

It suddenly felt colder. Ice crystals in the air made it look like it was snowing in slow motion. The streetlights cast a bluish glow that made the world seem harsh and unfeeling. She hunched inside her down coat and pulled her red scarf closer around her neck, but they could not protect her from the frostbite that was forming around her heart.

By the time she reached her apartment and hung up her things, the internal frost had melted and poured out as tears. She curled up on one end of the couch and muted the TV. One day. One whole day. Her future depended on whether Braydon could stand to be apart from her.

After half an hour of tears, she got angry. After all, there were two people involved here. No, three. What about little Jake? She adored him, and he was finally coming around about the piano.

She decided to go read in bed. She picked up the library books off the table, but her eyes filled with tears again and their titles were blurry. She couldn't even remember what she'd selected. No matter. She set them back on the table and went to bed.

The next morning, it snowed. Tatum had been so busy with Braydon and Jake that she didn't have anything in the house to eat except the bag of candy she'd bought last Saturday.

"One week," she mumbled. "How can my life take such a total turn in one week? And now I don't even know if there's a future for us." She turned up the heat and tucked her feet into bunny slippers. It was going to be a long day. She heated water and made tea. It went well with the root beer candy she popped into her mouth.

It was bleak outside. Her Christmas tree would shine brightly in this gloom, but when she plugged it in, every flash stabbed her in the heart.

"At least I have one miracle I can count on." She ran her hands over the keyboard and turned it on. As she played, her fingers took over, and after half an hour, she felt better...all the way up to her elbows. "Where did I put my piano books?"

She found them on the bookshelf and spent a pleasant hour playing tunes from each. The last book had a keyboard manual stuck inside. It must have belonged to the original owner. Tatum set the manual on the music stand and flipped through the book from back to front. It was boogie-woogie and there were handwritten notes in the margins. At the front of the book, she froze. At the top of the first page was a name.

Shelly Farmer.

Her hands trembled. Did this keyboard once belong to Braydon's wife? Giving it to One-Two-Three was sort of like giving to a charity.

She decided that the manual should stay in the case, so she wouldn't lose it. In the lid of the long black box was a velvet pocket. She tucked the manual inside it, but it caught on something. She slid her fingers in and found a pale green envelope. Written on the envelope was "To the new owner."

Tatum's fingers fumbled as she opened the card. It read:

"I pass this keyboard on to someone who needs it more than I. May you love it and play it and cherish it. And when the time comes, please find it another good home. Shelly Farmer."

Tatum's tears flowed again, but this time it was with a sense of grief. She felt that Shelly could have been her best friend had they met earlier in life. She fought the urge to call Braydon and tell him what she'd found, but he said he needed a day. So she sat down at the keyboard and played until her back threatened to snap in two.

It was past one p.m. by the time she moved to the couch. Her tea was cold, but she drank it anyway. She consumed three small Tootsie Rolls and a handful of melt-in-your-mouth peppermints. Once again, she fought the urge to call Braydon.

Instead, she wandered into the kitchen and picked up her

library books. She carried them to the couch. Well, her original plan had been to eat candy and read. It looked like she was going to have a chance to do just that.

Before she could sit down, there was a knock at the door. Tatum wasn't expecting visitors. She peeked through the peephole, and her heart soared. She nearly destroyed the sliding bolt in her haste to get the door open.

"Braydon! Jake!"

Jake ran past her and threw himself on the sofa face down.

Tatum looked a question at Braydon. "What's up?"

Braydon looked chagrinned. "I'm an idiot. I was miserable all night and all morning, too. I think I should make a new future instead of worrying about—"

Jake lifted a library book in the air. "Look, Daddy. This book has Mom's name on it."

Braydon closed the door, and Tatum took the book from Jake. It was from the romance section of the library. She gaped at the title, then held it up for Braydon to see.

He read, "Shelly Says Yes." His mouth dropped open in disbelief.

Jake hopped on one foot to the Christmas tree and dropped to his knees in front of it. "Your lights are twinkling," he said. "Daddy, look, here's my part of the paper chain. I signed Jake on all my pieces. Wait. Someone wrote on this one." He tried to pull it away from the tree. Braydon moved quickly to save the fir.

"Let's not pull the tree over," he said firmly.

"Look."

Under Jake's name, someone had drawn a red heart.

Braydon looked at Tatum. "Did you do that?"

She mouthed a silent, *No*.

"Cool, Jake. That's an excellent chain, by the way."

Jake said, "There aren't any presents under the tree." He sounded disappointed.

Braydon responded, "Santa hasn't come yet."

Jake gave him a look. "Really, Dad? Tony Pesca says his parents are Santa Claus."

"So you don't believe anymore?"

Jake shrugged. "Tony has lied before."

Tatum hid her laugh behind one hand. Then she said, "Braydon, the book title has to be a coincidence. I got these books from the library more than a week ago, before I met you."

Braydon nodded. "I guess signs from the beyond only happen in movies."

"You sound disappointed." She moved close and hugged him. She could feel his body heat even through his winter jacket.

"I guess I am," he said, hugging her back. "I'm like Jake. I'm not ready to stop believing in miracles."

Tatum gave him an impish smile. "Good. Because I have one for you." She let go of him and retrieved the note from the keyboard case. "Read this."

Braydon took the note. He read it once, then twice. His eyes filled with tears. "Oh my God. This was Shelly's old keyboard!"

Jake went to the keyboard and turned it on. "You mean this used to belong to my mom?"

Braydon nodded, marshaling an effort to speak. "That's right, Jake." His voice quavered.

Jake said, "Look, Dad. There's a playback button. Maybe Mom left a message."

Before Tatum or Braydon could say anything, Jake pushed the playback button. The sound of a boogie-woogie version of "Jingle Bells" floated through the room. And right afterward came a sweet organ version of "I'll Be Home for Christmas."

"Tatum plays really well, doesn't she, Jake?"

Tatum squeezed Braydon's hand. "I didn't record those songs." She looked up at him. "Along with the note, I found this book of boogie-woogie with Shelly's name on the first page."

Braydon sagged onto the couch. He ran his fingers over the

book, and then over her signature. "All I knew before I got here was that I couldn't stand being away from you. And here you are, playing Shelly's old keyboard, handing me a note from the past." He pulled Tatum down beside him and embraced her. "I love you, Tatum Price. I want you in my life. In our lives."

Tatum felt joy swelling within her. "Me, too." They kissed warmly.

Jake held his nose. "Ewwwwww. Love birds."

Braydon laughed. Then he squirmed. "Oh, it's the other library book." He pulled it out from under himself and held it up and read the title. "Sweets for the Heart."

Tatum shrugged and her eyes twinkled. "What can I say? I love romance."

Jake was playing with the ornaments on the tree. "I love Star Wars and Transformers," he announced.

But no one answered. Tatum and Braydon were lost in another kiss.

Jake shook his head. "If you're going to kiss a lot, you better get married."

Tatum and Braydon laughed.

Braydon framed Tatum's face with the palms of his hands. "What do you think? Can you be happy stepping into a ready-made family?"

"Yes," said Tatum. "Very happy. What woman wouldn't jump at the chance to marry a man who makes his own chocolate?"

"But TaterTot, you can't get married so far away! Your mother wants to see you in a wedding gown."

Braydon swayed back and forth, holding Tatum in his arms as she spoke to her parents. He mouthed silently, *TaterTot?*

Tatum made a face, then said to her father, "Don't worry, Dad. Braydon wants to meet you all. We're going to stay engaged a while. But after school is out, we're coming to California to get married."

"Oh dear," said her father.

"What? What is it?" asked Tatum.

"Your mother already has a copy of Brides magazine in her hand."

Tatum laughed. "I'll send you some pictures, Dad. I want you to see what a handsome family I'm marrying into."

"Ha! You're giving me my first grandson. How's them apples?"

"It's all candied apples here, Dad. Braydon is a candy maker, and he has his own shop in the Village."

"No wonder you said yes," teased her father. "Sweets for my sweet girl. Your mother says it should be a June wedding. Hello? You there?"

Tatum couldn't answer because Braydon's warm lips had claimed her own.

The Christmas Light

Regina Duke

HANNAH Gordon loved the cabin in Truckee. Her grandfather had left it to her because she was his only living relative. He'd raised her from the time she was five years old, and it had never occurred to Hannah that his being her grandfather meant he would get old so fast.

Even when she went away to college, she came back every chance she got. And then there was that new job in Reno and that darned snowstorm that hit right after Thanksgiving. She wanted desperately to blame the weather for what happened last year, but she'd had several months of grief therapy since, and she had come to grips with the fact that it was just Grandpa's time to go.

The memory of that last Christmas still haunted her. Even with six feet of snow on the ground, she'd chained up her car and made the drive to spend Christmas with her last remaining relative. She had his high cheekbones and amber eyes, complete with baby laugh lines, and although his hair had turned completely white, she'd seen the pictures of him in his youth with the same thick black mane she had.

At least she'd arrived in time to say goodbye. She found him at the foot of the stairs, looking gray and barely able to speak.

He motioned her close and whispered, "I'll always be with you. Don't be afraid."

She took a moment to call 911, but it was too little too late, and Grandpa expired right there on the floor.

It didn't make sense. She was only twenty-three. How could he be eighty-five?

Her therapist had reminded her, relentlessly, that Hannibal Gordon had married late. He'd been forty when her father was born and sixty-two when her parents insisted on naming her after the old man. Hannibal became Hannah, and she was proud of her uncommon name.

Hannah's parents had died in her father's Piper Cub as they tried to fly out of an unexpected thunderstorm. They were on a second honeymoon, during which five-year-old Hannah had been staying with her grandfather.

From that day forward, he'd become her sole legal guardian. They already had the same name, pretty much. She started school right there in Truckee, and she had so many fond memories of running through the trees or snowshoeing up the hill to the house and having hot chocolate waiting for her when she arrived.

Losing her grandfather at Christmas had soured her completely on the holidays.

When she called the phone number he'd written on the will tucked into the drawer of his bedstand, she was stunned to learn that he'd left her everything. The surprise had not been so much that he made her his heir, but rather how much she was going to inherit. The cabin was clean and modern, with the bedrooms downstairs and the living areas upstairs so that light could still come in when winter hit and the snow got really deep. When the lawyer told her it would appraise at over a million dollars, her jaw dropped.

"Location, location, location," said the lawyer. "But don't worry, the upkeep is taken care of for another twenty years.

And your grandfather wanted you to take your inheritance in monthly payments. He didn't want you to pull the capital and kill the golden goose."

Hannah had stared at him blankly. "What goose? We don't have a goose. Only Grandpa's Siamese cat."

The lawyer scanned the documents spread out before him. "Mr. Gordon lived a spare and simple life, but he held about twelve patents from his days in Silicon Valley. You will have an income for the rest of your days, if this Arturo fellow doesn't cause any trouble. Is he a relative?"

Hannah sagged in her chair and shook her head. "Arturo is the cat. Not a goose. A cat."

The lawyer finally seemed to realize that Hannah was still in shock. He had been the one who recommended a therapist for grief counseling. And he had reassured her that her future was bright. Hannibal Gordon had provided well for his only grandchild.

Now, almost a year to the day after that frantic call to 911, Hannah contemplated putting on her snowshoes and walking down to town. She'd been out and about over the last year, but summer had passed in a haze. The fall was cold and wet, and fitted her mood. But when the first snow came, her grief had threatened to overwhelm her again. Getting outside today sounded like a good idea. But when she looked out the window, flakes were coming fast and furious, and she knew she would not be walking to the shops in this storm.

All the suffering that had been so tidily corralled by the therapist who'd explained all the stages of grief— and actually gave her a timetable to use while she read book after book about the grieving process—all those feelings clawed their way out of their cold storage unit and flayed her heart wide open. Grandpa had loved the snow. He taught her to snowshoe, ski, sled, build snowmen, and he also taught her how to survive if she was ever lost in a snowstorm.

He had prepared her for everything except the most horrible thing of all—the day when her grandfather would no longer walk the earth.

She'd ended her therapist visits right before Thanksgiving. It seemed a smart thing to do, since the therapist was in Reno and she didn't want to be driving back and forth when the snows came. In November she had checked her timeline and seen that she should be well into acceptance by now. So much for psychology. She spent almost all of December—the first twenty-two days—holed up in the cabin, staring out at the forest as the snow came down, thicker and thicker.

At long last, today—the twenty-third—she longed to leave the house but the storm showed no signs of ending. She settled for spending a while on the upstairs balcony. Bundled in sweatshirts and a down jacket, she turned off all the lights in the cabin, took a mug of hot tea out on the deck, and sat in a plastic chair until the snow piled up six inches thick on her legs and forearms. Her tea was filmed over with ice, and she wondered if she could stand to stay out there long enough to go join her grandfather.

At that moment a breeze rustled the thousands of evergreen branches in the forest, and she could almost make out a voice.

Always.

Was that the word? She stood up, surprised by how much snow was displaced by her movement. How long had she been sitting there?

The breeze was picking up, the snow pelting her now.

"Okay, okay, Grandpa," she muttered. "Freezing to death was a stupid idea. I get it." She shook off the snow, emptied her tea cup over the edge of the balcony—the snow was already three feet deep—and retreated into the cabin.

She wasn't really suicidal. She was just so heartbroken, still, after all these months. She unbundled herself and turned the water on for another cup of tea. The room was filling with gloom. In all the

Christmases she'd spent with her grandfather, there had been a glorious tree, decorated as brightly as a lighthouse, in the corner of the living room. This year, she hadn't been able to bring herself to put up any decorations. Without a tree to brighten the space, she needed to turn on the reading lamp by his chair. Her chair now. She could still imagine traces of his cherry tobacco hanging in the air.

Arturo had settled on the back of the small sofa, waiting for a ray of sunshine to warm him, and if that failed, he was strategically located three feet above a floor vent. He had looked for Hannibal for a week after he died, but finally seemed to realize the old man wasn't coming back.

Hannah envied him his ability to keep going, as if adjusting to the new normal was what cats did. She wished she could do the same. When the teakettle whistled, she poured water over her tea bag and spooned a glop of honey into it.

The ringing of the phone on the coffee table was not what she wanted to hear. By the third ring, she decided she had to pick up.

"Hannah, where are you? I thought you were coming to the party." The disappointment in her friend Eva's voice filled her with guilt.

"Oh my gosh, I lost track of time."

"Well, it's not over yet. And don't give me any excuses. I'm sending my cousin to pick you up. Well, sort of my cousin. Okay, second cousin. I think. He's related to me, I'm pretty sure."

The doorbell rang.

"Eva, someone's at the door."

"I know! That's what I'm trying to say! My cousin should be there by now with his four-wheel-drive. His name is Trevor. If the person at the door gives you a different name, don't go with him."

Hannah had plenty of time to walk to the front door—also on the upper level of the house—while Eva babbled on. She opened the door and stood there, staring in disbelief, at the hunk of manhood shaking snow off his cap and ear flaps. He wore no winter coat, just a pale blue long-sleeved tee shirt that clung to every ab, individually. After six she lost count. He was smiling broadly, pretending that his teeth were not chattering.

"Hi. I'm Trevor. I'm here to take you to Eva's party."

Hannah nodded, unable to form words for the moment. She handed him the phone, waved him inside, and retrieved the down jacket she'd just taken off.

"You been outside?" he asked. Then he spoke into the phone. "She's fine, Eva. I didn't get lost. And I thought you said she was the Plain Jane of your group of friends."

By then, Hannah had her coat on, and when he said that, she grabbed the phone. "Eva! Did you really say that?"

Eva was laughing. "No, of course not. I told him you were a looker. He thinks he's funny. See you soon!" She hung up.

Hannah set the phone on the entryway table and zipped up her jacket. "I guess I'm going to a party."

Trevor looked concerned. "You sound miserable. I thought party invitations cheered people up."

He had a lovely voice, deep and musical. How come Eva had never mentioned him before? "You need a coat," she said.

"I just came straight here when Eva said you needed a ride. I'll be fine once we get in the SUV."

Hannah said, "Looking at you makes me cold." She opened the coat closet, then realized the only men's clothing in there was her late grandfather's. But she'd already offered. She pulled out a navy blue down jacket. "Put this on."

"I'm really fine," protested Trevor. He held up his ear-flap cap. "I'm keeping the heat in with this. Does it make me look like a logger?"

Hannah suppressed a snicker. "It makes you look Canadian. And considering the snow coming down out there, it also makes you look really smart. Too bad that impression is ruined by your tee shirt."

Trevor surrendered with grace. "In that case, I shall accept your loan of a jacket." He whisked it on quickly. "Nice. Shall we go?"

Hannah saw no way out now. After all, this beautiful man had driven to her house in a snowstorm. She picked up her house keys and shoved them in her pocket. "I'm ready. Hold onto the banister because the stairs can be icy."

"So I noticed," said Trevor.

She was surprised by the brand new Ford Explorer waiting at the foot of her steep driveway. When Eva said he was a cousin, she'd expected an open-air Jeep. That was the kind of woman Eva was, wild and woolly and broke all the time.

"Nice car," said Hannah as she got in.

Trevor turned up the heater. "Thanks. How do you ever get up your driveway? No offense, but I tried it once and slid downhill, so I gave up and parked in the road."

"How manly of you to admit it."

Trevor laughed out loud. "Eva said you had a great sense of humor." He made sure the hot air was defogging the windshield, then pulled slowly forward.

"I'm sorry," said Hannah. "I didn't mean to sound so snarky. I really appreciate the ride. As you discovered, my driveway is treacherous. At this time of year, I stay in shape by snowshoeing down the hill or skiing. My car is in the garage. His name is Steely Dan, and when I miss him, I sit in the driver's seat and we talk about the wonderful places we'll go when the snow melts."

Trevor nodded. "I see. Perhaps I should find a garage for Kimberly."

Hannah pulled back and stared at him.

He shrugged innocently. "Doesn't she look like a Kimberly? Women aren't the only ones who name their cars."

Hannah suppressed a grin. "Nice to meet you, Kimberly." She patted the dashboard. "I must admit, I admire your ability to navigate the winter roads."

"Kimberly's or mine?" Trevor kept glancing sideways at Hannah.

"Is something wrong?" she asked. "I'd feel safer if you watched the road." She winced as a small red Toyota slid in slow motion down the hill in front of them.

"No worries," said Trevor. "Take a closer look. Some poor fool is trying to drive around without snow tires or chains. We're fine."

Hannah said, "Good." But she had a white-knuckled grip on the handle above her door.

"Have you lived here long?" asked Trevor.

"Most of my life. I just hate driving in the snow. But at least the tourist traffic slows down in the winter."

"That's the right attitude. Find a silver lining."

Once they reached the bottom of the hill and the narrow road leveled off, Hannah relaxed a bit. "My grandfather always drove."

Trevor made an understanding noise. "Eva told me he passed last year. I'm so sorry. I know what that's like."

"Oh really? You lost the man who raised you as his own?" She didn't mean for it to come out icy, but talking about it still hurt.

Trevor reached out and squeezed her hand, just for a moment. "As a matter of fact," he said softly, "yes. My father...thirteen months ago."

Hannah sucked in a breath. "Oh, I'm so sorry. Please forgive me. I guess I'm so wrapped up in my own loss, I forget that the rest of the world is subject to the same pain."

Trevor murmured teasingly, "Surprise."

Hannah sank against the soft leather seat, then sat up straight. "Is my bottom supposed to be warm?"

"Heated seats," said Trevor.

"Awesome." Hannah relaxed again. In dry weather, Eva lived about ten minutes from her place, but in a snowstorm, it was more like half an hour. She might as well make small talk. "What do you do?"

Trevor looked at her like she was speaking a foreign language. "Beg pardon?"

"Your job. Your career. What do you do for a living?"

"Oh. I guess you could say I freelance."

"You're a writer?"

His perfect eyebrows met in a small frown. "I think I have to sell something before I get to claim the title."

Hannah smiled.

"What about you?"

She thought about her answer for a few seconds. "My last position was working as a paralegal."

"But you take winters off because of the snow?"

Hannah didn't want to tell him she had inherited a fortune. If she'd learned anything during the year since the funeral, it was how many men suddenly found her interesting because she could play all day and pay all the bills. Or so they thought. As if grief hadn't shut her off from the world enough, that realization had made socializing a nightmare.

Instead of replying directly, she tilted her head to one side. "I should get better tires on my car."

"I can help you with that, if you like." His tone was playful. "Being a man and all, I know all the right words to use at the tire store."

Hannah felt a genuine smile light up her face. It warmed her heart as it rose, and she couldn't remember the last time she'd smiled from the inside out. "I will probably take you up on that," she said. "Because I'm a woman, and phrases like 'P-metric' and 'Euro-metric' make no sense to my delicate princess brain."

"Good one!" Trevor was grinning from ear to ear. "I think we're here, but I've only seen the front of her house once. With all this new snow…"

Hannah pointed forward. "One more driveway."

"Thanks."

Enjoying a Christmas party was the last thing Hannah ever thought she would do again. A large part of it was having a handsome attentive man seeing to her every need and desire. The icing on the cake was the fact that they shared the same whimsical sense of humor. At one point, he bowed to her and offered her his arm while announcing in a perfect plantation drawl, "I believe this dance belongs to me, missy."

Hannah didn't think her southern accent was nearly as convincing, but she gave it her best shot. "Why, sir…" *Suh.* "…I do believe I've misplaced my dance card." *Cahd.* "Is your name Birmingham Jefferson Trevor Gatlin of the Mississippi Gatlins?"

"Why, your memory is outstanding, young lady. I shortened it to Trevor." *Trevah.* "Much easier when signing checks."

Hannah giggled. In her normal voice, she asked, "Do you have roots in the south?"

"I have distant relatives all over," said Trevor. "The first Gatlin came over on a ship before the Revolutionary War."

"I've got you beat," said Hannah. "My grandfather was half Cherokee."

"Fascinating," said Trevor. "Does that mean we get to dance?"

"I love your non sequiturs," said Hannah. "Maybe we could just assume the position, and sort of sway back and forth. I'm not sure my inner Hannah is ready for rock-and-roll."

"Neither is my inner Trevor," he murmured, pulling her close.

When they browsed the array of party food, they decided they were French for a while. That went beautifully until one of Eva's guests actually spoke to them in French.

Red-faced, Hannah confessed. "I don't really remember much of my French."

Trevor, however, answered the woman with an elegant fluency that Hannah found quite marvelous. She watched as the two of them conversed for a bit. She wasn't sure what Trevor was saying about her, but the other woman looked…jealous?…as she walked away.

Hannah leaned close. "What did you say to her?"

"I told her I'm a vampire and I never drink…wine." Now he sounded like Bella Lugosi.

One of Eva's other friends, three sheets to the wind, came up to hug Hannah and ogle Trevor. "Oh Hannah, darling, I hope your cloud of grief is starting to lift." She was not subtle about eyeing Trevor. "It must be a big weight off your shoulders to know he left you all that money."

Eva arrived too late. She turned her friend around and shoved her gently toward the open bar. Then she whispered to Hannah, "Everything's fine. Trevor isn't a gold digger."

The episode momentarily dashed cold water on Hannah's sputtering Christmas spirit. On the other hand, Eva knew what she'd been going through. She decided to trust her friend. Eva was kooky, but she would never do anything to hurt Hannah. At least, not intentionally. She tried to relax and let Trevor refill her punch glass.

The hours flew by. Before she knew it, the clock struck midnight. She stared down at her feet. "My slippers! My glass slippers! They've disappeared."

Trevor had grown very comfortable with his arm around her shoulders. "It must be time to go back to reality." He sounded disappointed.

Hannah turned to face him and stood on tiptoes. "Will the carriage last long enough to take me home?"

Trevor hugged her close. "Definitely."

Hannah was quiet as Trevor drove. She had done her duty as a friend. She went to Eva's party. Now she could go home and…what? Just sit all alone in the dark? Before the party, she'd expected to have popcorn for dinner, an old movie on cable. Just like every other night. But now that she'd met Trevor, she realized she didn't want to be alone. She didn't want their conversation to end.

She turned to tell him that, and the Christmas lights caught her attention. "Were these lights up on our way to the party?"

Trevor craned his neck to see the colorful decorations that were strung at intervals across the street. Snow was still falling softly, and the flakes glinted with reds and blues and greens. "They must have been," he said at last. "I was so busy trying to look at you, I didn't even notice."

Hannah was flattered. "Look, I hope this doesn't sound too forward, but would you like to come inside for hot chocolate?"

"That sounds delicious."

It took both of them to navigate the snow that had accumulated on the front stairs. It was so quiet, they could hear their breath flow in and out, and when the porch light hit them just right, they could see the moisture in their breath turning to ice.

"Don't fall," they said in unison. Then they laughed, and of course they fell, but it was more like a long slide to the bottom of the stairs.

Trevor helped Hannah stand upright. She let him hold her for a few seconds. Snowflakes hitting her face interrupted the moment. "Let's try again. We should be able to make it up twelve stairs."

"Fourteen," said Trevor. "Counting the landings."

"Well, if you're going to be like that, fifteen, if we count the step up into the entryway."

"Actually," he panted, "we just slid down eight, so by the time we arrive, it will be twenty-three."

Hannah giggled. "Don't make me laugh. I'm trying to breathe and hang onto the rail."

"We should have worn gloves. My hands are freezing."

"Check your pockets. Grandpa always kept gloves in his pockets."

Trevor stopped on the landing and pulled gloves out of his

pockets. "My dad used to do that, too." He slipped a hand into one glove. "Here. You take the other. Your fingers are turning blue."

Hannah accepted, and they continued up the stairs, placing their feet carefully and alternating their handholds on the snow-covered railing. She said, just a half-second too late, "Look out for that patch of ice we fell on before."

And down they went. At least they were laughing. Trevor was plopped against the solid wall of snow that lined the steep driveway, and Hannah tried to crawl off him but found herself unable to get traction. Her plan was to gain some footing and stand up, but the ice and snow had other ideas. "Catch me! I'm sliding!"

Trevor reached out and grabbed her ankle to stop her slide. Panting heavily, he said, "I can't believe your grandfather went up and down these stairs in the winter."

As Hannah righted herself with Trevor's help, she said, gasping for air, "He didn't. He went in through the garage."

As soon as the words were out of her mouth, they both burst out laughing. She hung on to Trevor as they found fresh snow to crunch through and made their way to the automatic door opener, where she punched in the code. The garage door groaned, but it lifted, and a warm yellow light came on inside.

"Nice car," said Trevor. Then he took a second look, and his jaw dropped. "This is a Rolls!"

Hannah winced as if caught in a lie. "It was my grandfather's. It's the smallest one they make, honest."

As the garage door closed behind them, Trevor said, "No wonder you don't want to drive in the snow. A fender bender would break your heart."

Hannah led the way to the back of the garage. She opened a door, and another light came on in the stairwell. "These stairs come out next to the kitchen," she said. "And they are dry, dry, dry."

"Excellent."

When they emerged upstairs, Hannah thought she saw a light move. Or maybe a shadow. "Oh, it's you, Arturo." The big Siamese leapt up onto the kitchen counter. "He loves hot chocolate. Well…warm chocolate, at least."

Trevor took in the kitchen and the living room like he hadn't seen them before. And maybe he hadn't. He'd been too busy looking at Hannah. There were no drapes on the sliding glass doors, and the balcony was completely hidden under the snow. He perched on a bar stool at the butcher block counter in the middle of the kitchen. "No tree?"

Hannah looked around. The only light shone in from the open door to the stairwell. She pushed a button over the stove, and the cook light came on. She felt the need to apologize for the bleakness of the place. "Sorry. I usually watch TV for a while and then sack out on the sofa. The bedrooms are downstairs, and you can't see out the windows in the winter."

"No need to apologize," said Trevor softly. "I didn't have the heart for a tree this year, either."

"I'm surprised you're here and not with your mother." Hannah pulled mugs out of the cupboard almost by feel.

"I'm the oldest sibling," said Trevor. "She took the rest of the family on a ski vacation. Trying to start a new tradition. You know."

Hannah nodded. "Without your dad."

"Right."

"But you're here, visiting your…second cousin?"

Trevor's lip curled in a smile. "Eva and I found each other on one of those DNA sites. We think…we're not sure, mind you…that her great-grandmother was my great aunt. Or something like that. We hit it off and didn't really care."

"Oh." It was a hollow syllable, empty and disappointed.

A moment later, Trevor seemed to follow her thoughts. "No, not like that. We really are related. We just don't know how close. Besides, if cousins marry cousins, it's going to happen on my mother's side of the family."

Hannah was relieved and puzzled at the same time. "So you're not dating Eva?"

"Correct."

"But your mother's family might have cousins who married each other?"

Trevor tried to make light of things. "Hey, we can't pick our family, just our friends. Our very close friends." He could finally see well enough to spot a teapot, which he filled with water. "I assume we're sitting in the dark for some reason other than non-payment of power bills."

Hannah finally slipped out of her jacket and held out a hand to take his. Her grandfather's. "It just feels cozier this way." She put the coats away and returned.

Out of the blue, Trevor asked, "Do you believe in life after death?"

With only a moment's hesitation, Hannah said, "Yes."

Trevor put his arms around her. "Are you hoping for some sign from your grandfather?"

Hannah let herself fall into his hug. "Shall I plead the Fifth?"

"Will admitting it do you some harm or injury?"

"Not if you agree with me."

She could feel his smile through the hug. "I totally agree. In fact, it wouldn't surprise me in the least to find my dad and your grandfather sharing a whiskey on the couch and congratulating each other on getting us together."

"Are we? Together?"

"I'm here. You're here. We have a ton of stuff in common."

"Except the marrying cousins thing."

"Except for that." Trevor cupped her face in his hands and planted a soft kiss on her lips.

Hannah was suddenly flustered. Should she? Shouldn't she? Did she want to? Oh yes. Did she feel the time was right? Oh no.

Once again, Trevor read her mood as if she were an open book. "Don't worry. That was a solidarity kiss. We both know it's too soon."

The teakettle whistled, and Arturo meowed loudly. Hannah lifted the kettle off the stove. "Arturo thinks it's another male cat, challenging his territory." She tore open two packets of instant hot chocolate and emptied them into the mugs.

Trevor said, "Maybe I'd better not pet him right away. Let him get used to me."

"I meant the teakettle," she said.

"I know." He took the kettle and poured water into the mugs.

"Can we just talk? Like, forever?"

"At least that long," said Trevor.

A faint green light glowed in the living room.

"I thought you didn't have a tree."

"I don't." Hannah hated to ruin the mood, but the green light went out, then glowed again a moment later, and she was forced to flick a light on in the entryway.

"Traffic light?"

"You just drove up my street twice. No stoplights. Even the stop sign is optional in this weather." She led the way into the living room. There was her sofa where she liked to fall asleep in front of the TV. It was off, so no light there.

Off.

On.

"Oh, I left the night light plugged in."

"Good place for a tree."

"That's where Grandpa always plugged his lights in. I just couldn't do it without him."

Off.

On.

Trevor went to check the bulb. "Here's the culprit. The bulb is loose. We probably jarred it a bit when we fell down the front steps."

"The first time or the second?" Hannah watched him tighten the bulb, commenting, "That's odd. I could have sworn I put an orange light in it. Not green."

"It's green, and it's shiny, and it slopes upward toward a point. Let's call it a tree."

Hannah laughed softly and was startled when her eyes filled with tears. She wiped them surreptitiously.

"Maybe we should sing to it," said Trevor. He sang very softly, "O Christmas Tree."

Hannah felt silly, but she joined in. At the end of the song, she reached out and touched the greenish glow on the wall.

"What was your grandfather's favorite tree ornament?"

She smiled. "He had a collection of dreamcatchers, and at Christmas, he would put them all over the tree." She caressed the green glow. "He told me they originated with the Ojibwe, but he loved them, and my bedroom was full of them."

"Where are they now?"

Hannah answered without hesitation, "In my bedroom. Downstairs."

"Don't you have one upstairs where you're sleeping?"

"Yes, of course." She was a little slow on the uptake, but after a few seconds, she tilted her head and said, "I can bring some up and decorate our green glow tree."

Hannah took him with her. Truth be told, she disliked being downstairs in the winter. Even with the heat on, it was chilly down there, and when she was little, she sometimes thought she saw ugly faces in the snow pressed against her window. Hence, the dreamcatcher collection.

No ugly faces against the window tonight. When she flipped the light switch, it turned on the little lamp on her bed stand. She heard Trevor's inhale and turned to see his face light up as he tried to take in the sight. Dreamcatchers of all sizes and colors hung from the ceiling. They covered the whole room.

"How many are there?" he whispered.

"About a hundred. Do you feel it?"

To his credit, Trevor took a few seconds before he replied. "I feel…safe…and comforted."

Hannah hid her smile.

"Which ones do you want to use for your tree?" asked Trevor.

"Hmm. We would always decorate with the small ones." She pulled the chair out from under the student desk she'd used all the way through high school and stepped onto the seat. One by one, she collected small dreamcatchers, from two inches to six inches across. They were hung by string to tacks in the ceiling. Trevor didn't need a chair. He began selecting small ones as well.

"I find it ironic that such magical little pieces of art are hung up with matter-of-fact string and tacks." He was hanging three to a finger on his left hand.

"This should be enough," said Hannah. Then she responded to his comment. "They protect children against bad dreams. If you put them in a case or an artistic frame, they can't catch the bad dreams in their webs. They have to hang free."

"Will they mind being hung on the wall?"

Hannah shrugged. "I think they'll survive."

When they returned to the living room, the little green light was still casting its glow on the wall. In reverent silence, Hannah began pinning the dreamcatchers to the wall, letting them hang on their strings. Trevor followed suit. After half an hour, they had a dreamcatcher Christmas tree.

Hannah approved. "I think they're happy. They'll be in the room with me while I'm sleeping."

Trevor pulled her close. "I keep learning things about you that I really like."

"Such as?"

"The way you infuse everything around you with life. From Steely Dan to your dreamcatchers. As if they all had souls."

"Maybe they do."

They stood there together for several minutes.

At last, Trevor said, "I guess I should go. It's three a.m."

Hannah nodded reluctantly. "Eva is expecting you?"

"Gee, I hope she's asleep by now. If I call, I'll wake her up."

They moved together into the entryway. "I'll get you Grandpa's jacket."

Trevor pulled the door open, and the heavy silence outside muted the noisy lights and electronics inside. "I don't think I'm going anywhere in this," he said. "I can't even see my SUV."

"Wow, what a snowfall. I don't think it's going to look any better from the garage door." She pushed the front door closed.

"Let's find a Christmas movie on TV," he said.

"Okay. I'll make popcorn."

"You don't have to go to any trouble. Just being with you is enough."

Hannah blushed. "Thank you. But I was planning to have popcorn for dinner, so it's no big deal."

Trevor laughed.

They caught the last half of an old version of "Christmas Carol." And fueled with popcorn and cocoa, neither wanted to waste time sleeping. They talked all night. Hannah figured they must have nodded off at exactly the same time because when she awoke, they were still sitting up on the sofa, and the blanket they had shared was still in place. The TV was still on. Cartoon reindeer were competing in reindeer games.

Hannah got up carefully. They were both still fully clothed, but she turned the heat up a couple of degrees. Then she went into the kitchen and made coffee.

When she returned to the living room, Trevor was up and standing by the glass doors to the balcony. Snow had piled up on the balcony about chest high. Hannah handed him one of the mugs of coffee. "Good morning."

When he smiled at her, she melted inside and decided it was already warm enough without turning up the heat. "Eva will tease us without mercy."

"I know." He wiggled his eyebrows. "Don't answer any of her questions. Let her think whatever she wants."

Hannah laughed softly.

Trevor tilted his head toward the balcony. "Do you think we're totally snowed in?"

Hannah shook her head. "No. The balcony always fills with snow. We have to look out front to see how much we got."

As one, they moved to the front door.

"Don't let the cat out," said Trevor.

Hannah snorted. "Arturo wouldn't go out in the snow if a mouse did a strip tease on the top step." She opened the door. The sight took her breath away.

"Ten feet. Bet you a quarter."

Trevor cocked his head to one side and squinted at the blanket of white. "I say eight. I can still see the radio antenna on my Explorer."

Hannah looked up at him apologetically. "I hope you weren't planning on leaving early."

Trevor grinned. "I'm good. Is there food in the cupboards?"

"Soup and crackers."

"Mmmmm. My snowstorm favorite."

Hannah shook her head, smiling. "You are scoring points left and right. Maybe you should call Eva and let her know you're safe."

He got Eva's voicemail, so he left a message.

"More TV?" asked Hannah half-heartedly.

"My dad would always insist on board games on Christmas Eve. It is, you know."

"Christmas Eve?"

"Yes. And we would gather next to the tree and play games and sneak peeks at our packages."

Hannah pressed her hands against his chest. "Well, thanks to you, we have a tree."

Trevor murmured, "It's the prettiest tree I've ever seen."

"How about spin the bottle?"

"There are only two of us," said Trevor.

"All the better." She melted into a warm kiss. After several seconds, the small green nightlight began to flicker, on and off, on and off.

Trevor ended the kiss. "I think your grandfather wants us to go slow."

Hannah stared deeply into his eyes. "Very wise. As long as you don't mind?"

Trevor took a deep breath. "It's probably a good idea to see what kind of board games you like before we let ourselves get serious. Besides, without games, it doesn't feel like Christmas Eve."

"That's a wonderful idea." She nuzzled his chin. "I never thought I would enjoy Christmas again. I tried to put it out of my mind. But thanks to you, I think I'm getting in the spirit."

"And I think we should have a dreamcatcher tree every year. Do you have any board games?"

"A closet full." She pinned him with a challenging stare. "Prepare to lose big time."

"At what?"

"Doesn't matter," she teased. "I'm really good at everything."

Now it was Trevor's turn to blush.

Three hours later, they were deep into a game of Scrabble when the lights flickered and went out. A second or two later, they flickered back on again.

"Brown out?" asked Trevor.

Hannah shook her head. "Too much snow on the lines. Probably a transformer somewhere. Don't worry. The house has its own generator."

"Sweet." He laid down a seven-letter word.

"No way!!!"

Trevor laughed. "Beat that, Princess I'm Good at Everything."

"Oh, game on," she taunted with a smile.

She was just about to lay down her own five-letter word when Trevor's cell phone rang. "Don't distract me," she warned.

He grinned and checked his phone. "Oh. It's Eva. Hey, Eva. What's up?" He tapped speakerphone.

Eva sounded stressed. "Hi, Trev. Power is out all over town. I still have four party guests who got snowed in, and they're getting hungry. Is Hannah's generator working?"

Hannah leaned toward the phone. "Do you need a ride?"

"We thought we'd ski over."

"Good idea. Pack food because all I have is soup and crackers."

Eva laughed. "Will do."

"Don't get lost. If you're not here in thirty minutes, I'm sending out the Mounties."

"Very funny. See you soon."

Trevor looked alarmed. "Is it safe for them to ski here? It took us almost half an hour in the SUV last night."

"When the roads are like this, skis are faster than cars. Eva's an expert, and she has made the trip to my house a dozen times on skis. Oh! I think I have cookie dough in the fridge. I'll bake some while we wait."

Forty-minutes later, the doorbell chimed. Trevor said, "I'll get it."

Hannah said, "Just push the button to open the garage door. I'll go greet them."

Eva looked pink-cheeked and refreshed. Her guests, not so much. By the time everyone got out of their ski gear and gathered in the living room, Trevor had a fresh pot of coffee ready, and the new arrivals were thrilled. Hannah carried the two backpacks full of food into the kitchen and returned with a tray of warm chocolate chip cookies.

"Everyone okay?" asked Trevor.

The four stranded guests were couples, and it was clear from their expressions that the guys thought skiing over was a great idea and the gals had not had fun. But it was equally clear they were happy to be inside with power and heat and cookies fresh from the oven.

Eva babbled a mile a minute about the drama and excitement of skiing to safety. Then, when everyone else had their mouths full of cookie, she asked casually, "So Trevor, are we supposed to call you Your Highness or anything?"

Trevor froze.

Hannah stared. "What are you talking about?"

Eva looked like a woman who wanted to shrink down to nothing. "Sorry," she said to Trevor.

Hannah insisted. "Come on. Out with it. Since when do you have cousins who are Highnesses?"

Trevor patted the air with both hands. "I am not a Highness." He glared at Eva. "We're cousins on my father's side of the family."

Eva nodded eagerly. "The poor side. It's his mother who's royal."

Trevor pushed his hands back through his hair and then closed his fists around an imaginary throat.

"He's upset," said Eva to Hannah, "because when women find out how well connected he is, they swoop in like hawks. That's why I introduced you two. You're perfect for each other! Trevor is almost a royal, with tons of moolah, and Hannah, your grandfather left you money from all those patents. You said you were constantly worried that every man you met was after your money." She spread her hands and made a happy face. "Problem solved! For both of you."

Hannah and Trevor stood and stared at each other for several seconds. The other two couples watched them expectantly.

Trevor shrugged and said softly to Hannah, "Actually, it does feel good to know you like me for myself. You do like me, right?"

Hannah answered by moving in for a warm hug. "I'd tell you how much," she murmured against his chest, "but not in front of company."

Six months later...

Trevor carried his morning coffee onto the balcony where Hannah was waiting.

"Good morning, my love." He set his coffee down and planted a warm kiss on her forehead.

Hannah smiled, one of those deep, happy-to-the-core smiles that had become the new normal. Arturo meowed and jumped into her lap.

Trevor said, "He was an adorable ring bearer. When did you teach him to walk on a leash?"

"Oh, that was the easy part," said Hannah. "Grandpa and I needed all four hands to get him into his first harness when he was a kitten. After that battle, attaching a leash was comparatively easy."

"My mother was delighted," said Trevor.

"Are they enjoying their stay at South Shore? They're so close to Lake Tahoe."

"Yes. Of all the places she's traveled—and she has been everywhere—she says Tahoe is the most breathtaking sight she's ever seen. And then she complained about the crowds."

Hannah smiled. "She's starting to sound like a local. We get our share here in Truckee, too."

"It was brilliant of you to choose a Tahoe hotel for my family," said Trevor.

"And brilliant of you," said Hannah, "to insist on a small wedding."

"Believe me, that was not easy. But then, with the Euro the way it is, and the hassle of air travel these days, Mother limited herself to the number who could fly on her private jet."

"The look on Eva's face!"

They both laughed at the memory.

Hannah said, "We owe her a lot."

Trevor took her hand. "Yes, we do. And I was thinking, maybe before the first snowfall, we might invite one of my cousins on my mother's side over for a visit."

"Really?"

"His name is Tony—Antoine, actually—and he's not a Highness either, but his father is a Duke, so she can call him royal if she wants."

Hannah lifted her coffee in a salute. "I'd call that a regal idea."

The Christmas Carnival

Colleen Ladd

He was the most gorgeous man she'd ever seen.

In the two years she'd worked at The Caboose, Carey Langley had seen a lot of handsome men come through the restaurant. Pullman Siding wasn't exactly Vail, but it was a popular destination town, winter and summer, and even a few movie stars wandered through now and then. She'd served Sam Elliott breakfast one memorable morning and had a minor breakdown in the back room when Chris Evans sat down for lunch as if he were just your average Joe.

But none of them held a candle to the guy who'd just walked in the door.

He wasn't enormously tall—which she preferred, being just a hair under 5′4″ herself—and his chest was pleasingly broad under his Aran sweater. His hair was black as a raven's wing, his face all perfectly chiseled planes, and his eyes a light color she couldn't make out from behind the counter. Carey made herself look away before he caught her staring, and didn't know whether to be pleased or seriously freaked out when he took a stool at the counter. Damn! With him there distracting her, there was every chance she'd burn herself on the grill inside fifteen minutes.

She plastered on what she hoped was a friendly smile without too much evidence of drool and snatched up a menu and silverware on her way down the counter to greet him.

"Good morning and welcome to The Caboose. My name's Carey. What can I get you this morning?"

"Morning, Carey," he said, giving her a smile that made her heart skip a beat. His eyes were a light, piercing blue, and they had a decided twinkle in them. "You all alone this morning?"

"As you see," she agreed, gesturing at the empty restaurant. The Caboose opened at six every morning to cater to the locals who stopped by for coffee and pastries, and occasionally something more substantial, on their way to work. They'd all cleared out already, and she was on her own until a quarter after seven, when the cook arrived. In the meantime, the grill was hot and ready and the breakfast menu simple enough that she was confident of her ability to provide for the few tourists who could be bothered to be up and about that early. "But don't worry. I can get you anything you want. Within reason," she added quickly, suddenly acutely aware of how that had sounded. And jeez, but that only called more attention to it.

"Let's start with some coffee," he said, and though he acted as if he hadn't noticed her unintentional innuendo, there was a smile tugging at the corner of his mouth.

Flustered, she set a cup on the counter in front of him and managed to fill it without spilling anything. The sugar and creamer were already on the counter, but he didn't reach for them, just swallowed a mouthful of the coffee as if it weren't scalding hot and sighed with audible satisfaction.

"An excellent start. The coffee at my hotel is execrable."

"Ten-dollar word," Carey said automatically. Then, mortified, wished she could shove her apron in her mouth.

Thankfully, he only laughed. "Perhaps, but appropriate. It's one of the ski-in, ski-out places. Spacious room, amazing views, but very bad coffee. Guess you can't have everything."

Even when you look like that? Carey bit her tongue hard. Oh God, she didn't say that aloud, did she? He wasn't looking at her funny, so maybe she hadn't. "So, what can I get you?" she asked hastily, before she could say something else stupid. For the first time, she sympathized with the poor men who couldn't get their feet out of their mouths when talking to well-endowed women.

"What do you feel like cooking?" He hadn't even opened the menu; he just sat there with his hands resting on it, fingers laced together, looking expectantly at her.

"I..." She gestured helplessly toward the grill. "I'll cook whatever you order."

"I'm ordering whatever you'd like to cook." He leaned back in his stool and lifted his coffee toward her in a kind of salute. "If it's anywhere near as good as the coffee, I'm sure to enjoy it."

"I... Okay... Anything you don't like?" she asked as she moved down to the grill, trying to shake off the confusion. She'd had customers ask what she recommended but never before been given carte blanche to make whatever she wanted.

The Caboose didn't have a separate kitchen—everything was cooked on the grills, griddles and gadgets sandwiched between the counter and the back wall. They only served breakfast and lunch, and customers seemed to enjoy having the cooks out there for all to see.

"It's too early for jalapenos, but aside from that..."

"My roommate says it's never too early for jalapenos," Carey commented as she began gathering up the ingredients for a hearty omelet.

"Roommate?"

Not able to read his tone—was he irritated at something?—she glanced over the ingredients she'd collected, seeing nothing that was likely to be objectionable, then up at him. Deciding he might just look quizzical, she answered, even though it really wasn't any of his business. "Yeah, Maria. Rent's expensive around here, so I'm sharing a place with one of the other waitresses."

"Oh." He smiled brilliantly again, and she was irritated to discover that repeat exposure did nothing to stop her heart from doing flips. "Sorry, didn't occur to me that you'd have to share a place. Should have thought of it—ski town, after all." He picked up his coffee and moved down the counter to sit as close to directly opposite where she was cooking as he could—none of the counter seats directly backed the grill for obvious reasons. She'd definitely burn herself now. "Hunter, by the way."

"I'm sorry?" she asked, a bit absentmindedly, as she was focused on cracking eggs into a bowl without dropping any shells in.

"My name. Hunter."

Of course it was. With his looks, how could he be anything else? Carey was quite certain that he caught anyone he cared to. "Good to meet you, Hunter."

"Same here," he said with another of those heart-stopping smiles.

Pay attention to what you're doing, girl, Carey's mind told her in perfect imitation of her father. Flustered, she dragged her eyes back from Hunter's face to her cooking.

"So," he said after a minute, "The Caboose, huh?"

"Owner's joke," she said, answering the question she got variations on at least a dozen times a day during tourist season.

"The owner's got an interesting sense of humor," Hunter said, glancing around the restaurant, which was long and thin, every inch of it visible from the counter. It had been shoehorned into one of the old brick buildings that were squeezed in cheek to cheek along Main Street and was deliberately rather rustic, but well-appointed, with top-of-the-line furnishings and equipment on both sides of the counter. Its shape was the only thing about it that resembled a train car.

"You have no idea." Carey smiled, thinking of the man who wrote her paychecks and fostered the working environment that had kept her waitressing and part-time cooking for two years when it was the last job she'd ever have thought she'd like. Working at The Caboose was a bit like being part of a large, boisterous family. Three parts enjoyable and one part irritating as hell.

She got everything plated up—a large omelet with damn near everything in it, plus bacon, sausage, and several pieces of toast—and set it in front of him. She could have sworn his eyes lit up as he picked up his fork. She wanted to stay and see whether he liked the results of his experiment, but the bell at the door jangled just then, announcing the arrival of some more early risers. Not locals, so she had to go greet them and get them seated at a table near the wood stove, which was definitely not just there for ambiance. By the time she got the couple set up with coffee and juice and returned to the counter, leaving them to look over the menu, Hunter was halfway through the omelet.

"I suppose that means it meets with your approval?" she asked, unable to keep a teasing note out of her voice. Even though she'd come up behind him, she didn't see any sign she'd startled him. She reached past him to refill his cup, taking a surreptitious breath as she did so. He smelled *very* nice.

"Definitely!" He sat back, taking his coffee with him, and turned to face her. "So, what is there to do in Pullman Siding on a lovely winter morning?"

Carey leaned her hip against the counter, angling herself so she could keep the other customers in sight. "Besides ski, snowboard, snowshoe, and sled?"

His laugh was loud and delighted, and she saw the couple by the wood stove turn to look. They were an older couple, both rotund with rosy cheeks and white hair. They looked like someone's benevolent grandparents, and Carey wondered briefly if the man was in town to play Santa in the Christmas Carnival.

Probably not—they usually got old Charlie to do it, and she was certain she'd have heard if he couldn't this year for some reason. They smiled, first at Carey, then at each other, before going back to their menus.

"I suppose I was asking for it," Hunter said, still chuckling.

"We *are* Ski Town USA, after all," Carey said, smiling herself. "Though if you don't want to ski, hm.... Well, there's snowmobiling, horseback riding, mountain biking—"

"In the snow?"

"Yup. Ice climbing, sleigh riding, dogsledding... Oh, and there's the shopping," she added brightly, as if she'd nearly forgotten it.

He laughed again. The Caboose was right smack in the middle of Old Town, surrounded by all the ski apparel stores, art galleries, and nifty little knickknack "shoppes" anyone could ever want. "Right, so you've pretty much got all the winter sports covered."

"It *is* December," she pointed out. "And we *are* in the mountains in Colorado."

"Point taken." He managed to stop smiling long enough to swallow more coffee.

"If you're looking for fun things to do, you've got pretty good timing—the Christmas Carnival started yesterday."

"Is that why it was so hard to find a hotel room?"

She gave him a teasing look. "Winter. Colorado. Mountains. It's pretty much always hard to find a hotel room this time of year."

"I suppose so. Surprised you're not busier."

"Give it another..." She glanced at her watch. "Ten minutes."

"Guess it's a good thing I'm an early riser. Otherwise, I'd never have had you to myself."

His tone was teasing but his eyes were appreciative, and she suddenly found herself completely tongue-tied.

Luckily, he took pity on her and went on almost immediately. "So what kinds of things happen during this Christmas Carnival?"

"What doesn't? Let's see… Well, you've missed the opening ceremony and parade—that was yesterday. But there's still tons of things to do. A lot of ski contests, of course—jumping, slalom, obstacle courses. And snow bike races. And some exhibition skiing, ending with fireworks over Howelson Lake."

"Sounds impressive."

Carey smiled. "It is," she said, proud of her adopted city. "The Carnival has been going on more than a hundred years. There's also a lot of street events, which take place out on Main Street there. They'll be getting set up for the ice carving tomorrow, and there'll be a couple more parades—the high school band marches on skis, can you believe it? And then there are the skiing contests in town…."

"Skiing in town… you mean on the streets? The snowplows are doing a better job than that, if you ask me."

Without thinking, she smacked his arm with the back of her hand, as if he were just one of her roommate's friends and not the most gorgeous man she'd ever seen. "Silly. No, they stockpile it and spread it back out on the streets for the events. It's mostly races, with the skiers pulled through the streets by horses—slalom and obstacle and skijoring…"

"Skijoring?"

"Well, I suppose by definition all the street events are skijoring. It's like water skiing, only on snow, and pulled by a horse instead of a boat. Pretty amazing to watch."

"Amazing," he repeated, but it didn't sound like a question. "Well, it looks like you've given me another reason to stick around town."

"Another?" she asked, wondering what business had brought him here during the Carnival. Wondering also if he'd stop by The Caboose again before he left town… and reluctantly admitting it was too much to hope that it would be when she was working.

He held her eyes for a long moment, his smile warm, then winked. Carey felt a hot blush spread across her cheekbones. Out of the corner of her eye, she saw that the older couple had put their menus down, and she bustled over to serve them, thankful for the excuse to escape her embarrassment.

As predicted, business at The Caboose began to pick up, with two more groups coming in while she was cooking the older couple's order—one three-top and one family of five with three kids under seven. She knew it was only the beginning of the flood and was grateful to see Barry come in—bald, bearded, and tattooed, the cook looked anything but reassuring, but she knew that under all that, he was a teddy bear. Without a word—just the gentle bump of his hip against hers—he took her place at the grill and got to work finishing up the eggs she was cooking, the handoff as smooth as if they did it every day. Which they did. She switched her focus to waitressing, not sure whether she was sad or relieved to no longer be working directly under Hunter's appreciative gaze. She'd somehow succeeded in not burning herself but wasn't entirely sure that any of the meals she'd produced with him so near were exactly right. At least no one had complained.

He hadn't tried to speak to her again, perhaps not wanting to embarrass her further. But she'd felt those piercing blue eyes on her everywhere she went, even when it seemed he wasn't looking. She was careful not to neglect him, though he'd finished his meal some time ago and was just lingering over his coffee. He smiled when she topped up his cup before going to check on her tables but didn't say a word, and she found herself disappointed. *Good lord, woman,* her father's voice said in her head, *make up your mind! Do you want him to talk to you or not?*

She was wiping down a booth when the guy at the next table over reached out and touched her sleeve. "What can I do for you, Walter?" she asked. She'd thought he was good, his usual order in Barry's capable hands and his coffee in front of him.

Walter had retired two years ago and shifted the time he came in from just after six to nearly seven-thirty, but that was apparently as much change to his routine as he could tolerate. "That guy at the counter," he said. "His name Hunter by any chance?"

"Hunter, yes." She straightened up, startled. "How did you know? I thought he was just passing through." Though she realized that was just an assumption on her part.

"Hunter Cameron, the world-class skijorer?" Walter said, as if he couldn't believe she didn't already know.

Righteous indignation filled Carey. She stalked back over behind the counter, ignoring the startled looks from her regulars and Barry, and tossed her rag at Hunter. It bounced off his chest and plopped damply onto the counter. "You!" She had enough presence of mind to keep her voice down.

"Me?" he said, half-laughing and all innocence. "What did I do?"

"You let me blather on about water skiing behind horses and the whole nine yards when you already knew everything there was to know about skijoring."

"Not everything," he protested, sounding utterly serious. "I had no idea the sport had such beautiful fans." Carey blushed hard again, sputtering as she was forced to shift suddenly out of irritation and into pleased embarrassment with a grinding of gears that made her wish for a mental clutch. She still hadn't quite gotten into a gear that would produce a response when he rescued her, saying, "But you're right; that was unfair of me. I deserve more than a damp washcloth thrown at me. Perhaps a slap?" He leaned toward her, his eyes closed and his head tilted to present one cheek, for all the world as if he actually expected her to take him up on the offer.

Much to her own surprise, she did take advantage. But not by slapping that chiseled cheek. Oh no. She bent in quickly and kissed him instead, drawing back with a fleeting impression of razor-smooth skin and a spicy cologne that would linger in her senses for hours afterwards. Her heart was pounding wildly, and she felt as if the entire world had gone silent and still. Or perhaps just the restaurant. Remembering suddenly where she was, she glanced around quickly, but no one seemed to be paying any attention, although Barry had a smile tugging at one corner of his bearded mouth.

Hunter remained precisely where he was, his eyes still closed, for another moment, during which Carey helplessly held her breath. Then he sat back, grinning delightedly. "That's the nicest slap I've ever felt."

Oh heavens, Carey thought as her heart stopped beating again.

Hunter had reluctantly left The Caboose at about the time the breakfast rush went swooping into the lunch rush. He really couldn't pretend he had any legitimate reason to continue holding down a stool by the counter. Not when there was a line starting to form to get in. He calculated how many customers might have taken his place over the time he sat there and made sure to leave Carey a tip big enough to cover the ones she'd missed because he'd planted himself there all morning.

It was chilly out on the street, but not particularly cold, despite the snow that iced up the street and sidewalk and was piled high in every unused corner. The famous Colorado sun was shining brightly, glittering off everything and making it feel warmer than it ought to have been in winter this high in the mountains. He'd been told that Colorado enjoyed as many sunny days as California, but had assumed that it lagged during the winter and caught up during the summer. Apparently not.

Hunter ambled down the street, his hands in his pockets, lips pursed in a whistle that was sometimes silent, sometimes loud enough to be heard over traffic. On the surface, he was admiring the "old town America" Main Street backed by breathtaking views of the snowy mountains that loomed up on all sides, right on their doorstep. Or perhaps watching with interest the preparations for the Carnival—huge blocks of ice being set up on every street corner, all ready for carving, and every storefront and lamppost decorated with Christmas tinsel. By and large, however, he actually took in little of it. His mind was on a different breathtaking view. Carey. Carey Last-name-unknown, but damned if he didn't want to make it Cameron. And wasn't that putting the cart so far out in front that the horse couldn't even *see* it?

Sure, she was beautiful. Petite and brunette and just curvy enough to be really interesting. With a face that was not, perhaps, classically beautiful, but a quirky reflection of her lovely personality, allowing her happiness and love of life to spill out her emerald eyes. Or turn them tempest-tossed with anger, he thought, smiling to himself. Pissed off, she was a little spitfire. And just as appealing.

He was nominally on his way from the Salt Lake area, where he'd been training, to the first skijoring event of the season in Michigan. But that didn't take place until near the end of January, so he was in no hurry. Pullman Siding wasn't exactly on his way, but it was a place he'd heard was well worth visiting, so he'd adjusted his route to take him through there. He was very glad he had. Well worth visiting indeed!

The Caboose closed its doors at three, and Hunter was waiting out front when it did, lounging on a wooden bench, his feet stretched out and his head tipped back to catch the warmth of the sun. Someone had cleared most of the snow off the bench and the sun had finished the job, so he wasn't getting wet, and the cold wasn't getting into his bones yet. In fact, it was just about perfect—just cold enough to keep the large flocks of tourists rushing from one store to the next and not loitering on the sidewalk, obscuring his view of the restaurant. He'd already wandered around the block and determined that The Caboose's back door was used only to carry trash out to a dumpster, the tracks in the snow going no further than that. She'd have to come out the front when she ended her shift.

When she did and saw him there, she came to a stop so sudden that the cook—a huge bearded fellow who looked more at home in a biker gang—nearly ran her down. "Something the matter, love?" he said in a voice like gravel. He followed her gaze to Hunter and bristled menacingly. "This guy bothering you?"

Just when Hunter thought he'd spend his afternoon in a fight and his evening in the emergency room—he was sure he could take the fellow if he had to but wasn't fool enough to think he could do so without injury—Carey gave herself a little shake and said, "Not at all, Barry." She laid a hand on his tattooed arm that made him visibly relax. "Say hi to Stephanie for me, okay?"

"If you're sure?" He waited to see her nod, gave Hunter a look that told him in no uncertain terms what would happen if he gave her grief, then headed off.

"Thanks," Hunter said when Barry was out of earshot. "I didn't have a visit to the hospital on my schedule for today."

"Barry?" she said, sounding surprised. "He's a marshmallow."

"Sure. Just like the Stay Puft Marshmallow man in *Ghostbusters* was just a marshmallow."

She laughed, and he smiled, thinking it sounded like a peal of bells. Yup, he had it bad. "What are you sitting around here for?" she asked, still shaking her head, hopefully at his joke and not his boldness.

"Waiting for you," he said, his heart pounding in a way it never did when he was skiing. He felt like a teenager asking his crush to the prom.

"Me?" she asked with far too much surprise. Someone needed to do something about her self-esteem, and he was just the man to give it a shot.

He stood up and offered her his arm. "I was thinking you might like to meet my skijoring partner."

"Your... partner," she said, sounding doubtful and a touch suspicious, but she took his arm and went with him up the road. He was sharply aware of her petite form so close to his own, the weight of her hand on his arm through his jacket, the smell of her perfume, still faintly lingering about her despite the hours spent working around stronger scents—in fact, he wasn't entirely sure whether it was the floral scent of her perfume or the mouth-watering smell of bacon he liked better. He decided it would be best not to tell her that.

She didn't hang back when he turned from Main Street onto a side street. In fact, her hand on his arm drew them a little closer together, each depending on the other for balance on the icy sidewalk. A block later, his SUV came into sight, and with his hand still buried in his warm pocket, Hunter pressed the remote buttons to unlock and raise the rear gate.

"Hey, Rusty, say hi to the lady."

"Oh my," Carey said as she caught sight of the large dog wiggling and dancing in his excitement to meet her. She immediately reached out and buried her fingers in his thick, mottled fur and let him enthusiastically lick her face.

Hunter smiled, pleased. She'd passed the first test—he didn't waste his time with women who didn't like dogs. No point when they were so much a part of his life. He reached to scratch down through Rusty's ruff, scritching the dog between the shoulderblades the way he liked. He pushed back a foolish swell of jealousy at the love and kisses his dog was receiving from Carey and said, "That's enough now, Rusty. Don't slobber all over the lady."

Rusty instantly sat down, regarding the two of them with brilliant blue eyes that looked as savvy as Hunter knew Rusty to be. His tail kept thumping away, but he didn't try to jump up again. Just regarded Carey for a solemn, panting moment, then held out his paw to her. Laughing, she shook it. Then again, when he held it out again the moment she'd let go. Then again.

Hunter laughed. "He's a pushy boy, and he wants to hold hands."

"Well then, why didn't he say so?" She laughed, and this time continued to hold the paw that was extended for a shake. Rusty made a soft wuffing noise and began to pant with his mouth open, his tongue lolled out, an expression of pure joy. "What is he?"

"He's a bit of a whatsit—Australian Shepherd, Husky, and Malamute for certain, with a healthy dose of who knows what else."

"Oh dear, you have your hands full with this one," Carey said, proving she did more than just like dogs.

Hunter laughed. "Yeah. He's a bright boy and very stubborn. But the thing he likes best is something we can both agree on—he loves to pull."

"Oh!" Carey said. "When Walter told me you were a skijorer, I just assumed with a horse, since that's what they do here. You skijor with Rusty!"

"Wouldn't know one end of the horse from the other," Hunter admitted, reaching out to scritch Rusty again. The dog had finally had his fill of holding hands and was lying in the back of the SUV with his head between his paws, his eyes locked on Hunter and Carey.

"So you don't do jumps and the like?"

"No, it's more like dog-assisted cross-country skiing. Less exciting than your version."

She shook her head. "I wouldn't say that. You get to go skiing with your best friend." She petted Rusty again, getting her hand licked in return.

Hunter grinned. "You got it. I mean, you get it—skijoring is my life."

She was silent a moment, apparently focused on petting Rusty. "I suppose the competition prizes and endorsements must be pretty good?"

He snorted. "Hardly. I said it was my life, not my livelihood. No prizes, no endorsements; just the joy of competing. Rusty and I are two of a kind—we love to race through the woods."

For a moment, Carey seemed almost to retreat from him, even though she didn't move an inch. He wondered what he'd said wrong and was about to issue a blanket apology when she seemed to shake it off and said, "Walter said you were world-class."

He scoffed. "As much as any American can be. It's hard to compete with the Norwegians in… well, anything skiing-related," he finished with a grin. "You stay, Rusty," he told the dog, who put his head on his paws with a whine and watched the rear gate lower again with the kind of resignation only a dog can project. "Rusty and I are on our way to Minnesota for the first event of the season. No rush though… it's not until late January."

When Hunter took Carey's arm and began walking back toward Main Street, she came along absent-mindedly, her brow furrowed a bit and her mind clearly elsewhere. "I guess," she said after a minute, "that I always assumed we'd invented skijoring. I'd never heard of it before I fetched up here, so I thought it was one of Pullman's little quirks. Odd to think of it as an international sport. Though I suppose the name's a dead giveaway it's Scandinavian. If it'd been invented in America, it'd be called skrodeo or something like that."

Hunter laughed so hard he staggered, driving them both off course for a second. When they reached Main Street again, they paused in front of a candy and ice cream store doing surprisingly brisk business. "Can I get you an ice cream and walk you to your car?" He wanted to do a great deal more than that but didn't want to frighten her off by coming on too strong.

She smiled. "No ice cream. No car. But if you like, you can get me a hot chocolate and walk me to the end of Old Town."

"Why the end of Old Town?"

"From there, I can either take a shuttle or walk the rest of the way home."

"I have a car," he protested. "I could take you."

"I know," she said solemnly, only a hint of a smile showing the tease. "But you'll never find a parking space if you leave that one. And I'm used to getting around town without a car. Believe it or not, I enjoy walking."

Hunter realized suddenly that there was a break in the stream of people making their way into the ice cream store. "Hold that thought." He dashed inside, coming out a few minutes later with a large cup of steaming chocolate for her and a butter pecan ice cream cone for himself. There was something charming, and very "Colorado," about wandering down a snowy street eating ice cream. "Now, will your path home take us back past my car?"

Carey took the lid off her drink and inhaled the steam, her lips curling in a smile he wished was directed at him. She licked daintily at the liberal mound of whipped cream floating atop her hot cocoa before taking a hearty drink. "I told you," she said when she came up for air, "I like walking."

"So do I. And so does Rusty."

"Oh!" she said, putting the lid back on her drink to keep the heat in. "By all means, let's go get him."

She had the cutest smudge of whipped cream on the tip of her nose. Hunter couldn't resist—he bent down and kissed it off. She said "oh" again in an entirely different tone, and when he drew back, she gazed at him with an expression that was half confusion and half... something else, something that looked vaguely starry eyed that he'd very much like to see again. Frequently.

"You had some whipped cream, just there," he explained, then grinned suddenly. "Besides, I owed you a 'slap.'"

"I ought to slap you more often," she said in a dreamy voice that matched the starry-eyed look. She blinked. "Oh! No, I meant—"

Laughing, he said, "I know what you meant." Then leaned in close to murmur, "I feel exactly the same way."

She blushed charmingly and took another sip of her drink, which he decided was his cue to take pity on her. He focused on nibbling off the ice cream that was bulging on one side of his cone before the whole thing came tumbling down.

"I don't know how you can eat that."

Hunter shrugged. "It's very good."

"It's December."

"It's *very* good." He grinned, extended his arm to her, and was delighted when she took it. They ambled back up the street to his car, saying little, each focused on their sweet treat. The warmth of her hand in the crook of his arm felt like it was burrowing its way through not only his jacket but his heart. Who needed hot chocolate?

After getting Rusty out of the car, Hunter stuffed the dog's leash in his pocket in case he needed it later, and they walked another block away from Main Street and its crowds before turning down a road parallel to it. Rusty trotted along at their heels, wandering to one side or the other of the sidewalk to sniff as the mood took him but never straying far.

"So," Hunter prompted, his ice cream half-eaten. The hand holding the cone might be getting a little cold, but the rest of him was toasty warm. "Why no car? I'd think that would be inconvenient in this climate."

"A bit," Carey admitted. "But Pullman's not that big a place, so walking's not too bad. And I don't live far from the bus line, which hits all the important parts of town." For a moment, he thought she'd go no further than those bare facts, but then she shrugged a little and added, "I didn't intend to end up here, you know. I was actually on my way to Denver for a job interview when my car broke down just outside town—Settler's Pass was just too hard a climb for the poor thing. Craig's Towing got it to town, but I didn't have the money to fix it. By the time I'd worked a bit and scraped enough together, I'd put down a few roots here, and it made more sense to use the money as first month's rent."

"What about that job in Denver?"

She sighed. "It wasn't anything special, and they certainly weren't going to hold it for me with everyone and his brother applying."

"Do you like waitressing?" He took one last bite of his ice cream, the cone crunching between his teeth, and gave the end of the cone to Rusty, who wuffed happily and scarfed it down.

She shrugged. "It pays the bills. And I like the people. The locals *and* the tourists. Not sure I'd want to do it anywhere else, though—there's something special about Pullman. Where else can you sit on your porch—" She gestured at a house just up the block that seemed to have sprouted more than the usual number of balconies. "—and look at that?" Now her gesture took in the snow-covered mountain peaks surrounding them.

Her smile was entirely too enticing, and Hunter couldn't have stopped himself if he wanted to. He ducked his head and kissed her, short and sweet at first, and then longer when she only moved in closer with a pleased sound. Her mouth was very warm and tasted sweetly of chocolate. He wondered if his was cold and if the butter pecan tasted as sweet.

When he finally made himself draw back, she said, "More whipped cream?"

"Something like that." He almost said something else, but just then, Rusty decided that if they were done walking, it was time to sit down on Hunter's feet. He was a big dog, and his maneuvering shoved them apart, nearly knocking Hunter on his butt.

Laughing, Carey took a step back to keep her balance and ruffled the dog's ears. "Aren't you a sweetheart?"

"He's something alright," Hunter grumbled, shuffling his boots out from under Rusty's furry butt. "Now… where were we before we were so rudely interrupted?"

"Just about home," Carey said, much to Hunter's chagrin. He'd hoped to get back to the kissing.

Ah well. Regretfully, he followed her lead, pointing to the balcony-festooned house she'd indicated earlier and asking, "That one yours?"

"Part of it." And yes, in addition to the overabundance of balconies, it did seem to have more exterior doors than typical in a single-family house. Broken up into apartments, no doubt.

"Unfortunate," he murmured. "Oh, not the house," he explained quickly when she turned hurt eyes on him. "That's lovely. I'd just hoped we had further to walk."

She blinked. Rusty wagged his tail, which made a loud thwapping sound against Hunter's jeans. "Oh, of course," Carey said, petting Rusty. "I'm sorry. I'm sure that's far too short a walk for you, boy."

Rusty tipped his head back to look at Hunter, panting happily, his tongue hanging out the side of his mouth. *Don't look so pleased with yourself*, Hunter thought, but he couldn't help but grin. "Yes, that too. But mostly, I'm sorry we're here already because I wanted to spend more time with you."

"Oh!" Carey looked at him wide-eyed, a blush blooming slowly on her cheeks. After a frozen moment, her eyes flew down to Rusty, who she started petting again as if it was some kind of refuge. Her shyness was adorable. "Thank you," she said without lifting her head, for all the world as if she were talking to the dog instead of Hunter. "So did… do I."

Hunter's grin turned into a beaming smile. He couldn't believe how light his heart felt at hearing her say that. Such a simple thing—that she'd like to spend more time with him. Lord, what *was* happening to him? Before he could think better of it, the words, "Spend the day with me," came blurting out. "I mean," he added before she could speak, "I'm sure you're tired after work today, so not today. But a day. When's your day off? Come to the Carnival with me?"

She was looking at him now, rather than Rusty, with an expression that might be… bemused? There was a smile tugging at the corner of her mouth. Surely that was a good sign?

"Sorry, that was stupid," Hunter said suddenly, wincing at how ridiculous he sounded. He was definitely babbling, but utterly unable to stop. If he stopped, she'd have a chance to say no. "Of course you wouldn't have time off during the Carnival. All those extra people in town…"

Then he did finally stop because she was laughing. "Actually," she said when she'd caught her breath, "Steve—that's the owner of The Caboose—says everyone should have an opportunity to go to Carnival. So the restaurant is closed for the next three days."

"Closed," Hunter said, needing to verify that he'd heard right. He needed to focus on the business side of things. If he thought too long on the rest, he might scare her off with how much he wanted that to have been an offer to spend the whole three days with him. "Can't be good for business."

"Well, Main Street is closed off for the skijoring, and there are a bunch of street venders selling food during the events, so…"

"So, more a business decision than an 'employees are family' decision."

"Let's say it's both. And either way—" She tucked her hand into the crook of his arm and tugged him forward, walking right past her house. "—I don't have to work tomorrow."

Carey had only meant to spend the first of her days off with Hunter—show him the sights, attend some of the more entertaining Carnival events with him, spend as long as she thought she could get away with looking at that handsome face and listening to his enticing voice—but somehow, when the sun began setting on her last day before starting work again, she'd managed to spend every waking moment of every single one of her days off with him. And the sleeping ones dreaming about him.

It was foolish—she knew it could never work. She'd known from the moment he said that skijoring was his life. She knew all about men chasing impossible dreams. Her dad had spent his life, and hers, on the rodeo circuit. She knew all about chasing the next race, the next thrill. And all she ever wanted to know about dying destitute, your body broken by the obsession you'd chased all your life. Skijoring might not take the same toll on a body that bronc riding did, but it was obviously just as much about finding the next fix. Carey had loved her father, but growing up, they'd never had anything. Not even a fixed address.

After spending her first eighteen years like that, what Carey wanted out of life was simple—a steady job and a place to stay. Emphasis on stay. Her dream wasn't one you chased—it was one you stuck around for.

And Hunter… God, if it weren't for the skijoring, he'd be absolutely perfect. He *was* perfect. Perfectly handsome, with a smile that took her breath away, even after three days' exposure to it. A perfect gentleman, offering her his arm, opening doors, buying meals, always checking that she was happy wherever they were and whatever they were doing—all those things she'd scoffed at anyone thinking they still needed in this day and age, which absolutely melted her insides when coming from him.

And they were perfect together, every minute spent with one another so effortless, so wonderful, that it seemed more like three hours than three days. But of course it was days—no way they could have packed in so much in just a few hours. All the events of Carnival—at least, every one that looked interesting and more than she'd ever attended before. She wasn't surprised that he was interested in the exhibition skiing and racing—just surprised that she could enjoy them so much in his company. And he'd gone to all the bits she liked best without a whisper of complaint... with, in fact, every sign of enjoying looking at the ice sculptures, cheering on the parade (the marching band was amazingly good at keeping the proper tempo despite not *marching* at all—surely shuffling along on skis should have made it harder to keep to a beat), and poking through the local art galleries. She'd even dragged him to see the delicate blown-glass hummingbird in the window of the Mountain Crafts Gallery that she'd admired for ages but couldn't justify buying.

And now the three days were nearly up. Three magical days of pretending Hunter could truly be part of her life. And Carey couldn't think how she could have possibly imagined only giving him one. Couldn't think how she was going to go back to work tomorrow, knowing he was still out there. Still not right for her, even though he was absolutely right for her.

"Penny for your thoughts?"

"Hm?" Carey looked up to see Hunter stepping out onto the balcony, two flutes of champagne held expertly in one hand so he could close the glass doors with the other. Rusty zipped through the door past him and padded over to flop down next to Carey's chaise, totally unconcerned about the cold. "Nothing important." She turned back to watch the setting sun paint Howelson Lake red.

The hotel with the "execrable" coffee had turned out to be the fanciest hotel in town, with an absolutely amazing view of the surrounding mountains and the lake. Carey had at first wondered how in the world he could even afford it, let alone manage to get a room on short notice in the middle of Carnival, and with a dog to boot—he must know someone. Someone really important. Later, she found out that he *was* someone important. Over dinner that first night—eaten on his balcony overlooking the lake—he'd admitted (and it had been an admission, voiced with the sort of shamefaced hesitation typically reserved for having relatives in prison) to being one of "those Camerons," as he put it. One of the wealthiest families in the country. So no, skijoring wasn't his livelihood—he didn't *need* a livelihood. Just one heck of a fat bank account that, according to him, he was better off leaving alone than messing with. To hear him tell it, he could live comfortably his entire life off the interest alone.

She couldn't imagine what it would be like not to have to work for a living. Not to have to work at all. No wonder he could simply take off and travel around with his dog, following his "life."

She'd tried to think—when she wasn't with him, as thinking when she was with him was very difficult and, as she'd discovered, thinking when she was *not* with him about anything *but* him was absolutely impossible—about whether that changed things. And though part of her wanted to say it did, that it wouldn't be so bad following someone's dream if you didn't have to do so in third-rate motels and broken-down cars, the voice of reason said that it didn't matter. It was still *his* dream, not hers, and chasing dreams like that was nothing but an exercise in never getting anywhere that mattered and losing everything you had.

"Sure it's nothing?" Hunter handed her a flute of champagne and settled into the chaise next to her. They were both wearing heavy winter clothes, including ski pants and parkas, in anticipation of the drop in temperature when the sun set. Tonight—the last night of Carnival—was the fireworks display, and Hunter's balcony would have a prime view. "Looks pretty serious."

Carey shook off the depressing thoughts and forced a smile. This was her last night with Hunter, her last night in the fantasy world where this could really work, and she was determined to enjoy it. "Actually, I was thinking about your expression when you saw the first skijorer come down the street." Just thinking about it made her smile for real, and then Hunter made exactly that same expression and set her to laughing.

It must have been a startling sight for someone whose experience of skijoring involved barking dogs, cross-country skis and poles, and probably far too much spandex. Oh, the barking dogs were still there, though their spectator-owners were trying to keep them quiet to avoid spooking the horses, but as for the rest.... The look on Hunter's face had been indescribable when first the horse, then the skijorer burst into view, the horse running for all it was worth, kicking up powder and blowing out its breath in great clouds like a locomotive. As for the skijorer... no ski poles in sight, both hands clinging for dear life to a rope attached to the horse's harness, and aside from the skis and ski boots, dressed head to foot like he'd just come off a ranch, complete with a cowboy hat and chaps. Hunter had pressed his face to her shoulder to muffle the sound and laughed until he couldn't breathe.

"Hey," she said now, fighting to keep the laughter under control, "don't diss the locals—it's how we Coloradoans do things. Get used to it."

He held up both hands. "Peace. I freely admit that they were all excellent skiers and amazing on the obstacle course and jumps. No matter how much they looked like fish on motorbikes."

Carey shot him a pretended glare. "I'd accept your apology, but I think there's an insult lurking in there somewhere."

"No insult," he assured her earnestly. "I'm quite fond of Colorado. In fact, you might even say there are some things in Colorado that I absolutely adore." If she was at all uncertain about his meaning, his shifting his chair closer and putting an arm around her removed all doubt.

She wanted to sink into his embrace, bask in the warmth she could feel even through both their parkas, but she couldn't. She knew this was coming to an end, but he didn't, and that was unfair. She licked her suddenly dry lips, wondering how to say it, wishing she didn't have to. Couldn't she just enjoy the evening—

their last evening together in this holiday from normal life and responsibilities? Did she really need to say anything? Men didn't start holiday flings with any expectation of them turning into real relationships, did they? And a man who was always just passing through—surely he didn't expect anything more than they'd had. Surely he'd always planned to move on. Oh heavens, she thought, her breath catching, that thought *hurt*.

He cleared his throat, and she jumped, startled. His arm tightened around her shoulders as if to steady her. Or perhaps keep her close. "I... I'm going to have to get back on the road soon... A day or two, perhaps."

She knew she had no right to feel so hurt. For one thing, she'd just been thinking about how to let him know it wouldn't work between them. For another... That was just what men following dreams did. They left. She knew that; she'd known it from the beginning.

With Carey unable to find any words to force through her tight throat, Hunter went on. "I don't want you to think that this, that I—"

Carey moved out of the circle of his arm, holding up a hand to stop him from having to say anything he didn't mean. "You don't need to say anything more. We both knew from the start that this was a short-term thing. I've got my life here, and you've got your... your skijoring... and—"

"Come with me."

Stopped cold, she stared at him.

He took her shoulders and pulled her gently forward until their foreheads were resting against each other. His eyes were closed, and she stared, fascinated, at the dark smudge of his eyelashes on his cheeks. "Come with me," he repeated. "These last couple of days have been..." He laughed softly, sounding astonished. "Amazing. I want to see where this goes. I want you to come with me."

Every single word had fled her mind, and all she could think to do was stare. His breath was warm on her face.

"You're stuck here, unable to chase your dreams because you don't have any way to get there. Let me take you. Anywhere you want to go." His eyes opened and looked directly into hers. She felt like she was drowning in a sea of blue. "Someplace you can use as a jumping-off point. Follow your dreams, Carey. Come with me."

It was her turn to close her eyes. She couldn't, she simply couldn't bear to continue looking into that earnest blue gaze, feeling like Hunter was looking right into her soul.

She was tempted. Oh God was she tempted. She wasn't as stuck as he seemed to think—how can you be stuck when you're precisely where you want to be? But it was certainly true that she'd probably never have the resources to get much of anywhere; nothing like what he could achieve if he put his mind to it. The thought of the unlimited options his money could give her... It was almost as tempting as the mere thought of simply being able to stay with him. That part would have been enough all by itself, even if he were poor as a church mouse. Almost enough...

Ultimately, however much she wanted him, what he offered wasn't for her. Part of her wondered if it was even smart to go off with some guy she'd only known for a few days, while the rest was confident that she'd known everything she needed to know about him that first afternoon. She knew she'd be safe with him. But she didn't know that she'd be happy.

Ultimately... It made Carey feel too much like her mother, leaving everything to follow her father into a life she neither valued nor enjoyed. Her mother had never stopped loving her father, but Carey wondered if she'd ever been truly happy with him either.

Slowly and regretfully, she began shaking her head. "I can't. I..." Seeing he was about to speak, she raised a quick hand to his lips, putting two fingers against them and marveling at how they could look so chiseled but feel so soft. "I did follow my dreams, Hunter. I followed them here. Mountains and woods, snow and serenity. Hearing coyotes howl at night. Sitting on my porch watching the deer eat my neighbor's rosebushes. That's my dream."

The lips under her fingers twisted up in a reluctant smile, and he nodded gently. His hand wrapped around her fingers, but instead of pushing them away from his mouth, he pressed them to his lips and kissed them. "You do know," he said, the faint lilt of a tease in his voice, "that other places have mountains and woods and snow?"

"And rosebush-eating deer?" she said, trying to tease back. She was appalled to realize that there were tears in her voice, which would soon be on her cheeks if she didn't get hold of herself.

"I'm sure of it," he said bracingly. And though he must surely have heard the regret in her voice, he didn't try to force the issue or make her change her mind. Instead, he said, "I understand. I can't say I like it…" His finger traced a line down her cheek and came away wet. "…but it's your dream. Who am I to argue with that?"

"I just, I…" Carey didn't even know what she wanted to say. She swung her legs off the chaise, but Hunter's hands were on her shoulders before she could stand.

"Where are you going?"

"I can't…" She couldn't just stay there. She'd killed the fantasy, the dream they'd spent the last three days in. He shouldn't *want* her to stay.

"Please stay," he said quietly. His arms came around her from behind, and he pressed his face into the hair at the nape of her neck. For all that, his embrace was loose enough that she could have left it, if only she had the willpower to. "The fireworks'll start soon and…" He took a deep breath and let it out in a gust. There was a bit of a shake to it, and she almost thought she felt something wet on the back of her neck. "The night isn't over yet. You don't have to go back to reality until tomorrow. Please stay."

Carey was in tears again, the cold night air beginning to freeze them on her face. Without a word, she took his hands and pulled his arms closer about her, shifting back until they were both on the same chaise, her arms tight over his where they wrapped around her.

The sun was gone, and the glow had faded off the lake. The fireworks were about to start.

Carey walked to work the next morning, her head bent and arms wrapping her coat tight around herself to keep in what little warmth she had. The temperature was the same and the sun just as bright as the last three days, but the world seemed damp and entirely too cold.

They'd spent almost all night together, just sitting out on his balcony, bundled against the cold and wrapped up in each other, looking up at the sky. After the fireworks were over, they watched the stars, talking of... nothing really. There was nothing useful to be said. But she took some comfort in the rumble of his voice through his chest, the feel of his heart beating against her back. She did her best not to think that it was their last night together.

Eventually, she had no choice but to go home and get some sleep. It was after one and she'd be wrecked in the morning as it was. The bus had stopped running hours ago, and Hunter drove her back to her apartment and insisted on walking her to her door.

"I'm sorry," he said when they stopped, "I can't not..." And then he was kissing her.

And she was kissing back, falling into the kiss like a rock plummeting off a cliff. For what felt like an eternity and an instant, she was wrapped in his arms, lost in a world where this could work, where their dreams didn't collide but combined. Too soon—it could never be anything but too soon—he pulled back. She stared at him, dazed, her eyes already starting to glaze over with tears, then turned quickly to shove her key into the lock.

"Wait."

Carey turned back reluctantly—it would take only a blink to send tears cascading down her cheeks—to find him fishing something out of the pocket of his jacket. He pressed a box into her hand.

"Open it tomorrow. After I'm gone." He kissed her again, a quick press of his lips to her cheek, and with that, he was gone, walking back down the path with his hands in his pockets and his head bent.

Gone. Blindly, she turned back to the door and went inside. She couldn't bear to look back and see him gone from the street. Gone from her life. Not at her side, not taking her hand when the sidewalk got icy, not sitting down in her restaurant to eat. At some point after midnight, he'd told her, his arms tight around her, that he and Rusty would be leaving first thing in the morning. His tone had been more sad than bitter when he explained, "Not much for me to stick around for."

Carey had fumbled on a lamp and opened the box by its light. What difference did it make if she opened it now or waited until morning?

Inside was the blown-glass hummingbird she'd shown him. She wondered when he'd had time to go back and buy it for her.

She held it up to the lamp and watched the light shine through its delicate body, making it glow a brilliant ruby red. Then she sat down and cried.

By the time she reached The Caboose, she felt like ice through and through. Even though it was fairly warm inside, she kept her coat on until after she'd gotten a fire going in the big potbelly stove. Then, brushing bark off her hands and jeans, she made herself take off the coat and get the day started.

The first wave of customers was a relief, taking her mind off Hunter, even though the locals' orders never varied and she could nearly handle this part of the day in her sleep. But despite having had almost no sleep the night before, what was dragging her down today had nothing to do with shut-eye, though she felt as if exhaustion dragged at every limb. Perhaps it would have been more accurate to say sorrow.

Because she wasn't so busy that she didn't have time to think, and the more she thought (always about Hunter—she could scarcely get her mind on any other subject), the more she realized that she'd let something special slip through her fingers. No, shoved it away.

She'd never felt like that about anyone before. Not in three days, not in three months. He'd become so important so quickly that it almost felt as if he'd been part of her forever, as vital as a limb or internal organ. You couldn't cut off an arm or rip out your heart—why had she thought she could let him just walk away from her? Shove him away, she thought again, whipping herself viciously with the truth. He hadn't wanted to walk away; he'd wanted her to go with him. And why couldn't she? Some stupid idea that he'd turn into her father and she'd turn into her mother and they'd both be miserable? Piffle! She was miserable now...

As the morning went on, the locals ate up and went about their business and the tourists began to descend on The Caboose. Barry came in, relieving her of cooking duties, which only gave her more time to think.

She could go to Hunter's hotel; he might not have left yet. No, no use. It was well after nine now, and she'd learned over the last couple of days that Rusty was even more of an early riser than she was and most certainly didn't have a snooze button. Besides, what was it Hunter had said? Not much to stick around for. No, he wouldn't still be at the hotel.

She could follow him... But she didn't have a car, nor any way to get one. Not quickly enough. Hell, not at all. And she could hardly borrow a friend's. All the people she knew needed their cars to make a living; they certainly couldn't simply hand them over to her when she didn't know where she was going or how long it would take to find him. She hadn't gotten his cell number or given him hers—there'd been no need when they'd practically lived in each other's pockets these last three days. And she hadn't thought it would do any good once he left—just a tether tying them both to a dream that couldn't be.

"Dammit," she swore under her breath when she was in the walk-in refrigerator getting more orange juice. It was the only place in the restaurant where no one could hear her or see her wipe away the tears that kept filling her eyes. What an idiot she was!

She took a deep breath of cold air, told herself to buck up and do her job, and went back out with the orange juice to refill the glasses of the elderly couple that were her only remaining table. The rest of the breakfast rush had cleared out, except for a few people at the counter who Barry was keeping an eye on.

She vaguely remembered seeing the couple the morning Hunter came into the restaurant. He filled her memory of that morning, making everything else seem a bit hazy, but she remembered them because of their resemblance to Mr. and Mrs. Claus—put them in red suits and they'd fit the parts to a T. They were even wearing Christmas sweaters, complete with snowflakes and reindeer, though thankfully at least not matching ones. Despite her distraction the first morning she saw them, she must have given acceptable service, because they'd seemed perkily glad to have her as their server again. Even when they had to remind her that they'd need syrup for their waffles.

She'd just finished filling "Mrs. Claus's" orange juice when the woman said, "I don't mean to pry, dear, but is something wrong?"

"Wrong?" Carey scanned the table desperately, afraid she'd forgotten something else. Her mind was definitely not on her work this morning.

"You were so happy the other morning, dear. And on the other occasions we happened to see you with your young man during the Carnival. Not so much now. I hope nothing has gone amiss."

"No, no, it's just..." To her horror, Carey's eyes started filling with tears again. Thank God there was no one near enough to see... except the gray-haired man and his wife, who looked at her so sympathetically that before she knew it, it all came spilling out. How wonderful Hunter was, how perfect for her, and how horribly she'd screwed up. Even why she hadn't followed him and the kind of life she feared she'd have if she *did* somehow manage to find him again. She finally wound down, dabbing miserably at her leaking eyes with a napkin and utterly shamefaced at she'd dumping all that on strangers, no matter how sympathetic.

"I understand exactly how you feel, dear," the woman said, patting her hand. "Mr. C travels a great deal for work as well." She smiled at her husband.

Carey shot the man a startled look. He smiled, seeming content to let his wife handle the conversation, and turned his attention to a clipboard absolutely overflowing with papers. Unlike most men, however, he didn't seem at all unnerved by Carey's emotional outburst; she had the oddest feeling he was retreating for her sake rather than his own. Still, she stepped closer to his wife's side of the table and lowered her voice to avoid interrupting his work any more than she already had. "He does? Even now?" He didn't look a day under seventy. A spry seventy, but still...

"Oh yes, of course!" Mrs. C said, as if it should be obvious. "Always has, always will. He's in his busy season now, and I shan't see him for a donkey's age after this. The trick," she said, leaning toward Carey conspiratorially, "is to make time for yourself. And make the most of that time. This is part of my time with him, and it'll tide me through until after the holidays are over."

"But is it worth it? Chasing some guy while he chases his dream?"

"It is if he's not just *some guy*. If you love him, his dreams become your dreams. And vice versa, of course!"

"And what are your dreams?" Carey couldn't help asking. Mrs. C seemed so calm, so serene in her relationship, that Carey couldn't help hoping her answer would give Carey herself some answers.

Mrs. C's smile was oddly mysterious. "My dreams involve sun and sand and warmth for the other half of the year. Though I will admit that neither of us looks as good in a bathing suit as we once did."

"Yes," Carey said distractedly, then quickly changed it to, "No." Then added, "Thank you," and walked away without remembering to say goodbye or ask if they needed anything else. Her mind was buzzing with what Mrs. C had said and what she now knew with absolute certainty she had to do.

Without giving herself any time to think, she marched right up to her boss, who'd come in about an hour earlier to figure out what was wrong with the credit card machine, which kept glitching on them. He looked up, his expression a little frustrated, changing to bemused. "Something I can do for you, Carey?"

"If it's okay— No," she corrected herself, "I'm sorry, but I'm going to need to leave early today. And use that vacation I've saved up."

Steve's expression shifted to concern. "Something wrong?"

"No. Yes." Carey closed her eyes and told herself to stop acting like a ninny. She took a deep breath and said, "There's something I really need to—*must*—do, and I have to go do it now."

He just looked at her for a moment. She held her breath. She did *not* want to just walk out on him—not when he'd been so good to her—but she would if she had to. Finally, he nodded. "Okay. Maria's due in in a minute, and it's always quiet immediately after Carnival. Normally, I'd never be able to let you go during winter season, but a young man just came by with an outstanding resume." He paused and looked closely at her. "Understand, I don't know that I'll be able to fit you back in the schedule when you get back…"

"I understand. Thank you. For everything."

"Well, I don't know what's going on, but I can see it's very important. Wait a moment before you go, okay?" He disappeared into his tiny back office, leaving Carey relieved. Thank heavens it was enough for Steve that it was important to her. She really didn't want to explain further—how do you tell someone whose opinion you value that you're ditching everything to go chasing after some guy? No, she corrected herself, remembering Mrs. C's comment—not just some guy. The man she loved.

Steve returned a moment later with an envelope, which he handed to her. "Vacation pay," he said in response to her questioning look. "I get the feeling you're going to need the cash, so waiting for a payroll check won't do."

Carey peeked in the envelope and was struck speechless. It was far too much—no way he owed her this much, even with all the unused vacation time she'd piled up. "I…" Her throat closed up. She swallowed hard and tried again. "I can't—"

"You better take it, cause I'm definitely not putting it back in the safe." He gave her a paternal look. "We'll figure out the withholding and whatever else when you get back."

Carey threw her arms around him and squeezed hard, surprising him. He cleared his throat and patted her gingerly on the back, muttering, "Well… so…"

Her eyes were wet when she pulled away, and she was surprised to see a suspicious shine in his. Steve pasted on an unconvincing scowl and stumped back to his office, saying, "Go on, before I change my mind."

Carey rushed over to where the employees hung their coats and dragged hers on, depositing the envelope securely in an inside pocket. She got a quick one-armed hug from Barry, who claimed he was "all over grease" and didn't want to get it all over her coat, then skidded to a stop next to Mr. & Mrs. C's table. The elderly couple were in the process of gathering themselves to leave.

"Thank you *so* much," Carey said, bending on impulse to drop quick kisses on each of their cheeks. Despite having just eaten breakfast, complete with bacon and orange juice, they both smelled of… vanilla? As she hurried out the door, she thought, *No, not vanilla. Cookies. Christmas cookies.*

She ran all the way home, slowing only where she knew the sidewalk was icy, and started throwing things into a bag the moment she walked in the door. She was too scattered to pack properly—the process took three times longer than it should, and when she was done, she had no idea whether she'd packed what she really needed or had shoved both snowsuits and swimsuits into the bag. Had she even packed underwear?

The entire time, her mind was spinning with plans. How was she going to find him? First step was to get out of Pullman Siding, of course. But the regional bus wouldn't be by until next week, and anyway, there was really no reasonable chance it'd be headed in the right direction. Whatever the right direction was. That first day, Hunter'd said something about where he was heading next. Now where was it…. Michigan? Minnesota? Yeah, Minnesota. Gee, couldn't be too difficult finding one man in the whole state of Minnesota.

Breathe, she told herself. It'll work out. You can do it. If nothing else, you can google skijoring events and go to every damn one of them until you find him.

In which case, she was going to need a car. She fished out the envelope Steve had given her and, holding her breath, took out and counted the money. When she was done, she sat back and cried. She had such generous friends here—surely it would be foolish to leave them.

But when she thought of Hunter, her determination returned. She had enough to buy an old car. Or rent. Renting might be quicker, and she'd be back eventually—all her stuff was here. "Eventually," though... that could get pricey if she were renting. Perhaps, it not exactly being the busy season, one of the used places had a car they'd be willing to do a monthly rental on.

She left a note for Maria, with an explanation that she very much feared wouldn't make any sense to the other woman, along with her half of the month's rent.

Then she sat down and started calling the car rental places and used car dealers in town, looking for the deal that would keep her on the road the longest. On the road looking for Hunter.

Hunter got as far as Settler's Pass before his car broke down.

When he first sputtered to what sounded very much like a final stop in one of the turnouts for putting on chains, all he could do was laugh. If he didn't, he very much feared he might cry. It was just too damn coincidental.

It had taken him a long time to get out of town. Everything—from repacking his stuff to checking out of the hotel to running Rusty until he was sufficiently tired to be a good car companion and not a complete nuisance—seemed to take three times longer than it usually did. And he wasn't certain if things were truly going that poorly or if he was sabotaging himself. Because he didn't want to walk away from her.

But he had to. Carey was a strong, independent woman who knew her own mind. If she said—with every indication that it was the last answer she *wanted* to give—that she simply couldn't go with him, well... he had to believe her. If he didn't—if he tried to convince her otherwise—he could only see two outcomes. Either he failed to convince her and burned his bridges with her forever by trying to coerce her, or he succeeded in getting her to go with him, taking her away from the place she loved and making her miserable. Either way, he'd lose her.

When the laughter got too close to tears, Hunter straightened up, hit the steering wheel with the flat of his hand a couple of times for good measure, and got out, telling Rusty to stay put.

He opened the hood and took a look inside. He knew enough about cars to suffice under most circumstances but couldn't see anything that looked wrong under the hood. Great—first he got going much later in the morning than he'd intended and now his car broke down, despite being nearly new and in good shape. He'd had it serviced before he left home—nothing should be wrong. He pulled out his cellphone and scowled at the "no service" warning. Dammit.

He climbed back in the car, rubbing his hands together to try to restore some of the warmth. Should have put his gloves on before getting out. Now, with the car unusable, the only sources of heat were his own and Rusty's body heat. Rusty shoved up between the seats and rested his head on Hunter's shoulder, panting loudly in his ear.

"I know, boy. But the highway is hardly untraveled. Someone'll come along soon."

Rusty made a wuffing noise right next to his ear that nearly deafened him, then apologized by licking a broad wet stripe up the side of his face.

"Hope they like dogs."

The highway, which once looked rather welcoming, remained empty for a great deal longer than he'd expected. Which gave him all the time in the world to think, and to regret his decision. Sure, trying to make her come with him was a losing proposition all around, but what said he had to go in the first place?

He loved skijoring. It was his life—it was the thing he'd always wanted to do, that he loved more than anything. He'd promised himself, back when he was slogging through law school to please his father, that the moment he was free to do what he wanted, he'd never again waste time on things he didn't. And what he wanted, more than anything, was to race with his dog. He couldn't imagine giving that up.

He couldn't imagine never seeing Carey again.

He loved skijoring, but did he love it more than he loved Carey?

Hunter leaned his head against Rusty's and started laughing again. Three days—it had taken him all of three days to fall head over heels in love. No. More like three minutes. He'd always thought that "love at first sight" thing was a load of romantic drivel, but here he'd gone and done it. Fallen hard for a woman he'd just met. If his emotions were running this high after only three days, what would five days bring, a month, a year? He couldn't imagine being any more in love with her than he was now, and yet he couldn't imagine not falling deeper in love with her every moment they were together.

Dammit! What a situation! She couldn't go with him; he couldn't stay here. Sure, he could go back to town (if someone ever came along what was looking increasingly like a deserted road), ski during the winter, do touristy things the rest of the year. And if he did, what really was there for him? Beautiful scenery, etc, but really, what else? Just Carey.

There was nothing "just" about Carey.

Hunter was seriously contemplating slamming his hand in the car door to take his mind off the mess he'd made of his life when a car appeared in his rearview mirror. It looked absolutely ancient, and he watched with his heart in his throat as it slowly crested the same rise that had proven the death knell for his own car. Amazingly, it kept coming, even though it was an absolute wonder that it chugged along on the flats, let alone pulled these mountain roads.

He got out as the car neared, and it slowed to a stop near him with a polite beep of the horn... which played a cheerful chorus of *Jingle Bells*. The passenger window slid open, and Hunter ducked down to peer in at the occupants, who looked like refugees from a Christmas village. All that was missing were the red outfits and funny hats.

"Car trouble?" the elderly lady asked him. She was smiling. Hunter had the feeling that she always smiled.

"Fraid so. Wonder if I could get a ride someplace where I can call for a tow?"

"Well," the lady said thoughtfully, "the next town's pretty far to go when you'll only have to come back. But we could take you back to Pullman Siding."

"That would be wonderful." He hesitated a moment. "Uh, I have a dog with me. I can't really leave him here."

"Of course not! Both of you hop in," she said cheerfully. Hunter ducked his head a little further to look at the man who was driving—a dead ringer for Santa if he ever saw one—and got an approving nod. Not much of a talker, apparently.

He went back over to his car, leashed Rusty, checked to make sure he hadn't left his phone or wallet behind, and locked it up. He was very careful lifting Rusty into the ancient car—the dog would have been happier jumping in himself, but he could be a bit of a bull in a china shop, and the back seat was absolutely full of wrapped Christmas boxes. There was just barely enough room for both Hunter and Rusty, who opted to sit on Hunter's feet as soon as he was seated. There really wasn't room for the large dog on the floor between the seats, so he was mostly lying on Hunter's legs with his head on one thigh. Panting contentedly as Hunter's legs slowly went to sleep.

The driver got the car turned around, and they began chugging back down the hill to Pullman. Back to Carey, but Hunter didn't want to think about that. He'd barely made it out of town the first time; he wondered if he had the willpower to do it again.

"So," he said after a bit, hoping to escape his own thoughts, "you must have a lot of grandkids." He cast an eye over the dozens and dozens of presents.

The man driving laughed at that, a cheerful rolling laugh that fit his appearance to a T. The woman giggled and said, "Mr. C and I do have rather a lot of deliveries to make this time of year."

"I hope I'm not going to make you late for your next stop," Hunter offered, feeling guilty that they were having to backtrack so far on his behalf. He hoped to God this old jalopy could make it up the mountain a second time.

"Don't worry about that, dear," Mrs. C said cheerfully. "I just hope *you're* not too late."

"Me?"

"To go back after that beautiful brunette, of course."

"Carey? How—"

"Anyone with eyes could see the love," Mrs. C assured him, as if there was anything comfortable about her comment. Geez, did Carey have a stalker or did he? "We saw you around town during the Carnival," she added, clearing up at least some of her remarks.

Hunter was silent a moment. Ultimately, though, he couldn't hold back the question. "Love?" he said, not quite certain what he was asking.

"Of course love. In *both* of you," she added, and how could she have known what he was asking when he didn't even know? But that was precisely the answer he needed to hear. He knew it because hearing that made him feel grounded, as solid and sure of himself as when he whisked down a snowy trail, his skis buried in the powder, a harness linking him and Rusty.

He was in the habit of keeping his emotions hidden, playing everything close to the chest, but there was something about Mrs. C, and the silently listening Mr. C... "But what good does it do if she doesn't want to come with me? I asked," he added, unable to keep the misery out of his voice. "She said no."

"Of course she refused," Mrs. C said, and he bristled at her matter-of-fact tone. How dare she take sides in something she knew nothing about? "You have to feed her dreams too, you know; not just your own."

Oh, he thought. "But how can I do that?" His dream was to skijor, which meant traveling the event circuit. Hers was to stay here.

She reached back and patted his hand sympathetically, reminding him of his own grandmother, even though that lady was tall and thin and nothing like this round, rosy-cheeked woman. "You'll find a way."

"Will we?"

"Of course." She said it with such absolute certainty that he found himself truly believing her.

There was silence in the car for the rest of the trip, aside from the sounding of the *Jingle Bells* horn, which Mr. C used liberally and without rhyme or reason, laughing and waving whenever he did and inevitably getting cheerful waves back. When they hit the city limits, Hunter expected to be dropped at the nearest restaurant or gas station—any place he and Rusty could safely wait for a tow truck. He hoped he'd be able to get out of the car—Rusty would hop out the minute the door was open, but Hunter's legs were all pins and needles from the dog's weight. But Mr. C didn't pull in anywhere and Mrs. C didn't ask where Hunter would like to be let off.

Just when he was about to ask where they were headed, Mr. C pulled up to the curb in front of a familiar house. Carey's house. Hunter got Rusty off his legs and out of the car, then climbed gingerly out himself, holding onto the frame until he was sure his legs weren't too numb to hold him. He closed the rear door and looked in the front window—Mrs. C patted his hand again and wished him luck. Then they pulled away with a cheery wave, "Merry Christmas" floating back to him over the rattle of the old car engine.

He wondered how they'd known where to drop him.

However, that little mystery seemed of minor importance when he looked up at the house. He paced around on the sidewalk a little, telling himself it was to give Rusty a chance to sniff around and get the circulation back in his legs. In truth, he knew he was stalling. What if she said no again?

Finally, he made himself walk up to her door and knock. It seemed to take forever for her to answer—long enough for Rusty to sit down and lean against the back of his legs; long enough for Hunter to realize she was surely still at work. No matter—he could wait. Just then, the door flew open.

Carey was already talking. "You're early—I wasn't expecting the taxi for another... Hunter?!"

"Hi," he said inanely, all thoughts flown at his first sight of her after thinking he'd never see her again. Wincing, he dragged his senses together enough to ask, "Uh... can I come in?"

Wordlessly, she stepped back, ushering him and Rusty in, giving Rusty a pat as he went by. Hunter stepped into the tiny living room and stopped short, seeing a suitcase and backpack sitting near enough to the door it was clear Carey was on her way somewhere.

He turned to her, asking, "Where are you going?" at the same moment she said, "Why are you here?"

They both laughed at that, and while they both sounded nervous and uncertain, Hunter was heartened by their shared amusement.

He saw Carey's perfect lips open and rushed to say, "I want you in my life," before she could speak. Before she could send him away. "I don't care what it takes." And he meant it. Even if it meant giving up skijoring. Even if it meant living in the same place for the rest of his life and never going anywhere.

"You…? Really?" She blinked quickly, her train of thought apparently derailed. "I…" She shook her head, laughing. "I was about to say exactly the same thing."

"Really? Exactly?" he asked, smiling.

"Exactly," she said firmly. "Word for word, even."

"Wow."

They kissed for a long time, her luggage at their feet. At some point, Hunter felt Rusty give up leaning against his legs and wander off. The creak of the couch springs a moment later telegraphed his decision to sit on the furniture if the humans weren't going to pay him any attention. Hunter smiled into the kiss and felt Carey smile back.

When they finally came up for air for more than a moment, they found themselves both speaking at the same time again.

"I can give up skijoring."

"I can come with you."

They broke off and stared at each other.

"You would?" she said, wonderingly.

"In a moment. You?"

"In a second."

He laughed. "Tell you what. I will do the winter circuit and spend the rest of the year here with you."

"I've got a better idea. *We* will do the winter circuit and spend the rest of the year here together."

There was nothing to do but kiss her again.

He broke off a moment later to say, "Did you hear that?"

"Hear what?" she said dreamily, laying a row of kisses under the edge of his jaw that made it very hard to think.

"I thought I heard someone call Merry Christmas."

"Well, it is," she said, her lips drifting back up to his.

"Yes, but…" Her lips were soft, and he really didn't feel like talking anymore. Or thinking, when it came to that.

The notes of *Jingle Bells* drifted through the cold mountain air.

The Christmas Champion

Colleen Ladd

"Come on, Maggie," Jamie muttered under her breath. "You can do it. You can do it." She was crouched over the steering wheel, her fingers clamped hard around it, leaning forward as if she could push her little car up the mountain pass by will alone.

Maggie, her ancient yellow hatchback, seemed almost to hear her, rallying and gamely chugging up the steep, snowy road. But Jamie's relief was short-lived. She tried to convince herself it was just her imagination, that her headlights weren't dimming, her windshield wipers going slower and slower. But as the snow began to build up on the glass, that became impossible.

"Come on," she urged between her teeth. "We're almost there. You can make it." She had no idea whether she was lying or not—she'd never driven to Tahoe before and wouldn't have been able to tell where she was even if she had. Snow had started falling soon after the road began to climb and had gotten steadily heavier the further up she went. Given a choice, she'd never have opted to drive a road she didn't know in the dark during a snowstorm. But her new employer—one of Tahoe's fancy hotels—had given her no choice and very little warning, moving up her start date and sending her scrambling to get there in time.

Now she wondered if she was going to get there at all.

Maggie's wipers were moving with glacial speed across the glass. Jamie wanted to rub her straining eyes, but she didn't dare take her hands off their white-knuckle grip on the steering wheel.

"Come on," she urged despairingly.

But she was having to go slower and slower, no longer able to tell with certainty where the edge of the road was, or the neighboring lane. The other vehicles on the road were clearly not having the same problem. They objected to her poking along, cars blowing past her on the left, their angry horns wailing irritation as they zipped by.

"God, please," Jamie murmured. She couldn't see the road, or the other cars, or even if there was anything resembling a safe place to pull off. She was terrified her wipers would stop altogether or the headlights go out entirely. Not that that would be a huge change from how little they were doing now.

A cheery sound cut through the storm-driven wind. *Jingle bells?* Jamie thought. Who the heck would be playing Jingle Bells out here? It certainly wasn't coming from her radio, which didn't work.

The notes of the song came again from immediately to her left, where a car had pulled up alongside her. It must have been the car's horn. He apparently wasn't in the same hurry the rest of the drivers were, because he stayed beside her. She wanted to turn and see what he wanted, assuming her side window wasn't completely frosted over—it was as cold as the north pole in her little car—but she didn't dare take her eyes off the barely visible stripe that marked the edge of the road. After a moment, he pulled ahead, once more with a cheery blast of Jingle Bells. Then he switched over into her lane, she had his taillights in sight, and her breathing eased a bit as she began to follow him.

He went slow, thankfully, and she clung tightly to his bumper, terrified of losing sight of his lights as the snow piled up on her windshield. Her wipers were moving about once a minute now, and her headlights were barely visible where they reflected anemically off the chrome of his rear bumper. Only the periodic (and perversely cheerful) sounding of the Jingle Bells horn confirmed that she was still following the same person. Or anyone at all.

Just when she knew she couldn't take it anymore—her heart pounding, breath coming fast through tight teeth, fingers clamped so tightly around the steering wheel that she couldn't feel them anymore—the vehicle ahead flipped on its turn signal and began inching toward the right side of the road.

Were they in Tahoe? Surely they were—she felt like she'd been driving so long that they must surely be past Tahoe and halfway through California by now. She followed the taillights to the right and was dismayed when they didn't turn sharply enough to be turning off the road. She was quite certain—when the car in front came to halt and she did the same, Maggie's dashlights and headlights flickering weakly—that they were on the shoulder, just barely off the road. As if to confirm that, three cars sped by in quick succession, blasting Jamie with their protesting horns and rocking poor Maggie in their wake.

Why had the other car stopped? This was hardly the safest of places. Though she had to admit that she'd needed the break. She was shaking, and not from the cold inside her car. Jamie slowly forced herself up from her tight hunch over the steering wheel and set her back against the seat. It took a minute to pry her fingers off the wheel—they felt like they were glued there.

For a minute, all she did was breathe. Not that that was easy with cars and trucks blasting past her every few seconds. Snow had piled up so much on the windshield that she couldn't see the car in front of her. She wondered why the driver hadn't tried to come and talk to her. Perhaps he was wondering the same about her. Seemed silly to get out and perhaps run smack dab into him in between their cars.

She gingerly turned off the wipers, which weren't moving at

all anymore. Then, holding her breath, she turned them back on, hoping they might work properly. They swept up in a quick arc, clearing half the windshield. Relief swept over her. Too soon. The wipers began to slow down, making the descending sweep at a snail's pace.

"Dammit," Jamie muttered. Her cousin had said he thought there might be something wrong with the electrical system of her "junker," as he so rudely called Maggie. She'd figured... well, as long as she could get the little car started, she'd be fine, right? At least until she could put some hours in at her new job and save up enough to have Maggie fixed properly. She'd thought wrong.

Her eyes fixed on the wipers inching along, it took her a moment to realize she couldn't see any taillights through the partly cleared windshield. She leaned forward, peering over the steering wheel, then used the sleeve of her sweater to scrub at the frost forming on the inside of the windshield, clearing a small section. They'd just turned their lights off for a moment, surely. She was just looking in the wrong place. But no. There was nothing but blackness ahead of her, barely lit by the anemic glow of her headlights. The glaring sweep of light from a passing car fanned over the area. Nothing.

"No. Oh no. Please," Jamie cried. How could they? How could they just abandon her like that, on the narrow shoulder of a busy highway? At night. In a horrendous snowstorm. Perhaps they'd thought she was behind them when they started up again? Perhaps they didn't realize she couldn't see them at all. "Oh God."

Now what?

Jamie pressed her head against the backs of her hands, once more cramped around the steering wheel, and tried to convince herself that she just needed to restart the engine. That if she shut Maggie down, turning the key would return her to life, all her bits and pieces working properly. Ha! At this point, if Maggie died, restarting her was not in the cards. And if Jamie *did* somehow manage to get her little car restarted, she ought to go straight to a convenience store and buy a lottery ticket because today was her lucky day.

Jamie shivered and tried to think what to do. Other than regret ever heading out for Tahoe when there was a major storm forecasted. But what choice did she have when she was expected to start her new job in the morning? She'd hoped to beat the storm. Foolish. Now here she was, sitting on the side (barely) of Highway 50 in what was quickly becoming one of the worst snowstorms of the decade, with all her worldly possessions jammed into a car that was clearly going nowhere.

"Buck up," Jamie told herself. "You can do this." It wasn't any more reassuring directed at herself.

She took a deep, shuddering breath, and reminded herself that she couldn't just sit there all night. She was already shivering in the freezing car. Maggie's heating had never been the best, and it had been the first thing to cut out when she started up the pass. And God knew, there wasn't a soul in the world who would ride to her rescue.

"So..." she said aloud. "How do you drive in a snowstorm with no wipers?" She briefly considered rolling down the driver's side window and sticking her head out. Then looked at her windshield, already completely covered again, and decided the snow was falling too heavily. No way she'd be able to see anything in that.

Well, what if she *did* try shutting Maggie down and restarting her? It worked with computers, and it was the electronic part of the car that wasn't working. So maybe... She had one of those battery jump boxes in the back. She'd have to dig it out from under everything else if Maggie didn't restart on her own, but maybe all she needed was a jump.

Jamie took another deep breath and let it out slowly. "Okay." She pulled the hood release and pushed the door-unlock button. Nothing. Even the power locks weren't working. She'd need the key to open the back. And if she took out the key... Well, she'd been planning on turning Maggie off anyway. Might as well do it now. Holding her breath, she turned the little car off. Then, after a moment's hesitation, turned the key again. Nothing. Not even a click. Swearing under her breath, though it was just as she'd expected, she fumbled the key out of the ignition and shoved it in her pocket. Better to have it on her anyway—the last thing she needed was to get locked out in this weather.

She manually unlocked the driver's door and shoved it open before she could talk herself into delaying any longer. Incredibly bright light bounced off the frosted window, blinding her, and she yanked the door closed with a gasp. A semi thundered past, horn wailing, Maggie shuddering. Her heart pounding, Jamie couldn't help but think her little car was as shaken as she was at the close call. That truck would have taken the door clean off, probably pancaking Jamie in the process.

She was clinging to the steering wheel again, her head pressed to the cold plastic between her white knuckles, her heart beating itself out of her chest. It couldn't possibly go any faster.

She found out just how wrong she was when something pounded on her window with a noise like thunder. Jamie jolted back in her seat, her mouth open in a silent scream, and stared at the crazed window. She couldn't see a damn thing except that all the windows on that side were now lit up brilliantly.

White light. No red or blue. Not a cop then? Probably not a cop.

She couldn't see who was out there, and she couldn't roll the window down with the power out. Not even a crack. No way was she opening the door at night on the side of the road. The stories about women who made that sort of mistake usually ended "and she was never seen again."

"You okay in there?" called the deepest voice she'd ever heard. Jamie huddled in her seat, shaking like a leaf. God, what was she going to do?

Before she could even begin to think of an answer, the man outside yanked the door open. Jamie barely held back a shriek. She'd unlocked it—she'd forgotten she unlocked it.

"Are. You. Okay?" he asked impatiently. Not waiting for an answer, he added, "What the hell is the matter with you? Don't you know—"

Her eyes dazzled by the headlights glaring off the frosted inner window of her open door, all Jamie could see was a looming shadow. She shrank instinctively away, and the deep, angry voice broke off suddenly.

"Jesus," he rumbled softly, "you're white as a sheet. You must be frightened to death."

Gloved hands clamped down on her arms, pulling her out of the car and against a warm brick wall. Chest, she thought, dazed—a really nice chest... He was incredibly warm, heat pouring off him in waves, and she instinctively burrowed against him.

He smelled really nice too—something spicy and piney. His warmth immediately began thawing not only the parts of her half-frozen in her cold car but the icy fear filling her chest.

His arms—as strong as his chest—wrapped around her, and she tried not to think of anything except his warmth and his scent. And certainly not of the chances of being found in a shallow grave sometime in the spring. Though that thought had receded rather a lot—how could anyone who hugged this wonderfully be bad?

Another semi rumbled past, its horn sounding like a roll of thunder, the wind of its passage slamming into them. Had Jamie been standing there alone, it would have knocked her on her butt. The man scarcely moved.

"Come on," he said, his voice rumbling through the chest under her cheek. "We can't stay here. We have to get you off the road and someplace warm." His arms loosened, and he slid one around her back, urging her to move with him. "My car's right here." He'd stopped smack in the middle of the right lane, flashers on, his car protecting them from being hit by passing vehicles. The headlights were blinding.

When he stepped away from her, the cold rushed back in, along with all the horrible stories she'd ever heard. Jamie dug in her heels, visions of shallow graves dancing in her head. "I'm—I'm fine," she gulped out. She wrapped her fingers around the frigid frame of the driver's door and held on as if he were pulling at her. "I just need a jump. Then everything'll be fine."

"This isn't a good place for that, and frankly, I doubt it would do any good. If your car stopped while you were driving, it's going to need more than a jump."

Jamie winced, knowing that he was right, much as she wished otherwise. "I'll, I need to stay here. My whole life—everything I own is in here," she babbled. "If you could just call a tow truck...?"

She ought to have been able to do that herself, but her phone was dead and her charging cable wasn't working—though now she thought perhaps it was Maggie's ability to charge anything that had been the problem, rather than the cable. She'd thought she could just plug it in when she got to the hotel. Stupid.

"I don't have cell service here," the shadowy man said, "and you aren't going to get a tow truck out in this weather anyway. Not this far out of town."

"I'll, I'll just, I'll wait here until morning."

"You'll freeze if you stay here in an unheated car." He took a quick step toward her, and she backed into the open V of her car door. Another semi lumbered past, this one throwing up slush from the road. None of it spattered her, blocked by the man's broad back. He didn't react to the icy mess hitting his black coat. "Look," he said, sounding incredibly patient, "just take a few steps toward the back of your car, where you can see me in the headlights. I'll show you my driver's license, so you'll know who I am."

So she'd know the name of the guy who killed her? No, surely she was being too suspicious—he'd stopped when she needed help, when her previous Good Samaritan had (accidentally or otherwise) left her in the lurch and no one else was likely to spare her little car a glance. And surely there were easier ways of picking up victims, if one was inclined to do that. Warmer ones, at least.

She walked, a bit stiffly, to the rear of her car, hesitating there. Snow swirled around them, dancing in his headlights. Under other circumstances, she would have found it pretty. He fished his wallet out of the pocket of his coat and handed the whole thing to her, then turned so the light reached his face. Jamie sucked in a breath. His hair and eyes were dark, his features a bit rugged. Combined with his height and broad shoulders, they probably made him appear forbidding to some people. She thought she'd never seen a more handsome man. After a moment, she remembered to look down at the wallet in her hand.

She flipped it open to the driver's license. The picture was definitely the same man, the name Devin Stanton printed next to it. The credit card opposite the license showed the same name. Feeling like she was snooping, Jamie closed the wallet and handed it back. He immediately opened it again, took out his license, and handed it to her.

"Put this in your car—hide it anywhere you like. That way, you know I'll deliver you safely wherever you need to go." His smile was charming. "After all, if you don't get there, my ID will be in your car and the cops will know exactly who to question."

"I wasn't thinking—" she stuttered, mortified.

"Of course you were," he said, not seeming in the least offended. Nor did he seem to even notice the snow building up on the shoulders of his black coat. She was certainly aware of it—her old ski jacket was not as waterproof as it had once been. "You're a beautiful young woman traveling alone. And you don't know me from Adam."

"I..." She couldn't continue to say she hadn't been thinking it, not without lying through her teeth. The idea seemed more and more ridiculous the longer she spoke with (and looked at) him. "But what if you get pulled over?"

He smiled, showing even white teeth. "Then I shall have to throw myself on your mercy and hope the nice officer will understand why I had to leave it behind. Go on now," he urged. "We can't keep standing around out here—your lips are turning blue, and if we stay here much longer, the snow will bury us both."

Jamie felt stupid doing it, her fears now seeming entirely ridiculous, but she dashed up to her driver's door, stuffed his license between the passenger seat and the console, and snatched up her purse. Then she locked the door, patted Maggie gently, hoping she hadn't witnessed the end of her trusty car's working life, and dashed back to Devin.

"Ready?" He didn't wait for an answer, but took her arm and led her back to his car, opening the passenger door for her. A blast of warm air hit her, feeling almost too hot and entirely too welcome at the same time. "Get in and start warming up."

"What are you going to do?" she asked when he started toward the back of his car instead of going around to the driver's door.

"There won't be many more people up this road tonight— they've almost certainly shut it down by now. But we've got to do something to make sure those that still *are* on the road can see your car. Usually, that bright yellow would do it, but tonight..." He walked off after once more urging her to close the door and get warm.

She pulled the door shut, sinking back into buttery soft leather seats that felt almost fever-warm to her frozen hands. The front and reader windshield wipers were going, and it was amazing how crystal clear her view of the road, the passing cars, and the falling snow was after fighting for so long to see out of her own car. She watched him take something out of the trunk and walk back up to her car. A moment later, the things in his hands began flashing—red lights that rotated through a series of patterns. He attached them to the back and driver's side of her car, the thump of strong magnets audible even inside the intensely quiet car. She realized she could barely even hear the large trucks speeding past and looked around the spotless car. Leather seats, wood inset in the dash, a front console display almost overloaded with muted lights...everything about it screamed "money." And she'd all but accused him of being some kind of predator.

"Oh dear..."

As Devin walked back to the driver's door, he swept the snow off his shoulders and out of his hair and climbed in with only a rime of snow on his coat. Jamie realized belatedly that she should have shaken off some of the snow before climbing in herself—her damp clothes were probably ruining his upholstery. She tried to apologize, but Devin just shook his head and flashed her another of those devastating smiles.

"Stop worrying. Now... where are we going?"

"Anywhere in Tahoe would be fine," she answered, not wanting to put him out. Surely she could get where she needed to go from wherever he dropped her. Though she had very little cash on her to pay for a taxi. Assuming she could find one in this.

He gave her what could only be described as a *look*. "Where do you need to go?" he asked, emphasizing every word.

"The Silver Star hotel," she said, and was rewarded with a smile. For some reason, he seemed to find that amusing.

"The Silver Star, is it? All right then." He ran the driver's side window down and back up to clear some of the snow off, then pulled smoothly out into traffic, the car quickly and quietly ramping up to speed to match the vehicles around them.

Only after he'd pulled away did it occur to Jamie that taking her suitcase along would have been... helpful. But she wasn't about to ask him to go back. She could manage—sleep in her underwear and the camisole she had on under her turtleneck and sweater, use the little complimentary soaps and shampoo, etc—but it reminded her of everything she'd have to do tomorrow. Get her car towed... to where, she didn't know—someplace that would hold it until she could afford to get it fixed and hopefully wouldn't charge her an arm and a leg. Get her suitcase and other necessities to the hotel. Start looking for an apartment... All without a car and all while starting her first day on the job. The thought was daunting.

"You know my name," Devin said after a couple of minutes. He shot her a sideways glance. "Might I know yours?"

"Oh! I'm so sorry! I'm Jamie. Jamie Drake. Thank you so much for rescuing me. I wouldn't normally even think of driving into the mountains in this kind of weather, but my boss at The Silver Star called me up and told me I had to start work tomorrow, and..." Realizing suddenly that she was babbling, Jamie swallowed the rest of the words piling up on her tongue and finished lamely, "And so here I am."

"It was the least I could do. Frankly, it's the least anyone could do—no one deserves to be stuck out on the road on a night like this."

Perhaps not, though Jamie's experience was that things like this were just the way of the world. One way or another, her life never did seem to run smooth, and there was no one to fix all the things that went wrong but her. Other people might have the leisure of waiting around for someone else to ride to their rescue—Jamie did not.

As such, it was absolutely par for the course that, upon arriving at The Silver Star, she walked up to the desk and discovered that they did not have a room for her.

"I don't understand," she told the harried desk clerk, fighting hard to keep the irritation and growing dismay out of her voice. It wasn't his fault, after all. "I was told they'd be putting me up for a couple of days while I settled into the job and found a place of my own. Are you sure? Jamie Drake," she said again, though she knew it would do no good.

"Yes, we put new employees up for a little while," the clerk said, not bothering to hide his irritation, "but not over *Christmas*."

"But *you're* the ones who decided to move my start date up to before Christmas," Jamie argued. "What am I supposed to do now?"

"Get back in your car and go find someplace else to stay," the man snapped. "*We* are booked up for the holiday."

Jamie became aware that someone had come up behind her just before a familiar deep voice said, "Is that any way to speak to a fellow employee?"

Her heart gave a startled (and pleased, if she were honest) kick, and she turned to find Devin standing behind her. He looked even more handsome in the bright lights of the lobby. She'd known she would see him again—after all, his driver's license was still in her car—but she hadn't expected him to come into the hotel after her. The last she'd seen him was at the drop-off area, where she'd taken the card he pressed into her hand and promised to call in the morning, then dashed into the hotel before she could make a fool of herself by asking if he wanted to have dinner with her. She flushed, wondering how long he'd been standing there and just how much of her desperate pleading he'd overheard.

"She's not *my* fellow employee," the desk clerk snapped, his eyes focused on his computer, as they had been throughout the exchange, though Jamie didn't think he was actually *doing* anything. "She's working in one of those froufrou boutiques, and it's her own damn fault if—" He finally glanced up, and all the color washed out of his face. "Mr. Stanton!"

"I trust you haven't lost *my* reservation," Devin said, his face like stone and no hint in his voice of the pleasant friendliness he'd shown Jamie.

"No, sir," the desk clerk stammered. "I want you to know, sir—"

"Then you shouldn't have any trouble getting me checked in."

"Yes, sir," the man muttered, shooting Jamie a venomous look, as if *she* were at fault here. The three of them stood in a frigid and uncomfortable silence while the clerk fumbled through the check-in process as quickly as possible, not even bothering to ask Devin for an id or credit card. Or perhaps, Jamie thought, thinking of how the clerk instantly recognized Devin, he was just so important they didn't *need* any of that. She wished she were anywhere else—Devin's cold anger at the clerk made her extremely uncomfortable and she wanted nothing more than to walk away. But she had nowhere to go and no choice but to wait until Devin was checked in and the clerk could return his attention to her. Though she very much feared that her chances of being treated with any kind of consideration, poor to begin with, had fled entirely the minute Devin got involved. She knew he was only trying to help, but she wished he'd just kept out of it.

It felt like an eternity before the clerk pushed a keycard across the counter. "You're in the Silver Suite, as usual, sir."

Devin didn't take the card. "I'll need two," he said without expression.

The clerk's face got, if anything, grayer. "Of course, sir. I should have asked." He had the second keycard done in a matter of seconds.

Devin took it, and Jamie's arm, and walked away while the clerk was still trying to stammer out something about having a good evening. Not wanting to make a scene, Jamie didn't dig in her heels, but she drew the line at getting on the elevator with him.

"Thank you, but I can take care of myself," she said, drawing her arm out of his grasp, trying not to be too rude about it. She glanced over at the reception desk, but the clerk was now helping a couple who were dead ringers for Mr. and Mrs. Claus. Jamie wondered if the hotel was planning some kind of Christmas party or show for its guests. It seemed too... kitschy for the quiet, high-class aura of the place. She found that idea singularly depressing—

she loved Christmas, and the thought of working in a place that didn't have time for it....

"Of that, I have no doubt."

Her eyes flew back to Devin's face. There hadn't been a trace of sarcasm or irony in his voice, but she was sure it was there. It always was when people said things like that—and was especially likely from the man who'd literally plucked her off the side of the road. But she could see nothing but that pleasant friendliness in his face. She sighed. "Look, I'm sure it made you feel good to tell that clerk off, and I won't pretend I didn't enjoy seeing him taken down a peg or two, but I've still got to get a room for the night and it's going to be three times as hard now."

"On the contrary, it's going to be impossible," he said, as if it were a simple statement of fact and not akin to tossing her out in the storm. Jamie sucked in a breath, but before she could say any of the things warring to escape her mouth, he went on, "But he's not going to refuse you a room because of anything I said. He's going to refuse you a room because he's a snobby little man who thinks he's better than you because he works Reception and you work retail."

Which was entirely true, if more blunt than Jamie would ever dare put it. She gaped at him. What would a man like Devin Stanton—with his fancy car and his expensive suit and his rented *suite* for the holidays—know about the world she occupied and the hardships that came with it?

When she found her voice, it was sharp and irritated. "And what exactly do you propose I do about that? I can't exactly go find myself another hotel, now can I? I have no choice but to throw myself on his mercy and hope the little rat actually has some."

There was a gleam of amusement in his eye at that. "I very much doubt he even has any mercy for his fellow rats."

"Great. Then I'll just go sleep on the street, shall I?" She could barely believe the words coming out of her mouth. But she was tired, and still cold, and absolutely fed up with the whole situation. And she had no idea at all what she was going to do—even trying to catch some sleep in the lobby was probably out. The hotel almost certainly had staff watching out for that—it was too nice a place not to—and if by some chance it didn't, that jackass of a desk clerk would doubtless see to it himself.

"You could do that," Devin said equitably, as if she wouldn't freeze to death in a few hours, assuming she lasted even that long. "Or you could take this and have a good night's rest in a warm, safe place."

He was holding out the second keycard to her. The second keycard to *his* suite.

She stared at it, and him, for a long moment. The elevator arrived with a muted ding, opened its doors, and sat there waiting. It had given up and closed the doors again before she found her voice and said, "I appreciate all you've done for me, but—"

He was shaking his head, the expression on the rugged face tipping more towards amusement now. "No, it's not like that. No strings—of any sort. For anything. I have a suite, and my family's not coming in until tomorrow. Why shouldn't you take one of the rooms for the night? It'll just sit empty if you don't." When she still didn't reach out for the keycard, he added, "Separate rooms, Jamie. With locks on the doors."

Jamie flushed painfully. She'd done it again—accused him (by implication if nothing else) of having ulterior motives when he was only trying to help. Shamefaced and apologizing, she reached for the keycard.

He waved away her apologies as if he scarcely heard them. His fingers brushed hers when he handed over the card, so warm they felt almost burning. He smiled. "Have to say, though... you're cute when you blush."

Behind them, the elevator dinged and opened its doors again.

Devin almost, *almost* asked her to have dinner with him.

But by the time the elevator reached his penthouse suite and he showed her into one of the rooms off the central living area, she was drooping so visibly, he didn't have the heart to. Instead, he wished her goodnight, surprised them both by dropping a quick kiss on her hair—which was as fiery as a bonfire... or her personality—and retreated to his own room, feeling the weight of her eyes on his back the whole way.

He stood just inside his closed door, listening until he heard the soft sound of her door closing. And then the even softer sound of the lock engaging. He grinned, imagining her turning it slowly and carefully, trying to make as little noise as possible. As if it were offensive for her to lock her door, even after he'd made it a selling point for taking him up on his offer.

Perhaps Devin ought to have found her suspicion offensive. After all, he wasn't the kind of man who took advantage of women, in any sense of the word. He'd never before been accused (let alone several times in the span of a couple of hours) of having ulterior motives... or worse—he was quite sure she'd thought him some kind of sexual predator on the road. It was, paradoxically, almost charming. Or would be if it didn't say something about what Jamie had come to expect of the men in her life. That made him grit his teeth and want to go hit someone. Even if he had no idea who the someone or someones were.

Or maybe he'd find anything she did charming. He was certainly taken with her. On the road, she'd been an intriguing combination of damsel in distress and miniature firecracker. In his car, a quiet presence smelling damply of lilac and watching his every move with large green eyes. In the hotel, an irritated and exhausted woman, bearing up as best she might under impossible circumstances and doggedly determined to take care of herself. She was also, under the bright lights of the hotel lobby, so beautiful she took his breath away. He'd actually slowed as he walked up to the counter in order to have just a moment longer to take in her petite perfection. She scarcely came up to his chin, and she was as enticing to look at as she'd been to hold.

Devin made himself move away from the door—standing there listening for any movement from her room made him feel like the perv she'd all but accused him of being—and picked up the phone to call room service. The storm had slowed traffic so much that the trip up had taken much longer than he'd anticipated. A journey only lengthened by stopping to help Jamie, which was a delay he could only be thankful for. He thought of knocking on her door and asking if she wanted anything. Surely she'd also missed dinner. But she'd looked so completely exhausted—who wouldn't be after fighting their car up the mountain like that?—and he couldn't see any light under the door.

He reluctantly decided it would be best not to disturb her. She might be sleeping, and even if she wasn't, there was no saying an invitation from him would even be welcome. Her expression when he first saw her—pale as a ghost and terrified nearly out of her mind—was burned behind his eyes. He'd never been looked at like that before and he never wanted to be again. Especially not by Jamie.

He'd never realized before how much he took the way people reacted to him for granted. It was rare to do more than exchange a few words with anyone who didn't know who he was. Like it or not, his family's reputation (and especially their money) preceded him. He was met with gratitude, cheerful assistance, obsequious bowing and scraping, and occasionally resentment. Never suspicion. It had taken him longer than he liked to understand why she was hesitating, longer still to determine what to do about it.

Absolutely starving, he ordered two hamburgers and all the fixings, which he took into his room to eat, and a bowl of fruit and plate of muffins, which he left on the table in the common room in case Jamie got hungry in the middle of the night. It didn't seem like enough, but he couldn't think offhand of anything else available from the kitchen that would still be appetizing after sitting out for several hours. The suite had its own refrigerator, of course, but he couldn't be sure she'd think to look in it.

After he ate, he stood looking out the window at the wintery landscape. It was still snowing heavily, fat flakes blotting out the city lights. If it kept up, the rest of the Stanton clan would not be making it to Tahoe for the holidays. He couldn't say he found the idea entirely disheartening. If they didn't come, he'd continue to have a spare room for Jamie. If he could convince her to stay. He thought he could. Probably. There was, after all, literally no room at the inn. *Any* of them, if he knew Tahoe this time of year. Which he did.

It would certainly be easier to get to know her better if he didn't have to track her down first, come up with a believable excuse second, and convince her to spend a little time with him third.

He thought again about how she'd questioned his motives in the lobby and cold reason washed over him. Even if everything fell into place perfectly, it wouldn't be easy. He'd have to talk very fast indeed to stay ahead of her suspicion. Someone had clearly hurt her very badly, and Devin wished he knew who so he could go flatten the bastard. Wished even more that time travel were real and he could do it before the guy betrayed her.

Devin leaned his forehead against the cold window and sighed, his breath fogging the glass. He was getting very emotionally invested *very* quickly. Stupid, the rational part of him said. Inevitable, said the side that could still feel Jamie's petite frame pressed to his heart... and the absolute necessity of protecting her that had filled him in that moment.

If she'd let him. She was damned independent.

Oh hell, even if she wouldn't.

Speaking of... Her car could not stay out on the highway indefinitely. Especially as he'd been so focused on getting her warm and safe in his car that he'd forgotten to bring along her luggage.

A final sigh fogging up the window, Devin went and sat in one of the immensely comfortable chairs—one that just happened to have a clear view of her door—and pulled out his phone. Scrolling through his contacts, he found the mechanic who'd done an excellent job on his Lexus two years ago.

"Jerry. Sorry to call so late…" Though when he glanced at the clock, he was surprised to see it was barely seven. Between the snow blotting out the light and the long drive in, it seemed much later. "Got a job for you in the morning, assuming anyone can get out."

It didn't take him long to describe the car and its location, as best he could determine, tell Jerry he didn't have the key but the owner was there in the hotel, and ask him to have it towed to his shop as soon as possible and the luggage delivered to the hotel.

"I know you typically only work on high-end vehicles, but I'd take it as a special favor if you'd see to the repairs. Bill it all to me." Devin hesitated, thinking of Jamie's determined, dogged independence. "I need a second invoice in the name of Jamie Drake for not more than fifty dollars. I don't care what repair you put on it—just something that could reasonably explain the car breaking down. Send that one to me here as well."

Jerry was not only an excellent mechanic, he was a very smart man. He didn't question the request or say a single word about its oddity. Just agreed cheerfully and hung up after promising to get the car as soon as he could.

Devin held his phone a moment, deliberating. There was another call he wanted to make. If Jamie was starting a job here in the morning, she'd most definitely be doing so in the clothes she'd driven up in. He wanted to smooth the way with her new boss—make the excuses he was certain she wouldn't—but didn't know which "froufrou boutique" she would be working in. And calling around to find out could cause her problems and resentment later. He reluctantly decided it would have to wait until morning.

He even more reluctantly decided that Jamie wasn't going to come out of her room tonight. And if she did, that it would only scare her to find him sitting there staring at her door.

He retreated to his own room and set about unpacking his personal travel bag, the rest of his luggage having been brought directly to the room on his arrival and unpacked into the bureau.

When he finally climbed into bed—his alarm set for what ought to be an early enough hour to catch Jamie before she slipped out (which he was certain she would try to do)—it took him an eternity to fall asleep, the phantom feeling of her in his arms taunting him with the desire for the real thing.

Jamie slept like the dead, waking to a world rimed with ice. The sun shone fitfully through the frost-encrusted window, and for a moment as she stretched in the sinfully comfortable bed, she could not remember where she was. Then it came to her, and she scrambled out of bed with a gasp.

Her phone, plugged in on the desk, showed that it was still early, and her heart rate slowed slightly. She wasn't late for work, thank god. She even had time to shower and eat… and figure out how to make herself presentable using only what was in her purse.

Shower first. There was soap, shampoo, and lotion by the sink, which smelled wonderful and worked even better. None of the usual sub-par toiletry giveaways here. She wondered if all the rooms got stuff this good or if it was reserved for the penthouse.

The shower was strong and hot, and she basked in it as long as she dared, her eyes closed, imagining Devin's arms around her again. Strong and hot—that was him, the heat of his body warming her more thoroughly than the shower. She wondered if he was up yet—perhaps showering, like her—or maybe still in bed, his dark hair tousled, eyes sleepy.

"Oh, for pete's sake!"

Jamie flipped off the water and stepped out, toweling herself off roughly. She had tons of things to worry about today—there wasn't time to moon over a guy she knew nothing about. Except that he had hair and eyes like midnight, a voice so deep she could feel it in her bones, rugged good looks, and a boyish smile.

"Get a grip, Jamie!"

However roughly she toweled herself, the towel itself felt like... velvet or something. Softer than any towel she'd ever touched. Which was, she told herself sternly, just one more reminder that the man had money. As if the size of the room—hell, the *bathroom*—wasn't reminder enough. She'd had apartments smaller than this bathroom. Devin Stanton obviously had money. A lot of it. And a man like that would never be interested in a woman like her.

Oh, he probably wouldn't mind spending a few days with her. But guys like that didn't see *forever* when they looked at her.

She finished drying her hair and pulled on the clothes she wore the previous day. They passed the sniff test, thank God, and the wonderful scent of the shampoo and lotion provided by the hotel would mask any lingering odor that might give away that they were yesterday's clothes. What it couldn't do, she thought with dismay when she looked at herself in the mirror, was change her knockabout driving clothes into anything she'd have chosen to wear to work. Especially on her first day at a—what had that jerk called it?—froufrou boutique.

But there wasn't a thing in the world she could do about it. Except not look quite so defeated, she reminded herself, forcing a smile that didn't look as fake as it felt. Just grin and bear it, like everything else.

Jamie set about using the small brush from her purse to tame her out-of-control hair. It was like trying to harness a dozen cats to a dogsled. She finally gave up and managed to weave her long red hair into a credible braid. She put on some makeup, rinsed her mouth with water, and stepped back to take stock.

Well, she was presentable, at least. It could have been a lot worse. She could have slept in her car on the side of the road. She could still be there. Would be, if it weren't for—"

"Jamie?" Devin's deep voice was accompanied by a sharp knock on the connecting door.

"One minute," she called, hoping there wasn't a tremor in her voice. Her heart was pounding, and she didn't know if it was surprise or the reminder that he was only a door away. All she had to do to see him again was open it.

"Well, of course he is," she scolded herself quietly, shoving everything back in her purse. Adding the little shampoo and lotion bottles after a moment's hesitation. She might need them later. "What did you think, he was just going to *leave* you here? In his suite?" In the suite he was supposed to be sharing with his family. Her heart sank—family that'd be arriving sometime today. No doubt he wanted her out. And the sooner the better. So his... What? Sister? Mother? *Wife?* Could sweep right in the moment she arrived.

Jamie shoved that aside. Shoved aside worry over where she was going to sleep tonight. And shoved open the door, nearly hitting Devin with it, if his startled expression was anything to go by.

"Sorry," she muttered, ducking her head instinctively. "I'm just leaving."

But he was between her and the hall door, and when she forced herself to lift her eyes, he was smiling that boyish, engaging grin that seemed both at odds with and perfect on his rugged face.

"Surely you don't have to be at work just yet. You must have time to eat." He gestured at the table that was the central feature of the room, its entire surface crammed with covered dishes. "They say breakfast is the most important meal of the day," he coaxed. "Share it with me?"

"I..." Oh geez—how did anyone ever say no to him? He

probably always got everything he wanted. "Okay. Thank you," she added after a moment, remembering her manners.

He pulled out a chair for her. Who did that anymore? Certainly no one had ever done it for her before. Then he began taking the covers off the plates. "What would you like? Eggs? Bacon? Pancakes? French toast? Fruit?"

"What did you do?" Jamie asked, stunned at the array. And he was only half done. "Order everything on the menu?"

He looked at the table, then back at her. "...Yes?" He put the covers on a room service cart nearby and stood, his hands on his hips, looking at the table. "I didn't know what you'd want." As if simply ordering everything was the most natural and obvious solution in the world.

It was Jamie's turn to hesitate, overcome with confusion. No one had ever done anything that sweet for her before. Finally, she found her voice and said, "Eggs and toast would be nice, thank you." She didn't think she could eat anything more substantial.

Forcing her frozen muscles to move, she reached for the nearest plate of eggs—scrambled, good enough—and mutely accepted the toast and juice he offered her, this time without the litany of choices.

He sat down opposite her and pulled the nearest plate to him, for all the world as if it didn't matter which he took. For several minutes, they ate in silence. Jamie wasn't sure which she was more aware of—the pressing need to make some kind of conversation to break the awkward silence or the necessity of eating and getting out of there as quickly as she could. Not only did she not have the slightest idea what to do with herself in his presence, but she was terrified that she'd do something she didn't mean to but desperately wanted to. Like ask him how long he was going to be in Tahoe. Or how often he visited. Or if he'd hug her again—she'd felt so safe and secure in his embrace...

Yeah, she definitely needed to get out of there. Besides, she still had to get her car towed and a whole host of other things done. So many that her head reeled if she let herself think beyond the most immediate ones. If she didn't make some calls now, it might have to wait until she got off work that night. She had no idea what the break and lunch rules might be like here. And if she couldn't call until tonight, there was no way she'd get her car before tomorrow, and…

As if reading her mind—and oh my God, was she in trouble if he could—Devin said, "I made some calls last night. A repair place I know in town will pick up your car as soon as the road is clear and take it to their shop. I hope that's okay? I thought you might be too busy to deal with it today."

Realizing she looked far too much like a startled guppy, Jamie snapped her mouth shut. She quashed her first instinct—a semi-articulate "how dare you?" And the second—to tell him she could take care of herself, dammit. And managed to remind herself that she did not, in fact, know when she'd be able to deal with it and he was only try to be helpful. It wasn't his fault she couldn't afford his help.

"Thank you," she said, hoping she didn't sound like a teenager forced to be grudgingly grateful for what she was given. "But could you just have them leave it in the hotel parking lot?"

For a moment, he looked at her as if she'd grown a second head, and she thought, mortification turning her stomach hot and killing her appetite, that she'd have to actually say she couldn't afford to fix Maggie. If she was very *very* lucky, she might earn enough to repair it before the hotel ordered her to get her old junker out of their hoity-toity parking lot. Maybe.

Then he blinked and said, "Sure. I'll have Jerry bring it over after he runs the diagnostics." Before she could object, he added, "Might as well find out what's wrong with it first. There's no charge for that part."

Her cheeks were hot with embarrassment, but she hurriedly agreed, knowing it could have been so much worse. Then, partly for an excuse to look away from his too-kind eyes, she dug her car keys out of her purse and handed them to him. "Guess this Jerry person will need these."

"They'd help, I'm sure," he said easily, taking the keys with fingers that burned where they brushed hers. "Still got the keycard for the room?"

She flushed painfully—she hadn't known she could get any more embarrassed or any redder—and fished that out from where it had fallen to the bottom of her purse.

"Good," he said, completely focused on his coffee, as if he didn't see her trying to hand it to him. "I'll probably be here when you finish work today, but if by some chance I'm not, you can let yourself in. If Jerry gets the keys back to me by then, I'll leave them on the table for you. If not... you'll have a place to wait."

He finally looked up and caught her gaping at him with her mouth open again. At least she didn't have food in it! In fact, she wasn't sure she could eat a single bite more—her chest was entirely too full.

"Besides," he added when she couldn't find any words, his eyes kind again, "I'm going to have to get my license back from you somehow." His smile ensured there was no sting in the reminder of her accusation—an utterly ridiculous one, it was becoming ever more apparent. She... had no idea what to say, to that or anything else. What she really wanted to do was apologize for thinking so poorly of him, but she couldn't even begin to figure out how to broach the subject. Once again, he took pity on her, asking, "So, which of the boutiques are you working in? There are four of them, if memory serves. Or maybe five now."

"Um... The Silver Queen," she said, and only then thought to wonder why he wanted to know. *Stop it,* she told herself sternly, *not everyone has an ulterior motive, and second-guessing his is what left you wanting to apologize in the first place.* Still, the change of subject was a perfect excuse to get out of there before she did something she'd regret. Like throw herself into his arms. Or just sit there, staring at his face, which only got more handsome and more perfect the longer she looked at it. "Speaking of… I've got to get going," she said, glancing at her watch for show.

He smiled. "Have to make a good first impression," he said, sounding rather distracted as he pulled out his phone. No doubt he had business to attend to and didn't need to waste any more time on her.

Standing, she brushed at her clothes ruefully. "Much as I can, anyway."

"Jamie," he said, and she looked up to see that his eyes were on her, not the phone. He smiled again, an intimate smile just for her. "You look wonderful."

Bright red once more, she stammered her way out the door, both relieved and disappointed when it clicked closed behind her. In the elevator, she put both hands to her hot face and willed the blush to go away. She didn't really have to leave immediately to get to work on time, but she'd really needed to escape his overwhelming presence. And more importantly, the overwhelming urge to just throw herself in his arms and beg him to fix everything. And never let her go.

Wanting someone else to take care of her was something she'd grown out of long ago. And for good reason too, she reminded herself sternly. It wasn't safe to put your fate in someone else's hands. Nor your heart.

And why did she keep thinking about her heart? Or a life with Devin? He was just a remarkably nice man who'd decided to help her out. He hadn't offered her forever, and she wouldn't have believed him if he had. Jamie snorted aloud and was never more grateful to be in an empty elevator. He hadn't offered anything, actually, which was just as well, as she'd probably have jumped at it. He was, she decided, far too handsome for her well-being or peace of mind. It was just as well that she'd be getting her living situation sorted out today, at least temporarily, once she talked to her new boss and straightened out the confusion over getting her a room. After that, she probably wouldn't see him again.

What an utterly depressing thought.

Jamie did a couple of laps around the hotel's public spaces to calm down and get a feel for the layout. Gift shop, gift shop, boutique, restaurant, restaurant, restaurant... In the process, she passed through the lobby a couple of times, earning herself a nasty look from the jerk behind the reception desk, who was either still on duty or back on duty. If he was still on duty from the night before, she didn't fault him for his bad mood *now*, though it was no excuse for being an ass last night. She ignored him.

Finally, five minutes early by her watch, she took a deep breath, braced herself, and walked into The Silver Queen, trying desperately to project calm and confidence and not sheer despair over the workaday clothes she was wearing and her far-from-sophisticated hairstyle.

"Be with you in a minute, dear," the lady behind the counter called before going back to her phone conversation. She was an older lady of indeterminate years, her frosted hair swept into a complicated knot. Her outfit probably cost more than Jamie's entire wardrobe.

The bottom dropped out of Jamie's stomach. She'd done all her interviewing by phone—if she'd seen either the woman or the boutique, she'd never have dared apply. Even with all her luggage at hand and her entire wardrobe to choose from, she wouldn't fit in here. Hell, even if some fairy godmother bought out the store for her, so she could dress the part, she still wouldn't be the least bit suited for it. Elegant, she was not.

She squeezed her hands tightly together where they were instinctively clasped behind her so she wouldn't touch and possibly damage anything and told herself to buck up. She could do this. She had to. She had no place to go and no car to get there. She'd earned this job with her resume, her references, and her interview, and by God, she could absolutely do it.

Though she wasn't entirely sure she believed her own pep talk, it did give Jamie enough courage to say, "Mrs. Nevins?" once the older woman hung up.

"Oh, call me Cora, dear." She came out from behind the sales counter, and seeing her from head to toe only reinforced Jamie's impression that she was an extremely sophisticated lady. But her expression was friendly, and she was already reaching out to take Jamie's hands. "You must be Jamie. I've been so looking forward to meeting you. You must be quite exhausted if you drove up in that horrible storm yesterday. Come, let's put your bag in the back and I'll give you the tour. Not that there's much to see in our little shop."

And she continued in that vein, sounding very much like Jamie's grandmother. The tour did not, as promised, take long, and before she knew it, Jamie found herself sitting in the back room ("We'll hear the bell if anyone comes in, dear. Not that they're likely to this early.") with a mug of hot tea warming her fingers, telling Cora everything. All about the awful drive in whiteout conditions and poor Maggie and how everything she owned was stuck out there with the car. She was very vague about her rescuer—she couldn't think of any way to explain Devin (or where she'd spent the previous night) that wouldn't make her sound like the kind of woman she most definitely was not.

"Oh my dear! How horrible! How frightening that must have been. I can't imagine." She patted Jamie's hand again, shaking her head sympathetically. "You might have called, you know, and told me you couldn't make it in today. I would have understood. In fact, we don't really need you here until tomorrow. I don't know who it was that called and told you to come earlier, but I'm very cross about it."

Looking at her, it was hard to believe that Cora was ever cross about anything. Jamie couldn't believe she'd thought the woman unapproachable. Despite the trouble this whole mess had caused her—if she could have waited until after the snowstorm to come up, perhaps Maggie wouldn't have broken down—she couldn't help but smile into her tea at Cora's "cross" expression, which reminded her a bit of her three-year-old nephew's. Besides, if she hadn't driven up yesterday, she'd never have met Devin, and that thought made her stomach sink ridiculously inside her.

"In fact, I distinctly recall telling Andre that we would need a room for you starting *tomorrow* night. I don't know how anyone could have mixed that up."

Jamie's smile fled. No room until tomorrow night? For half a second, she thought about just asking if Cora could change the reservations for her. But then reality intruded with the memory of that snobby jerk at the desk saying there were no available rooms in the hotel. Probably none in all of Tahoe, it being nearly Christmas and all. Not that she could have afforded one if one *were* by some miracle available. Lord, where was she going to sleep? In Maggie? Assuming the car could even be towed by then? She'd freeze. The lobby was out—not only would she get kicked out in no time flat, she certainly couldn't afford to be seen acting like a bag lady in her own place of employment. Talk about reflecting badly on the boutique! No one would walk into this shop and buy anything from her if they'd seen her sleeping in the lobby the previous night. Perhaps there was some kind of all-night diner or something nearby. Though how she was going to get there, or back, or manage to look the least bit presentable for her first actual day on the job…

She struggled to hide her dismay. No matter how friendly Cora was, she was Jamie's boss and Jamie *really* needed the job, which meant she really needed to impress Cora.

Who was still talking, thankfully having missed Jamie's reaction to her revelation. "I'm terribly sorry about the mix-up. I'll certainly be having a talk with Andre and whoever called you. Bad enough we had to ask you to come before the holidays, but to get you here unnecessarily early…"

"It's no problem," Jamie lied, pleased to hear herself sound calm and unconcerned.

"Still," Cora said. "I despise putting people out, and asking you to move up here before Christmas is appallingly bad of us. Getting you up here a day early just makes it worse." She sighed. "If we hadn't had to let one of the shop assistants go, we wouldn't be in this pickle. I would normally never fire anyone right before Christmas, but it wasn't like I could just ignore the fact that she was brazenly stealing from us." She was talking mostly to herself, reaffirming the rightness of a decision she'd clearly not wanted to make despite the theft. Definitely a kind-hearted woman, Jamie thought, feeling a lot better about her new job, no matter how desperately worried she was about how she'd get through the next twenty-four hours. "And all that's neither here nor there," Cora said briskly, her attention coming back to Jamie. "Drink up, dear. And then you can head off. I'm sure you have a lot of things to deal with, with your car and all, so go on and I'll see you tomorrow morning."

"Tomorrow?" Jamie said, feeling all at sea. She obediently swallowed her lukewarm tea.

"Yes, tomorrow's soon enough to start. Go do what you need to do and come back then."

A few minutes later, Jamie walked out of the boutique feeling rather as if she'd been swept out the door by a whirlwind. A very kindly one, but…

Now what was she supposed to do?

The odor of cinnamon and icing drew her to a little shop that sold hot cinnamon rolls. It smelled like heaven and made her mouth water despite the worry roiling her stomach and despite having already eaten… perhaps not enough, given that she'd only been able to pick at her breakfast thanks to sheer nerves and Devin's presence. His wife or girlfriend or whatever must be thin as a rail—how could anyone eat when they could be looking at his handsome face across the table? While she was hesitating by the door—she really wanted one, but she *really* shouldn't—the couple she'd noticed the previous night, the ones she'd privately dubbed Mr. and Mrs. Claus, came out looking highly satisfied. Mrs. Claus smiled and waved at her, for all the world as if they knew each other. Mr. Claus *twinkled*. No other word for it.

Smiling, the world suddenly seeming a great deal brighter, Jamie walked in, ordered a plate full of cinnamon and sugar, and ate every bite without feeling the least bit guilty. Then, fortified by her second breakfast, or perhaps just hyped up on a sugar rush, she went back to the elevators, enduring the evil eye from the desk clerk again (what in the world was his problem?), and pushed the button for the penthouse.

Maybe he'd be gone. Maybe the suite would be empty. She didn't know if she was hoping it was or would be horrifically disappointed to find Devin gone.

She didn't have to find out, as he was right there when she slipped the keycard in the slot and pushed the door open. Sitting in one of the chairs by the windows, his legs crossed comfortably, talking on his cellphone.

Jamie headed quickly for her room, tiptoeing to make as little noise as possible. If she could have stopped breathing entirely, she would have. But Devin shook his head, waving her over to the other chair. He was nodding as if the person on the other end of the line could hear him doing it. Finally, whoever it was apparently stopped talking for a moment, and Devin said, "I understand. Not like we can wave a wand and change the weather. We'll get together after Christmas. Love you."

Jamie felt as if her whole body was drooping with disappointment. She'd assumed he had a girlfriend or wife—a man like him couldn't possibly not already be snapped up—but hearing him express his love was another thing entirely. *Oh good grief, girl,* the part of her that usually had more sense grumbled. *You've known him less than a day!*

Yeah, but….

Devin put his cellphone on the table and smiled at her. "Sorry about that. I love my mother dearly, but she could talk the hind leg off a mule." Jamie felt instantly relieved. Then stupid. What difference did it make whether he was taken or not? Either way, he was well out of her league and wouldn't even be looking twice at her if he hadn't had to rescue her off the side of the road. "You're back early," he added, looking concerned. "Everything okay?"

"Fine," she said, surprised at his worried tone. It sounded like he actually cared whether or not her first day had gone well. Why would it matter to him whether or not she still had a job? He'd known her less than a day.

Yeah, but….

He looked at her expectantly, obviously wanting more than a bare bones answer.

"Apparently, I'm not needed until tomorrow, so I have a chance to work out some of the things that need doing." Except the car was taken care of, at least for now, and she wasn't sure what the rest of those things were. Especially not since looking at Devin had driven most coherent thought from her brain. Embarrassed, she grabbed a thought at random. "I should look for an apartment."

He grinned. "I doubt anyone's showing any today."

"On account of Christmas?" Jamie said skeptically—in her experience, apartment managers with open units would show them anytime.

His grin widened. "On account of the snow. Look outside—the whole city is shut down, or nearly so. If you can't get there on foot, you can't get there."

He was silent a moment as she looked out the frost-framed window. Part of her quailed at the sight of all the snow blanketing the landscape, leaving very little moving down below and certainly no traffic. But the larger part was awed by the beauty. Snow covered everything, lying like thick icing on the ground and roofs and spun into delicate filigree in every nook and cranny. It was gorgeous.

"So no long-term housing resolution today," Devin said after a minute, during which she'd felt his eyes on her but couldn't turn, a little afraid of what might be in them. "What about tonight? Did they get you a room?"

Was it her imagination or did he sound ambivalent about that, almost as if he didn't want her to have a place of her own? As if he was reluctant to have her leave?

Or was it just her own reluctance she was projecting on him? "No," she admitted, holding her breath as she waited for his response.

"How convenient."

"Convenient?" Jamie said sharply, uncertain which of them he thought it convenient for that she had no place to say. Or perhaps he meant it as an accusation. Women must throw themselves at him all the time, some of them obviously and unscrupulously. Her cheeks burned at being lumped in with that kind of person.

"Well, yes," he said, sounding nothing but pleased. "My family can't make it because of the snow. I have a room. You need a room." He waited a moment, and when she didn't say anything, added, "Convenient," as if it were a done deal.

"I can't just—" Even if she wanted nothing more.

"Of course you can," Devin said, as if it were silly to object. "It's already paid for. If you don't use that room, no one will, and that would be a complete waste, don't you think?"

Well, when it was put that way… "I suppose it would be."

Devin smiled brilliantly, and Jamie was helpless to do anything but return it. She ought to have felt reluctant or embarrassed to be so reliant on the kindness of this near stranger, but all she could feel was relief. And anticipation. Now she could spend more time with him. She tried to tamp down the triumphant feeling—after all, he'd offered her a room, not his companionship.

Well, that effectively drowned her delight in ice water.

Suddenly, as if that dose of harsh reality had invited others, she realized that the state of the roads almost certainly meant that Maggie would be staying beside the highway for now. However good Devin's mechanic might be, he couldn't tow her car through several feet of snow. And no car meant no luggage. Which meant no clothes. Dismay filled her. She couldn't possibly go to work in the same clothes tomorrow—that really would be the kiss of death for her job, no matter how kind Cora was.

"What?" Devin leaned toward her, looking concerned again.

Jamie was surprised at his intuition—he seemed almost able to read her mind. Which, given the tenor of some of her thoughts around him, would be… unfortunate. She shook off that thought in favor of something more immediately important—clothing for tomorrow, and not from any of the places in the hotel. The boutiques (including the one she'd be working at) were too expensive and the gift shops didn't have anything suitable. "You know Tahoe—are there any clothing stores nearby that might be open?" She hesitated, then added, "Inexpensive ones," her cheeks burning. Not that she was ashamed at having to be frugal—everything she owned, she'd worked for, and she was proud of that. But a man like him, with his money… she didn't imagine he had any idea what it was like to have to be careful. Come to that, did he even know what "inexpensive" meant? His concept of it and hers were probably very different things.

"Clothing stores, yes. We're a couple of blocks from Heavenly Village—it'd be a bit of a slog through the snow, but reachable. And with the hotels near it, at least some of the shops are likely to be open, even with the roads impassable. Inexpensive? Depends on what you mean." Now he was the one to hesitate. "If it's work clothes for tomorrow you're needing, would you let me help?"

Jamie was already shaking her head.

Devin held up his hands as if surrendering, but what he said was, "It's *Christmas*," as if that made all the difference. And Jamie must have been addled because a large part of her wanted to believe it really did. "I'd like to help, and you can't think I don't have the money to do it. To be frank, you could buy everything that caught your eye, and it wouldn't even make a dent in my walking-around money." He eyed her hopefully.

Hopefully! Jamie felt like she'd fallen down a rabbit hole. The only thing she really understood was what her answer had to be. "I can't."

"No strings attached," he said again. His perfect lips opened once more, as if he were going to continue arguing, but then he seemed to think better of it and instead sat back, waiting with every appearance of patience while she looked at him, thinking hard.

No strings attached. He'd said it before... and apparently meant it. There'd been no pressure of any sort. Devin had been nothing but helpful and supportive. If it was an act, he was committed to it, but as she looked at him, staring into his dark eyes, she couldn't believe that it was. He seemed amazingly straightforward—what you see is what you get. And what she saw she liked very much.

"I'll pay you back later," she said finally, knowing her concession was less a considered decision than a foregone conclusion. She had to have clothes for work, and even if Maggie and her luggage were right there, she wouldn't have had the right ones. But she didn't have the money to buy something better—not and still have enough to put down first and last on an apartment. Let alone get Maggie fixed. If Maggie were working (and the roads clear), Jamie could take herself off to a thrift store and probably score some good outfits—she'd learned to do wonders with hand-me-downs—but if Maggie were working, she wouldn't be in this mess.

She also wouldn't have met Devin, and she was beginning to think that would have been a crying shame.

"Done," Devin said, but she could tell he didn't mean to hold her to her end of the bargain. Well then, he'd be learning something about Jamie Drake. She always paid her debts.

Somehow.

Devin stood up as if he'd just been waiting for her okay to get moving and said, "Get your coat—we're going out on the town."

The streets were snowpacked and slogging to Heavenly Village was a workout and a half, but the shopping area was open. Mostly. And there were others out and about, shuffling through deep snow in fancy boots, laughing and throwing snowballs, and just generally acting like children.

Before Jamie managed to get Devin out of the shops, he'd bought her far too much—several outfits for work, new boots that didn't let the wet in five minutes after she stepped out the door, a new winter coat that wasn't threadbare. He had the shops send everything but the boots and coat straight back to the hotel. Those, he had her put on, stuffing her old winter gear into a bag and sending *that* back. She couldn't say her frozen feet didn't appreciate his thoughtfulness.

After the first purchase, Jamie knew she was already in too deep—no way he hadn't spent more than a week's wages on her in just that one transaction. Devin didn't let her see any of the sales slips he signed; nor did he give her an opportunity to look at the price tags on the clothes he encouraged her to pick out. By the time she convinced him to stop, he'd spent more than she could repay for many months to come. But he put his arm around her and told her not to let it worry her, and somehow, it didn't. His arm felt right around her shoulders, the warmth of his body comforting even through her new coat.

When he suggested that they rent skis and boots and take the gondola from the Village up to the Heavenly Mountain ski resort, she agreed. There was nothing to be done today about her car, her job, where she'd live, or how she'd pay him back. She looked into his laughing face and did something she hadn't done since she was a child—she enjoyed the day without a thought for tomorrow. And she trusted. Trusted him.

The day was magical. Skiing with Devin, slowly regaining rusty skills—she hadn't skied since she was a kid, as it was too expensive and any money she had was better used for other things—and relying on his strong arm to steady her. Jamie fell entirely too many times, but the powder was soft and Devin was always nearby to help her get up and brush off the snow. And if his hands lingered, well, she enjoyed that too.

They had hot chocolate at the lodge to warm their fingers and their insides and sat laughing over it until it brought smiles to the faces of the other skiers. Later, after they'd returned to the hotel and she'd changed out of her damp jeans and into one of the gorgeous outfits he'd talked her into, he took her to dinner at the amazing restaurant in the very top of the hotel. It had 360-degree views of the lake and surrounding mountains, food that was melt-in-her-mouth delicious, and a hushed atmosphere that would have been intimidating if Jamie were on her own. Not that she'd ever be able to eat at a place like that under normal circumstances. Devin had ordered for them both without her ever seeing a menu, and she didn't want to see it—she didn't want to know how much it cost, didn't want to think about how many hours she'd have to work to pay for it. She wanted to end her day in the dream where this was her life and Devin was her own.

He kissed her when they got back to the suite, his mouth firm, lips hot and clinging sweetly to hers. Jamie wanted to melt in his arms and never come out. But reality intruded, as it must, and she slowly drew herself away. She had work in the morning, and she'd never been the kind of girl to be swept off her feet. No matter how much Devin made her wish she was. He looked regretful but didn't argue, just gave her one last kiss—a chaste one on the forehead—and wished her good night.

She took the warmth of his embrace and the heat in his eyes with her into her room and hugged it close as she climbed into the ridiculously comfortable bed in nothing but her skin. It felt sinful, no matter how necessary. But none of the stores they'd been in that day sold either nightgowns or underwear (nor would she have wanted to shop for such personal things with Devin never more than an arm's length away). So those garments had been rinsed out and left over the heater to dry and Jamie was naked in bed. Thinking of Devin and their magical day. She fell asleep with a smile on her face.

Even waking up to her alarm the next morning didn't dash ice water on her dreams. She might only be up because she had to go to work, but some of the starry-eyed delight of the previous day still clung to her. Her new clothing fit wonderfully, and she didn't have to think (yet) about how much it cost because there were no tags anywhere to be found. And though her hair was still not done up in anything like a sophisticated style, the rest of her definitely passed muster.

Jamie hesitated for several minutes on her side of the connecting door, almost afraid to walk out into that shared room and find out if the Devin of yesterday was real or only something she'd dreamed. Eventually, the desire to see him overwhelmed her nerves and she went through.

The smile that spread across his face when he saw her warmed her clear through. "Good morning."

"Morning," she mumbled, suddenly feeling shy.

He didn't say anything for a moment, and when she shoved

away the ridiculous bashfulness and forced her eyes up to his face, there was something bright and joyful there that was almost as dazzling as the brilliant sunlight streaming through the window.

Devin came across the room to her as if he couldn't do anything else and took her hands. "I'd like very much to kiss you," he said, as if he were asking permission.

"I'd like that," Jamie said, feeling bashful all over again.

His lips were just as soft and warm as on the previous night, his embrace just as strong. She felt so safe and secure in his arms... She felt like she could stay there forever.

But then someone's stomach growled, and they broke apart, laughing.

"Here," Devin said, still chuckling. "I've ordered breakfast."

There were just a handful of covered dishes on the table this morning—some kind of omelet for him, scrambled eggs and toast for her. Jamie's heart filled at the realization that he'd remembered what she liked—the gesture just as sweet as filling the table with food the other morning. He pulled out a chair for her, then took his own seat and smiled at her again before tucking into his breakfast. For a minute, Jamie couldn't bring herself to even pick up her fork. She was overcome by the warm, comfortable feeling of sitting across the table from him. As if they'd done it a hundred times before in the past and would do it a thousand times in the future. As if looking at his face across the breakfast table every morning was something she was destined to do.

After a couple of minutes, he looked up, perhaps confused by her stillness, and raised one eyebrow in question. Jamie didn't have to force a smile—he was just so cute with that quizzical look on his face—but she wasn't about to answer. She didn't have the foggiest idea what she'd say. She forced her eyes down to her plate and managed to put away nearly half her food before her gaze was drawn to him once again. This time, he didn't notice and she was able to look at him uninterrupted.

Somewhere along the line, he'd stopped being the rich, handsome stranger who'd insisted on lavishing his largess on her and become just Devin. Not that there was anything "just" about him. She'd never met a man so warm and caring, or one she wanted to spend every waking moment with as much as she did him.

Forcefully shaking off the feeling as best she could—no matter what she wanted or dreamed of, her job awaited—Jamie set her fork down and stood. "I have to be going," she said, wondering briefly if he was going to tease her about the time, which was much later than she'd left him the previous morning. Then she'd been anxious in Devin's presence; now she didn't want to leave it.

"If you must," he said, offering her a smile. Was he reluctant to see her go or was that just wishful thinking? "I'll see you later."

"Thanks for breakfast." Jamie leaned down and kissed Devin softly before heading out the door.

While in the elevator on the way down, she had plenty of time to think about how ridiculous that instinctive movement had been. And how telling. But also about how natural and comfortable it had felt. Maybe there was something there. Maybe there was something between them that could last. Sure, he had money—boy, did he—but he seemed unimpressed by it and unconcerned about her lack of it. She'd never met anyone like him: a man who'd give without expecting anything in return, who anticipated her needs and did everything he could to satisfy them, who seemed to genuinely like her for herself.

Work was surprisingly easy. Perhaps it was the light crowds, the snow keeping most everyone away. Or perhaps it was the lingering feeling that her feet were being swept along on a rose-tinted cloud. Whatever it was, she enjoyed every minute of it. Her boss was just as kind and friendly as she'd been the previous morning and looked approvingly at her new outfit, which fit in perfectly in the fancy shop. And if the customers were a bit spoiled, a bit demanding, well, that was fine too. Perhaps it was her new clothes, or perhaps it was Jamie's good mood, which nothing seemed capable of blunting, but none of them treated her like she was something they'd have to scrape off their shoe later, an experience she'd "enjoyed" in some previous jobs.

All in all, the day was going marvelously. Which made what happened just before closing time a rude shock, like being dunked headfirst in the icy lake.

When she saw the desk clerk who'd been so incredibly rude to her walk into the store, she thought nothing of it. She wouldn't have thought he made enough to shop there—probably only the executives did—but perhaps he was splurging on someone for Christmas. Or perhaps he was coming to apologize for his behavior the other night.

When he came charging up to the counter, she stepped back instinctively and glanced toward the back room. Cora had gone in there to make some phone calls, and the door was firmly closed. No help there. Not that she ought to be looking for any—she'd dealt with plenty of pissed off customers in the past; she wasn't any kind of shrinking violet.

Jamie braced her shoulders and stepped back to the counter. Some people moved like that—like they were conquering ground instead of just covering it. It didn't have to mean anything.

"Can I help you?" she asked in her best customer service voice.

For a moment, he said nothing, but his eyes travelled contemptuously up and down her, leaving Jamie feeling like she needed to scrub every inch of herself with lye. He sneered. "I see now why my girlfriend was fired. Wanted to play at having a job, did you? And you didn't care who had to pay for your little whim. You're the sort of woman who always gets what she wants; you get everything handed to you, no questions asked." He leaned across the counter, practically spitting his vitriol in her face. "You don't know what it's like to have to work for a living, to claw and fight just to get by. Putting an honest, hard-working woman out of a job is nothing to you. You don't care that we're only just getting by on the pittance I get paid for working my ass off for that slave driver. That means nothing to a woman like you."

"I beg your pardon?" Jamie stuttered, barely able to get the words out. Adrenalin flooded her, and she didn't know if it was fear or rage that shook her whole body. How dared he? How dared he when she'd fought for every little thing she had? When she'd crawl on her knees over broken glass for a job half as good as his?

"Come off it, you bitch," he snarled. "Don't pretend you're something special. We all know exactly what you are. You only got the job because the owner of the hotel gave it to you, and we all know why. Don't pretend you don't know what I'm talking about." He grabbed her wrist, his grip grinding the bones together. "We all know you spent the last two nights with him, you dirty—"

It was all Devin could do not to whistle in the elevator. If it had been empty, he wouldn't have stifled the urge, but as it was, he kept his eyes on his reflection in the doors and his cheerfulness to himself.

It was extremely difficult. Especially when the eyes of the female half of the couple sharing the elevator with him caught his and she twinkled at him. He didn't think he'd ever actually seen someone *twinkle* before, but that was the only word for it. He couldn't help but smile back. Might have smiled even if he weren't already in such a good mood—outside of a Christmas display, he doubted a couple existed that looked more like Mr. and Mrs. Claus.

Still smiling, he shifted his gaze back to his own reflection. It wouldn't do to stare, even if he was wondering whether they hired themselves out and if they were already booked for the holidays. Jamie would just *love* them. After a moment of looking at himself, he grimaced. Not only was he grinning like a lunatic, but he looked like a teenager gussied up for his first date.

He tugged at his tie, first just loosening the knot, then yanking it down, pulling the tie off over his head, and stuffing it in his pocket. Then he undid the top button of his dress shirt. Better. At least now he didn't look like someone had dressed him to make a good impression but succeeded only in making him look like some kind of tailor's dummy.

Jamie'd be more comfortable if he wasn't so formal anyway. Warmth filled him at the thought of her—closely watching him over dinner, as if afraid she'd pick up the wrong fork; walking through stores with her hands clasped behind her, as if brushing up against any of the merchandise might soil it; nervously modeling a dress for him, as if she needed his approval to decide it was acceptable. He ought not, he knew, find her uncertainty attractive, but really, she was capable of anything she put her mind to, including fitting into any environment she found herself in. She just didn't know it yet. And that untapped potential was very attractive.

Hell, who was he kidding? *Jamie* was incredibly attractive. Everything about her, from her determination to succeed on her own merits to her fiery hair to her equally fiery temper. She only got more attractive and more perfect every moment he spent with her.

The day had been deadly dull without her. Devin had tried to get some work done, and did manage to make several phone calls, but anything that didn't have to do with Jamie just didn't seem worth his attention. He'd suffered through an extremely boring phone conference before admitting that he just couldn't keep his mind on anything other than her and giving up the rest of that day's business as a lost cause.

Instead, he'd checked on her car, called around to find out which of the nearby restaurants were open for business, then spent an inordinate amount of time getting dressed to take her out for dinner. Devin didn't usually spend a lot of time on his appearance—he was who he was, and if he'd never be pretty-boy handsome, he did well enough for himself. But he couldn't help but want to look his best for Jamie. Besides, he had to really shine to look like he belonged with her.

And look how that had worked out—strangled by his own necktie and buttoned up like a ruddy choirboy. He really had to stop overthinking this.

But it was so damned important.

All the day had really proven to Devin was that he didn't want to spend even one more moment without her. If Jamie weren't so blasted independent, he'd have suggested that she ditch the job and just spend the week, or at least the day, with him. Better yet, spend all her days with him.

Well hell, if she weren't so blasted independent, she wouldn't have been Jamie and he wouldn't have been half so interested in her. Which was all well and good, but it didn't help in the least in knowing how to convince her.

And surely it was silly to be thinking about forever with her when he'd only just met her a couple of days ago.

"She'd be lucky to have you," a friendly voice said, and Devin turned, startled, to find the Mrs. Claus-alike regarding him with a smile.

"Pardon?" he said, wondering how she could possibly have guessed what he was thinking. Surely not.

"Handsome fellow like you," she said, smiling merrily up at him, "of course she'll say yes." She reached up with a grandmother's certainty and straightened his collar. Which Devin realized he'd been tugging at as if it were choking him. Perhaps it wasn't surprising she'd been able to guess his thoughts were on a woman.

"I…" The elevator dinged just then, saving him. Devin held the door open for the older couple, receiving a grandmotherly pat on the cheek from Mrs. Claus by way of thanks and a commiserating nod from Mr. Claus, who seemed to find his spouse amusing. But then, he looked like a jolly fellow who probably found everything amusing.

Adrift on a sea of confusion, Devin nearly allowed the elevator doors to close with him inside. He realized at the last minute that it was at the lobby and he wanted out there.

By the time he stepped out, the old couple were gone. Devin shook off the odd exchange, and the even odder feeling it had given him, and headed for the boutique Jamie was working in. He checked his watch and increased his speed—she should be off work any minute.

The moment he spotted her through the glass wall of her little fishbowl, warmth suffused his chest and climbed nimbly into his head. Just looking at her made his heart beat faster and his breath leave all in a rush. It was love, he knew, and it wasn't silly at all.

A moment later, as he came closer, he realized she was white as a sheet and broke into a jog. Who was the little weasel talking to her, leaning across the counter and clearly scaring her half to death? Devin was going to twist the man into a pretzel.

He dashed into the boutique just in time to see the bastard grab Jamie and call her something unforgivable. A different kind of heat filled him and turned his vision a deep crimson that throbbed with the pounding of his heart. Devin grabbed the man—that nasty little desk clerk from the first night—by the back of the collar and shook him violently.

"I can see," he said through clenched teeth, "that you're not capable of learning your lesson. Time to have a chat with your boss."

He dragged the little weasel out of the boutique by his collar, scarcely noticing how the man tried to dig in his heels and not hearing a word of his objections. The only thing he could see was Jamie's horrified expression.

"Are you okay, dear?"

Blinking rapidly, Jamie turned toward her boss, almost afraid to see her expression. If Cora had heard what the desk clerk was saying…. But Cora only looked concerned, which was almost worse because Jamie was this close to breaking down. "Fine," she said quickly, looking away before she could start crying. "I'm, it's…. fine."

"I suppose," Cora said doubtfully, then audibly perked up. "It would be, wouldn't it? Mr. Stanton is dealing with it. He always takes care of his employees. Those that deserve it, anyway," she added darkly.

"Yes," Jamie said without listening to herself, "I… Excuse me." Without waiting for a response, she dashed out of the boutique. She had no idea where she was going. Just away.

When she started noticing her surroundings again, she was tucked into the nook under the main staircase, a little cubbyhole that contained two chairs and a tiny table. Good. No one would see her there.

She was huddled in a chair with her knees drawn up to her chest, and she probably couldn't look more like the poor little girl from the wrong side of the tracks that she was if she tried. So much for the sophisticated clothes and snobby job—put her under pressure, and Jamie reverted to who she'd always been.

And she always would.

Even if dating was on offer—and she doubted now that it ever had been—she couldn't go out with a man like Devin. The world he lived in just wasn't her world and she wasn't capable of faking it. Yeah, she'd thought maybe she could, maybe it didn't matter, when she didn't know who he was. When he was just some dude with more money in his pockets than she'd ever had in her life.

Ha! "Just" that. Only that. She didn't know how she could have thought it wouldn't matter. Or that he could even be interested in her in the first place. Even if he didn't have more money than God, he obviously had far more money than her. She was so far out of his frame of reference, he wouldn't even have noticed her if her car hadn't been blocking his lane. He'd been doing his good deed for Christmas, nothing more.

It made her cheeks burn just to think of it. Being someone's charity case, letting him buy her things and put her up and take care of her. Nothing good ever came of that sort of thing. There were always strings.

Even if he didn't tie them on there, other people would. Other people would make assumptions, make judgments. Even if there was something more between them than charity, something that could be fought for, how could she stand knowing what other people thought of her? How could she stand people looking at her like that?

Especially when she could never be sure that they weren't right. What if she was just seduced by the idea of an easy life, of someone else dealing with her problems for her? What if it wasn't love after all?

"Dear? Are you okay?"

Jamie shied violently, startled by the sudden appearance of someone else in her hiding space. Not so hidden, apparently. When she looked up, it was to see the elderly lady who looked like the sweetest, kindliest stand-in for Mrs. Claus anyone could ever want. Jamie sniffed, tears battering at the backs of her eyes, nearly undone by the woman's concerned and sympathetic look.

"Oh, you poor dear." Mrs. Claus sat beside her and took her hand, patting it gently. "What a horrible way to be treated, and right before Christmas, too!"

"I..." Jamie stopped, hearing her voice break. She closed her eyes, clinging to Mrs. Claus's hand, and fought herself under some kind of control. Finally, she opened them again, hoping the tears were at bay now, though they felt like they could come roaring back any second. "I don't remember seeing you…" Mortified, she couldn't finish.

"Oh, don't worry your head about *that*. I find my way into all sorts of places I'm not supposed to be." It was said in the sweetest voice imaginable, and it took Jamie a moment to absorb what the woman had actually said. She did a double take, then another one upon seeing the woman's crafty smile. She still looked like someone's kindly old grandma, but one with a seriously steely backbone and a nose for trouble. "And don't you worry about your young man. Mr. C will find him."

"My young man?" Jamie said, more confused than she'd ever been. She felt like she was playing catch-up to this woman, who steamrolled ahead so vigorously that even managing to dangle along behind was a triumph.

"Such a handsome fellow," Mrs. C gushed, patting Jamie's hand again. "And with such wonderful resources at his fingertips. I don't mind telling you, dear," she said conspiratorially, "that's the wonderful thing about marrying someone who doesn't need to worry about where his next meal is coming from."

"What is?" Jamie asked, lost. There didn't seem to be any doubt that Mrs. C was talking about Devin, but Jamie couldn't imagine how this little old lady could know who he was, or who Jamie was, or put the two of them together in any meaningful way. And yet, listening to her left Jamie feeling strongly that she spoke nothing but truth and only a fool would ignore a word she said.

"Why, all the good and wonderful things you can do!" Mrs. C said, as if it were the most obvious thing in the world. "Not just for yourself or your friends, but for people you've never met before and never will again. My life would be so much poorer if I couldn't help people who've lost their way find the right path again, the one that'll lead them to their best and brightest future."

"I… don't think I understand," Jamie admitted. It was all too much, and she felt the tears prickling at the back of her eyes again. When she closed them, a tear squeezed out, running down her cheek.

"No matter, dear," Mrs. C said, patting her hand again. "You will."

There was a sudden commotion, and Jamie found herself wrapped in strong arms and pressed to a hard chest that smelled so familiar that more tears escaped her. Devin. Warmth and safety surrounded her, infusing the very air she breathed. She clung to him, her arms as tight around his waist as his were around her.

"God, Jamie, I'm *so* sorry!" His breath stirred the loose hair against her neck. "That jackass should never have been working here, and he never will again. Or anywhere in Tahoe, if I have any say in the matter."

Instinctively, Jamie started shaking her head. "No," she said, pushing back against his strong embrace. "He was an ass, but no one deserves to be—"

"He does," Devin said adamantly. He let her leave his arms, but entwined his fingers with hers, almost as if he couldn't bear to let her go. "A guy like that, you think he hasn't done something like that to someone else? Besides, he's as much of a thief as his girlfriend, and we've got the security tapes to prove it. My fool of a general manager was just too softhearted to fire them both before the holidays. If I'd known any of that was going on, I'd have put a stop to it immediately."

"It *is* Christmas," Jamie said hesitantly. Despite the desk clerk's behavior, she did feel for him and his girl, out of a job at that time of year. But she couldn't pretend it wasn't a relief to know she would never have to see him again.

"Yes." Devin's smile transformed his face. "It is, and against all the odds, I've somehow found myself a Christmas angel."

Abashed, Jamie looked away. "Don't tease."

He tucked an errant lock of hair behind her ear with a gentleness that made her heart ache. "I'm not," he said earnestly.

He might have been about to say something else, but Jamie suddenly realized… "Where's Mrs. C?"

"Who?"

"Little old lady, looks just like—"

"Mrs. Claus?" Devin finished. "You ran into her too?"

"She was just here," Jamie said, confused. "Just before you came."

"I didn't see anyone but you." His warm fingers touched her face gently again, lightly skimming down her cheek to touch her lips. "Not sure I'll ever again be able to see anyone but you."

"No one but me?" Jamie asked, her thoughts confused but her heart filling with warmth as if it understood perfectly.

"Not in the whole world," Devin murmured, bending to kiss her. "Stay with me?"

"For how long?" Jamie's mouth said, on autopilot. The rest of her already knew the answer.

"For always."

He kissed her before she could answer. But then, she thought dreamily, he already knew it too.

Christmas Magic

Sandra Edwards

EVE Langdon lived a charmed life. She had the job of her dreams. A gorgeous high-rise apartment overlooking the river walk. And a bevy of friends who were always vying for her attention. But—

Something was missing. Something Eve couldn't quite put her finger on, but she knew it was absent just the same. And it often filled her heart with melancholy.

Ancient memories and not-so-distant regrets flooded her thoughts daily. She didn't need a prompt, but today—on Christmas Eve, of all days—fate had dropped a biting reminder right into her lap.

"I can't do this pitch," she said to her friend and colleague, Patricia. Even as she pushed the file across her desk, Eve knew her boss, Larry, would not be pleased.

Tough. She wasn't doing it.

"Why not?" Patricia asked, taking a seat in the empty chair in front of Eve's desk. "I'd kill to pitch a campaign to First Star Security Services. Have you seen the owner's pic?" She pointed toward the file, a giddy grin spreading across her face.

"That's why I can't do it."

"I'm not following you." Patricia's brow furrowed. "Do you know Jake Mitchell?"

Eve nodded. After a moment of silence, she said, "Well, I used to."

Patricia leaned in to prop her elbow on the desk. "Do tell."

"I was in college, my last year." Eve glanced up at Patricia. She wouldn't risk telling this story to anyone else at Bartlett, Burrows, and Gaines Advertising. "I met Jake on New Year's Eve. Eight years ago." Eve shrugged, hoping to hide her mounting discomfort over talking about this. Oh, she'd gone over it in her mind plenty of times, but saying it out loud somehow lent weight to her colossal mistake. "He was in the Navy. A week later, he shipped out to Italy for a year."

"And you never saw him again?"

"I'm afraid it's worse than that." Regret filled Eve's voice. "He asked me to go with him. To marry him."

"And you said no." It wasn't a statement so much as a realization for Patricia.

Eve shook her head. "I was young and stupid. Naïve. Scared." Her words stopped, hindered by the lump of regret rising in her throat. She swallowed around the bulge. It stayed put.

"Jake Mitchell is your *one that got away*." There was a hint of glee in Patricia's tone now. She was enjoying this far too much.

With a shrug, Eve let out a strangled, "Yeah, I guess so."

"When's the last time you saw him?"

"When I said *no*."

"Oh, man." Patricia giggled and nodded. "You have got to do this pitch."

"No." Eve shook her head. "I don't want to know how perfect his life is. How perfect his *wife* is. How perfect their *kids* are."

Patricia jumped up. "Let's Google him."

"No!" Eve screeched. "I certainly don't need confirmation of his *perfect* life." She cleared her throat and squared her shoulders. Patricia was determined, but so was Eve. She wasn't doing that pitch and she wasn't Googling Jake Mitchell.

"Oh, come on, Evie..." Patricia's words trailed off in laughter. It'd been a long time since anyone but Patricia had called her Evie. And that was a corner of her mind she'd rather not visit. Patricia carried on, "Where's your sense of adventure? Besides, he could be single."

Patricia dangled it out there, but Eve wasn't biting. "There are some things that are better left in the past. This is one of them." Eve scribbled 'handle this for me' on a sticky note and attached it to the front of the manila folder. She grabbed her purse from the bottom desk drawer with one hand, took the file in the other and headed for the hallway. Patricia followed her.

Eve slipped into a deserted office a few doors down and put the file on the center of Coleman Rink's desk. Coleman would take the pitch, and with pleasure. He was, after all, the biggest glory hound Eve had ever met.

Patricia paused in the doorway of her own office across the hall. "I'll see you day after tomorrow," she said. "Sure you don't want to head out to the country with me? It's going to be boring enough at my parents' house as it is."

"It'll be a lot of things at your parents' tomorrow," Eve said, "but I doubt boring is one of them."

A good laugh settled between them. Patricia went back to her office and Eve headed for the lobby.

Eve sleeved into her coat, turned up the collar and palmed open the door. Santa was outside, standing beside a pot and ringing a bell. She fished out her wallet, pulled out a twenty and dropped it in.

"That's very nice of you," he said. "Santa's got a little something for you, too." He reached into his pocket and came out with a candy bar. "Here ya' go. Sweets for the sweet." On the ring finger of the hand holding the candy bar, Santa wore a gold ring that reminded Eve of a Christmas wreath. Unusual enough for her to take notice, but she didn't give it extra thought.

Eve didn't want to appear rude, so she took the candy and moved on.

Eve entered her apartment on the thirty-second floor of Riverview Towers, an exclusive residence that tenants often sublet for twice their rental rate. It was the place to live in Laurel Hills, Washington, an enterprising community on the western side of the state. A few weeks ago, some hotshot from Seattle had offered her three times her monthly rent, but she'd turned him down. She liked living here and she wasn't about to give it up.

She went to her bedroom, pulling off her coat. She draped it across the chair by the door, and the candy bar she'd gotten from the sidewalk Santa slid out. Eve picked it up and tossed it onto the bed. It might come in handy later when she was watching *It's a Wonderful Life*.

After she stuck the frozen apple and pumpkin pies in the oven (she'd promised her mother she'd bring them for tomorrow's dinner), she made a bowl of popcorn, grabbed a glass of wine, and headed for the comfort of her bed.

She'd forgotten about the candy bar until she spied it on the bed. No biggie, though. Chocolate and popcorn made a good combo. She chuckled at the thought as she climbed onto the bed. Bring on *It's a Wonderful Life*.

Eve turned on the television and cued up the movie. As the opening credits began to roll, she picked up the candy bar. Blue snowflakes scattered over a white wrapper gave it a magical feel. Big, red letters spelled out *Christmas Magic* in a pretty cursive script. Beneath the name, and in a smaller, standard font was the phrase: *If you've ever wanted a second chance.*

"A second chance?" she said out loud, then laughed. "At what?" Like she needed a second chance at anything.

Well, hardly anything.

She wouldn't try to kid herself that she never thought about

Jake, or that she hadn't often wondered how things would've turned out if she'd married him. But that ship had sailed. It wasn't coming back to port, no matter what went down at work. And Eve didn't need or want to have it thrown in her face.

Whatever. Thank goodness she had some chocolate. She had a feeling she was going to need it.

Eve peeled back the outer wrapper, then the gold foil sheathed around the candy bar, and took a bite.

Tasty.

She took another bite and settled in to watch *It's a Wonderful Life*.

When Eve Langdon woke on Christmas morning, even before she opened her eyes, she knew she wasn't in her bed. She didn't know how she knew it; she just did.

Man, had she cracked open a bottle of wine last night and then gone out without remembering it? Her heart pounded against her chest as she prepared to open her eyes. Where the hell was she?

"Hey, sleepy head..." a vaguely familiar voice said, then an arm draped around her. The feel of it was oddly, yet distantly, familiar. A firm masculine body snuggled her close. "I'm gonna need you to pick up the kids from school today," he whispered. "It's a half-day. Remember?"

Who?

Eve's eyes shot open. A wall of windows with sheer white curtains masking the scene outside (trees) was the first thing she saw. Eve rolled her eyes around as much as she could without moving her head. She saw yellow walls and a half-opened doorway reflected in the floor-to-ceiling mirrors behind the headboard. The floor was not carpeted, but light-colored hardwood. She could see the corner of a brown and tan striped rug at the foot of the bed. It was a pleasant enough room, but one she did not recognize. Eve gasped.

"You okay, Evie?" His voice sounded worried now.

It was at that moment, when he said her name, that she knew who was lying beside her on the bed. But how could that be? She hadn't seen Jake Mitchell in eight years.

Eve sprang from the king-size bed, dragging the yellow sheet with her. She swung around to see Jake Mitchell lying on the bed in dark slacks, a blue dress shirt and matching tie, and looking completely scrumptious, if a bit older. Understandable, she thought. It had been eight years.

She tried to say something. To form the words to ask where she was and how she'd gotten here, but they wouldn't come.

Jake leaned toward her and reached for her hand, giving her that smile of his. The one that made her melt. He climbed off the bed and pulled her to him. "Are you still worried about leaving the kids with your mom over New Year's?" He studied her face for a moment and then brushed his lips against hers.

Eve's first instinct was to back away, but when the familiarity of his kiss washed over her, she remembered just how much she'd missed him and his kisses. "Jake..." she whispered as his lips spilled his recognizable touch through her soul.

Ending the kiss, he said, "You're gonna get the kids, right?"

She nodded, trying to break free of the stupor his lips had put her in.

He grabbed his blazer off the back of the chair, slipping into it as he headed for the door.

"Jake...?" she said, following after him. When he stopped in the hallway and turned to look back at her, she added, "Whose kids?"

Jake scratched his head and his face filled with worry as he moved toward her. "What's the matter with you, Evie?" he asked, latching onto her elbow. "Our kids."

"We don't have any kids," she said softly.

"Yes, we do." He nodded and his voice took on a questionless tone. "Two of them. A boy and a girl."

Her mouth dropped open as she prepared to object. Again.

Jake flashed her a serious look. "This is not funny."

"Tell me about it!" She snorted as the fog began to clear. "Who put you up to this? Coleman?" She peered at him through slanted eyes, unable to reconcile that Jake would willingly participate in a prank like this—and at Christmas.

"Evie..." He gave her a confused look, and shook his head. "What are you talking about?" he asked, leading her back to the bedroom. He sat on the foot of the bed, then pulled her down beside him. "What's going on?" he asked. His eyes were darkened by fear now. "Who's Coleman?"

"My co-worker."

He looked more confused than ever. "You're not...." His voice trailed off as distrust filled his gaze and he looked away.

"Me and Coleman?" That was too disgusting for words. "Oh God no!"

"Then what's going on, baby?" He shrugged helplessly.

Eve glanced at his hand. His left. He wore a wedding band. The rings sparkling on her own left hand caught her eye. Wedding rings. She studied the rings on her finger—a diamond solitaire alongside a band of gold that looked like the one Jake was wearing—and began shaking her head. She looked at him. "Where'd these rings come from?"

"From me. I gave them to you the day I married you."

"We didn't get married."

"Yes, we did. Eight years ago on New Year's Eve."

Okay, so apparently Jake was going to see this prank to the end. Maybe it was his version of payback.

"Yeah, okay. That's right." She shrugged. "You asked me to marry you and we got married on New Year's Eve," she said. Only that's not what happened. They'd met on New Year's Eve. He had asked her to marry him a few days later (as he was shipping out to Italy), but she'd said no.

Eve had wanted to finish school. She was one semester away from her degree. She also had reservations about marrying a man she'd only known a few days—even if she was convinced she'd fallen in love with him the moment their eyes first met.

"Actually..." His tone held a measure of mischief. "You asked me to marry you."

He was baiting her, and it was in her best interest not to bite. She looked at him and said, "Why are the kids in school? It's Christmas." She was sure that'd trip him up.

He squinted. "Christmas is tomorrow. They get out at noon today." Jake got this genuine look of worry on his face. Either he was a damned good actor, or he genuinely believed what he was saying. "I'm gonna call Gloria and have her cancel my appointments today."

"Gloria?" she asked.

"My secretary." Jake sucked in a shallow breath. "I'm calling the doctor."

"No, don't do that." Eve shook her head. Doctors had a tendency to want to stick you with something that always hurt more than they said it would. Seeing a doctor was the last thing she wanted, even though she thought it quite possible that she might need to see a shrink because if Jake wasn't pranking her, then she was going crazy. Either that, or she was dead.

"I'm not leaving you here alone," Jake said in such a way that Eve knew that option was now off the table.

But Eve needed answers. She clearly wasn't going to get them from Jake. He thought she was acting crazy. And so did she. A little. "Don't cancel your day on my account," she said. "Just drive me to my mother's." It was better if he drove her. Plus, he probably wouldn't let her drive right now anyway. And that suited her just fine. Who knew if her mother still lived in the house Eve grew up in? There was nothing at all familiar about this crazy dream she was mixed up in—except maybe Jake. She looked at him and couldn't help smiling. "I'm sure I'll be okay in a little while. She can drive me to pick up the kids from school."

Jake studied her face for a moment, then said, "All right." He nodded. "I'll take you to Ann's house."

Ann? He said her mother's name like he *liked* her or something. Wasn't a person supposed to have a natural aversion to their mother-in-law? This was getting weirder by the minute.

Eve dressed in a pair of jeans and a long-sleeve blouse. After she went downstairs, Jake took his coat from the closet in the hallway leading to the garage and sleeved into it before pulling Eve's jacket from the closet and handing it to her.

She followed him into the garage, where he opened the passenger door of a black Unlimited Rubicon X for her. Inside, the 4X4 smelled new. As he climbed behind the wheel, she looked out her window at the blue Lexus GX. Sporty and cool, yet effective for hauling kids around. *Is that mine?*

The garage door opened and light filtered in as Jake backed the car out onto the driveway and then the street. It didn't take long for Eve to realize they were in the affluent Richland Hills neighborhood.

A nice house in Richland Hills. Decent vehicles in the garage. Somebody wanted Eve to think that she and Jake were doing all right. Or would've done all right—if she'd married him. Which she hadn't, and she was counting on her mother to set the record straight.

Ten minutes later, the Jeep rolled to a stop in the driveway of a house that Eve did recognize. It was the house she'd grown up in. Well, at least something about this dream—that's what Eve had decided this was, a dream—was making sense.

Eve reached for the door handle, and Jake touched her arm gently. "Evie, I don't know what's going on." He shrugged. "But I've never not opened a car door for you, and I don't plan to start today."

That's right. Jake had been a perfect gentleman, and it was probably one of the things about him that'd swept Eve off her feet. "Sorry," she said, barely above a whisper.

Jake turned his collar up as he trotted around the Jeep. Once he opened her door, she found out why. It was cold, bitingly so. She climbed out and he held her hand as they walked up to the front door of her mother's house. He turned to Eve, studied her face approvingly, then dipped his head to brush his lips against hers. Eve felt herself growing weak against his soft, unhurried kiss. When he backed away, she stood there gazing at him, wondering why he was doing this. It had to be a joke. Right?

"I'll be done about three. I'll come back to pick you and the kids up then." He smiled, then stepped back.

"Wait?" she said. "You're not coming in?"

He shook his head. "I've got a meeting."

"Okay," she said and pushed the door open. Eve felt a measure of relief after crossing the threshold. Now the world would make sense again. She'd go inside and call her office to tell them she'd be in directly. Whatever this game was that Jake Mitchell was playing, he could finish it without her.

Eve closed the door and stepped inside the living room. "Mom?" she called out, gazing around at all the Christmas decorations, including a heavily decorated tree beside the fireplace.

"Evie?" her mother responded. "I'm in the kitchen."

"I'll be right there. I'm just gonna use the bathroom." That'd give her time to call her office without her mother jabbering in the background.

Inside the bathroom, Eve put the toilet seat down and sat. Going through her phone, she looked for "the office" in her contacts, but it wasn't there. *What the...?* she wondered. Did somebody delete it from her phone? Jake? Was it a ploy to make the ruse seem more real? Boy, he'd thought of everything.

Eve flipped through the contacts until she came to Patricia. It rang twice and Eve prompted her impatiently to answer.

"Eve?" Patricia's cheery voice said. "Is that you? Man, I haven't talked to you in ages. How's Jake and the kids?"

He'd gotten to Patricia too? "I'm fine. They're fine. We're fine." Eve was beginning to feel helpless. Either she was trapped in some weird dream, or she was dead. Neither one held much appeal for her. "I just wanted to wish you a Merry Christmas."

"And a very Merry Christmas to you too, Eve," Patricia said. "Let's get together for lunch after the New Year." She sounded like she really meant it, but Eve got the feeling it'd never happen.

She disconnected the call and glanced around the bathroom, wondering what the hell she was going to do. Given her two options, death or dream, she decided to focus on the latter. Okay, so if this was a dream, how was she going to get herself to wake up?

But isn't this what you always wanted? she asked herself. *What you've always thought you missed out on?*

Heck, if this was a dream, she might as well enjoy it. Besides, it was probably as close to being Mrs. Jake Mitchell as she was ever going to get.

Eve stuffed her phone back inside her purse, washed her hands and left the bathroom.

The scent of pumpkin and spices wafted around her. Mom was baking pies for tomorrow. Boy, as far as dreams go, this one was first rate, complete with smells and everything.

"Hey, Mom," she said, entering the kitchen. She went to her mother's side and kissed her cheek.

"Good morning, dear." Ann looked up from the bowl of ingredients she was attending to, and said, "Is Jake with you? Where are the kids?"

"Jake dropped me off. He has to work. The kids are at school."

"On Christmas Eve?"

Eve shrugged. "So it would seem."

"You want a piece of pie?" Ann said to her persuasively.

"Pumpkin?" Eve asked. Childhood memories of she and her mother cutting into the first pumpkin pie out of the oven on Christmas Eve washed over her.

"Fresh out of the oven."

Without a word, Eve went to the cabinets for saucers, then the silverware drawer for forks and the pie server. Her mother poured coffee into two cups while Eve served up the pie. They took the pie and coffee into the dining room and sat down at the table.

A nostalgic feeling washed over Eve. She regretted being so busy with work these days that she hadn't had a chance to do this with her mother in years.

Eve devoured several bites of her pie, then said, "Mom..." She glanced at her mother. When their eyes met, she continued. "Have you ever woke up one morning and felt like you'd dropped in on someone else's life?"

Ann hesitated, then said, "No. I don't believe I have." She looked at Eve. "What's this about?"

"This is not my life. I don't belong here with Jake."

"You mustn't say that, Evie." Ann's tone turned sharp. She pushed herself up from the table and reached for a framed photograph on a nearby shelf. She set the picture down in front of Eve. It was a snapshot of Eve and Jake on their wedding day. They were standing cheek-to-cheek and smiling for the camera. Both looked incredibly happy. It left Eve with an empty feeling. Ann pointed at the couple in the photograph. "What you and Jake have is something special. Something that most people only dream about."

Yeah. Including Eve. She was not the Eve in this picture. And the Jake in this picture was not *her* Jake. She'd turned her back on him eight years ago.

Eve didn't understand what was happening, but her mother would never perpetrate this fraud on her. Eve had to be dreaming.

Eve shrugged and told herself, *well, I guess I'll go with it for as long as it lasts.*

As if her mother had heard her thoughts, she said, "You must treasure your time. Every moment that you have with Jake, Jacob, and Annie are a gift," Ann said. While Eve silently thanked her for telling her the kids' names, Ann pointed her finger at Eve. "You could wake up tomorrow and it'll all be gone."

By the time Ann and Eve had arrived at school to pick up the kids, the wind had picked up and dark clouds had started to billow in. On the way over, Eve had pretended to be looking for something in her wallet, while searching for pictures of the kids. She at least wanted to look like she recognized her own children.

They may not be *her* children exactly, but they did belong to another version of herself. They wouldn't know she wasn't their mother, and she couldn't bear the thought of traumatizing them.

Annie was a beautiful child, with Eve's strawberry blond hair and Jake's coffee-brown eyes. Jacob looked like his father, but he had Eve's smile. That empty feeling that'd wrapped around Eve when she looked at her and Jake's wedding picture plunged down in her gut as she looked at the photographs of *their* kids.

Kids began pouring out of the school. When Eve saw Jacob and Annie running toward the car, she stepped out to greet them. Annie leaped into her arms and Eve's heart filled with joy as she held the little girl. As Jacob passed her by, going for the car door, Eve tried to give him a one-handed hug.

Jacob yanked away. "Mom!" he complained.

She helped the kids into the car, then reclaimed her seat up front. Closing the car door, Eve looked at her mother and said, "Did you see that? He wouldn't even let me hug him."

Ann laughed and stepped on the gas. "I wonder where he gets that from?"

Eve scoffed indignantly. "Not me!"

"By the time you were Jacob's age, you hated when anybody, including me, tried to hug you."

"I did not." Eve discounted Ann's version of her childhood.

"Did too," Ann said.

Annie giggled. "She lets Daddy hug her."

"Mommies and Daddies are supposed to hug," Ann said.

Eve looked over her shoulder, wondering how old Jacob and Annie were. If Annie was in school, she had to be at least five, right? "How old are you?" she asked Jacob.

"Mom!" He complained about this inquiry worse than he had about her attempted embrace.

"I'm seven," Annie said.

"No, you're not," Jacob corrected her. "I'm seven. You can't be seven too, stupid."

Ann glanced into the rearview mirror. "That's no way to talk to your sister. Tell her you're sorry."

Jacob looked at Annie and said, "Sor-ry," in a sing-song voice, the way kids do when they're not really sorry at all.

"That's better," Ann said.

"Better?" Eve looked at her mother.

Ann shrugged. "People rarely mean it when they apologize. What's important is that they say the words."

Eve kept staring at her. "Who are you and what have you done with my mother?"

"Being a grandma has mellowed her," Jacob said. Annie laughed.

Ann tossed Eve a quizzical look. "I wonder where he got that from?"

Eve chuckled. She didn't need help answering that one.

Ann glanced at the sky through the windshield. Eve did the same. The clouds were getting darker.

"Do you want me to drop you and the kids at home?" she asked. It made sense, since their house was closer than her mom's.

"Sure," Eve said. She'd call Jake after she got home to let him know he didn't need to drop by her mother's.

Moments later, Ann pulled into the driveway. Eve unfastened her seatbelt and looked at her mother. Ann said, "If the roads aren't too bad, I'll be over about noon."

Eve leaned across the seat and kissed her mother's cheek. "Bye, Mom. I'll see you tomorrow."

"Bye, Grandma!" the kids bellowed in unison, scrambling out of the car.

Eve stood in the driveway, watching her mother's car back out into the street. Ann waved. Eve waved. The car rolled down the street, and once it was out of view, Eve went inside.

The kids peeled off their coats and shoes, staying in their socked feet and headed for the kitchen. Eve checked her cell phone for Jake's number and set the call.

He answered after the second ring. "Hey, babe...you feeling better?" There was genuine concern in his voice, and it was wrapped up in sexy. Eve just about melted.

"Yes," she said softly. "The kids and I are home. Mom dropped us off."

"Great. I'll be heading home in about an hour."

"Good. It looks like snow."

"I'll be home before it sets in and messes up the roads."

"Wonderful. I'm looking forward to a quiet evening at home," Eve found herself saying. She knew she shouldn't get wrapped up in this fantasy. It wasn't real. At least, not for her.

Jake chuckled. "On Christmas Eve? We'll be lucky if we can get the kids to bed before midnight."

"I've got it all planned out," Eve said. "I plan to load them with milk. I hear it has a sleeping agent."

"Good. I've got a little mistletoe that I'd like to put to good use," he said in a soft voice that echoed through her like a lingering caress.

Eve's mind had just started to wander when she heard Jacob call out, "Mom! We're hungry!"

"I gotta go," she said. "Hurry home."

"Love you," Jake said.

"I love you, too." Eve sighed and disconnected the call. She never thought she'd ever have the chance to say those words to Jake again. She laid her phone on the table in the entry and headed for the kitchen.

The kids had claimed stools at the snack bar. "You guys hungry?" Eve asked. Annie nodded. "Did you have lunch at school?" Annie laughed at Eve's question. "I'll take that as a yes," Eve said, widening her eyes.

Eve made the kids peanut butter and jelly sandwiches, gave them a cookie (because it was Christmas Eve), and poured them each a glass of milk.

She leaned against the counter, watching the kids eat. She needed answers and she figured the kids could be a well of information—if they didn't know she was grilling them. "You guys want to play a game?" she asked, munching from a bowl of mixed nuts sitting on the snack bar.

Jacob shrugged. Annie said, "What's it called?"

"It's a question game," Eve said. "I'll ask you a question, then you can ask me a question."

Jacob rolled his eyes. Annie nodded, stuffing a huge chunk of her sandwich into her mouth. "Me first," she said over her mouthful of food.

Eve tapped her nose. "You'll get a turn after you've chewed and swallowed your food." She looked at Jacob. She would love to figure out how to get him to open up to her. "Jacob, you want to go first?" Eve asked.

He shrugged as a pensive look crossed his face. When his

eyes brightened, she knew he'd found his question. He snorted, then said, "What'd you get me for Christmas?"

Annie clapped and joined him. "Yeah! What'd we get for Christmas?"

"Quite frankly..." Eve chuckled. "I have no idea." She looked at the kids who were preparing to mount a protest, and said, "But I'll bet it's good."

"This is a dumb game," Jacob said.

"If you keep playing," Eve bargained, "you both can open one present after dinner."

Annie's eyes lit up. She looked at Jacob, who nodded.

"Okay. My turn to ask both of you a question," Eve said. She looked at them, letting her silence build the suspense. Jacob had already said he was seven, but she didn't know Annie's age. She settled her sights on Annie. "How old are you?"

"Five." Annie giggled.

Eve looked at Jacob. "Do I have a job?"

His brow crinkled. "You said your job was to take care of us."

Okay. That was reasonable. Eve could easily see herself putting as much effort (if not more) into raising her children as she did her job.

The kids finished their snacks and went into the family room to watch TV. Eve looked around the family room off the kitchen and dining room. The television the kids were watching hung above a wood-burning fireplace that looked like it'd been used quite often. The kids had claimed seats on the couch and were watching some cartoon that Eve couldn't name. She'd bet her counterpart, the woman who really belonged here, would know.

Eve's gaze skirted the room, checking out the cabinets on the back wall behind the couch. She stepped toward them and one by one opened the doors to see what was stored there. In one of the cabinets, she found several photo albums. Eight of them.

She took the albums to the end table sitting next to the nearest chair. Taking the top binder off the stack, she glanced at the kids. They were engrossed in the TV. She opened the album and settled her gaze on it.

The picture of Eve and Jake—one from a long time ago—jumped off the page at her. It was from that New Year's Eve when they first met. Her friend, Ellen, had snapped a picture of them, declaring that they looked like the perfect couple.

Briefly, Eve wondered whatever happened to Ellen. Where was she now? Last she'd heard, she married some guy from the Bay Area down in California. She'd probably moved down there.

Turning the page, Eve returned her focus to the photo album. On the second page was an eight by ten of the wedding picture she'd seen at her mother's. Jake was in a tux, and she was wearing a white dress complete with a veil. Jake had told her they'd gotten married on New Year's Eve. Maybe they'd communicated during that first year (at least in this time and place) and had gotten married the following New Year's. It was kind of romantic, she thought, getting married one year to the day after they met.

Eve leafed through all eight photo albums and got a crash course on their life together. Pictures of both pregnancies, the kids as babies and then toddlers, family vacations, holidays. It was all picture perfect, and left Eve feeling empty inside because she'd missed it all.

Eve learned the traditional Christmas Eve dinner in the Mitchell household was pizza, which always delighted the kids. After dinner, the kids got to open one present each, as they'd been promised. An Ultra Stomp Rocket for Jacob and a fifty-piece Squigz set for Annie.

As Eve watched the kids practically bouncing off the wall, probably from the anticipation of what they'd find under the tree in the morning, she was surprised at how much fun she was having. Just her, Jake, and the kids sitting in front of a cozy fire. Everybody was happy. It truly was a wonderful life.

Jake said to the kids, "Time for bed." After boisterous complaints from both, he added, "If you're still awake when Santa comes by, he won't stop."

That got their attention. Eve chuckled.

Jake whispered against her ear, "I'll see them to bed. Why don't you pour us a couple of glasses of wine?"

She watched him scoot the kids upstairs. After Jake and the kids disappeared, Eve went into the kitchen. She returned with two glasses and a bottle of Cabernet Sauvignon. After filling each glass, she took one and settled back on the couch, tucking her feet up underneath her.

Sipping the wine, she gazed at the fire snapping and crackling in the fireplace. Over the years, she'd played out the what-if scenario in her head many times. What would've happened if she'd married Jake? None of her fantasies had ever come close to the bliss she was feeling right now.

Jake returned, scooped his glass off the table, and settled in beside Eve, draping his free arm around her.

"Merry Christmas," he said, brushing his lips against her cheek.

She smiled and turned to meet his kiss. "Merry Christmas," she said against his lips.

"Everything okay now?" he asked. "You seemed to be a little upset this morning."

"I must've been having a bad dream or something. Things were a little foggy when you woke me."

"You're safe and sound now," he said. "Right here with me."

Eve laid her head on Jake's chest and said, "Right where I've always wanted to be." She might want to be here, but Eve knew she didn't belong here. She was not this Jake's Eve. No matter how much she wanted to be. Wherever *his* Eve was, she probably wanted to get back to her family just as much as Eve wanted to take her place. Permanently.

"Is there something going on that I don't know about?" Jake asked, as if he sensed her inner turmoil.

She glanced up at him. "I think maybe I dreamed last night that *this* was all a dream." The words shattered through her. "I guess I'm afraid of waking up now and finding out that you've built a life with someone else."

Jake merely shook his head. "Do you remember what I said to you just before you asked me to marry you?"

No, she didn't. But she would like to know. And what was this business about her asking him, anyway? He had asked her. She had said no. And they went their separate ways. End of story. "Yes," she lied, "but tell me anyway."

"Well, to make a long story short, you wanted to know if I'd ever married." He shrugged. "I told you that no matter how much time had passed, I had never stopped loving you so I never married because I didn't think it would be fair to pledge my heart to someone else when I'd already given it to you." He tipped her chin up with his forefinger and lowered his mouth to hers, meeting her lips with a slow, smooth kiss. She let out a soft moan. "This is real," he whispered. "We're real."

"Let's go to bed," she in a soft voice filled with desire.

Jake stood, set his wine glass on the coffee table, retrieved hers and placed it beside his, then scooped her into his arms and headed upstairs.

Eve giggled while her heart jolted and her pulsed pounded all the way to her head, dizzying her. She tried to grab onto something inside her head, anything concrete, as her thoughts weakened.

But everything around her began to disappear as her consciousness faded.

Eve's eyes shot open. Her heart deflated when she realized she was back in her apartment overlooking the river.

She grabbed her cell phone off the nightstand and glanced at the display.

December 25th.

It was Christmas, and she was here alone. There was no Jake in the bed beside her. Their children weren't sleeping down the hall. Eve was right where she'd put herself eight years ago. Alone.

A pang of longing shot through Eve. She'd had a taste of what might have been, and she wanted it more than ever now. But that wasn't going to happen, was it?

Just when Eve was about to dive so deep into her own melancholy that she'd never find her way out, a thought crossed her mind. She was supposed to handle the pitch to First Star Security Services tomorrow. Essentially, Jake Mitchell.

But she'd passed that off to Coleman. She'd put it on his desk yesterday. Chances are, though, he hadn't seen it. He hadn't come into the office on Christmas Eve.

All she had to do was go back to the office and remove the file from his desk, and he'd never know. She could do the pitch to Jake tomorrow; at least she'd see him.

Better yet, she could probably find his phone number and address in the file. Why wait until tomorrow? She could call him today. No, she'd go see him. If she ended up intruding on his family holiday, she'd make up some reason for being there and then excuse herself. At least, she'd know once and for all. She didn't think she could stand to wait until tomorrow to see him. To find out if he'd moved on without her.

Excitement coursed through Eve as got out of bed and headed for the bathroom. No matter the outcome, she was going to see Jake Mitchell today. For real. And not in some dream world where she'd spent last night.

Half an hour later, Eve left her building, stepping out into the brisk December day. Today's forecast called for temps in the low forties and clear weather. The crystal-clear sky supported the no-snow or rain prediction. It did seem a little chilly out, though. She shivered and tucked in her arms to ward off the chill as she walked the three blocks that separated her apartment building from her office building.

The front door was locked, but Eve simply punched in a code on the keypad and the door swung open. The lobby was empty, as she'd expected. She went to the elevators behind the information desk, punched in her code again, and traveled up to the twelfth floor.

She found the file for First Star Security Services, with her sticky note affixed to the exterior, still sitting on Coleman's desk. Eve snatched the file up and took it back to her office. Inside the file, she found Jake's home address, work address, and several phone numbers, including a cell, and jotted them down before ripping off the sticky-note and stashing the file inside her desk drawer. She tore the sticky note into several pieces, then dropped them into the trash.

Heading out, Eve folded the paper with Jake's info and stuffed it inside her coat pocket.

She walked back to her apartment building, went inside the garage and climbed into her car. She keyed Jake's home address into her phone's GPS and discovered it was on the other side of town.

She dropped her phone onto the passenger seat, started her car, and headed out. The streets were unusually quiet. Typical for Christmas Day. Everybody else was home with their families. Eve didn't have a family. The only one she'd ever known apparently existed inside her dreams.

The drive across town went quickly (thanks to the absence of traffic), and once she arrived at Jake's address, Eve was able to park practically at the front door. The interior doors inside the lobby were locked. On the left wall, she found a directory with the tenants' names and a bell beside each. There were double names for some of the tenants, like Mark and Emily Sharp, Carl and Jackie Foster, or Jim Reilly and Adam Cox. Jake Mitchell was listed alone.

Eve hit the buzzer beside his name and waited. Nothing. She hit it again. Still, there was no answer. She reached into the pockets of her coat and retrieved her cell phone from one and the paper with Jake's info from the other. She keyed his cell number into her phone, hit the call button and waited.

It went to voice mail. "Hi, Jake," she said into her phone, "it's Eve Langdon from Bartlett, Burrows, and Gaines Advertising. We have a meeting tomorrow morning. I'm sorry to interrupt your holiday, but if you could give me a call, I'd really appreciate it." She pretended like he was any other client, just in case he was married. That way, she wouldn't cause him any trouble or end up looking like a complete fool. She disconnected the call and glanced inside the lobby.

A man in uniform, probably the bellman, walked across the lobby. He saw her and redirected his course, heading to the door. Opening it, he said, "I was just about to leave. Is there something I can help you with before I go?"

"I'm looking for Jake Mitchell," she said, eyeing the man. There was something oddly familiar about him. Something she couldn't quite put her finger on.

He chuckled. "Knowing Mr. Mitchell, he's probably at his office."

"His office?" she asked. That must mean—

"He doesn't have any family to speak of here, so yes, I'd imagine that's where he went this morning."

"Thank you." She backed up toward the exterior door. "I'll see if I can catch up with him there."

Eve went back to her car and keyed the address for First Star Security Services into her GPS. It was located six blocks away, and due to the nonexistent traffic, she arrived quickly. She recognized this area of town. She'd always envied the businesses lining the perimeter of a one-block park. It must be enjoyable to look out at the square as you went about your daily duties.

There were no cars parked along the street in front of First Star Security Services, but that didn't deter Eve. She knew there was parking on the next street over.

Eve stepped up onto the sidewalk. She peered through the windows lining the front. The darkened interior suggested no one was inside.

That was not an option Eve had considered on the drive over, and the thought of it now was yanking the rug right out from under her.

Her heart thudded as she tried the door. It was locked. Damn. She knocked, then waited for what seemed like eons. Nothing. Double damn.

She went back to her car, found First Star's phone number on the info sheet and dialed the number. She wasn't surprised when it went to voice mail. She disconnected the call without leaving a message. She'd already done that.

The thought of leaving without seeing Jake left her feeling despondent. But what else could she do? She was probably the only person out on the streets of the city right now. Everybody else had somewhere to go. Some place they wanted to be. The one place Eve wanted to be—she couldn't get to.

With her finger on her car's electronic ignition, she glanced around. The neon sign on the window of the coffee shop a couple of doors down from First Star caught her eye. The hot pink color stood out, and she realized it was on.

A coffee shop that's open? she thought, getting out of her car. *On Christmas?* As odd as it seemed, she went inside.

"Good morning." The man behind the counter smiled at her. She looked at him. Forties, graying hair, tired eyes. There was something familiar about him. He wasn't the guy she'd just seen at Jake's apartment building, was he? No. Couldn't be. "Could I get you a vanilla latte?" he asked.

Funny, she hadn't drank one of those in years. Since college. "Sure." She nodded.

Moments later, he slid a steaming cup of coffee across the counter toward her. She fished a twenty out of her wallet and handed it to him. He said, "No charge. Merry Christmas." As he waved the money off, she noticed the gold ring on his left hand. It reminded her of a Christmas wreath. Where had she seen that before? Somewhere.

"Thank you," she said, stuffing the twenty back into her wallet and pulling out a five. She stuffed it into the tip jar. "Merry Christmas to you too."

"Thank you." He nodded.

She went to a table at the front windows and took a seat. "If you want to close up, just let me know," she said.

"I'm in no hurry," he said and disappeared into the kitchen.

Eve laid her phone on the table and sipped her coffee while gazing at the square across the street.

What kind of hell had she tripped into? First, she was thrust into a world that was by all accounts perfect, but it was not hers. And then, just as quickly, she'd been yanked back into this world. Sitting here in this coffee shop, she realized just how lonely her world was.

Eve's phone vibrated on the table. She glanced at the display. Jake's number. Her heart pounded against her chest. All she could think of was Jake's arms around her. His lips against hers. "Hello?" Her shaky voice shredded the word.

"Evie?" He said her name in such a way that it made her think he was asking, *'Is it really you?'*

She smiled inside. "How are you, Jake?"

"I'm fine," he said. "And you?"

"Never better." She sucked in a breath, trying to calm her nerves. "I hope I'm not disturbing your holiday," she said. "Merry Christmas, by the way."

"Merry Christmas to you, too," he said, and she thought she heard a bit of a chuckle in his voice. "And no, there's nothing to disturb here. I'm at work."

"Work?" She laughed anxiously. "I just knocked on the door."

"You're here? Now?"

"Well, I was a few minutes ago."

"Where are you now?" he asked. "You didn't leave, did you?"

"No." She shook her head. "I'm a couple of doors down at this coffee shop, which I am frankly surprised is open today." She realized she was rambling, so she stopped and waited for him to say something.

"Give me five minutes," he said. "I'll be right there."

It seemed more like ten minutes before she saw him walk through the door, but maybe time was just dragging for her because she was so anxious to see him. Jake was dressed smartly in black slacks and a black pullover sweater. He hadn't changed much. His tall frame was still clean-cut and athletic. His black hair was a little longer than it had been when he was in the Navy, but not much. He was as handsome as ever. As he strolled toward her, a smile tipped the corners of his mouth.

Eve stood when he was no more than a couple of steps away from her. His dark eyes danced and sparkled. "Evie…" Her named trailed away as he enveloped her in his arms. "It's great to see you."

She clung to him as if he were a lifeline. "I can't begin to tell you how wonderful it is to see you." She hid her anxiety behind a nervous giggle.

His hands slid slowly down her arms, then he tangled his fingers around hers. Still holding her hands, he sat down in the empty chair behind him. She followed his lead and returned to her seat.

"To be honest, I was a little shocked to get your voicemail," he said. "I hadn't anticipated running into you today."

She said weakly, "No?"

"I knew it was you, though, the minute I heard your voice." He shot her a grin that set her at ease. "And I couldn't be happier."

"I was a little surprised myself when a file for your company landed on my desk yesterday."

"Seems like fate, doesn't it?"

She nodded, but she couldn't get the image of their home in the suburbs and their two children out of her head. She found herself asking, "Did you ever marry?"

Jake shook his head. "You?"

"No." Eve shrugged. "It would've been awfully crowded. Me, him, and your ghost." She laughed at herself now.

"I get that," he said. "That's why I never married. The years flew by, but it didn't seem to matter how much time passed...I never stopped loving you." He gave a shrug to accompany his words, which were starting to sound vaguely familiar. "How could I marry someone else when I'd already given my heart to you?"

Okay, so the words weren't verbatim, but they were close. Very close. Close enough to make her wonder about the dream world she'd visited last night. She'd taken for granted that this might be one of those *what might have been* scenarios. But what if it wasn't? What if it was more of a *what was to come* or *what could be* type of thing?

Eve's heart swelled with hope. That'd mean the children—her children—that she'd met and fallen instantly in love with were destined to be born to her. That also meant that she would have to propose to Jake.

Hoo boy.

The fact that he'd obviously said yes, at least in her dream world, didn't offer Eve much comfort.

The clerk—Eve had a hard time calling a man in his forties a barista—came out of the kitchen. He smiled at Eve.

She looked at Jake. "Could I persuade you to take a walk with me in the square?" she asked, then glanced across the street.

"I'd love to." Jake stood and offered his hand. She took it and let him pull her to her feet.

As they stepped outside, a chilled wind whipped against Eve's cheeks. It did little to faze her. She was with Jake. That was all that mattered.

He offered his arm and she draped her hand at the crook of his elbow as they started across the street. The sky was filled with clouds. When had that happened?

"What are the odds that all these years later, you'd be looking for an advertising agency…and the pitch falls on my desk?"

"I'll confess, I had a little something to do with that."

"Huh?" she asked as they stepped up onto the sidewalk leading into the square.

"I researched the top three advertising agencies in town," he said. "Yours was one of them. Once I realized you were an ad exec there, I insisted that you handle the account."

"Really?" That made her feel good.

He led her to a bench in the middle of the square and they sat together. "I just really wanted to see you again," he said. "If for nothing else—" He shrugged. "—closure."

Closure? Eve's heart plummeted. Closure was not what she had in mind. She looked at Jake. "Would you like to have Christmas dinner with me? At my mom's."

He studied her face for what seemed like an eternity before saying, "I would." Then a slow grin spread across his face. "But how are you going to explain the stray you're bringing home for dinner?" he asked with a chuckle.

Well, it was now or never. She'd better clue him in about her intentions. If she didn't, the next thing she knew, they could be saying *goodbye* instead of *I do*. "I'm going to introduce you as the man I'm going to marry!"

"I suppose you call that a proposal?"

"Yeah. Yeah, I guess it is." She nodded. "So what do you say?" she asked. "Will you marry me?"

He peered at her suspiciously. "Are you serious?"

"I am." Eve sucked in a breath, preparing to spill her guts. "I'm trying to rectify the mistake I made eight years ago." She shrugged. "Give or take a few days." Eve bit back the urge to cry. "You have no idea how many times I've wished for a do-over. A chance to go back and say *yes* instead of *no*. I figure this is the closest I'll ever get, so…how about it?"

Jake's smile lit up his entire face, including his eyes. "You're serious, aren't you?"

"Very."

"All right," he said. "I'll bite. When are we getting married?"

"New Year's Eve."

"This New Year's Eve?"

Hell, yes, this New Year's Eve. She didn't want to wait an entire year. Besides, if her dream world was to become reality, Jacob should be born before the next year was out. "Yes. *This* New Year's Eve," she said with confidence.

Jake pulled Eve into his arms. "Are you absolutely sure?"

"I'm absolutely positive." She laid her head on his shoulder. "I love you. I've always loved you. By your side is where I want to be for the rest of my life."

"New Year's Eve it is." He kissed the top of her head. "I'll make sure you never regret marrying me."

As they hugged, tiny snowflakes began to drift down around

them. So much for the weather forecast. It looked like they were going to have a white Christmas after all. But most importantly, they were going to spend it together, and they were going to be married in less than a week.

Sometimes things do work out—even after eight years. All you need is a little Christmas Magic!

Made in the USA
Lexington, KY
04 May 2018